Dark September

Brendan Gerad O'Brien

Dark September

Chapter One

The tram came clattering out of the thick mist and rattled down Stow Hill. When it reached the King's Head Hotel it shuddered to a halt with a screech of metal as the wheels struggled to grip on the wet tracks. Sparks hissed from the overhead cables and fluttered off in the bitter cold wind that came straight in off the River Severn.

The wind brought a heavy drizzle, blowing it in sheets along the road. The street lamps rocked with each gust and threw fragmented shadows onto the huge shop windows on either side of Newport High Street.

The tram doors slid open just as Danny O'Shea came around the corner of the Post Office, and the group of men standing in the doorway of the hotel jostled to get on board out of the rain. O'Shea tried to hurry but he just didn't have the energy. He felt totally drained.

It normally took less than fifteen minutes to get from his house in Henry Street to the tram stop, but today his legs had turned to jelly. It was as if he was sleepwalking through a horrible dream. His collar was pulled up tight but the rain that dripped from his cap still found a space and dribbled down his neck. He gave it an angry wipe as he tagged onto the end of the line and shuffled along behind the others.

Once on board he dropped into the first seat he came to and Elwyn Jenkins squashed in beside him. The doors slid shut and the tram gave a shudder as it rattled on through the dismal wet dawn that was creeping over the colourless rooftops of Newport.

'Did you hear the latest rumour, Danny?' Elwyn pulled a newspaper from his pocket and unfolded it. His eyes were disturbed, wide and anxious. They darted from O'Shea to the newspaper and back to O'Shea again.

'Do you mean about …' O'Shea felt his throat tighten. He really didn't want to think about it. But at the same time he desperately wanted to know what was really going on. He rubbed a hole in the steamed up window and watched the lights from the tram flicker on the curtain of rain. 'I heard something on the wireless before I came out. But I'm not sure *what* I believe on the radio anymore.'

'Well, there's nothing in the paper about it.' Elwyn rattled the wet pages as he tried to separate them. 'They'd put in the papers, wouldn't they? What d'you think, Danny? Wouldn't they put it in the papers if there was any truth in it? Or do you think it's just another pack of lies from that lunatic Lord what's-his-name? D'you think it's another one of his tricks to upset us, like? Make us panic?'

O'Shea glanced around at the other passengers. The tram was full and the steam from wet clothes misted up the windows. He recognised most of them. The men all worked in the dockyard. The few women on board were heading for the nice warm Tax Office.

It was obvious they'd heard the rumour too from the way they held their arms across their bodies, and the tension was like a fine mist. But nobody spoke. There was no idle chatter, no swapping gossip behind gloved hands. Instead they sat in silence and looked out of the window with faces blank and mouths drawn into thin, anxious lines.

A desperate sigh rippled up from O'Shea's chest. What in God's name was he doing? How could he even think about going to work at a time like this? If the rumour *was* true, why wasn't he at home with his wife and child? They'd still be in bed, unaware of the drama unfolding around them.

O'Shea usually took Heather up a cup of tea before he left for work. He'd just poured her one this morning when he heard the pips for the BBC news coming from the old Bush radio in the corner. He went over and twiddled the knob on the front, shifting through the static until he found what he was looking for.

'Germany calling, Germany calling …'

He gave a satisfied nod. He couldn't face listening to the BBC today. It would be the same old depressing stories - desperately needed food convoys from America blown up by U-boats out in the Atlantic. Cities all over Britain pounded to smithereens by German bombers during the night. The German army mustered on the French coast poised to invade at any moment. Nothing but doom and gloom.

It was already raining outside. Why add to the misery? He needed to lighten the mood so he tuned to Hamburg Radio instead. And as the nasal tones of Lord Haw-Haw filtered through the screech of the radio waves, O'Shea chuckled at the way he pronounced *Germany* in his strange Irish-American-English pseudo posh accent. He made it sound like *Germaine.*

More often than not Lord Haw-Haw had the British people laughing out loud at his absurd stories - the war was already over, Churchill was on the verge of surrendering, the Navy had abandoned them and absconded to America, the generals were staging a coup and taking over the country before joining with Germany.

Sometimes he touched a nerve when he gave precise details of an air raid - the exact damage, the number of casualties. Information only someone high up in the

German command could know. And the people would howl with rage. But mainly he only succeeded in making them chuckle when they needed it most.

But this morning as O'Shea picked up the cup of tea and headed for the stairs, something about *this* broadcast made him hesitate. There was something different in the tone, something odd about the inflection of the words. The usual verbal swagger, the sarcasm, the mocking voice, were missing.

Lord Haw-Haw sounded subdued. His words were heavy and tinged with sadness. There was even a hint of regret as he told the world that Winston Churchill, the Prime Minister of Great Britain, had died during the night.

The cup shook in O'Shea's hand and splashed tea all over the kitchen floor. Love him or hate him, it was Churchill - the bulldog at the gate - who made Hitler hesitate about invading the British mainland.

Now when he looked across the Channel and saw the gate was unguarded Hitler's next move was *so* predictable.

O'Shea's instinct was to race upstairs and wake Heather, grab their son and get over to the railway station. If they could get there in the next half hour they could catch the train to Fishguard and be in time for the afternoon ferry to Rosslare. They'd be in Ireland before the Germans had time to respond.

He ran to the stairs. Then he stopped. Persuading Heather to go to Ireland would be impossible. He'd lost track of the times they'd argued about it. Every day since the war started he'd tried to convince her they should take Adam and go. Ireland was neutral. And O'Shea had family there so they'd have somewhere to stay.

But she was not prepared to leave her home, her family, everyone she loved to go to a strange country, and that was that.

Anyway, why did he think they'd be any safer in Ireland? If the Germans invaded wouldn't they just sweep across Ireland too? No, it was not going to happen.

So all O'Shea could do was squeeze his fists into balls of frustration.

But was this really true? Or was it just another pack of lies to de-stabilise the country? Wasn't this what Lord Haw-Haw was *supposed* to do, spread disinformation, cause maximum distress by cranking up the fear? Right now he was doing exactly that.

O'Shea twiddled the knob on the radio again, setting it back to the BBC. The news had finished. Soft chamber music flowed out instead. Everything appeared to be normal.

The music faded and the cultured voice of the announcer introduced the latest offering from the country's all-time favourite - Vera Lynn. An orchestra began to play an upbeat tempo and O'Shea stared at the dial trying to read the meaning of it all.

If Churchill *was* dead, surely they'd be making a bigger fuss of it than this? Wouldn't people be telling the country what to do, explaining what was going to happen next, telling them who was going to take his place as Prime Minister?

But there was nothing. Surely that meant it really *was* just empty propaganda - nothing to worry about?

The chime of the clock in the hall told O'Shea it was time to leave for work. His head felt light and he couldn't think straight. He went to the bottom of the stairs and looked up. Then he turned away and got his coat from the hook on the door. Maybe it *was* best to go to work, see what the rest of the lads were making of it. Then he could decide what to do next.

So he let Heather sleep, crept out the front door, and closed it quietly behind him.

Chapter Two

Elwyn was muttering to himself as he grappled with the newspaper. He was trying to shake the pages apart but was getting into a worse mess as they glued together even more.

'There's nothing in here.' He had a nervous squeal in his voice. 'Not a bloody word. If it's true surely they'd have to tell us. Wouldn't they have to tell us, Danny?'

'I'm not sure, Elwyn.' O'Shea looked out of the window again. 'I don't think they'd just broadcast it to the whole world, though. Would they? In these critical times? Surely they'd keep it quiet for as long as possible so's not to cause mass panic.'

'Yeah, but ...'

'And they certainly wouldn't want the Germans to know about it.' O'Shea continued. 'They'd close this down tighter than a duck's eyelid. And you have to ask yourself, how the hell would that Lord what's-his-name know about it in the first place? How would he hear about it before the British people? Naw, the more you think about it the more it sounds like another one of his cock-and-bull stories. Doesn't it?'

'I hope to God you're right, Danny,' Elwyn sighed. 'I can't think of anything worse right now.'

'Rubbish!' Brian Williams turned around in the seat in front. 'If it *is* true then it serves the bastard right, that's what I say.'

'For God's sake.' Elwyn rattled the newspaper. 'What are you talking about? You're ...'

'Oh, come on!' Brian's eyes sparkled with fury. 'Churchill's a fat arrogant prat. He should have stayed well away from those Germans. But no! He had to interfere, didn't he? He sent our boys over there to fight a war that's nothing to do with us. He didn't have to. It was none of our business. That man could have avoided all this by signing a peace pact with Hitler. But no, we were the mighty British. We were going to sort it out *our* way. And our boys ended up being slaughtered like pigs on them beaches in Dunkirk and nowhere for them to run. It's bloody scandalous.'

'That's absolute tosh and you know it!' Elwyn stabbed the air with his finger. 'Churchill didn't start this war. It was a Government decision, a proper ...'

'*He* was the Minister of War.' Brian had dribble on his chin. 'He could have stopped it if he wanted to. You *know* that.'

'*How* could he have stopped it?' Elwyn gripped the newspaper so hard it was scrunched into a ball. 'Hang out the white flag? Invite Hitler to tea in Buckingham Palace and beg for a treaty? You can't trust those bleedin' Germans as far as you can spit. They're out of control, and *you* know it. They're a serious threat to us. Our lads went over there to try and stop this war happening in the first place.'

'Well it didn't bloody work, did it?'

'You can't blame Churchill for *that,*' Elwyn yelped. 'No one expected the Germans to do what they did, come down behind them through Holland and that. Churchill did his best to prevent a war. And when it all went wrong he desperately tried to get our lads home again.'

'Well he shouldn't have sent them to begin with, should he?' Brian spat back. 'Hitler didn't want a war with us. He made that perfectly clear. If we'd left him alone, he'd have left us alone. Now look at the state of us. Coventry, Birmingham, Cardiff! Nothing left. All blown to smithereens!'

Brian drew on the last of his cigarette before flicking it out the gap in the window.

'And look at the date!' he added, picking a bit of tobacco off his lip. 'It's exactly one year since he started this bloody war. So if he's gone and popped his old slippers, well good riddance to him. That's all I have to say about it.'

Elwyn unfolded the newspaper. 'What do you mean, one year ...?'

O'Shea pointed to the date at the top. 'The third of September. The day our lads went across the Channel.'

'Good God.' Elwyn continued to study the paper. 'Just one year ago? My good God, it feels a damn sight longer than that.'

He took out a packet of cigarettes and handed one to O'Shea, and the match fizzled as he cracked it against the box and held it out. O'Shea sucked the smoke in deep as Elwyn lit his own then shook the match out. O'Shea rubbed another hole in the steamed up window and looked out. But all he could see was his ghostly reflection with gloom written all over his face.

'The problem with Churchill ...' Brian Williams spun around again and jabbed a finger at Elwyn.

'Oh, for God's sake!' Elwyn turned away from him and rolled up his newspaper.

'So what are you going to do, Danny?' he asked O'Shea, deliberately not looking up at Williams. 'Are you going back to Ireland?'

'I wish to God I knew, Elwyn.' O'Shea flicked ash from his coat. 'Heather's determined to stay here, take her chance in her own home. I can't see me changing her mind.'

Williams gave a loud snort. 'Typical bloody Paddy, isn't it? You come over here and take the jobs from decent Welshmen. But as soon as things get a bit rough, what do you do, eh? You trot off back to Boggyland, that's what!'

Elwyn grinned at O'Shea and rolled his eyes. 'Just ignore him, Danny.'

O'Shea grinned back. He wished he could, but it wasn't easy to ignore Brian Williams. Especially since he was the foreman down at Turner's Marine Engineering. It didn't pay to upset him if you valued your job. The last time O'Shea crossed him he spent two miserable weeks trying to replace a rusty old pump in the bowels of an African freight ship,

'Well, I suppose tis understandable,' O'Shea sighed. 'God knows, everyone's feeling a bit tense at the moment.'

'Tense?' Elwyn laughed. 'I'm not tense, Danny Boy. I'm bloody petrified.'

O'Shea let out a splutter, but there was no humour in it because he knew exactly what Elwyn meant. Thin, bony fingers of dread had snaked around his heart the moment he heard Lord Haw-Haw talk about Churchill. And they were squeezing tighter with every minute that passed.

He couldn't get Heather and Adam out of his mind. Heather *knew* Adam was in mortal danger if the Germans ever came. But still she wasn't prepared to take him to Ireland out of harm's way. The frustration of not being able to persuade her was making him physically sick.

'And another thing, O'Shea...' Williams turned around in his seat again just as strange glow lit up the inside of the tram like a sudden burst of sunlight. There was a moment of stunned silence then an almighty thud blew the windows of the tram into fragments of flying glass.

Everyone leapt from their seats, clutching frantically at each other as they fell over themselves, pushing blindly to find the way out.

'For God's sake, Danny.' Elwyn grabbed at O'Shea's coat. 'Get out, get out!'

More explosions were coming down the street towards them. The building on their right erupted and spewed out a cloud of debris like a blast of buckshot.

The tram bucked and started to roll over, and it skidded across the road in a screech of torn metal and flying sparks. Then it hit a building with such force the impact bounced it upright again.

And the noise stopped as suddenly as it began. An eerie silence fell down around them.

'Oh, my God ...'

The groan came from somewhere behind O'Shea. He opened his eyes but all he could see was the side of Williams' head. It was pressed back against his face.

He drew back instinctively and went to sit up. And he froze when something sharp dug into his back, high up under his shoulder blade. He sagged back down and took a deep breath before working his hand around so he could reach behind him.

What he felt was cold and long. It was also wet and sticky.

It felt like a steel rod. He gave it a tug but there was no movement in it.

'Brian!' It was a right in his ear but Williams didn't move.

O'Shea brought his arm around to the front again and gave the head a gentle shove. And he yelped as it rolled sideways and dropped on the floor with a dull thud.

The spear dug deeper into his back as his whole body convulsed. Tears filled his eyes as he struggled to control the heaving in his stomach. Then he retched.

It was several before minutes he was back in control and he wiped his mouth on the sleeve of his coat as he tried to look around.

But it was impossible to see what was happening from where he was pinned into the seat. Rain sprayed him through the broken windows. He was sure he could hear the sound of something burning close by. He had to get out. He couldn't just sit there waiting for something to happen. No one was coming to help. He had no choice but to help himself.

He tried bending his knees and sliding down the seat to dislodge the spike. But it made no difference. He was trapped.

But it wasn't just the spike that was stopping him from getting out. Something heavy was wedged across his back as well, pinning him into the corner. He closed his eyes and whispered a prayer.

Gradually he noticed a flurry of activity outside. Fire engine bells clattering in the distance as they raced through the streets. He hoped they were coming in his direction. Inside the tram people were beginning to groan as they struggled to get themselves out from under the carnage. Things clattered on the ground as they were thrown out of the way. Then the sound of someone climbing on board and shuffling around in the wreckage.

'Are you all right there?' A voice somewhere in front of O'Shea.

'I think so,' was the feeble answer. 'If I can just get out from under this rubbish I'll be able to stand up.'

O'Shea raised his head but when he tried to speak his throat dried up.

'There's someone down by here.' A different voice.

'Is he all right?'

'Don't look like. He looks like a goner to me.'

'Best leave him then, isn't it. Concentrate on the live ones. You don't look too good yourself, mind. Maybe you should be sitting down, take it easy, like.'

'No, I'm fine. See, it's only a bruise on the arm. I get worse knocks than that when I'm in work. Come on.'

More rattling and shoving, then O'Shea sensed someone standing close by.

'Poor bastard, he didn't even know what hit him.'

'What about this one by here? Is he still breathing?'

'Good God! That piece of metal's gone right through the seat, right through him, and now it's stuck in that poor sod in front.'

When O'Shea groaned a hand touched his shoulder. 'Glyn, this one's moving. Quick, give me a hand by here.'

'Better not move him, then. Who knows what the damage is. We might kill the two of them.'

'Well it's already too late for this one, I'm afraid. See if we can lift him back a bit.'

O'Shea could feel them struggling and he groaned as the point pressed deeper into him.

'Can you hear me, mate?' One of the men held O'Shea's head.

'Yes,' O'Shea whispered.

'Then try to keep calm. We should wait for a doctor before we move you. But in the meanwhile we'll see if we can stop the bleeding, though it looks bad, you see.'

He took a penknife from his pocket and started to cut at O'Shea's overcoat. 'If it hurts too much let me know.'

After a few minutes of gingerly picking away he reached bare skin.

'Well, well, well. I don't believe it. It's gone right through your clothes and it didn't even break the skin on your back. You'll have a nasty bruise, mind you. But you'll certainly live to talk about it.'

'But all that blood?' the other man. 'It's everywhere. It looks like a bad cut from here.'

'No, no. It looks like the blood's coming from young Elwyn here. He took the full force of the blow. That's what probably saved this lad's life.' He patted O'Shea on the face.

'Elwyn?' O'Shea tried to look behind.

'Elwyn Jenkins. He worked down the docks. I've known him for years, poor bugger.'

'Listen,' the other man said. 'If you hold on, we'll try and prise the spike away from you. All right?'

He pressed O'Shea's shoulders against the seat while the other man tugged at the metal. It gave a soft plop, and suddenly he was free.

'Sorry, Elwyn,' someone said. 'We couldn't help it, you see. We had to get the lad out, didn't we?'

They helped O'Shea to stand up. And when he glanced back he cringed at the look of shock on Elwyn's face. The eyes staring into space and the mouth open in a silent cry.

'Come on, you'd better get going,' Glyn gave O'Shea a pat on the arm. 'Go on home, now. And you can thank God He spared you today.'

Chapter Three

'Where were the bloody sirens?' The woman's hysterical cries echoed off the battered walls of Shaftsbury Street as she staggered through the piles of rubble scattered all over the road. She held a cloth to her head. The cloth was saturated with blood.

'I didn't hear no sirens,' she sobbed. 'Why wasn't there no sirens?'

All around her little knots of people were pulling at what was left of their homes. Some of them looked up at her and one or two of them even nodded in agreement. Then they turned back and carried on searching through the wreckage for their loved ones.

The miserable rain had created streams that poured down both sides of the road. It washed into O'Shea's shoes as he stared in shock at what was left of Shaftsbury Street. How long he'd been standing there he didn't know. He couldn't even remember how he got there.

All he knew was he'd walked up this street on the way to work less than one hour ago and now there was nothing left of it. A huge crater split the road in two. Everything was peppered with lumps of shattered masonry and broken chimney pots. Bits of green and blue window frames jutted out of cracked walls like accusing fingers.

Thick clouds of smoke wafted in from all sides carrying the heavy smell of death and destruction with it. Pockets of flames danced around wooden rafters and caused roofs to crash down onto the shells with a deep grumble.

Dark September

A policeman stood in the middle of the street with his hands hanging loosely by his sides. From the dazed look in his eyes it was obvious he wasn't prepared for something like this. Yes, Newport docks and the steelworks had been bombed many times over the past few months. But this was different. This was far more ferocious, far more intense. He looked totally bewildered.

'She's right, you know,' O'Shea called to him.

'What?

'The sirens! There weren't any air raid sirens.'

The policeman shook his head, causing droplets to fly off his wet helmet.

'That's because it wasn't a bloody air raid.' His eyes were red in a pasty grey face. 'We were bombarded by warships out there in the Channel. They came at the crack of dawn and bombed everything along the coast with rockets and missiles. They hit Swansea, Cardiff, Newport. The English side too. Bristol.'

'Oh my God ...'

'Right now, even as we speak, Germans are coming ashore all over the country. They'll be concentrating on securing the docks, the steelworks, the collieries.' He gave a dramatic sweep of his hand. 'It looks like Hitler has waited long enough. He's coming over to sort it out himself.'

He glared at O'Shea for a moment before turning sharply and walking away down the street with his shoulders hunched and his head bowed.

O'Shea's heart gave a sharp thump. Henry Street was still two blocks away. Suddenly there wasn't any time left. He spun on his heels and sprinted back down Shaftsbury Street. If he hurried they could still get the train to Fishguard and catch that ferry to Ireland.

Dark September

A rough shortcut took him across the wasteland at the back of the school, and it took him less than four minutes to reach the embankment at the end of Henry Street. But as he scrambled through the thick undergrowth and slid down the other side he knew he was already too late.

One side of Henry Street had taken a direct hit. Several houses were completely gone, and the ones on either side were just broken shells. Others had dense smoke billowing out through broken windows and cracks in the walls. Ugly shards of flame belched up through the shattered roofs.

Number fourteen was on fire and O'Shea howled as he charged down the road towards it. At this time of day there was only one place Heather and Adam would be – at home in bed. He had to get them out. There was no hesitation. He threw himself at the door.

It crashed open with a shriek and he fell in with it. But a wall of flame came bursting down the hallway and the searing heat drove him back out into the middle of the street.

As he landed on his knees he heard a deep, sinister rumble inside the house. Then the roof crashed down through the top floor. Sparks and dust spurted up in a swirling cloud and mingled with the dancing smoke.

O'Shea fell back and covered his ears with his trembling hands.

The crackle of burning wood sent another wave of smoke across the street. The rain had stopped now, but thick grey clouds still hung low in the sky and shrouded Henry Street in a miserable damp haze.

Dark September

An hour, maybe two, had passed. O'Shea was curled up in a doorway on the other side of the street. He was too distressed to care what was going on around him.

Houses still burned fiercely, throwing fingers of flame in whichever direction the breeze blew. And smoke billowed around the group of men passing buckets of water to each other in a desperate attempt to stop the fire spreading to the others properties.

Farther down the street some women were piling boxes and suitcases out on the pavement, getting ready to move to a safer place. Their neighbours were trying to reason with them, saying it would make more sense to stay in their homes until they knew what was happening. Others just wandered aimlessly, misery etched on their faces and their haunted eyes darting all over the place as they looked for some kind of guidance.

O'Shea just sat there and ignored it all. His senses were torn to shreds. He couldn't believe he'd been so weak, so incapable of making a simple decision about the safety of his family. Why didn't he just take control and move them to Ireland? What madness made him hesitate like that? They should have gone months ago! Now he was consumed by the guilt of it. It welled up in his throat and almost choked him. He had to swallow hard to stop himself being sick.

Someone shuffled through the door behind him and he glanced up.

'Are you all right, Danny?' Mrs Evans put a hand on his shoulder.

'I'm fine,' he lied, shifting out of her way.

Mrs Evans wore her usual wrap-around housecoat. O'Shea had never seen her in anything else in all the years he'd lived in Henry Street. It was her trademark.

'You haven't seen our Harold, have you, Danny?' There was fear in her voice. 'Only I'm waiting for him to come home. He went to see his brother Sam to find out what's happening. But he's been gone ages. I hope to God he's all right.'

'I'm sure he is.' O'Shea wiped his mouth with his sleeve.

'I wish the bugger would hurry up, though.' Her face screwed up in a frown. 'I'm terrified waiting here on my own. I don't know what to do. What *are* we supposed to do, Danny? Should we just stay here or should we pack our things and get the hell out of Newport?'

When O'Shea didn't answer she gave another sigh.

'So what are you and Heather going to do, Danny?' she asked absently, her eyes still scanning the street. 'Are you going to stay here or will you ...?'

She gasped and her hand went to her mouth as she realised what she'd just said. 'Oh dear God, Danny, I'm so sorry. I wasn't thinking. I didn't mean ... I'm so, so sorry. I ...'

'Ah, there you are.' A gruff voice made Mrs Evans spin around and her knee knocked O'Shea on the arm.

'Harold!' she yelped. 'I didn't hear you come in. Where the hell have you been?'

'I came in the back way.' Mr Evans was over six feet tall and his enormous frame filled the doorway. 'Sam and I had a scout around to see what's going on. I came back through the lane.'

'So what are we doing?' Mrs Evans took his hand. 'Are we staying here or what?

'Well, according to Sam there's a massive crowd trying to get out of town.' Beads of sweat glistened on his forehead. 'Every road is choked solid. Sam says if the Germans come it'll be bad news for anyone in their way. They'll just bulldoze their way through. He says it would be suicide to get caught up in that.'

'So are we staying put, then?'

'Aye, we're staying put.' Mr Evans gave her hand a gentle squeeze and they both shuffled back down the hallway.

A moment later Mr Evans was back behind O'Shea. 'I'm sorry about your loss, Danny. And your ... look, you can stay here with us if you want. Until you sort something out. That's if you want to, like.'

O'Shea scrambled to his feet and wiped his hands on his shirt. 'I ... yes. If that's all right with you and Mrs Evans. Thank you. But I don't want to be a burden.'

'Then why don't you go and fetch that boy of yours and bring him over.'

'Harold!' Mrs Evans jabbed him in the ribs and nodded towards the shell of O'Shea's house. Her husband looked at it and then at O'Shea, and he scratched the top of his head.

'But I've just seen him. I recognised that check shirt he wears. You know? The one Danny said was a real cowboy shirt his cousin sent him from America. It was definitely him.'

'Where did you ...?' O'Shea's voice cracked and his head was suddenly light. He felt himself sag and he had to lean against the doorframe. 'Where did you see him? Was he on his own?'

Mr Evans looked at O'Shea for a second before his eyes dropped to his hands. 'Yes. He *was* on his own, I'm afraid. He was sitting on a swing over in the school playground. That's probably why I noticed him because he was the only one there.'

O'Shea didn't hear the rest. He was already bolting down the street towards the redbrick schoolhouse.

Dark September

Chapter Four

As O'Shea rushed through the school gate he spotted the little figure in the far corner of the playground rocking back and forth on the solitary swing. And a cocktail of emotions caused tears to smart his eyes. He wiped them away with his fingers as he hurried across the yard and wrapped his arms around his son.

Adam looked startled and gripped onto the chains. And when he looked at O'Shea it was like he'd never seen him before in his life.

'It's all right now, son.' O'Shea ruffled the boy's hair and kissed him on the top of his head. 'Everything's all right now. Your Da's here.'

It took a few moments for Adam to focus properly on the man kneeling on the ground in front of him. Then he gave a huge smile of recognition and threw his arms around his father. And he buried his face in his neck.

A gust of wind rustled the trees on the other side of the wire fence and spattered them with raindrops as O'Shea looked around the yard. It was empty. Adam was alone. He took the boy's arms from around his neck.

'Adam, where's your mother? Where's your mam?'

Adam blinked a few times. 'Mam's in bed.'

'Adam, listen to me, son. This is very important. Do you understand? I need to know where your mother is.'

'She's in bed, though.' Adam was looking everywhere except at his father.

O'Shea rubbed his eyes again. 'Adam, you wouldn't be out of bed all by yourself at this time of the morning. Now would you? And you certainly wouldn't be out in the street. Not on your own. If you're up then your mother would be up too, wouldn't she?'

The boy's face had gone blank again. He lowered his head and started to rock on the swing, pressing his toes hard on the ground. O'Shea sat back on his heels. He knew all it took to get a sensible answer out of Adam was a little patience. But right now he felt only frustration. And fear. And they were quickly eroding what little patience he had left.

'I heard something,' Adam said suddenly. 'I got up to see what it was.'

'And what was it, son? What did you hear? Was it your mam?'

Adam let his head roll back and he stared up at the sky. The vacant look was back in his eyes.

'Mam's in bed,' he said again.

'Then why are you dressed and out in the street?' O'Shea snapped. The tone of his voice startled Adam and he jerked up straight. And his lip quivered.

'I heard a big crash.' As he sputtered over the words his eyes filled with tears. 'I got up and put on my clothes and I went into Mam's room and the window was all broken and it was all over her bed and she wouldn't talk to me. Her eyes were open and she was looking at the fire but she wouldn't talk to me so I came downstairs. There was black stuff everywhere and I couldn't see. It was making me cough and I was sick so I said I was going outside but she never answered me.'

O'Shea's stomach heaved and he sagged back on the ground, gagging on the bile that stung the back of his throat. He didn't want to hear this. Adam must be confused. He was often confused. Heather would never let him wander off on his own like that. She'd be out looking for him right now.

But deep down O'Shea knew he was grasping at a thin wisp of hope. And right now Adam was in grave danger out here in the open like this. He wouldn't survive closer scrutiny if the soldiers came.

So for the sake of his son O'Shea needed to get a grip, drag himself back to reality and get out of there fast before they were spotted.

He looked around the school playground one more time and his chest tightened with the dreadful sadness that filled his heart. He took the boy by the hand and headed back over to Henry Street.

Chapter Five

Mrs Evans had closed her front door. O'Shea gave the brass knocker a quick rattle and listened to it echo in the hallway. After a few moments he heard the shuffling of her feet on the tiled floor.

'Hello?' Mrs Evans' voice had a cautious tone as she pulled the door open just enough to see who it was.

'Tis only us.' O'Shea put his hand on Adam's shoulder and guided him into her view. She gave a relieved sigh and opened the door wider.

A motorcycle roared into the street and they both jumped. The shiny black sidecar with German insignia lifted off the ground as the driver did a tight turn before sliding to a stop in a shower of dirt.

Everyone in the street turned to look at it. The men fighting the fire stopped in mid swing. And one or two lowered their buckets on the ground. Some women grabbed their children. Others shot back into their houses and slammed the doors.

In less than half a minute the only sound in the street was the purr of the motorcycle.

The soldier in the sidecar took off his goggles and his eyes narrowed against the watery sun. He looked startled by the sea of faces staring back at him. There was a map open on his lap. He glanced down at it then looked up again. The driver sat perfectly still. They both seemed very young. And very nervous.

'Stupid bastard's got himself lost.' Mr Evans came out of the door and squeezed past O'Shea onto the pavement.

Nothing moved and the tension crackled in the stillness. The soldiers were getting increasingly anxious at the way everyone just stood gaping at them as if waiting for something to happen.

The man in the sidecar muttered to the driver and they both looked down at the map.

Then someone dropped a bucket and the sudden crash made the soldiers jump. The driver gave a strange squeal and revved the engine, making it roar like an angry bear. Then the motorcycle shot forward and tore off down Henry Street scattering everyone in its path.

They didn't know Henry Street was a dead end. When they reached the bottom of the road they skidded to a halt. Obviously flustered now, the driver took a wide swing as he tried to turn around. But he misjudged the width of the street, bounced up onto the pavement and pinned the sidecar against the wall. And he got a flurry of abuse from the man in the sidecar.

The driver tried to move the bike backwards and in his panic he stalled the engine. Ripples of laughter from the watching crowd threw them into even more of a flap and their embarrassment was quickly turning into irritation.

It took three attempts to restart the engine. Then they roared back up the street. Everyone scattered again, running in all directions to get out of the way.

Little Elsie Taylor couldn't run fast enough. The sidecar caught the back of her legs and threw her up in the air. And her head collided with the soldier's helmet before she flipped over his back and landed in the middle of the road.

The screams of horror were drowned out by the roar of the motorcycle as it careered off the road onto the pavement. It clipped the wall of a house and spun back into the middle of the road. And once more the engine stalled.

A dreadful howl exploded from Mrs Evans as she charged out from behind O'Shea and ran up the road to where Elsie Taylor was sprawled on the ground.

Mr Evans followed her, mumbling incoherently and slapping his hands against his head. His lips were pulled back in a horrible snarl and words were coming out. But O'Shea couldn't catch what he was saying.

Then the big man gave a heart-wrenching cry as he staggered across the road towards the motorcycle. 'You mad bastards. You've killed our little girl. You've killed our Elsie.'

The driver looked shocked. The man in the sidecar was holding his head in his hands. Blood oozed from between his fingers. The driver yelled at him but he didn't respond.

With the furious figure of Mr Evans rushing towards them the driver jumped on the pedal and tried to kick-start the engine again. But all he got was a dull sputter.

Mr Evans kept coming. The soldier pulled a pistol from his belt and waved it in the air. He was yelling. It was in German but the meaning was clear.

'You stupid, murdering, sausage eating bastards.' Mr Evans had spit dribbling down his chin. 'You killed our little Elsie.'

The German pointed the pistol at the big man's face but Mr Evans was having none of it. He reached out to grab the soldier and the soldier clipped him across the face with the pistol.

Mr Evans staggered back and his face glowed bright red with anger. He glared at the German as he held his cut jaw with shaking hands. Then, foolishly, he tried to grab him again.

Two shots hit him in the head. He dropped in the road and lay perfectly still.

All over the street people threw themselves to the ground. The man in the sidecar was suddenly alert, shaken by the gunshots. He whipped out a machine gun from somewhere and swung it in a wide arc. The look on his face was total alarm.

A woman screamed and dashed across the street to drag her children out of harm's way. Another woman wrapped Elsie in a coat and was carrying her towards an open door. She froze for a second, glanced around then carried on.

The driver kicked at the motorcycle pedal again and squealed in rage when nothing happened.

A stone came from somewhere and clattered off his helmet. He gave a surprised cry and held his head. When he realised he wasn't actually hurt he leapt off the motorcycle and waved the pistol around as he tried to spot the culprit.

What he saw was Mrs Evans stomping towards him with mad eyes and a ferocious snarl on her face. He staggered back against the motorcycle. His hand started to shake and he howled at the other soldier again.

In his rush to get out of the sidecar the other soldier slipped and his leg got caught in the seat. He toppled out onto the road still holding the machine gun. And as he hit the ground there was a long burst of gunfire. Bullets sprayed all over the street and took large chips out of the masonry. In the confusion the driver fired too. Mrs Evans danced for a fraction of a second before dropping onto her back.

Everyone was scattering now, crawling along the ground to keep as low as possible before disappearing into any opening they could find and slamming the door behind them.

Dark September

Arthur Martin and his wife barged past O'Shea and ran into the Evans' house. O'Shea grabbed Adam and went to follow them but the door had already slammed shut. He gave it a push, then an angry kick as he yelled for Martin to open up. Martin didn't answer. O'Shea kicked the door again and shouted through the letterbox. But still no one responded.

He couldn't see anyone either. They must all be hiding under the stairs. O'Shea and Adam ran to the house next door. That door was locked too.

O'Shea looked around in desperation. He was horrified that in less than a heartbeat every door in Henry Street was shut and bolted. Now he and his son were the only ones standing in the open.

The soldiers watched them warily. The one with the handgun had a weird sneer on his lips. He gave an arrogant wave of his hand and beckoned O'Shea to come closer.

A painful cry made the soldier jump. He crouched as he spun on his heels, holding his gun out straight. And he aimed it at the only thing he could see. A figure struggling to get back on her feet.

Mrs Evans managed to get on to her knees, then stand up into a crouch. Blood dripped from her hands.

The soldiers looked at each other and gave a chuckle of relief. The woman glared at them through bloodshot eyes. And as she staggered towards them the driver aimed the pistol at her head.

O'Shea didn't have time to think. In a split second he had a brick in his hand and he threw it with all the strength he could muster.

The driver glanced up and the brick hit him in the face with such force he dropped flat on his back. The pistol flew out of his hand and clattered along the ground.

The other soldier was still sitting on the ground where he'd fallen and he didn't see what happened so he was slow to react.

But when he spotted O'Shea racing towards him he rolled away and let off a burst from his machine gun. It tore lumps out of the tree behind O'Shea's head as his fingers scratched the ground and snapped up the pistol.

And he got off one shot before he too rolled away. It hit the soldier in the middle of the chest. He jerked with the impact and dropped his gun, and he looked down in horror at the hole in his uniform. His hand came up to touch the wound. Then surprise turned to fear and he sagged back and closed his eyes.

O'Shea dropped the pistol and scrambled to his feet just as Mrs Evans reached him. He went to hold her but she shrugged him away.

'Thank you, Danny boy,' she said. 'But you should have left them to me. I wanted to rip their bastard guts out.'

She took a kick at the driver.

'You're hurt' O'Shea tried to see what was causing so much bleeding.

'It's just a flesh wound.' She pushed him away again. 'Nothing's broken.'

Then her gaze fell on Mr Evans and she gave a soft sob as she sagged down beside him and cradled his head in her lap. 'Oh, my poor wee man,'

Doors began opening again and people filtered out, cautiously looking up and down the street. Someone covered Mr Evans with a coat and took a distraught Mrs Evans into one of the houses.

'What are we going to do now?' a woman asked in a shaky voice that was close to hysteria. 'There's soldiers coming down the next street. We'll all be killed if they see what you've done.'

Her eyes were fixed on O'Shea. His whole body was shaking. He wanted to run away but fear had paralysed him. Reaching out to Adam, he took him by the hand.

'You'd better get off the street,' a voice called from one of the upstairs windows. 'The soldiers are almost here.'

'They'll see the bodies and think we killed them. They'll take it out on us!'

'Well I'm not staying here to be killed. I'm off.' Mr Allen from number eleven was well into his seventies. He'd seen enough during the Great War to last him forever. He shuffled off down the road.

'Why don't we hide them?' Gary Fredrick stuttered and his hands were flapping all over the place. 'Before their friends get here. If they don't see them they won't know anything happened.'

'Hide them where? We haven't time to ... what are you saying? Hide them in someone's house?'

'Yes!' Peter Redman was O'Shea's next-door neighbour. Still in his early twenties, he'd already lost most of his hair apart from a sprinkling of wispy bits around his ears. They'd lived side by side for over six years and they borrowed bits and pieces from each other. But O'Shea could never warm to him. There was something too serious about Peter Redman. 'We can hide them in one of *those* houses.'

'What?' They all turned and looked at the burning ruins. 'How're you going to do that? You'll never get close enough. It's too hot. You'll roast alive if you try to drag them in there.'

More people were carrying boxes out of their front doors and scurrying down towards the wasteland at the back of the street. They probably thought they wouldn't meet any soldiers if they kept off the roads.

'Look, smash out the rest of that window,' Redman said. 'Drag them over to it and we'll throw them in as far as possible. There's enough of us to do it. Then we can throw something in on top of them to make sure. No one will ever know what happened to them. So come on. We haven't got much time.'

The soldiers were unceremoniously dragged by the arms and legs across the street. Two men pulled the remains of the window frame from the wall. Spurts of flame snaked dangerously close to them as they threw the bits of wood back into the fire.

The rest of the men lifted the bodies one at a time, swung them back and forth to get momentum and threw them as hard as they could in through the gap. They disappeared in a shower of sparks. Then the men all hurried back into the middle of the road and stood in silence as they pondered on what to do next.

'What about the motorbike?'

Young Michael Jenkins took a closer look. Apart from a few dents it appeared to be all in one piece. He climbed onto it and fiddled with the bits and pieces, twisting the clutch and crunching the gears. Then he jumped hard on the pedal.

To everyone's surprise the engine shuddered and gave a throaty growl. He revved the accelerator and made it roar. And the spontaneous burst of laughter was followed immediately by relieved clapping.

'Now take it and dump it somewhere.'

'What?' Michael Jenkins shot off the bike. 'I'm not taking it anywhere. I've got a wife and … no, not me, I'm afraid. I'm not getting caught anywhere near it.'

'Well we can't just leave it here. It'll defeat the whole object of burning the bodies.'

'Can't we roll it into the house as well? It'll burn too.'

'How?' Malcolm Taylor was spinning in little circles, apparently trying to decide if he should stay or if he should run after the others who were disappearing around the corner at the end of the road. 'It wouldn't fit in the door, would it? And we couldn't possibly lift it in the window.'

'Well we have to get rid of it. And quick. Someone has to take it away from here or we're all in the shit up to our necks.'

'Not me. If you're seen on that thing they'll shoot you on the spot. No thanks.'

'Then who? If we don't shift it now we'd all better start running. And keep running. There won't be any coming back.'

A shudder ran through O'Shea. If he was to keep Adam safe he needed to get him away from this place. And he needed to do it now. There was nothing left for him here anyway. His only hope was to go to Heather's mother in Tredegar.

But Tredegar was a long way from Newport. It would take days to get there if they had to walk. And every step would heighten the chance of being discovered.

'I'll do it.' The words were out before he could stop himself. And there was an awkward hush as everyone looked from him to Adam and back again.

'Danny, are you sure?' Paul Redman's face showed real concern. But there was relief in his eyes as well. He patted O'Shea on the arm.

'No,' O'Shea answered in a hoarse voice. 'I'm *not* sure. But we can't stay here. I need … we need to get to Adam's grandmother.'

'It'll be an awful big risk, you know. Where does she live? Will this machine take you that far?'

O'Shea hesitated. He was suddenly aware the less his neighbours knew about where he was going the safer it would be. 'She lives way up there in the Brecons,' he lied. 'If I make it I'll dump the bike down some old mine shaft.'

Someone patted him on the shoulder, and someone else shook his hand.

'Thank you, Danny Boy.'

Malcolm Taylor went to hug him but tapped him on the chest instead. 'Good luck, Danny. And God bless you. Now go. Get out of here while you can.'

'Come on, son.' O'Shea put his arm around Adam. 'Climb into the sidecar there.'

'Mam?' Adam looked over at the burning house.

'Quickly now, son. We have to go *now*.'

Adam pulled away and shook his head. Tears filled his eyes. 'What about Mam?'

'Adam, please. Just get in.'

'No. I want Mam. I want to stay here.'

'For God's sake,' O'Shea snapped. 'How the hell can you stay here?'

'My mam's here. I want to stay with Mam.'

O'Shea sighed bitterly and wiped his face on his sleeve. The fingers of panic were squeezing tighter around his heart and he felt the bile rise up in his throat again. He grasped Adam tightly by the arm and when the boy whimpered O'Shea let him go again. Damn! He took a deep breath. A bit of reasoning was all that was needed.

'Look, Adam, I'll tell you what we'll do. We'll go and see Nana. We'll go and find Nana and then we'll come back here. And Mam will make us a nice cup of tea. Wouldn't that be nice, eh? A nice cup of tea. And maybe she'll have some Welsh cakes for us as well. And we'll put lots of butter on them. What do you say?'

O'Shea held out his hand. Adam stared at it for a moment, unsure, his eyes anxious. He glanced at the house then back at O'Shea. Then he walked over and put his hand in his father's.

'Welsh cakes, Dada?'

O'Shea lifted him into the sidecar and wrapped the heavy army blanket around him.

'Welsh cakes, son. And plenty of butter.'

There was a set of goggles on the ground where the soldier had dropped them and O'Shea put them on before climbing onto the motorbike. He glanced around at what had been his life, at the wreck of his house, at the neighbours who gave self-conscious waves. He put the motorcycle into gear and gave a few turns of the handle. The engine roared and he pulled away and drove out of Henry Street.

Chapter Six

By the time they got to Malpas Road it was already swarming with people pouring in from every side street and moving in a solid mass along the main route out of Newport. Women pushed prams and men dragged wheelbarrows stacked high with things they were desperate to save.

Bicycles had huge bundles on them, and the men wheeling them were pulling children along too. Even the children staggered under piles of baggage.

But some people only had the clothes they were standing up in. They were the most frightened. They barged through the crowd, desperate to put as much distance between them and the advancing soldiers as they could.

And all around them buildings were on fire and smoke billowed across the road.

O'Shea couldn't go any faster than a walking pace as he weaved through the swaying wall of bodies, and he was struggling to control the panic that simmered up inside him.

What if someone noticed the Nazi insignia on the sidecar? He wouldn't be able to accelerate away. They'd tear him to shreds. He rearranged the blanket on Adam's lap so it fell down over the side and dragged along the ground. Hopefully the crowd would be too engrossed in their own survival to take notice of a motorbike with a child in the sidecar.

He glanced back to see how far behind the Germans were. If they were getting too close he'd abandon the motorcycle and take their chance amongst the crowd. But as far as he could make out the Germans were concentrating on the massive steelworks across the river. Most of the smoke came from there.

It took well over an hour just to get to the outskirts of Pontypool. Then a left turn took him onto the long road that sliced through the massive slag heaps clinging to the side of the mountains above Crumlin town.

The people there were spilling out of their homes too but it was hard to decide which way they were trying to go. They crossed from one side of the street to the other and sometimes even staggered back in the opposite direction to the rest of the crowd.

On the other side of Crumlin the people thinned out and O'Shea was able to open the throttle. And as he followed the narrow road up to Blackwood the sun was a watery disc behind the clouds sitting on top of the hills. They wiped out all the colour and shrouded the world in a dismal grey haze. The damp air clung to their faces and fogged up the goggles.

At a junction where several roads converged a rusty sign told them Tredegar was now only three miles away.

O'Shea glanced down when Adam tapped him on the leg. And the look on the boy's face made his heart sink. He pulled onto the grass verge and shut off the engine. Removing the goggles, he wiped his face on his sleeve, got off the bike and helped Adam out of the sidecar.

'I'm wet, Dada.'

'I can see that!'

O'Shea took him into a field through a gap in the hedge, and he could tell by the smell that Adam hadn't just wet himself.

'For God's sake, couldn't you have waited? Just a few more miles and we'd be at Nana's.'

'But sorry, Dada.'

O'Shea closed his eyes and gave a slow, deep moan. He'd had to deal with this kind of stuff so many times over the years and it had never bothered him before. Adam was his son. It wasn't a problem. Whenever Adam got worried or excited he wet himself. O'Shea understood and he cleaned it up.

But this time it felt so different. It was like being hit in the chest by something from a nightmare. And it caused a bitterness in O'Shea's heart that he'd never felt before.

It took him a minute to regain his compose. None of this was the boy's fault. What happened to Adam all those years ago was just an accident. A terrible, cruel accident. It could have happened to anyone. A simple twist of fate that turned all their lives upside down.

It was just an ordinary day. Heather took Adam for a stroll around Shaftsbury Park and down by the river Usk. He waddled along ahead of her, standing on his toes to reach the handle of the pram as he pushed it through the long grass that was peppered with daisies.

Heather looked away for the briefest of moments. She saw a neighbour sitting on a bench and waved hello.

Adam's distressed yelp made her jump. And when she turned around the pram was gone. A huge wedge of riverbank had broken away. The child and the pram had dropped into the river.

Before Heather could react Adam was pulled away by the ferocious tidal current and swept out into the middle of the river. It was dragging him towards the town bridge.

Heather's screams alerted two young men on the opposite bank of the river and they scrambled down through the thick mud to a small boat tied to a beer barrel. And they rowed frantically after the child for almost a mile before they came into sight of the giant Transporter Bridge, a huge metal structure that straddles the river.

Built in 1906 when Newport was a busy port, the Transporter Bridge was basically a suspended ferry designed to connect the two sides of the river. A boom is suspended from 240 foot high towers, one on each bank. The boom has a rail track and a carriage operated by twin 35 horse power electric motors.

Hanging from the carriage on steel ropes is a gondola, large enough to carry six cars and numerous foot passengers. And this is pulled from one side of the river to the other by means of a hauling cable.

Now the tide was turning and the river was at its highest as Adam was dragged towards it. The gondola was only ten feet above the water as it headed back to the town side of the river. When the guard noticed the men in the boat chasing the struggling child he rang the alarm bell and shouted to the crew.

They dropped a cluster of buoys into the water and tied them to the railings. And as the driver manoeuvred the gondola into the path of the child three men slid down the ropes. Then as Adam swept by them they grabbed his shirt and hauled him out.

Back on the platform they couldn't get him to breathe so they piled him into the back of a cars and raced him off to the Royal Gwent Hospital.

It took a dangerously long time but the doctors worked a miracle and brought him back to life.

In the meantime Heather had run all the way along the riverbank to the railway bridge, gathering a crowd of people as she went. And by the time she reached the Transporter Bridge she was near to collapse.

But the news that Adam had been rescued gave her the strength to run up Mendlegiefe Road to the hospital. The relief of finding him alive reduced her to a flood of tears and she fainted on the floor. They put her in the bed next to her son.

When O'Shea got there later a doctor took him into a small room, sat him on a hard chair and told him the bad news. Because of the time it took to revive Adam there would have been a severe lack of oxygen to his brain. There was a strong possibility of permanent damage. He was very sorry but he couldn't say how bad it was going to be at this stage. Only time would tell.

Now Adam was ten years old and he had his mother's soft fair hair and big hazel eyes. And to look at him you'd think he was just another ordinary little boy.

It was only when you spoke to him you'd notice the difference. The lack of response. The vacant expression. The movements that were awkward and unsure.

Also if he was taken out of his own environment it made him anxious. And he often lost control of his bladder.

O'Shea snatched a handful of long grass and cleaned the boy as best he could. But there was no way he could get his clothes dry. He would just have to sit in them until they got to Tredegar. He pulled the boy's trousers back up and buttoned his coat.

All of a sudden O'Shea realised why he was feeling so resentful. It was because Heather wasn't there anymore.

She'd always been around before. Maybe she'd be in the kitchen doing something else but her presence was all he ever needed. It gave him the strength to do what had to be done. While she was there he knew he could handle all this, deal with whatever came his way.

But now she was gone and he was on his own. And he was no longer sure of anything.

'Better get back in the sidecar, son.'

When he looked into his son's eyes and saw Heather looking back at him it caused a sudden emptiness that made him gasp for breath. His eyes smarted and he couldn't stop the tears.

Adam took his hand. 'Dada?'

O'Shea turned away and wiped his face with his sleeve.

'Why are you crying, Dada?'

O'Shea swallowed and shook his head. Then he lifted Adam into the sidecar.

'Never mind,' Adam said cheerfully. 'Nana will make us some Welsh cakes when we get to her house, won't she, Dada?'

Chapter Seven

The old bridge over the Sirhowy River grumbled as the motorcycle rattled across it, and O'Shea slowed the vehicle right down as he turned it into the long deserted street on the edge of Tredegar town.

The eerie emptiness of the place was exaggerated by the intermittent gusts of wind that blew wisps of drizzle along the wet pavements and rocked the creaking signs that had ice cream advertised on them. The cluster of small shops had their shutters up and their doors locked.

A curtain fluttered in a window across the street and a face darted back out of sight when O'Shea looked up. He was suddenly aware the only noise in the whole place was the growl of the motorcycle.

Quickly switching off the engine, he sat still and listened. Then he realised that for the last couple of miles they hadn't seen a single person on the road. Everything was strangely quiet. A dog in the distance, a crow squawking on a rooftop, but no people.

Heather's mother lived on the other side of the town a few doors along from the old chapel in Church Street. O'Shea didn't want to draw attention by riding the motorcycle through the streets. The only safe thing to do was to hide it somewhere and walk the rest of the way.

He lifted Adam out of the sidecar and together they pushed it down a narrow lane behind Vale Terrace and through a gap in a hedge. It fell down the steep overgrown riverbank, crashed through a clump of thick bushes and rolled over twice before wedging itself behind a pile of rocks. Then they gathered a pile of old coal sacks and planks of rotting wood and threw them down on top of it to cover it completely.

Though they couldn't see a living soul it felt as if they were being watched by a thousand eyes as they crept along the wet streets keeping close to the buildings. Adam's hand squeezed O'Shea's as he too sensed the tension.

In the centre of the town four streets converged to form a wide circle. Standing on a big concrete plinth in the middle was a magnificent clock tower.

O'Shea looked up at it and smiled cynically. He didn't know what the clock represented but he guessed it was in memory of those who died in previous wars. If that *was* the case their spirits must be crying out at the madness that was erupting around it today.

When they reached the house in Church Street they stood looking at it for a moment.

'Is Nana in?'

'I hope so.' O'Shea gave a quick rap on the flaking brown door, taking some of the paint off on his knuckles. He waited a moment, and when there was no answer he knocked again.

Somewhere deep inside there was a sound, faint, but O'Shea heard it and he knocked harder.

'Mrs Mead?'

Still no answer. And no more sound either.

'Mrs Mead? Tis me, Danny. Tis Danny and Adam.'

High overhead a plane buzzed and they stood perfectly still until it vanished again. Then out of the corner of his eye O'Shea caught a movement, a flicker inside the window. He ran to the glass and peered in, blocking the reflection with his hand. But the lace curtain prevented him from seeing into the room. He tapped on the glass.

'Mrs Mead, tis only us. Danny and Adam. Let us in. Please! Open the door.'

He went back to the door and knocked again. 'Please!'

Inside the door a bolt clanged and a chain rattled. Then a key turned and the door opened a little bit to reveal a wary face that looked them up and down.

'Nana! Look, tis us!'

The eyes didn't blink but watched them in silence.

'C'mon, Mrs Mead, will you open the door?'

She drew it open slowly and stepped back. 'What are you ... how did you get here?'

'The Germans are after invading,' O'Shea said. 'They bombed Newport.'

'I know that,' she snapped. 'But what are you doing here?'

'Well, we haven't got anywhere else to go. The Germans are everywhere. Our house was hit. We had to run for our lives.'

She stepped back and waved them into the house. As they walked past her into the dark hallway she put her head out of the door and looked up and down the street. Then she turned back and looked at O'Shea. And her eyes had a terrible fear in them.

'Where's Babs?'

Heather was the youngest child and had always been called Babs. O'Shea cringed and looked away. He'd hoped to break it to her gently. But really there were no words on earth that would have made it easy for her.

'Oh, Sweet Jesus.' She closed her eyes and her hands went together under her chin. And her lips quivered. Then she turned to Adam and put her arm around him.

'My poor child. My poor, poor child.' She hugged him tight against her as she kissed his forehead. 'Babs, did she ...?'

'No.' O'Shea couldn't look at her. 'The house was hit by a bomb while she was inside. She wouldn't have known a thing.'

'Dear God.' Mrs Mead's face was creased in despair as she kissed Adam again. Then she took a deep breath and wiped her face with the hem of her apron.

'Come through to the kitchen.' She turned abruptly and walked ahead down the hallway.

She went straight across to the big black range and started shuffling pots and kettles around. O'Shea sat Adam on one side of the large pine table then squeezed through and sat down on the inside.

'That boy badly needs a bath.' Mrs Mead pointed at him with a wooden spoon. 'I'll get some water on. It won't take long.'

Adam gave a tired smile. Mrs Mead took a kettle to the sink and turned on the old brass tap, and it banged like a drum when the water gushed into it. Then she slammed it back on the range and dropped the lid onto it.

Mrs Mead was a tall dignified lady and you could tell from her eyes and the colour of the hair she was Heather's mother. But there was never any warmth between Mrs Mead and Danny O'Shea. She was strict Presbyterian and attended chapel four or five times a week. And though it was never said, there was a suspicion she couldn't quite accept her daughter marrying a Catholic. And an Irish Catholic at that!

Also she had great difficulty in accepting Adam for what he was. It was as if she was wary of getting too close to him. Maybe worried that his difference from her other grandchildren was some sort of curse from God. She'd became visibly upset when Adam got excited over something other children his age found trivial. As usual he'd wet himself and she'd struggle to hide her embarrassment.

Now O'Shea sensed she was struggling again. And he felt helpless because he just didn't know what to do for her. When he looked up she was holding onto the mantelpiece with one hand and the other hand had a handkerchief pressed to her face.

Her head was bowed and her shoulders rocked with the terrible sobs she could no longer hide.

Chapter Eight

'I wish Dai Jenkins would get some fresh vegetables in that shop of his.' Mrs Mead stuck a knife into another potato with a dull crunch. 'All these are soft and green.'

O'Shea glanced up at her. Although the sky outside was clear and blue, the day was bitterly cold. A biting wind swept in from the east and whistled as it came down the chimney. It made the windows rattle in the tiny kitchen. He drew his chair closer to the warmth of the range.

'Perhaps he's not able to get any fresh vegetables.' O'Shea shoved a poker through the little grill of the range and gave the coals a quick shuffle.

'Pah! It's his duty,' Mrs Mead snorted. 'He's the greengrocer, isn't he? He should give the people tidy vegetables, not this pile of old rubbish.'

'Why don't you go and tell him, so?'

Mrs Mead looked startled for a second then sucked in a gasp of air.

'Why would he listen to me?' She cut at the potato, took off a long sliver of peel and dropped it onto a sheet of newspaper on the kitchen table. 'But *we* know where all the best stuff is going, don't we? And they make bloody sure it gets there too, what with all those Gestapo people creeping around to see none of us objects about it. Not in public anyway.'

A shudder ran through O'Shea. When Mrs Mead came home from chapel that morning she was seething with anger. The pastor announced from the pulpit that a local policeman, Constable Gordon Pearce, was now the Gestapo Officer for the Tredegar area. He would be answerable only to the Bureau in Cardiff.

Dark September

Mrs Mead claimed Pearce he was a miserable little man with an appalling record of spite and petty bureaucracy. But what distressed her most was he came from the town. So he knew everyone. Worse still, he knew their business.

Almost five weeks had passed since the invasion but the people of Tredegar were still living in a strange kind of limbo. Apart from unconfirmed rumours they didn't know what was going on in the rest of the country. They had no contact with the outside world except for a battered wireless in the Post Office. It was switched on for one hour in the afternoon and it broadcasted German scripted news bulletins to the crowd on the pavement outside.

According to the BBC the British public was complying with the German administrators so life in the United Kingdom was returning to normal. However, it was stressed, this was subject to *all* the citizens of the UK behaving responsibly towards the new regime. Unfortunately some disruptive elements did not. And as an example the first public executions were carried out in Hyde Park on Sunday. Five members of the same family were hanged and their bodies left for the public to view until Wednesday. Other such reprisals were repeated in Sheffield and Newcastle. Regrettable as these measures were, they were necessary to discourage any further dissent.

Bizarrely, they never mentioned Winston Churchill. Nobody knew if he was still alive or not.

Apparently the Royal Navy had dispersed to the far reaches of the Empire. The captains were invited to return with their vessels immediately or their families and the families of the crew would be held accountable.

Some new British Army divisions were created but they would not serve overseas. They were commanded by German officers and would only be required to maintain order on the mainland. A Penal Corps was supposed to have been created too, made up of criminals and political activists. But that was never confirmed.

And despite the deluge of rumours coming at them day after day, the town was actually starting to get back to normal again. Most shops had re-opened and even the milk was delivered again at the crack of dawn.

Mrs Mead had taken the news of Heather's death far worse than O'Shea expected. And for the first week there was nothing he could do to console her because he was grieving too.

They both loved Heather and she'd been taken from the both of them. But there was a gulf between Mrs Mead and O'Shea even their common pain couldn't bridge. So instead of sharing the heartache and diluting it, they retreated into their own worlds and took their individual loss with them.

The way Mrs Mead dealt with her private torment was to sit in the kitchen and stare vacantly into the fire. She didn't have the will to eat or drink. Or even to speak. She was already waiting for news of her husband Brian who'd gone off to France with the army and never came back. Since Dunkirk she'd had no word, no letter to say if he was dead or alive. Every morning she'd wander down to the front door to wait for the postman.

Then O'Shea turned up with the worst news of all and she had no husband to turn to, no shoulder to lean on, no arms to hold her while she cried away the pain.

For O'Shea, though, the nights were the worst.

When the darkness closed in on him the nightmares came with it. He'd lie on the bed with Adam asleep in his arms and his eyes burnt from lack of sleep. He'd squeeze them tight and pull a pillow over his ears as if that was going to create a magic buffer to block out the torment.

It never worked. The terrors still came. Little wisps of dark, brooding misery slithered through every little gap in his defences and straight into his tortured mind. The scream of the bombs, the shattering, blinding flash, the horrific final thud that changed his life in the blink of an eye.

He'd see the two Germans lying in Henry Street and his home in flames. His mind would pound with the fear and the guilt. He would feel the heat of the flames that engulfed his house and took Heather away from him forever.

How in God's name could it happen so fast? One moment he was just an ordinary working man on his way to his job. Then the next he was catapulted into a world of unbelievable duress, stumbling blindly through events he had no control over at all.

And he ached with rage as he prayed for the morning to come.

Now, however, they were gradually starting to pick up the pieces again a little bit at a time. Mrs Mead put the pictures of Heather back on the sideboard and she could go a whole day without stopping to look at them. The desperate need to go down to Newport to find her daughter and give her a proper funeral started to wane.

She spent hours writing long rambling letters to her other daughters asking them to come and see her if it was possible. And every morning she still checked the hallway for the postman, though now she spent a little longer looking at the bare mat inside the door.

Dark September

In all that time Adam never said a single word. He crept around the house or played quietly by himself in the front room. He went to bed with his father, got up with him, and sometimes he would just come and sit on his lap and put his arm around his shoulder. But he never said a word.

One morning he suddenly stopped to look at the pictures of his mother on the sideboard. Reaching out, he touched the smiling face of the beautiful girl. And for a second a memory danced in his eyes. But it faded quickly and he went off again to play with a ball.

Chapter Nine

The kettle on the range began to boil and the lid gave a sharp rattle. Mrs Mead tutted and wiped her hands on her apron before moving it to the back plate and putting another pot in its place.

'Did you see that notice outside the Town Hall this morning?' O'Shea asked her.

The flames behind the open door of the range danced hypnotically as they turned the black coals into a brittle grey ash.

'Another notice?' Mrs Mead glanced up then went back to peeling the potatoes. 'What's it about this time?'

'Well, it says they want everyone to report to the Town Hall before Thursday so they can be given new papers and identity cards. Anyone who doesn't is likely to be arrested.'

'But we've already got all that.' She gave a long sigh. 'Ration Books. ID cards. What more do they want, for God's sake?'

'It's some sort of census, I think. I suppose they want to know who's living here in Tredegar. And what they're doing.' O'Shea gave a resigned shrug. 'The trouble is it makes it very awkward for me and Adam.'

'Why? What do you mean?'

'We can't go down to the Town Hall, can we? They'll want to know who we are, what we're doing here. Then they'll know all about Adam.'

'Oh, I don't know.' Mrs Mead thought for a moment. 'I should think he'd be all right if it's just to issue him with some papers.'

'No, he wouldn't.' It came out sharper than O'Shea intended. 'Anyway, I can't take that chance. Not with

Adam's life. Do you know what the Germans *do* to children like Adam? I've spoken to people who've been there and seen it happen! They're taken away from their family and …'

'I know, I know.' Mrs Mead dropped a potato into the pan. 'We've had preachers from Europe visit our chapel. They told us all about it. It's horrific. I can understand why you'd be concerned. But what are you going to do? How do you think you'll get by if you don't have the right papers?'

'Well, actually, I was planning to take him to Ireland.'

'Ireland? Why on earth do you want to take him to Ireland?'

'Because tis the safest place for him right now.'

Mrs Mead put the knife down and wiped her hands on her apron. 'Why do you think that? Why would Ireland be any safer than here?'

'Well, for a start, it's neutral. Ireland's not at war with the Germans. They're not taking sides in this war. The Germans will respect that and leave them alone. So I believe Adam would be safe over there.'

When their eyes met O'Shea thought he saw a flicker of relief in Mrs Mead's and he suppressed a smile. Of course he was aware that whatever bond there was between them when Heather was alive, it died with Heather. Now O'Shea and Adam living in her house was putting a great strain on her. And not just financially.

'But where will you go? How will you manage?'

'I have family over there. The only problem is I'm not sure how we're going to get there. I haven't got any money. But that doesn't matter at the moment. The thing is I'll have to go before this Town Hall thing starts to get serious.'

Mrs Mead scooped up the last of the peeled potatoes and put them into a saucepan and it spat when she put it back on the hot range.

'Would you like some tea, Adam?' She asked as she poured some into a mug and handed it to O'Shea.

Adam nodded. 'And a biscuit, Nana?'

'I wish I had a biscuit to give you. Or a piece of cake, even. But you know how things are.'

Adam frowned and took the mug from her. 'No biscuit, Nana?'

She gave a tired smile. 'No biscuit, son.'

A burst of gunfire out in the street made the windows vibrated. Mrs Mead gave a terrified yelp and let the mug fall to the floor.

'Oh, no!' Her hand went to her mouth. 'Please God, no!'

'Hey, take it easy, now!' O'Shea took her hand and helped her to a chair.

'That was a gunshot, wasn't it?' Her voice shook. 'Was that a gunshot? What was that?'

'I don't know what it was. But I'll go and look, all right? You stay here and stop worrying. It's probably nothing.'

He ran down the hallway to the front door and opened it just wide enough to see down the street.

The sharp wind was making the electricity cables whine as it blew through them, and it pushed huge lumps of cloud all over the sky. Weird shadows rippled along the tops of the houses after them.

Across the road an upstairs curtain fluttered and a child's face appeared at the window. Then a door opened in another house farther down the street and a young girl with a baby in her arms stepped out onto the pavement. She was followed by an older woman.

They watched in silence as two lines of soldiers came marching up the street, their boots crashing as they stomped along on either side of the road. Every few yards one of them stopped and stood to attention at the edge of the pavement.

Moving slowly along behind them was a big car with an open top. The man standing up in the front wore a black German uniform. His head turned from side to side as he shouted into a loudhailer but most of his words were blown away in the breeze.

'What is it, Dada?' Adam pushed his head under O'Shea's arm and tried to pull the door open.

'Shush! I can't hear him.'

'What's he saying, though?'

'Adam, will you be quiet! Look, go back and see if your Nana's all right. There's a good boy.'

'Nana's saying her prayers.' Adam was still pulling at the door.

'*What*?'

The car was closer now and the voice was very clear and very English. Everyone was to come out of their house and go down to the Circle immediately. If they did not they would be arrested.

To emphasis the point the soldiers turned inwards and faced the houses. O'Shea shut the door.

Back in the kitchen Mrs Mead was kneeling on the floor with her hands joined under her chin and her elbows on the chair.

'Come on.' O'Shea barged past her to the back door. 'We have to get out of here *now*!'

'What's happening?' Mrs Mead's eyes were wide with fear.

'They want everyone to go down to the Circle. I don't know why. All I know is we have to get out of here now. We'll go out the back way. Adam, get your big coat on. Quickly now.'

'What are you talking about?' Mrs Mead stood up. 'Where are you taking us?'

'We have to get away from here.' O'Shea was already pulling the door open. 'If we slip out the back way no one will notice us in all the confusion. So come on!'

'I can't go running all over the countryside at my age. I can't go with you. Where are you going? What do you think you're doing?'

'Am I wearing Nana's coat?' Adam yelled as he climbed onto a chair and took an old army jacket off the back of the door. It used to belong to Mrs Mead's husband before he went off to war. She'd taken the sides in and shortened the sleeves. Then she padded it with an old cardigan and now it fitted Adam like a coat.

'Yes.' O'Shea ran back to him. 'Just hurry up. I don't like the look of those guards out there. They might start kicking the door in if we don't come out soon.'

O'Shea retrieved his own coat and pulled it on.

'Where are we going to?' Adam asked.

O'Shea looked at Mrs Mead who was trying to tie a scarf around her head.

'Mrs Mead.' He held up his hand. 'I'm sorry. I didn't mean *you* were to come with us. You should do as the Germans say. Go down to the Circle with the others. Adam and I will sneak out the back door.'

'But why don't you just hide in here?' She sat back down. 'They won't even know you're in here.'

'Oh, but they will. They've already seen me. They *know* we're in here.'

'Dada, where are we going?' Adam asked again.

'We're just going for a little walk, son. Come on.'

He took Adam's hand and nodded to Mrs Mead. 'Are you going to be all right?'

'Yes.' She forced a smile and kissed Adam on the top of his head. 'God bless you.' She looked up at O'Shea. 'I'm sorry it turned out this way.'

'Me, too.' O'Shea went to give her a hug but she moved away. 'I'll be in touch,' he smiled. 'Let you know what's happening.'

They crept out into the tiny back yard and O'Shea opened the gate to the lane that ran along the back of the houses. The wall on the other side of the lane was about three feet high but it dropped down about eight feet into a field that sloped away up a hill to some woods.

O'Shea's first thought was to go that way. But they'd be too exposed. They'd be seen immediately. The only other way was to slink along in the shadow of the buildings until they got to the main road.

There was no one in the lane. O'Shea glanced back at Mrs Mead and she waved at them through the window. He took Adam by the hand and they walked away quickly.

Chapter Ten

Half way along the lane was a narrow alleyway which cut between the houses into Chapel Street. O'Shea could see people running past the gap and down the road towards the town centre. He took Adam's hand and they hurried along the lane hugging the shadow.

'Halt!'

O'Shea froze and Adam walked into him. Two soldiers stepped out in front of them carrying long sticks. One slammed his against the wall knocking a lump of moss off it.

'You're going the wrong way.' He pointed the stick back at the alleyway.

O'Shea's mind went blank. He looked at the low wall on his left. He could vault it easily enough. Then they'd have an open field in front of them. But in a flash he knew it was a stupid idea. How far did he think he'd get dragging Adam behind him? No, he didn't have much of a choice. Squeezing the boy's hand, he turned back towards the alleyway.

Adam smiled at the soldiers and gave a little wave as they walked away. The soldiers didn't smile back. They just stood there looking menacing.

Mrs Mead was pulling her front door shut as they came out onto Chapel Street. She looked startled when they caught up with her but she didn't say anything. And they all walked down the hill together.

When they got to the Circle it was already filling with people streaming in from all directions. O'Shea and Mrs Mead were forced along a narrow channel until eventually they were standing directly in front of the clock. Shouts and screams and a burst of gunfire came from the edge of town. And the crowd squeezed tighter as more bodies pressed in around them.

The black car was pushing a few stragglers along as it came back down the hill and drove into the middle of the square. Mrs Mead groaned as they were crushed by the surge of people trying to get out of its way.

It stopped in front of where O'Shea was standing and gradually the crowd stopped swaying. The noise dimmed into an anxious murmur. While they waited nervously for something to happen the bitter wind tore into them. And the hands of the clock ticked off the time.

'Holy shit!' O'Shea grabbed Mrs Mead's arm. 'I'm just after having an awful thought.'

'What?' She looked startled again and pulled away from him.

'Well, can't you see?' He waved his hand at the people around them. 'Why didn't I see this before? I can't believe I didn't notice this before. It's so feckin obvious now everyone is here.'

Mrs Mead glanced around then looked back at him with a dark glare.

O'Shea's breath was coming in fitful gasps. 'All the times I went to the shops and got the funny looks I thought it was because of Adam. You know, how he is and all that? But tis only just dawning on me now. Everyone around here is either female or very, very old. There's not another man my age in the whole feckin town.'

'Well, of course there isn't,' Mrs Mead snapped. 'They'll all have gone off to the war. Or else they'll be over in Ebbw Vale steel works. If not they'll be over in the colliery. Surely you must have noticed that before now?'

61

'No, I did not.' O'Shea slapped his hands together. 'Now I'm going to stand out like the proverbial spare prick at a wedding.'

'For God's sake!' Mrs Mead recoiled from him.

'Well, I'm sorry.' O'Shea sucked in a cry. 'But what am I going to do now? They're going to notice me straight away and they're going to take Adam away from me. Whatever chance I had of hiding in this crowd has just evaporated.'

Mrs Mead squeezed her eyes shut and her hands went under her chin again.

O'Shea pulled his collar high up around his face and sank deeper into it as he held Adam tighter.

A whole hour dragged by. They blew on their frozen hands and stamped their throbbing feet. And they hardly noticed the little man in the long leather coat strutting over to the car. He climbed into the back and stood up straight, and he clasped his hands behind his back. His small, cold eyes swept the crowd.

'Who's that?'

'Gordon bloody Pearce!' groaned the man on their left.

'The Gestapo man?'

As more people became aware of him, Pearce slowly and deliberately smoothed out an imaginary crease in his coat. And his face was a mask of smugness as he looked at his reluctant audience. He slapped his hands behind his back again and pulled himself up to his full height.

'Right!' He aimed the message at the people at the back. 'I want you all to listen to me very carefully now. You were brought here for a reason, see? And a very important reason at that. Now, you know me. I'm not a great believer in fun and games. So if I tell you that something is serious you can take it from me that it really *is* serious.'

Again the smugness. The crowd shuffled nervously and waited for him to continue. But he was determined to relish the dramatics for a few seconds more.

'It has been brought to my attention,' he continued, 'that an unusual item was found here in Tredegar and handed in to the police station. Now that in itself is a bit unusual around here, as you all know. But that's beside the point. The reason you've all been brought here is this. The object in question was involved in a serious incident down in Newport. Now my superiors in Gestapo HQ in Cardiff want to know *exactly* what happened down there in Newport, who was responsible for it happening in the first place, and how the object ended up here in Tredegar. So it has been bestowed upon my good self to acquire the answers to these questions. And I am to use whatever means I feel necessary to do so.'

His eyes scanned the faces again searching for a reaction.

'But first things first, isn't it?' He grinned at the way his words fell down on the crowd. And when he raised his arm the line of soldiers behind him stepped back to create a gap. Through the gap two men in black uniforms pushed a motorcycle with a sidecar across the cobbles and over to the car.

Chapter Eleven

O'Shea's stomach gave a violent heave. Shock filled his head and made everything around him merge into a blur.

'As you can see ...' Pearce's voice floated off somewhere into the distance. O'Shea put his arm around Adam and tried to sink deeper into the crowd. But they were too densely packed and the people behind couldn't move any more.

'... not just any old motorcycle, is it? It's a German motorcycle.'

O'Shea looked around for a way out. But all he could see was a mass of bodies and a wall of soldiers blocking off all the streets that led out of the Circle.

'Two German soldiers, one a senior officer as well, were brutally murdered by the person who stole this machine,' the voice droned on. 'Not only that, the person who killed them also shot dead a young policeman who tried to intervene!'

A murmur rippled through the crowd and Pearce strained to pick up its message. O'Shea's mind was racing. How could Pearce know what happened to the soldiers? It was impossible. They were swallowed up in the fire. Only the people in Henry Street knew what happened.

Was it possible someone from Henry Street betrayed him? Someone who was trying to save his own skin? Or maybe someone was trying to ingratiate himself to the Germans.

And what policeman was he talking about? That was a pack of lies.

'So whoever committed this foul deed brought this machine here to Tredegar.' Pearce's voice was suddenly higher. 'And whoever he is, he didn't go very far after that because the petrol tank is still half full. Now what does that tell us?'

He glanced at the soldier in the driver's seat who looked alarmed and shifted his arms in front of him. Then Pearce turned back to the crowd.

'It tells us that the murderer is still here in Tredegar, doesn't it? It tells us that at this very moment in time he is right here in our very midst. It also tells us that someone knows who he is, too. And maybe they're even sheltering him. Now you know me, don't you? Very reasonable, that's what I am. So I'll ask nicely, isn't it? Come forward now, whoever you are. And surrender yourself to me. Then everyone else can go on back to their homes.'

He let the words sink in. Only his eyes moved as he watched and waited. And the people of Tredegar shuffled and looked at each other as they braced themselves.

Pearce let the silence fill the Circle for what seemed like minutes.

O'Shea tried not to catch his gaze. For God's sake, what was he supposed to do? Terror rooted him to the spot. His senses reeled with a million reasons for not saying anything. What would happen to Adam? And what would they do to Mrs Mead? How could he tell Pearce he came here on that motorcycle and not involve both of them?

'Major Edwards!' The shout was like the crack of a whip. Everyone jumped and looked at the officer as he snapped to attention. 'Select five people and take them to the truck.'

It was only then O'Shea noticed the army truck on the pavement outside the cinema. As Pearce spoke two soldiers pulled back the canvas canopy. Underneath was a wooden frame. And hanging from it were five ropes. On the end of each rope was a noose.

The reaction was immediate. The crowd groaned and pulled back away from the soldiers who stepped forward with their rifles raised. Major Edwards pointed with his cane and the soldiers grabbed a man and pulled him out.

'Dada … *no*!' A young woman with flaming red hair ran to the car and screamed up at Pearce. 'For God's sake, Gordon Pearce, what are you doing?'

'Now stop that, Pauline Marshall,' he shouted back at her. 'You know very well what's going on here. Unless the murderer comes forward right now that man will swing by the neck until he is dead. Then there will be another. And another after that!'

'*What*? You're going to murder our dad so you can catch someone else? You always were a mad bastard, Gordon Pearce. *A mad bastard*!'

Pauline Marshall held onto the side of the car with one hand. The other hand held onto her heavily pregnant stomach.

Pearce's face turned bright red as he climbed down from the car and Pauline Marshall stared at him defiantly as he strode over to her. Then her head shook when he smashed his hand across her face and brought it arcing back up again. She held her cheek and staggered back against the railings.

'You can't do that,' she wailed. 'Who do you think you are? You can't do that.'

'Can't I just?' Pearce hissed.

'But that's our dad you're taking by there. Why are you taking our dad? He's never done anything to you. You ... you went to school with our Barry. You were best friends with our Barry. You were in the choir together, the two of you. Now you're doing this to our dad?'

'That's enough!' The little eyes were as cold as marbles. 'You've said enough now!'

Pauline Marshall straightened up and moved closer to him. Her eyes were streaming and her face pleading. 'Please, Gordon.'

She put her hands on his shoulders. And when she brought her knee up Gordon Pearce lifted in the air for a second before sprawling on the ground.

A shocked silence dropped over the Circle. Then Pauline Marshall gave a mad laugh and even some of the soldiers smirked. Pearce tried to compose himself as he clutched with his hands and struggled to his feet. His face was purple and his eyes wet.

He barked at two soldiers and they grabbed Pauline Marshall and pinned her arms to her side. Then Pearce pulled the pistol from his holster and put it to the girl's ear. When he fired she jerked so hard the soldiers dropped her.

'Jesus God!' A woman started screaming and the crowd surged forward. The soldiers tried to push them back by hitting out with their rifles.

Pearce looked stunned and his smug expression disappeared. He waved his gun in the air as he tried to scramble back into the car. A man ran to Pauline and tried to stop the flow of blood with his hands. Then as a soldier ran past he hurled himself forward and grabbed his rifle. And at point blank range he fired it into Gordon Pearce's face.

One of the black-clad soldiers dropped to his knees and sprayed the crowd with a machine gun. The man with the rifle fell first as the bullets cut an arc through the terrified people.

Bodies dropped and others trampled over them in their mad panic. Then more soldiers started shooting, cutting to pieces women and children and anyone else who got in the way. The car sputtered and shot forward, and the wail of the dying rose above the clatter of the guns.

O'Shea started running too, pushing off hands that grabbed at him in pain. And he dragged Adam and Mrs Mead along behind him.

A soldier crouched by a pillar-box on the corner of the street and fired at people as they ran past. A little girl sprang in the air and landed at O'Shea's feet. Then the soldier hit an old woman in the back, taking three shots before she went down.

When he turned and looked at O'Shea his eyes were as cold as death itself. And suddenly everything took on a bizarre slowness as if O'Shea was trudging through very deep water. And he knew if he turned to run he was dead. He had less than the blink of an eye to avoid being shot. His only option was to attack.

It took three long strides and the soldier looked astounded as O'Shea kicked the rifle out of his hands and slammed him back against the wall. Out of the corner of his eye O'Shea saw another soldier running up behind him. And at the same time he heard Mrs Mead scream a warning.

O'Shea grabbed the soldier and swung him around just as the other man fired his rifle. And the front of the soldier's jacket blew apart in a spurt of red mist. The bullet slapped against O'Shea's coat as it flew past. And above it all O'Shea heard Mrs Mead yelp in pain.

The dying soldier hung on to O'Shea's wrists as he struggled to stay on his feet and they both fell back against the wall. O'Shea saw Mrs Mead clasping her stomach and stagger backwards. A trickle of blood bubbled from between her fingers.

The metallic scrape of a rifle bolt being repeatedly slapped made O'Shea spin back around. The wounded soldier still gripped on to his wrists and groaned loudly. The second man was frantically trying to clear his jammed rifle by thumping the bolt with his fist.

O'Shea ripped the man's hands from his wrists and flung him at the second soldier. But the man danced out of the way as the jammed shell gave a ping and shot out onto the pavement. The breech was clear. He raised the rifle again.

Propelling himself away from the wall, O'Shea kicked out wildly and his foot caught the soldier between the legs. He crumbled and the rifle flipped out of his hands. But he still managed to grab O'Shea's coat and pull him to the ground with him.

They hit the pavement with a thump and clawed wildly at each other. And somehow O'Shea managed to pull the bayonet from the soldier's belt and ram it into his side. The soldier gave a howl of agony and did a little a jig before his grip eased and O'Shea was able to push him away and scramble back to his feet.

Chapter Twelve

'Run! For God's sake, run.' Mrs Mead was curled up in the doorway of a shop and she pushed him away when O'Shea dropped down beside her.

'No!' O'Shea took her arm and tried to lift her up. 'You're coming with us. Get up. Sure we're nearly at the house already. Come on, we'll get you home.'

'It's no use.' Her eyes rolled back and she fell farther into the doorway. 'Listen, in my bedroom ... the wardrobe ... there's a sock. Take it for the boy! Save the boy. Take him to Ireland.'

'Don't be talking like that. Please! Just try and get up.'

'Thank you, but no,' her eyes were unfocussed now. 'This way is best. Now I'll be with Babs, you see? And my Brian, too. This way is best.'

Then she gave a little sob and slipped back onto the floor.

The window of the shop exploded as bullets whined around them, digging grooves in the wall and spattering them with bits of flying glass.

O'Shea grabbed Adam, threw him back against the wall and shielded him with his body. The noise was deafening. Shots whizzed over their heads and cracked against the walls, whipping off little clouds of dust and taking chunks off the trees. Everything was happening in a fog of chaos, and all they could do was run.

Crouching low they scuttled the rest of the way up Church Street. They reached the door of Mrs Mead's house as an armoured car rumbled around the corner. The cannon spat and sent shells howling down the street taking mortar off the walls and ripping out windows.

Doors splintered and grit and dust scattered in waves across the street.

O'Shea dragged Adam into the house and down the hallway to the kitchen. He hurled himself against the back door but it was locked and he couldn't open it.

'Quick, upstairs. Come on!'

They took the stairs two at a time and threw themselves into Mrs Mead's room at the back of the house as tracers from the armoured car tore through the old walls. The paraffin heater in the front room exploded and sent flames shooting across the floor and up the walls.

O'Shea slammed open the window and put his head out. People were already dotted across the field behind the house as they staggered away to the safety of the woods at the top of the hill.

Directly below the window was an old shed with a rusty tin roof. It looked totally unsafe, but right now it was their only way out.

'Adam, get that mattress off the bed. Quick.'

Adam spun around in a circle as he tried to think. O'Shea grabbed the mattress and shoved it out of the window. He aimed for the top of the shed. He didn't expect it to bounce so easily and he cursed as it slid over the side into the yard next door.

'Shit, shit, shit!'

'Shit, shit, shit,' said Adam.

'Oh, shut up!'

O'Shea stuck his head out of the window again. A metal drainpipe was within reach. He leant out and gave it a tug. Dust dropped from the spikes and pattered onto the roof of the shed.

'Adam, throw those blankets out. We might need them later. Then I'll climb out and when I tell you, get on my back. All right?'

Adam nodded but he didn't look too sure. O'Shea swung his legs out and sat on the windowsill.

'What about Nana's socks?'

'What?'

'Nana said she wanted her socks.'

O'Shea swung his legs back into the room and ran across to the wardrobe, and he opened the doors. All he could see on the bottom was a row of shoes and a pile of boxes. He pulled them out onto the floor but he couldn't see any socks.

He ran his hands up and down the side panels and along the back behind the dresses and coats.

'There's nothing in here.'

Flames were crackling on the paint out on the landing and smoke was starting to filter under the door and smart their eyes. Out in the street they could still hear the roar of the guns and the screams of the dying.

O'Shea pulled down an old suitcase and ran his hand along the top of the wardrobe. But there was nothing there either.

'It's no use. We have to get out of here before we burn to death.'

As a last gesture he pulled the wardrobe forward and let it crash down onto the bed. Pinned to the panel on the back was a man's black sock. He grabbed it and looked inside.

'Wow!' It held a bundle of pound notes tightly bound with an elastic band.

A sudden whoosh brought a ball of flames through the bedroom door and Adam screamed and fell down behind the bed. O'Shea dived after him, pulled him up, and shoved him over to the window.

'Get on my back, son.'

Adam put his arms around O'Shea's neck and wrapped his legs around his body.

'Don't choke me!' O'Shea snapped and Adam grabbed his shirt instead.

O'Shea swung out and grabbed onto the pipe, feeling the full force of his weight pull on his hands and chest. Almost immediately there was a sickening shudder as the spikes began to slip away from the wall.

Adam gripped tighter as the pipe prized itself loose and dropped them with a thud onto the roof of the shed. He gave an almighty shriek when O'Shea landed on top of him.

O'Shea hauled the boy to his feet, pulled him to the edge of the corrugated roof and lowered him to the ground. Then he snatched up the blankets and jumped down behind him. And they ran across the lane and vaulted the little wall as soldiers came running around the corner a second too late.

The grass at the bottom of the wall was thick with nettles but they had no choice. They rolled back into it. The soldiers stopped right above them. People were still staggering up the field.

'Look at that fat bastard trying to run up that hill,' one of the soldiers laughed. It was a Scottish voice. 'A packet of Woodbines says you can't hit him from here.'

'Good grief. If I can't hit him from here I'll shoot myself through the head.'

'I'll tell you what, then,' the first one growled. 'I'll bet you a week's wages.'

The rifle cracked and made Adam jump, and his head slammed into O'Shea's face. Out in the field the fat man flew forward onto his face. The soldiers gave a shriek of delight.

Blood spurted from O'Shea's nose. He pressed his face against Adam's as he cringed in pain.

The rifle cracked again and another person dropped. In a very short time they were either all down or safely in the woods at the top of the field.

A crash of metal was followed by footsteps as someone came scrambling out of one of the houses. A rifle cracked again and a woman screamed.

'Don't shoot her, you prick!' the Scot bellowed. 'We can have some fun with this little one.'

Still shouting at each other they hurried off down the lane.

O'Shea let Adam go, covered his face with his hands and rested his head back against the wall. The pain from his nose arched up through his forehead like a hot poker. He took out a handkerchief to stop the bleeding.

Adam sat watching him, spots of blood glistening in his hair. When O'Shea looked at him he bit his lip.

'Dada?'

'I'm fine, son. I'm fine.'

'Dada,' Adam touched his father's hand. 'I'm wet.'

O'Shea felt something erupt deep in his chest and slither up to his throat. But he bit it back before it exploded out of his mouth in a scream. For one appalling moment he couldn't believe what the boy had said. Chaos was raging all around them and it was all his fault. He'd been stunned by a dreadful fear. No, the worst kind of *cowardice*! And his spineless action turned a quiet country town into a slaughterhouse. It was a nightmare that would haunt him for the rest of his days.

And Adam was totally oblivious to it.

This time it took O'Shea ages to gather his senses again. He wrapped the blanket around them, and he held his son in his arms until the darkness came.

The bitter cold starlit night brought with it an unnatural quietness. A ghostly moon glared down at them. But nothing stirred. No animal noises, no night birds squawking in the dark.

When he was sure the soldiers had gone O'Shea rolled up the blanket, took Adam's hand, and they walked across the grass to the dark and eerie woods.

Chapter Thirteen

The heavy rain spattered in the muddy streams that swept down both sides of the winding country road. And the wind slapped it against the two lonely figures as it gusted across the desolate countryside.

Slate grey clouds rolled down over coal black mountains and shrouded the whole valley in a dismal colourless haze.

They were cold and wet and very, very tired. O'Shea's shoes were full of water and grit stuck between his toes and under his feet. He cursed with frustration because they'd struggled all the way to the top of a long steep hill only to find there was nothing on the other side. The road just rolled away into the distance until it disappeared into the mist.

O'Shea's heart sank into his boots. He flopped down on what was left of an old stone wall and Adam climbed up beside him. They couldn't go on like this. They needed to rest and eat and get themselves dry. O'Shea was hoping to find some sort of shelter over the ridge, maybe a village or a town. But there was nothing. He rubbed his face with the sleeve of his coat and swore again.

The past couple of days had been a blur of panic and appalling fear. O'Shea couldn't stop when they reached the woods on the edge of Tredegar because an overwhelming terror pressed him to get as far away from the disaster he'd caused as he possibly could. So they pushed deeper into the safety of the trees and struggled on through the night.

By the time the sun came up they were battered and bruised and very weary. But still O'Shea couldn't stop.

They passed people who'd collapsed exhausted into the long grass and he knew they should rest too. But he just couldn't do it.

He was in shock. The fact he didn't have the guts to admit *he* brought the motorcycle to Tredegar stunned him. Innocent people were about to be hanged and still he didn't step forward. Fear had rooted him to the ground. He was terrified of what they would do to him.

And if they took him away, what would happen to Adam?

Anyway, who on God's Earth could have known what the Nazis were going to do? No one expected people to be *hanged* for something as trivial as stealing a motorbike. O'Shea really believed if he didn't say anything it would all just go away. He never expected *that*.

But even as he wallowed in a haze of self-pity he knew he couldn't keep running around the countryside dragging Adam with him. If they could get to Pembroke or Fishguard they could get a boat to Ireland. O'Shea had a sock full of money and that would make a difference. So now they were following the sun towards the west coast.

Sometime during the first day they came to a tiny village. By then they were ready to collapse from exhaustion and hunger. There was a small shop next to an ancient church. Fruit and vegetables were laid out on a table outside the window. Two doors along smoke from a turf fire floated up from the red brick chimney of a small hotel. The glow that fell onto the pavement from the little lattice windows was warm and enticing and it lured them inside.

O'Shea caressed the sock of money he'd hidden beneath his shirt and wondered how much a room for the night would cost. He took out a pound note and stuffed it in his pocket.

The bar was all low beams and there was a fire blazing in the big stone hearth. A sign pointed to a small reception desk and O'Shea went over and gave the bell a push.

It tinkled once and a severe-looking young girl came out from the office. She didn't look up as she shuffled some papers on the desk. When O'Shea asked about a room she grunted something about having to see their documents. O'Shea hesitated and this made her glance up. Her eyes were a stark blue and much too big for her face.

After taking a longer look at Adam she continued to tidy the papers on the desk.

She pursed her mouth when O'Shea said his papers had been destroyed when his house was bombed. She grunted again, told them to wait a minute and scurried back into the office. But the look on her face was dark and full of menace so O'Shea took Adam by the hand and they left.

Then the weather changed and brought down clouds that were so low and thick it was impossible to see where the sun was. When they found themselves on a long, winding road O'Shea couldn't tell west from east. He didn't have a clue which direction they were going and now they were totally lost.

O'Shea cringed when Adam tugged at his coat.

He looked down at the boy wrapped in the huge blanket that was covered in mud.

'Son, please don't tell me you've wet yourself!'

'Dada, there's a man over there and he's watching us.'

O'Shea turned to where Adam was pointing. A tiny cottage was tucked in amongst the trees about a hundred yards across a boggy field. The old walls were as grey and colourless as the countryside around it and it had a huge hole in the roof. What was left of the door hung open on one rusty hinge.

But O'Shea couldn't see a man.

As he turned back towards the road he noticed headlights rising and dipping in the distance, flickering faintly in the dim afternoon haze. They were coming up the hill in their direction. Then some more appeared behind it strung out like a necklace.

'Come on, son, we'd better hide in that wee cottage over there until those cars go by.'

O'Shea lifted Adam over the wall and he sank up to his ankles in the wet spongy ground. It was a struggle to drag his tired legs all the way over to a narrow gravel path leading to the cottage door.

'Where's your man?' O'Shea whispered to Adam as he hauled him along by the arm.

Adam looked around. 'I think he's gone.'

By the time they reached the path the first of the vehicles was roaring past them. Two motorcycles side by side with the riders bent forward against the driving rain.

'Come on.' O'Shea dragged Adam towards the door.

Next up the hill was a large black car and it slowed down as it passed the house. Three faces looked out at O'Shea and his son with a mixture of curiosity and caution.

Behind the car came two trucks and their engines groaned as they struggled in low gear to clear the brow of the hill.

Then just as O'Shea reached the door of the cottage a man came around the corner and threw something into the air. It landed on the roof of the second truck and there was a massive burst of light. And the truck flipped off the road into the ditch.

Chapter Fourteen

Soldiers came tumbling out of the wreckage. Two had their clothes on fire. The rest scrambled to their feet and sprinted for cover amongst the heather.

The car skidded to a halt but immediately tried to accelerate away again. And when a man waving a machine gun jumped out in front of it the driver threw his hands up. It didn't save him. A burst of gunfire shattered the windscreen and flung him over the seat on top of the two officers in the back.

The motorcycles came roaring back over the brow of the hill as another grenade erupted under the first truck. And the driver tore the door off as he flew out. The passenger was blown through the roof and the burning wreck took one of the motorcycles with it into the front garden of the cottage.

The motorcycle flew back out when the petrol tank exploded.

Soldiers came screaming through the smoke and were cut down in a hail of bullets from somewhere behind O'Shea.

The second motorcycle spun around and came racing back towards the house. The man in the garden let go with a shotgun and parted the rider from the bike and they both piled into the blazing wreckage of the truck.

Two more soldiers appeared on O'Shea's left and their bayonets glinted in the rain as they charged at him.

O'Shea threw Adam to the ground as the first one reached him. The blade thudded straight into his coat and sent a violent pain through his side.

He fell with the blow and the second soldier disappeared back through the bushes when a shotgun blast hit him in the chest.

The first soldier pulled the bayonet out of O'Shea and stepped back to try again. O'Shea grabbed at him in blind panic and the mud slid from under him as he lashed out with his feet.

The soldier was losing his grip on the rifle so he tried to get his hands around O'Shea's throat instead. But he wasn't strong enough and O'Shea got the rifle between them and found the trigger. The shot was stifled by the soldier's body, but the force threw him backwards into the grass.

O'Shea scrambled to his feet and waved the gun at anything that moved. And when the man came up behind him O'Shea spun around.

'Give me that!' The man snatched the rifle from his hands. Then he pushed O'Shea out of his way and hurried down the path.

'Right, get a move on, you lot!' he bawled. 'We haven't got all day.'

The shooting had stopped. Through the smoke and the rain O'Shea could see men picking things up and pulling at the bodies. One man was trying on a pair of boots.

'Dada ...' Adam was holding on to O'Shea's arm.

'I'm all right, son.' O'Shea wiped rain from his face with the palm of his hand. 'I'm all right, now.'

The man with the shotgun stormed over to the car and tugged at the handle of the trunk. It was locked. He gave a grunt as he walked back around to the side of the car and pulled the door open. The body of the driver fell onto the road.

'Dada, you've got blood on you.' Adam poked at O'Shea's wound with his finger.

'I know, son.' The blood was thin and watery as it saturated his shirt. He took a handkerchief from his pocket and pressed it against the cut to try and stop the flow.

'For God's sake!' A scream made him look up. 'There's no need for all this.'

A group of men had dragged one of the officers out of the car and let him fall on his face in the road.

'Open the trunk!' The man with shotgun prodded him with his foot.

'I can't.' The officer tried to get up on to his knees but he was knocked back down again.

'Open the trunk!'

'I've told you.' He had a cultured English accent. 'I haven't got the keys.'

Boots and fists rained down on him and his screams turned into a pathetic whimper. O'Shea turned away and put his arm around Adam.

A watch glistened in the mud. A watch on a hand. The trucks were well ablaze now. O'Shea searched for something to use as a bandage but there was nothing. He squeezed the handkerchief and put it back into place.

A cough made him spin around. The soldier who'd stabbed him was propped against the wall. His eyes were bloodshot in a grey face. He held a Luger in his right hand. His left hand was pushing his stomach back into the hole in his uniform.

He coughed again and blood trickled from his mouth. O'Shea reached out instinctively but he jerked back and pointed the gun at O'Shea's head. He tried to speak but his eyes rolled and his face contorted.

'Look, let me help …'

But before O'Shea could do anything a gun roared and the soldier's face flew apart. He spun backwards into the grass.

O'Shea dropped to his knees. The man from the house stood looking at him with the shotgun still smoking in his hand.

'What the hell did you do that for?' O'Shea screamed.

'Why do you think, boy?' the man sneered back.

'But he was wounded! He was ...'

The man raised the shotgun and touched O'Shea on the cheek. And his dark eyes studied him for a moment. Adam put his hands under O'Shea's arms.

'Dada, stand up.'

The man slapped the shotgun against his leg. Then he turned sharply and walked away.

'Hurry up!' he snapped to his men. 'We have to go *now!*'

The German officer on the ground was obviously dead now. The other one cowered in the car and his huge fat face quivered in terror. The trunk of the car was open and papers were scattered all over the road.

'Come on,' the man with the shotgun roared and a cattle truck appeared from the back of the house. It bounced over the rough ground and wobbled up onto the road.

'Idris, you drive the car,' the man yelled above the noise. 'We'll have to take the German with us. The rest of you get in the truck, right?'

He glared over at O'Shea. 'You, too.'

'Now wait a minute.' O'Shea held onto Adam. 'This has nothing to do with us.'

'The choice is yours, boy. I haven't got time to argue. Get in the truck.' He waved the shotgun at the body by the car. 'Or stay here!'

The men clambered into the back of the truck and one of them reached down to Adam. 'Pass him up, will you?' he said to O'Shea.

The man with the shotgun glowered. O'Shea held Adam up and the waiting hands lifted him over the tailgate. Then they grabbed O'Shea's arm and pulled him up too.

A pile of hay covered the truck floor. O'Shea crawled into the middle of it and Adam followed him. And he snuggled into his father as the truck moved away. No one spoke as it bounced along the winding country road and it wasn't long before Adam was asleep. O'Shea laid him down and pulled the hay around him.

When they came to a strange village that appeared to be just one very long narrow street the truck had to slow down. Two rows of houses were squashed between a high mountain on one side and a steep drop down to a river on the other. It was as if the whole village had been constructed half way up the side of a mountain.

But what made it even more peculiar was the way the whole thing was bent in the middle like a huge bow. The street plunged down steeply to a crossroads then rose up again just as severely on the other side.

The truck groaned and shook as it followed the road down the dip. And the driver had to scuffle through its gears to get back up the other side. When it eventually creaked over the top of the hump it stopped by a gap in the hedge and two of the men got out. The truck took a sharp right turn between two high walls and followed a rutted track that was barely wide enough for a vehicle that size. Bushes slapped against the sides and leaves fluttered in the gaps in the slats.

Half an hour later they stopped again. Someone got out and opened a gate, letting it clatter back against a large stone. The truck followed a smaller track that skirted the edge of a wide meadow.

At the top it turned into a yard by the side of a large house invisible from the road because of the enormous trees around it.

The German car had followed at a safe distance and now it swept past and crunched up to the front door of the house. A tall woman in a long overcoat was waiting for it and her sharp eyes were like a hungry eagle's.

She marched over to the door and whipped it open. The man with the shotgun shook his head as they spoke quietly for a moment. Then they went around to the back of the car and the man with the shotgun opened the trunk.

The woman was visibly annoyed. She started pulling at the papers in the trunk and shouting at the man with the shotgun. He jabbed with his finger and growled back at her.

The rest of the men in the truck were already jumping out and disappearing around the side of the house. O'Shea waited for a minute before he jumped out too and lifted Adam down. Adam rubbed his eyes and pulled the blanket tighter around him.

'Where are we, Dada?'

At least the rain had stopped.

'I don't know, son. I think we should go and find out, though.'

'Well, I know my information was correct,' the woman was screeching as O'Shea approached then warily. 'The time, the place ...'

'I'm not saying it wasn't.' The man's voice was struggling to stay calm. 'But everything went like clockwork at our end. All I can think is someone must be playing games with us.'

'*Who's* playing games with us?' The woman did an angry little dance and flung her hands in the air.

The man stormed back around to the side of the car, and when he pulled the back door open the German officer cowed away from him with a gurgled cry.

'*He* should be able to tell us.'

'Oh, my God,' the woman groaned. 'You've brought a bloody German back here. Are you mad? What the hell possessed you to ...?'

'I had no choice, did I?' His voice was starting to crack. 'He's a senior officer. He's part of this. He'll know *exactly* what was going on.'

The woman did another little dance and blocked a frustrated scream with her hands.

'You had better be right, Gareth Lewis. For all our sakes! Now get him into the house out of sight. Quickly, now!'

She turned to go back indoors when she glanced in O'Shea's direction. She stopped and took a second look. And her face clouded even more.

'For God's sake! And who the hell is this?'

Gareth Lewis shook his head.

'They got mixed up in things.' He beckoned for O'Shea to come forward. 'I couldn't just leave them up there, could I?'

'What do you mean you couldn't just leave them up there? Who the hell *are* they?'

'I'm Danny O'Shea.' O'Shea moved closer and manoeuvred Adam between them. 'And this is my son, Adam.'

'What the hell were you doing up there in the first place. In the middle of the Brecons in the middle of bloody winter? What in God's name were you ...?'

'I was minding my own business, so I was!' O'Shea snapped.

The woman frowned. 'Your accent ... are you Irish?'

'I am. Why?'

She rolled her eyes and clapped her hands together. 'This is getting worse by the minute.'

'What do you mean by ...?'

'Don't say another word.' She took an angry step forward and her eyes flashed at O'Shea. 'Not another bloody word!'

She pointed at one of the men behind them.

'Rhys, *you* sort them out. Gareth, come in the house, we've got things to sort out.'

Dark September

Chapter Fifteen

Rhys had a face like thunder as he led O'Shea and Adam around to the back of the house. Flicking the latch on the old wooden door he stepped back and nodded them into a tiny scullery. A young woman washing clothes in a porcelain sink had to shift awkwardly to get out of their way.

'Rhys!' She gave him a bright smile. Rhys scowled and barged past her into the kitchen.

The windows of the house were small square things set into thick walls and they let in very little light, especially on a dull wet day like this. An oil lamp hanging from a beam in the centre of the ceiling cast flickering shadows onto a large wooden table in the middle of a slate floor.

Smoke from an open turf fire danced in little waves around another young woman stirring something in a big pot hanging from a hook above the flames. More pots bubbled on a grate straddling the fire. She glanced up when she heard them come in.

'Rhys.' She smiled as easily as the girl in the scullery. 'You're back, then.'

Rhys put his shotgun on the table and pulled a chair out with his foot. He broke off a lump of bread as he sat down.

'Good evening, Cerys.' His tone was sour. 'And how are you?'

'I heard the truck.' Cerys wiped her hands on her apron. 'Where's everyone? Dinner's almost ready.'

'They've gone home.' Rhys bit into the lump of bread. 'I'd have gone home myself if your sister hadn't made me look after these two by here.'

Cerys squinted at them in the dim light. 'Hello. And who're you, then?'

O'Shea moved Adam closer to the fire and as Cerys stooped down to look at him thick curls of ash blond hair floated around her shoulders. The light from the fire made her eyes sparkle and they were bright and clear and startlingly blue.

She frowned when she looked up at O'Shea and he knew what she was thinking. The two of them looked like drowned rats. O'Shea's hair was matted and he hadn't shaved for days. Their clothes were in tatters and stinking dirty. Even their shoes were only held together by their laces.

'We found them up on the Brecons,' Rhys muttered.

It took a moment for Cerys to respond. She seemed startled by O'Shea. But she recovered quickly and ran her fingers through Adam's hair.

'Good grief.' She took the blanket from around his shoulders. 'You're soaked to the bone. What on earth were you doing up on the Brecons in this weather?'

She took a tea towel off the back of a chair and wiped Adam's face with it. 'And what's your name, then?'

Adam looked up at his father.

'His name's Adam.'

Cerys put her arm around him and moved him closer to the fire. The heat was already causing steam to rise from his wet clothes.

'Your accent,' Cerys glanced back at O'Shea. 'You're not from around here, then.'

'Irish,' Rhys interrupted.

'Irish?' Cerys frowned. 'Really? What on earth is an Irishman doing wandering around the Welsh mountains?'

'Tis a long story.' O'Shea gave a dismissive wave.

'But where did you come from?' Cerys persisted. 'Where do you live?'

'Well, we don't live anywhere now.' O'Shea didn't feel comfortable talking about it with these people. Especially in such a weird situation. But he couldn't stop himself. He was so tired and hungry his head buzzed.

'Our house was bombed when the Germans came,' he heard himself saying. 'My wife was in it. So now I'm trying to get Adam across to Ireland.'

Rhys gave a loud snort. 'That sounds about right. A typical Irish dope looking for a ferry up a bloody mountain?'

'You're a funny little maggot ...'

'That's enough of that.' Cerys moved between them. 'Look, you're wet and cold. And Adam badly needs seeing to. We have plenty of hot water here. Why don't you take a bowl into the scullery and give him a wash down. I'll fetch you a towel.'

'What?' O'Shea was still glaring at Rhys. 'Look, I'm sorry but I don't want your hot water. I don't want your towel either. All I want to know is why I was brought here in the first place!'

Cerys' eyes flashed and she threw the wet blanket at him. 'Well, how the hell do I know why you were brought here? But I have better things to with my time, see. I have a meal to get ready for everyone. So please yourself. But that boy badly needs seeing to.'

She guided Adam to a small stool by the fireplace. 'You just come over and sit by here, Adam. We'll get you nice and dry in no time.'

He looked around for his father. 'My Dada's been shot.'

'*What*?'

'I haven't been shot.' O'Shea opened his coat to show the dark bloodstain that had spread all over his shirt. 'I was stuck with a bayonet.'

'How on Earth did you get stuck with a bayonet?' Cerys pulled up the shirt and prodded at the wound with her fingers. O'Shea jumped and she slapped the shirt down again.

'It's not as bad as it looks.' She wiped her hands on her apron again. 'I've seen worse injuries than that on the farm and people lived to talk about it. But you haven't answered my question. How did you get yourself stuck by a bayonet?'

'Well, I guess I was in the wrong place at the wrong time.' He glared at Rhys again.

Rhys smirked back at him and nodded for him to sit down. His small, dark eyes watched O'Shea pull out a chair on the opposite side of the table and drop down on it.

'Look, what's going on?' Cerys waved the ladle at Rhys. 'How was he stuck with a bayonet? Were you there? And how come they were brought back here anyway?'

'You tell me, Cerys.' Rhys shrugged his narrow shoulders. 'No one tells *me* anything around here, do they?'

'So what does Bethan want me to do with them? How long are they going to be here?'

Again Rhys shrugged. 'You know what she's like. She just said see to them. I presume she'll elaborate when she's had time to think about it.'

Cerys went back to the fire and clattered some more pans on the grate.

'Mind you,' Rhys pointed at O'Shea with a lump of bread. 'It *was* a pretty stupid thing to do.'

'What do you mean?' Cerys put two mugs of cabbage soup on the table in front of them then handed another one to Adam.

'Well, just think about it.' Rhys gave a sinister grin. 'Now they know where we live they could tell the Germans. What would happen to us then? We'd all be in the poo-poos, that's what would happen.'

'Tell the Germans *what,* for God's sake?' O'Shea groaned. 'How could we tell the Germans anything? We don't *know* anything.'

Rhys rubbed his nose. 'Anyway, it wasn't my decision, thank God. I'd have left them out there. Left them to catch their bloody boat to Ireland.'

He snorted again as he pulled at another lump of bread, dipped it in his mug of cabbage soup and ate it noisily.

The heat of the fire wafted over O'Shea and he felt his eyelids droop. To keep alert he took a sip from his mug, rolled the hot soup around his teeth then let it trickle down his throat.

His head felt light and nothing seemed real anymore. It was like a weird dream. Even the fear rattling around in the pit of his stomach and the pain in his side seemed to be disconnected somehow.

'That woman out there,' O'Shea forced himself to sit up. 'Is she in charge around here? Is she the one who'll decide what happens to us?'

Rhys ignored him and slurped at his mug of soup. O'Shea looked across at Cerys. She glanced at him then turned away. 'I'll have you know that woman out there is my sister. Her name is Bethan and we run this farm between us. All three of us make the decisions around here.'

'All *three* of you?'

Rhys nodded towards the scullery. 'Rhianne. She's a half-sister.'

'Oh. So are you telling me ...?'

'We're not telling you anything, mate!' Rhys put his mug down on the table with a thump.

The door beside the fireplace crashed open and the tall lady charged into the kitchen followed closely by Gareth.

'Bethan,' Rhys pushed his chair back and stood up.

'Right,' Bethan shouted. Her voice was like shattering glass. 'What the hell's going on here?' She went straight to Adam and glared down at him. '*Well*?'

Adam looked startled and turned around to O'Shea.

'He can't tell you!' O'Shea jumped up and rushed over to him.

'Let him speak for himself. He's not a baby.'

'He *can't* speak for himself, that's what I'm trying to tell you.'

'Why can't he? He's a big boy. What's the matter with him?'

'You're confusing him.' O'Shea struggled to keep his voice under control. 'He had an accident when he was a baby. It left him with ... you know ... brain damage.'

'Oh my good God!' Bethan ran her hands through her hair. 'That's *all* we need. Of all the people to being here, you bring the bleedin' village idiot. What the hell possessed you to bring them here in the first place? And what in God's name were they doing up in the mountains anyway?'

'Well, like I just told your sister, we're trying to get to Ireland.' O'Shea stared back into eyes that were full of fury.

'Why do you want to go to Ireland, for heaven's sake?' Bethan was taller and thinner than Cerys but the resemblance was obvious. Bethan was also considerably older.

'I have family over there. We'll be safer there.'

'Safer? What do you mean safer?'

'From the Germans. Do you know what they do to children like Adam? They'd have him killed.'

'Well?' Her eyes were as cold as ice.

'Well *what*?'

'Well, wouldn't he be better off?'

'How could he ...'

'Surely it couldn't be any worse than what you're doing to him right now.' She flapped her arms in the air. 'You're dragging him all over the country like an injured animal. He's wet, cold, hungry. If he doesn't understand what you're doing to him why not just leave him to the Germans and get it over with?'

'What are you ... he's my son, for God's sake!' O'Shea felt the panic leap into his throat and he held Adam tighter. 'How can you say ... what are you saying? I don't believe you're ... he's my *son*!'

'He's my son!' Bethan mocked. 'Do you realise you've caused us a bloody big problem by coming here?'

'Well *you* dragged us here.'

'Whatever! But why were you farting about out there in the first place? You could have ruined everything. And you could have got us all killed in the process. So what are we supposed to do with you now? Take you out and shoot you too?'

'Bethan!' Cerys put her hand on Adam's shoulder. 'Stop it. You're frightening the little one.'

Bethan slapped her hand on the sideboard and glared at her sister. 'Don't you dare speak to me like that. Not in front of strangers. You just get on with the cooking. If that's what you call this rubbish. You can't even do that properly.'

She turned back to O'Shea. 'You'll have to stay here until we decide what to do with you. Sleep on the floor. Whatever. Doesn't matter. But we can't spare anyone to look after you. So just keep quiet and stay out of the way. Rhys, you can go home now.'

'Thank God for that,' Rhys muttered.

Bethan glanced around the room and pulled another face before flouncing out of the kitchen.

'We'll eat in here,' she shouted over her shoulder.

Chapter Sixteen

Rhys vanished as soon as Gareth pulled the door shut. Then there was a strained silence in the kitchen for a minute before Cerys rattled a pot on the grate. Her face was flushed and she sniffed.

Adam sat on the stool as O'Shea went back to the table and tried to ignore the thumping of his heart. The fire was throwing out a welcome heat and O'Shea rested his head on his arms and closed his eyes. His mind was scrambled. He knew he should be planning his next move and looking for a way out of this place. But what *was* his next move? He didn't even know where they were. If they *did* manage to get out of the house, where were they going to go?

He jumped when a hand touched his shoulder.

'Are you all right?' Cerys smiled down at him.

'What?' O'Shea sat up and almost knocked the mug off the table. 'I'm sorry, did I fall asleep?'

'Only for ten minutes or so. Then you started talking to yourself.'

She stood so close to him he could feel the warmth from her. 'I'm afraid you'll have to sleep on the floor tonight. There's no spare bed. I'll find you some blankets.'

'Ah, don't be worrying about us.' O'Shea picked up the mug and cradled it with both hands. 'At least we're out of the rain.'

'The rain has stopped.' She stayed close to him. 'And there's a huge moon out there.'

He moved his chair back a bit. 'Look, I'm sorry I was rude to you earlier. It's just that ... well, I was worried what you were going to do to us.'

'I know that.' Cerys pulled out a chair and sat down next to him. 'I understand how you feel. But I don't actually know what's going on myself.'

'Don't you? But you live here. You must have some idea what your own sister is up to.'

Her face clouded and she looked away.

'Oh, I'm sorry.' O'Shea took a sip of cold cabbage soup. 'If you can't tell me, you can't tell me.'

'It's not that I *can't* tell you.' She gave a little pout. 'It's because I really don't know. You know more about what happened today than I do. And I'm sorry you got caught up in it.'

'Caught up in what, though? What are you people up to? You're not just farmers, are you? Are you some sort of terrorists?'

'Terrorists?' She sat back in her chair. 'No! Of course we're not. Why do you think ... what do you mean? Why do you think we're terrorists?'

'Then what was all that about today? Why did you blow up those German trucks and kill all those soldiers?'

'*What*?' Alarm danced across her face.

'Your friends blew up some German trucks today and killed a load of soldiers and you're telling me you knew nothing about it?'

Cerys seemed too stunned to answer. She stared at her hands and ground her teeth.

'Look, I'm sorry if I upset you.' O'Shea rubbed his mouth with his hand. 'I thought ...'

'No, no.' Cerys took a deep breath through her nose and sat up straight with her hands joined under her chin. 'I'm not upset. Because I know if Bethan *is* involved in something like that she'll have a very good reason for it. I can assure you she never does anything without a good reason. You've seen her yourself. She will have a very good reason indeed to involve us in something that might cause trouble for us.'

O'Shea picked up a lump of bread. 'Well what I saw today certainly looked like trouble to me. Those Germans walked into an ambush. That was planned. It wasn't done on impulse.'

Cerys ground her teeth harder and sighed again. 'Well, no one told me about it.' There was a hint of rejection in her voice. 'Anyway, all I do around here is cook and clean. Me and Rhianne, we're the ones who keep the house going. Bethan runs everything else.'

'Yes. I can imagine.'

'She's still my sister.' Cerys gave the table a thump. 'I know what she's like and I moan about her. But she's my sister. Keeping this place going isn't easy for her, you know.'

O'Shea put his hand up. 'Sorry. I meant no offence. I'm just saying she was a bit hard on you, that's all. It wasn't right to speak to you like that front of other people.'

She thought about that for a moment. 'Thanks. But it's all right. Really. That's just the way she is.'

The fire crackled and they both looked at it.

Cerys leant forward in her chair again 'The problem is our family has a lot of history. And Bethan likes to remind everyone about it. She loves the glory of it all, you see. She believes people around here look up to us because of who we are. But I don't think they actually care one way or the other. The one thing they *do* know is we're fiercely proud of our name. And of our descendants. And of course our Welsh heritage. It's not easy being the descendants of the great John Frost.'

She saw the blank look on O'Shea's face. 'You *do* know who John Frost was, surely?'

He shook his head.

'The Charterist Uprising?' She looked incredulous. '1839? A hundred years ago? You *must* have heard of it.'

'I'm sorry,' O'Shea shrugged. 'What happened in 1839?'

'Well, I'm disgusted at you.' She pretended to slap him. 'Fancy not knowing who John Frost was. But you *are* Irish, so I suppose I should forgive you.'

She pulled her chair closer. 'Well, the story is this - back in those days people were denied their basic rights so the Charterist were inciting civil unrest. They organised protest marches and antagonize the Establishment in any way they could. They were demanding the right to elect their own Member of Parliament amongst other things. Anyway, when they organised a march on Newport the protesters came in their thousands from all over the country. They were supposed to have help from Ireland, too, but of course that never came. The Government was rattled and when the Charterist got to Newport the constabulary was waiting for them. But they were determined to make their voices heard so they pushed the constables out of the way. What they didn't know was the Army was waiting for them in the Westgate Hotel with orders to dispel the crowd by whatever means they thought fit. They immediately opened fire and the protesters were shot to pieces. You can still see the bullet holes in the foyer of the Westgate Hotel.'

'Good God! That's awful. So what happened to Jack Frost?'

'John Frost,' she corrected. 'They had him transported to Australia! They wanted to hang him, you see. Stick his head on a spike outside the Tower as an example. But typical English, isn't it, they thought he would become a martyr if he was hanged. And you know what? They were right. They had him sent away to the other side of the world and that was the end of it. Forgotten. But not by us. Not by his family.'

She got up and went back to the fire.

'Adam.' She ruffled his hair. 'Go and sit at the table. Supper's ready.'

She scooped something from the pot onto plates and put them on the table. 'Lamb stew. Not much lamb though, I'm afraid. But that's how it is now, isn't it? With the Germans taking most of our stock and leaving us with the scrag ends. So don't look too closely at the vegetables either, will you?'

She put two plates on a tray and took them into the other room. When she came back she sat down beside O'Shea again.

'All right, Adam?'

He nodded and dipped some bread in the stew.

'Nice stew though, isn't it? Lots of herbs and spices to make up for the lack of everything else. Just so's you'd think you were getting something substantial.'

'Tis *very* nice,' O'Shea assured her. 'We haven't had a lot to eat for a while so this is a feast fit for a king.'

Cerys frowned. 'You haven't been wandering around out there since the invasion, have you?'

'No, no.' O'Shea picked at the stew as he considered what to tell her. 'When our house was destroyed and my wife killed we were homeless. So the only place we could go was to Adam's grandmother in Tredegar.'

'Oh, my God. *Tredegar*? We heard what happened. You weren't there when it happened?'

'I'm afraid so.'

101

'Oh, you poor man. That's terrible. Adam must have been terrified. The poor child. But how did you get away? We were told only a handful of people survived.'

'We were lucky, I suppose.' O'Shea knew his guilty secret was making his face flush. 'I can't remember much about it. When the shooting started we... I just grabbed Adam and ran. We just ran and ran. We were still running when we came across your people today.'

Cerys put her elbow on the table. 'Your wife was killed, did you say?'

'Yes. She was.'

'That's dreadful. I'm so sorry. Was she Irish too?'

'Heather? No, she was Welsh.'

'Heather.' Cerys smiled. 'That's a pretty name. You must miss her terribly.'

Cerys pressed closer and when O'Shea straightened she moved back a little and reached for the bread.

'What brought you to Wales, then?' she asked through a mouthful of food.

'A boat.'

'Ha, ha!'

'No, really. I'm serious. I got a job on a coal boat. I was only a kid. I'd never been to sea before. We only got about a mile out when I felt the first sway of the decks. And, boy, did I get sick. I was so sick I had to spend the whole of the trip on the upper deck under a sheet of canvas. I couldn't eat or drink. I couldn't even stand up to be sick. I actually prayed I would just die, that's how bad I was.'

'Good grief, that sounds terrible.'

'Terrible isn't the word for it. When we docked in Newport the captain thought sailing was not a career I should pursue and he got me a job in the dockyard.'

'That was good of him.'

'It *was*, I suppose. But I think maybe he was worried I would go and die on him. What would he do with a body on a coal ship?'

Cerys chuckled and wiped her mouth with the back of her hand. 'You're a very lucky man.'

'Yeah, right. Lucky's my middle name.'

Cerys didn't seem to notice the sarcasm because she glanced over at Adam and smiled. He looked contented. He was warm and fed and oblivious to the world around him.

'How old is he?'

'He's ten.'

'Bless him.' She put her hand on O'Shea's and it was soft and warm. 'Still, you're safe here now.'

She looked up and the expression on O'Shea's face must have been sour because she frowned and took her hand away again.

'Well, you *are* safe here!' She sounded agitated. 'So stop looking so worried.'

She picked up a piece of bread and munched it, and an awkward silence settled between them. And as soon as O'Shea finished his stew she took his plate away.

She was pouring water into the sink when the young girl from the scullery came in the door behind them.

'Tell Bethan I'm off now.' She gave a beautiful smile and her face was the image of her sister's. Her hair was shorter but her eyes had the same intense sparkle. And she shook her head in exactly the same way. Cerys went over to her and kissed her on the cheek.

'Now you take care. And we'll see you in the morning.'

'Don't worry,' Rhianne laughed. 'I'm going to chapel. What could be safer than the house of God? He'll look after me.'

She gave a little wave and disappeared out the back door.

'It's her chapel night.' Cerys sat back down beside O'Shea. 'She stays over in the pastor's house. The pastor's daughter went to school with us. She's a great friend.'

She rested her hand on O'Shea's again, playfully tapping his fingers. 'So you think we're terrorists, do you?'

'*What*?'

'Well, do you?'

'I don't know.' O'Shea moved his hand away. 'I'm not sure what to think. It's just ... well, what I saw today ... you know what I mean.'

'No,' she smirked. '*What* do you mean?'

'I mean you lot were out there killing Germans, that's what I mean! So who are you? I just don't understand any ...'

'But what's worrying you, though?' The smile she gave was stunning. And totally disarming. 'Do you think we're going to do away with you too?'

'I don't know! Well, yes! *Maybe*.'

'So you think we're just as bad as the Germans, do you?' Her eyes had mirth in them.

'It's not *that!* It's just ... anyway, why do you think you can beat the Germans when the rest of the world can't?'

'We're not trying to beat the Germans. There's no way on God's earth we could ever beat them.'

'Then what was all that about today?'

'I've told you. I honestly don't know.'

She got up, pulled a blanket from a box and laid it on the floor in front of the fire.

'Come on, Adam.' She took the boy's hand and helped him lie down on the blanket. 'You're worn out, bless you. You have a good sleep, now. And we'll see you in the morning.'

Chapter Seventeen

'Thanks,' O'Shea said as Cerys sat back down at the table again.

'You're welcome.' She looked at the mug of cold cabbage soup and pulled a face. 'Can I get you anything else? Tea?'

'No.' O'Shea patted his stomach. 'I'm full, thank you. That was lovely.'

They sat in silence for a minute then Cerys went to put her hand on Shea's again but he pulled away. She tutted and rubbed her eyes. 'Look, I honestly don't know what went on today. I promise you. Whatever you're thinking it wasn't...'

'I'm not thinking anything. All I'm worried about is what's going to happen to us. How long will you keep us here?'

Cerys pursed her lips as if she was suddenly thought of something. 'There's been a lot of people coming and going around here lately. But of course Bethan is involved with the local council. It could have been that. They looked shifty, though. Like they were planning something. They were creeping around and whispering.'

She glanced at O'Shea and crinkled her nose. 'The thing is, Bethan is sometimes away with the fairies. She has a dream, you know? Autonomy for Wales. A Wales free from the shackles of the English. She said the other day how great it would be if she could convince the Germans that a free Wales would be a neutral country. Like Switzerland, say. Or Ireland. Then when the war is over we'd be independent. The Republic of Wales.'

'Was she serious?'

'*Yes*!' Her answer was sharp. 'Of course she was. *Very* serious.'

'And you think what happened today had something to do with independence for Wales?'

'Well, it could do. You never know.'

'Your sister *does* seem to be a very determined woman. Maybe we shouldn't put it past her.'

'She can be *very* strong-minded when she wants to be.' She picked at another piece of bread. 'She takes after our father, you know. He was an army officer.'

'Really?'

'Yes. A major.'

'Where's he now?'

'He ...' She leant back in the chair and gave a slight shrug. 'He went off to fight the Germans in Europe. His division was wiped out at Dunkirk.'

'Jeez, I'm sorry.'

'Don't be. He *wanted* a war. For years he spoke of nothing else. I don't think he realised it would be this ... *final.*'

'I know,' O'Shea agreed. 'I don't think anyone did. I watched the young lads down the docks. They all wanted to be soldiers. They all wanted to march. To wave the flag. But they didn't realise someone would die when the shooting started. Still, you must have been upset.'

'Oh, I was.' She moved close again and her leg touched O'Shea's. 'I was devastated. But I cried it out of my system. It took a while but there's too much to do on the farm to dwell on it.'

'And you said your mother is ...'

'Oh, she's gone too. She died giving birth to me.'

'Oh. I'm sorry. I ...'

'My father was!' Sarcasm laced her tone. 'He was so sorry he ran straight over to his fancy woman. She had his baby a year later, which was my sister Rhianne. Then she dumped the baby here and went off to America with her own husband and her four other children.'

She waited for a reaction. O'Shea shook his head and sighed. She continued. 'Rhianne's exactly a year younger than me. Bethan was only sixteen but she ended up having to rear the two of us. She was only a child herself. She had no childhood of her own. Makes you bitter and resentful, I suppose.'

'*Cerys*!'

They both jumped when the door crashed open and Gareth barged into the room. He pulled a cap from his pocket and put it on. His face was as dark as his beard.

'We're going out now.' He scowled at O'Shea. 'A bit of business to attend to, you see. We won't be long. You should be all right, though. I don't think Irish will give you any bother. But don't go wandering about now, will you, boy? There's traps out yonder, see. Farms, isn't it? Dangerous places to go wandering. Anyway, we shouldn't be long.'

Then he was gone. Cerys gave a nervous giggle. She went to the box and took out another blanket.

'Help me with this.' She knelt on the floor to spread it out. As O'Shea bent down her hair brushed his face. It was soft and scented with a faint hint of perfume.

She turned her head and smiled at him. And her eyes twinkled with mischief as she lifted her hand and touched his face. Then her lips brushed lightly against his cheek. But she pulled away and sat back on her heels, and she stared at the fire for what seemed like ages. Then she stood up and ran her fingers through her hair.

'I'd better be off to bed, then. My sister will be home any minute.'

She went to the door and opened it.

'Can I get you anything before I go?'

O'Shea sighed and shook his head. His mind was still buzzing, only now it wasn't just from the tiredness.

Chapter Eighteen

Something woke him in the night. He'd been in a deep sleep, dreaming he was strolling along the canal in Newport with Heather. It was a beautiful day. O'Shea was holding her hand and listening to her chatting about ordinary things. Normal everyday things.

But there was something peculiar about this dream. A shadow hovered in the back of his mind, dark and sinister. It seeped into his heart but it was too elusive, too vague for him to focus on. And he knew instinctively that if he didn't keep hold of Heather she would slip away from him and he would never, ever see her again.

All of a sudden she started to fade. She was evaporating right in front of his eyes, turning into a swirling wisp of colour. He tried to grab her, hold her, but he couldn't catch the mist. His cries died in his throat. And in the blink of an eye Heather was gone and there was only a cold, empty blackness left.

Now he was wide awake. He sat up and his breath came out in little puffs of vapour. The kitchen was bitterly cold. The fire had died down and left just a few orange embers glowing in the grate. He pulled the blanket up around his shoulders.

The full moon was low in the sky. A beam of silver light fell across the small figure of Adam curled up on his blanket and sleeping peacefully.

The rest of the house was still. O'Shea listened for a minute but there wasn't another sound to be heard. He couldn't decide what woke him. Maybe it was the dream when he cried out.

Now he needed the toilet. He cursed out loud. The toilet was a small corrugated lean-to beside the pig shed on the other side of the yard. Wandering outside on a fiercely cold night like this was the last thing he wanted to do. But he was desperate. And it was too uncomfortable to leave until morning.

Reluctantly he got up and rubbed his arms and legs to get some life back into them. Then he crept out the back door and across the cobbled yard.

The sky was amazingly clear and it sparkled with a sea of pulsating stars. The light from the moon cast dark shadows out across the valley, fusing the trees together in various shades of grey until they merged with the jet black of the mountains beyond.

A strange noise made him stop. It sounded like a muffled cry. He stood still, turning his head slowly as he tried to establish where it came from.

Something flickered. A tiny spark of light inside the little window of the whitewashed building in front of him. He moved carefully across to it, lifted himself up on his toes and peered in.

The German officer was standing naked in an old tin bath with his hands tied to a beam above his head. A rope snaked around his body and secured him to a post. The bath was full of water and standing on a square of bricks. A fire was burning underneath it.

Bethan and Gareth hovered in front of him and they appeared to be asking him something in loud whispers. The German just shook his head. A lump of cloth shoved into his mouth prevented him from speaking.

Judging by the steam wafting up from the bath the water was already very hot. The German looked distressed. He wriggled and pulled against the rope. But when Bethan threw more questions at him he grunted stubbornly.

His face was purple and his eyes bulged. Eventually the heat became too much for him. He gave a muffled howl and nodded his head. When Gareth pulled the rag from his mouth the German spluttered and gasped. Then he started speaking very fast.

Whatever he said made Bethan happy because her face beamed and she clapped her hands excitedly. Gareth grinned too, wrote something in a little notebook then put it back in his pocket with a satisfied sigh.

Now the German appeared to be struggling for breath. His eyes rolled back in his head and his face turned a deeper puce. His big stomach strained against the rope and his legs jerked violently as he started to convulse.

'What's the matter with him?' Bethan moved back behind Gareth.

'I think he's having a heart attack.' Gareth was obviously unsure of what to do.

Then the spasms stopped as suddenly as they began and the German sagged lifelessly against his bonds.

'Oh, shit!' Bethan stayed behind Gareth. 'Is he dead?'

'I think so.'

'Damn, damn, damn. I just hope he's told us the truth, that's all.'

They seemed to gape at the body for ages before Gareth reached up and cut the rope. He let the body fall onto his huge shoulders and he staggered under the sudden weight. Then he carried it across to the pigsty and dropped it over the low wall.

There was a flurry of excitement and the squeals from the pigs echoed around the bare walls. Gareth watched impassively as the evidence was devoured until a thin stream of blood shot up and hit him in the face. He stepped back in disgust and wiped it off with his sleeve. Then he stormed back into the building, kicked the bath of water onto the fire and everything went black.

O'Shea moved around the corner as the door swung open. Bethan was first out and they walked to the German's car, climbed in and disappeared down the winding drive to the front gate.

Chapter Nineteen

'How's the walking wounded this morning?' Cerys gave a beaming smile as she poured some tea into a mug and handed it to O'Shea.

The kitchen was warm and bright again. The fire blazed and pots were boiling on it. Eggs spattered in a frying pan.

Cerys watched O'Shea as she waited for an answer. But his mind was too numb to respond.

He hadn't slept any more during the night. Every time he closed his eyes the same images rolled around in his head. The sickening screech of the pigs made him want to throw up.

After everything he'd seen in Tredegar he thought he was immune to this kind of mindless violence. But he wasn't. He still felt the sickness, the fear. Nothing could sanitize him against that.

'I've got something for that cut of yours.' Cerys took something from a bag on a nail behind the door. 'Take off your shirt and I'll sort it out for you.'

O'Shea lifted his shirt and she dabbed at the wound with a piece of cloth soaked in hot water. Her hands were soft and she smelt of the same mixture of soap and perfume as last night. She looked up and smiled. And O'Shea's heart skipped a beat. How could she have such a pretty face and gentle eyes and be a part of this?

She tore a strip from a piece of sheet, poured some stuff on it and pressed it to the wound. And O'Shea jumped.

'What the hell is that? It's burning me. Get it off.'

'Sit down!' Cerys chortled. 'It's only medicine.'

She forced him back onto the chair and tied a bandage around his chest to keep the pad in place.

'It's excellent stuff. It'll do you good, I promise you. I know it stings now but that means it's working.' She leant down and let her lips brush his cheek. O'Shea jerked back and she grinned. Then she helped him tuck his shirt back into his trousers.

Bethan came charging in through the side door and she glared at the two of them. Cerys straightened up quickly.

'Oh my God,' Bethan groaned. 'I'd forgotten about you two. That explains the terrible smell in here. What the hell is it? Is it that boy? If it is can I suggest you take him outside and hose him down? You wouldn't let a dog in the house smelling like that.'

'What the hell ...'

'I'd be very careful if I was you.' She pointed a finger at O'Shea's face. 'I'm not at my best before breakfast. And you've just put me right off mine. So I'd keep well out of sight for the rest of the day. At least until I decide what to do with you.'

She put her food on a tray and took it into the other room, and she pulled the door behind her with a loud crash.

Adam sat at the table eating eggs on fried bread and O'Shea sat beside him. And when Adam finished he got the boy's coat off the back of the chair and helped him put it on. He took his own coat from the hook on the door and felt for the sock of money tucked inside the lining.

Cerys frowned. 'What are you doing?'

'We're leaving.' O'Shea avoided eye contact. 'I've had enough of this shite.'

'*What?*'

'You heard me. We're going.'

'Going where?' Cerys shook her hair from her face. 'What makes you think you're going anywhere?'

'Look, all I want is to take my son somewhere safe. Can't you understand that? Don't you realise if the Germans find him they'll kill him? Can't you see I'm petrified of what they'll do to him? And right now I don't think he's safe here either. So I'm taking him to Ireland.'

'Oh, come on.' Cerys forced a laugh. 'Surely you don't think Bethan was serious? You don't believe she'd harm a child, do you? No! She was only showing off. She'd never do anything like that.'

'Wouldn't she?' O'Shea went to say more but checked himself. 'The fact is I don't think Adam is any safer here than he would be out there. It's a chance I'm going to have to take.'

'And you think Bethan will just let you go?'

'So how's she going to stop me?'

Cerys put her hands over her face and gave an angry groan. And when she took them away again her eyes were dark and angry. 'You can't just walk away from here. You can't just get up and walk away if Bethan says you stay. Please. Don't even try it.'

'I have no choice.' O'Shea put his hand on Adam's shoulder. 'I have to go.'

'*No!*' Cerys moved between him and the door. 'Don't. Look, why don't you just stay here for now. Just for a few days. Please. By then Bethan will have calmed down and she'll probably tell you to go anyway. Only don't try to leave now. You'll only get her back up and she'll retaliate. And you won't like it if she throws a fit. Believe me, you're better off staying.'

She put her hand on O'Shea's face but he brushed it away. 'I can't stay. I'm sorry.'

'*Please!*'

O'Shea pushed past her and clicked open the door. And when he glanced back he was startled by the look on her face. There was a black fury in her eyes and a hardness in the way her mouth had set.

He took a sharp breath. 'Come on, Adam. Hurry up, now.'

They walked across the yard and around the corner of the white building. And when they reached the top of the driveway a man with a dog stepped out from behind a hedge. He carried a shotgun over his arm.

'Miss Frost would rather you stayed inside the house.' The dog sat down at his feet and let its tongue hang out.

Back in the kitchen they sat down at the table and Cerys put a plate of eggs in front of O'Shea.

'May as well have breakfast, isn't it.' She gave a disarming smile. 'Seeing as you're not leaving now.'

'I'm not hungry.' O'Shea pushed the plate away.

'Please yourself.'

Her mood had lightened as suddenly as it had darkened. She let her fingers brush O'Shea's face and they were as soft as the petals of a flower.

'It's best you stay, you know? Until things settle down, anyway.'

'Oh, don't start all that again.' O'Shea turned away from her.

'Start what?'

'You know what.'

'Do you mean asking you to stay?'

'Yes.'

'And what's wrong with that?'

'What's wrong with that? Because you don't know the first thing about me.'

'I do ...'

'Yeah? Do you? You don't even know my name.'

'Of course I know your name. Danny O' something. O'Reilly? O'Connor. Danny O'Connor?'

'Danny O'Shea!'

'I knew that.' Cerys gave a throaty chuckled and brushed his face with her fingers again.

A truck rumbled past the window and crunched on the gravel as it drove up to the front door.

'Who's this now?' Cerys went to look out the window.

From where O'Shea was sitting he could see three men get out of the cab. Another two climbed out of the back and they were all ushered into the house.

'Oh, it's that lot again,' Cerys said almost to herself.

'What lot?'

'The ones I told you about. You know? The ones who were creeping around and planning something. I wonder what they're up to now.'

Bethan looked around the door and Cerys jumped.

'Cerys, tea!' She glanced at O'Shea for a second. 'Quickly, now.'

'What?' Cerys picked up a tea towel and went to the fireplace. 'How many for?'

'Just bring a pot,' Bethan snapped. 'And enough cups.'

Cerys narrowed her eyes. She was obviously flustered. 'Well, do they all take sugar? Only we've not much left.'

'Just get on with it, will you?' Bethan shook her head in irritation. 'And find some biscuits. Or cake. Whatever! Bring it in here.'

She slammed the door again. Cerys stood looking into the fire with her head bowed. Her face was flushed as she waited for the kettle to boil.

When the lid of the kettle eventually rattled she poured the water into the teapot. Then she put a pile of cups on a tray and took it into the front room without looking at O'Shea.

And she stayed in there.

Chapter Twenty

About an hour later more men arrived and they joined the others in the front room. Their voices were loud and animated and they filtered through the thick walls into the kitchen. But O'Shea could only catch a few words and none of them made any sense to him.

He went into the scullery, clicked open the back door and looked out at the yard. Could this be an opportunity to get away? Could they just walk out and vanish into the countryside while everyone was distracted? He knew there would be someone watching the drive down to the gate. But what if they could sneak out a back way?

There was a wall across from the scullery but it was at least ten feet high. Adam would never get over that.

In the left hand corner of the yard between the wall and the toilet shed he could just make out a gate. Judging by the line of trees behind it there was some sort of path going back into the fields.

He darted back into the kitchen and grabbed their coats. Then he guided Adam out the door and shut it quietly behind them.

'Dada, where are we going?'

'To the toilet. You haven't been for ages.'

Adam skipped along happily and when they got to the toilet he went straight in.

'Wait by there, won't you, Dada?'

'I will, son.' O'Shea was already edging towards the gate, his eyes scanning for signs of a watchman. The gate was tied up with a chain and a big rusty padlock. It obviously hadn't been used for years because the bottom rung was embedded in thick weeds.

The narrow lane behind it was a quagmire. It was the route the cattle took from the cow shed to the fields. Churned up mud was mixed with copious amounts of cow dung. To make it worse, it was diluted by the recent rain and now it was a river of sludge. It was at least a foot deep, maybe even more in patches. And it reeked.

O'Shea gave the gate a rattle. They could climb over it. That wouldn't be too hard. But how far would they get in that lake of manure?

But surely it couldn't be any worse than staying here. And they might not get another chance like this. Go while the going's good. That's what his brain was telling him. He turned around to call Adam. Rhys was standing by the toilet door with a big grin on his face.

'Are you all right there, Irish?'

O'Shea felt his throat go dry. Just then there was a clatter against the toilet wall.

'Dada, I'm finished.'

Rhys looked surprised and stepped back as O'Shea walked around him and opened the door. Adam grinned up at Rhys as he waddled out hitching up his trousers.

'Hello.'

'Hello.' Rhys tipped the peak of his cap with his shotgun.

It was late evening before all the visitors left. They drifted out in twos and threes until eventually the house was quiet once more. Bethan and Cerys came back into the kitchen and Cerys made a fresh pot of tea.

'You'll be moving on soon.' Bethan gave O'Shea a cursory glance as she went and stood by the window.

O'Shea sat up straight and tried to read her expression. 'What do you mean?'

When she ignored him he looked at Cerys. But she didn't respond either.

'What do you mean *moving on*?' he asked again.

Bethan rolled her eyes.

'I'll repeat it for you. *Slowly,* as you're Irish.' She looked at him with a distasteful sneer. 'You will be moving on soon. Away from here.'

'Where to?'

Bethan thought a moment and sipped her tea. Then she grunted, put her cup down on the table and went back through the door into the front room.

'Cerys!'

Cerys glanced around.

'*Well*?'

'Well what?' She shook her head. 'I'm sorry, I wasn't listening.'

'You weren't *listening*? Your sister just said we'll be moving on soon.'

'Yes.'

'Well, where will we be going? What's going to happen to us?'

She pulled out a chair and sat down beside him.

'Can I ask you something?' She reached out and took his hands.

'Well, yes. Of course. What is it?'

'Yesterday, up in the mountains.' She looked around the kitchen and lowered her voice. 'Did you see any boxes?'

'Boxes? What do you mean boxes?'

'I don't know. Boxes! Did you see any boxes?'

'I don't think so. I don't know.'

She gave a heavy sigh. A shadow crossed her face and she bit her lip.

'Look,' O'Shea squeezed her hand. 'There was a lot going on at the time. People were shooting at me. They were sticking bayonets into me. What boxes was I supposed to be looking at?'

'Well, those men were up there for a reason.' She spoke softly, almost to herself. 'They were looking for something. They were planning this for weeks. I told you, didn't I? They put a lot of time and effort into this. And they came from all over the country. Top people. And it had something to do with those boxes. Now if the boxes weren't brought back here then where are they?'

She had that strange look again. Her eyes were cold and annoyed. They were on O'Shea but she wasn't looking at him. She was staring through him into the distance.

'I'm sorry.' O'Shea let go of her hand. 'Honestly. I don't know anything about any boxes.'

'Never mind. Don't worry about it.' She stood up and went across to the fire.

O'Shea turned around on his chair. 'Anyway, you haven't answered my question. *When* are we being moved on? And where are we going? What's going to happen to us?'

She ignored him. She seemed totally distracted.

When the front door slammed they both went to the window. In the light of the moon they could see Bethan and Gareth climb into the captured German car and cruise off down the drive.

O'Shea sat down at the table again but Cerys perched on the windowsill and looked out at the night. Her reflection looked back at her in the glass and her expression was hard to read.

Chapter Twenty-One

O'Shea took Adam into the scullery and lifted him into the huge porcelain sink filled with hot soapy water. Then he put the boy's clothes to soak in a bucket.

After washing his hair and scrubbing him from top to toe, O'Shea let him soak in the bubbles for a few more minutes. Then he wrapped him in a blanket, carried him back to the kitchen and sat him at the table.

With his face scrubbed and his hair combed flat against his head, it reminded O'Shea of the Saturday nights when Adam had his bath in the tub in front of the fire. The only thing missing now was the scent of the talcum powder Heather sprinkled all over him leaving imprints of his little feet on the kitchen floor.

Cerys was still sitting on the windowsill staring out at the dark. O'Shea looked in the pot on the fire. It was still half full of stew and it smelt delicious as it simmered quietly. Little bubbles popped and let off bursts of steam.

'Cerys, is it all right if I give Adam some of this stew?'

She half turned. 'Yes, of course,' she nodded then looked back out the window.

Using the copper ladle O'Shea scooped stew into two mugs and took them back to the table.

'Would you like some yourself?' he asked Cerys.

Her head gave the hint of a shake but she didn't answer. So O'Shea sat down and took a sip from his mug. Adam's eyes smiled as he sipped from his. He looked contented. As long as he was warm and had something to eat he never asked for much else in life.

'Cerys,' he said suddenly.

'What about her?'

'She's nice, isn't she, Dada?' He gave a shy smile. 'I like Cerys.'

O'Shea sensed Cerys looking at him and when he glanced over her eyes smiled. Her hair fell around her face and in the glow from the fire she looked very pretty.

But O'Shea also saw Bethan in that face and it disturbed him. He put his hands around his mug of stew and lowered his eyes.

Cerys frowned. Then she gave a deep sigh, got up from the windowsill and came across to the table.

'I think I will have something to eat, Francis. I'm a bit peckish after all.'

O'Shea gave a little cough and grinned to himself.

'Danny,' he said.

'Pardon?'

'My name is Danny.'

She tilted her head and her eyes asked the question.

'My name is Danny,' O'Shea repeated. 'You just called me Francis.'

'Did I?'

'Yes. You said I will have something to eat, *Francis*.'

'Oh.' She sat down beside him. 'I meant Danny, of course.'

O'Shea gave an exaggerated pout. 'Tis an easy mistake to make. Danny. *Francis*. So who's Francis? One off the farmhands?'

'No. Francis is my husband.'

'Your husband?' O'Shea spluttered. 'You have a husband?'

'Yes.' She grinned. 'It's no big secret.'

O'Shea put his mug down and sat up straight. 'Oh. Right! So where is he now, this husband of yours?'

'I've no idea. He disappeared after the baby died.'

'After the baby …you had a baby too?'

'Oh, it was a long time ago.' She waved it away. 'A lot of water has flowed under the bridge since then.'

O'Shea shook his head. 'Are you saying your husband just buggered off after your baby died?'

'Well, you couldn't blame him.' There was a bitter edge to her voice now. 'The way everyone ganged up on him. They drove him out, you know? My father and Bethan. They never liked him from the start so naturally they blamed him for everything that happened to us.'

She paused for a moment. 'God, it seems so long ago now. We were no more than children at the time, me and Francis. Everyone said it wouldn't last. *Couldn't* last. You know what people are like. But me and Francis, we were going to prove them wrong, see. We were going to show them.'

The shudder made her flinch. 'But it was all pie in the sky, wasn't it? How can you explain to someone that life isn't one big bunch of roses, eh? Certainly not the young folk. We had to find out for ourselves. And roses have thorns, don't they?'

The fire crackled and spat and a wave of heat floated over them. Cerys got up and moved some pots on the grate.

'I'm sorry.' She sat back down beside O'Shea. 'I shouldn't be telling you all this. It's nothing to do with you, after all.'

'Not at all,' O'Shea smiled. 'I'm not going anywhere, am I? So you carry on.'

'I knew you'd understand.' She smiled back at him and put her hand on top of his. It was soft and warm. He didn't resist. He was too tired and muddled to think clearly anyway.

'I knew you were a nice person the minute I saw you. Just like Francis.' She paused for a moment as if she was analysing the memories. 'Well, at least he used to be a nice person when I first met him. He was wonderful, kind. But the baby changed him, you see. That's when it all began to unravel. When the baby was born we were thrown together and everything was new and unfamiliar and confusing. Frightening too. Then came the squabbles. You know, when the baby wouldn't sleep and seemed to cry all the time? Then a bit of nagging, isn't it? Me nagging him to help me. Him nagging me because I was going on at him all the time. He couldn't cope with it all, see. The confinement, the responsibilities. Eventually it started to degenerate, become abusive. It all just fell apart, bit by bit.'

Cerys glanced at O'Shea and her eyes were wide and sad and looking for a reaction. O'Shea sipped his soup.

'Anyway, when he saw how bad things were my father decided I should go away for a while. Stay with relatives in north Wales until things sorted themselves out, see? And you didn't argue with my father.'

She looked across at the fire again. Her brow was creased and her eyes were lost in her thoughts. And O'Shea had a sudden impulse to put his arms around her and hold her.

'And they didn't, I take it,' he said instead.

'What?'

'Things didn't work out.'

'No, they didn't.' Her voice had a sob in it. When she looked back at O'Shea her eyes were wet. She wiped them with her sleeve.

'While I was away my baby died. I don't know how, and no one would tell me. I was so desperate, so alone. But no one came to help me. It was then I desperately needed Francis. But he never came to me. God, how I cried. For days and days. My baby, my poor little baby.'

Now the tears came freely and she turned away. O'Shea took a mouthful of the stew as he waited for her to compose herself. Eventually she dried her eyes with the hem of her apron.

'I'm sorry,' she sobbed. 'I shouldn't go on like that.'

O'Shea had to swallow the stew before he could reply. 'Ah, 'tis all right. I understand.'

'I know you do.' She took his hand again. 'You're just like Francis.'

O'Shea grimaced and she frowned.

'*What*? It's true. You *are* alike. You even look like him. Honest to God, Danny, I mean it. When you walked into this kitchen yesterday my heart nearly stopped. I thought you were Francis. I thought he'd come home. I wanted to run to you, hold you. I was almost in tears. But of course I realised you weren't him so I said nothing.'

O'Shea wiped his mouth with his hand.

'You don't believe me, do you?' Her eyes filled with tears again.

'It's not … I don't know.' O'Shea held the mug of stew against his chest and struggled for the right words. 'It's just you seem way too young for all this shite to have happened to you.'

'But I'm not. The thing is, I was fourteen when I met Francis. My father wasn't too happy about it, as you can imagine. But it wasn't just about the age thing. He just didn't like Francis. He was too brash, couldn't be trusted. Not safe to be alone with. My father couldn't accept we were just friends. That's all we were. Friends. Nothing else. Not like they all seemed to think. Bethan was really suspicious of him. But there was nothing to worry about. He did make one or two vague attempts to kiss me but when I hesitated, well, that was that.

Sometimes he would go quiet for a while, sulk like. But nothing too dramatic.'

She went silent again for a few moments. 'I suppose it would have fizzled out eventually if we hadn't gone to a stupid fancy dress party. I went as a Roman slave. You know the sort of thing, short little toga and all that. My father went mad, forbade me to go out looking like that. But that was all the more reason for going - defiance. Anyway, Francis had a drink or two and it made him very excited. He wouldn't leave me alone all night, dancing with me, buying me drinks, falling all over me, telling me how he admired me for standing up to my father.'

She brushed away another tear. 'I wasn't used to drinking so I got quite tipsy as well. And when he took me home we went the short way through the woods. That's when it happened. What I *wanted* to happen. To prove I was a real woman. A *real* woman. Not just a defiant little child.'

They sat in silence for another few moments. 'Anyway, a few months later our night of passion came back to haunt us. Of course Francis did the honourable thing and married me.'

She moved closer and brushed her fingers against O'Shea's face.

'So you see ...'

O'Shea pulled away and she snapped up straight.

'What's the matter now?'

'Nothing.'

'Yes there is. You don't believe a word of what I'm telling you. Do you?'

'Well, I ... I just don't know.'

'But why? I'm telling you what happened. Why don't you believe me?'

'I don't know *what* to believe anymore.' O'Shea ran his fingers through his hair. 'Tis just, well, this is coming at me a bit too fast, you know. I can't think straight. I mean, why are you telling me all this? I'm a complete stranger yet you're telling me all these things.'

'You're not, though.' She took his hand and squeezed it again 'You don't feel like a stranger to me. I feel I've known you all my life. I feel I can talk to you, tell you things. And I know you'll listen without judging me.'

Adam gave a big yawn and both of them looked at him.

'I'd better get his stuff ready,' O'Shea said. 'He looks like he wants to go to sleep.'

'No.' Cerys jumped up. 'I'll do it.'

She got the blankets and made him a comfortable bed beside the fire then she tucked him in and gave him a kiss on the forehead. 'Sweet dreams, sweetheart.'

Then she held out her hand to O'Shea. 'Come into the front room. We won't disturb him in there.'

'*What*?'

'Come on. It's much more comfortable in there.'

O'Shea hesitated. The front room was Bethan's domain. She could return at any minute and he dreaded to think what she'd do if she found him in there.

'I'm perfectly comfortable here,' he argued.

'Come on. Let's just sit and talk for a while in a comfy chair.'

'Talk about what?'

'Whatever you like.' She pulled him to his feet and slipped her arm around his waist. When she looked up at him he noticed the little cluster of freckles around her nose and the light dimples at the corners of her mouth. She let her lips brush his, then she turned and led the way.

Dark September

Chapter Twenty-Two

It was a comfortable room. A big iron fireplace had a large mantelpiece with photographs and ornaments scattered all over it. A bureau in one corner had the lid open and it was covered in all sorts of papers and official-looking documents. Cerys manoeuvred O'Shea towards the sofa and they sank down onto it.

'You've no idea what it's like living in this house.' She lay back in the corner and drew her legs up under her. 'No one ever just sits down and talks anymore. All we ever do is get up, cook, clean, scrub. We work until we're exhausted then stagger back to bed again. Every day's the same. We all pass like ships in the night. We mutter a few pleasantries and that's it. Sometimes there's not even the pleasantries, just a grunt or two. But there's never any conversation. It's years since I actually sat down with anyone and had a decent gossip. It's so long since I was able to just talk, confide in someone. Talk to someone who would understand.'

Her foot rubbed against O'Shea's leg.

'What about all those people I saw yesterday? Couldn't you talk with them?' He shifted awkwardly.

'What?' she sniggered. 'Who, for instance? Which one of that lot do you think I would wish to tell my troubles to? Rhys, with his bad breath and wandering hands? He's married, lives on the farm next door. He's got five kids and a wonky knee which is why they wouldn't take him in the Army. And if you so much as smile at him he thinks you're after his body. Imagine waking up to *that* first thing in the morning. I'd rather sleep with a bag of spuds.'

She swatted the thought away. 'Who else? Gareth? Older than my own father. Anyway, if I told him anything he'd repeat it word for word to Bethan.'

'Can't you speak to Bethan?'

Cerys sputtered.

'Okay, what about your other sister, then? You said you were only a year older than her. Don't you have a lot in common, girls your age?'

'No,' Cerys pursed her lips. 'The thing is, Rhianne's full of chapel, isn't she? I mean, I love her and all that. But with Rhianne every conversation turns to Jesus. She really believes Jesus will solve every little problem no matter how trivial. She includes Him in everything. I mean, it's wonderful to have such faith. I wish I did. But it's become an obsession with her. I know it's a great comfort to her and I wish her all the best with it. But it's got to the point where we really don't talk much now. I think maybe I've become too cynical over the years.'

She let her leg rub against O'Shea's again and she grinned when he moved away a little bit more and coughed into his fist.

'No,' she continued. 'There was ever only one person I could really talk to. Who I could trust with my most intimate secrets. Only once in my life did I have that kind of trust in someone and I had the heart ripped out of me because of it. I swore no man would ever do that to me again. But what happens? You turn up out of the blue looking like his double. And I'm making a complete fool of myself all over again.'

'*What*?' O'Shea slid farther back in the sofa. This was becoming surreal. The knot in his stomach was warning him he'd wandered into something that wasn't going to end well.

'Well, I am.' She pulled a face at him. 'I'm telling you things and you don't believe a word of it.'

Sweat tickled the back of his neck. 'It's not ... look, I'm just having difficulty trying to grasp it all.'

'But you *do* believe me.'

He studied her face. The impish smile looked playful enough but he couldn't tell how serious she was. Was she just playing with him now? Or did his answer really matter?

She drew her legs up under her chin with a tantalising slowness and let her dress slide up her thighs. And she opened her legs just a fraction.

And she made sure O'Shea could see she wasn't wearing anything underneath.

He dropped back against the arm of the sofa and tried to look away. But he wasn't strong enough to drag his eyes from the dark clump of hair that contrasted vividly with the whiteness of her skin.

She sat up quickly and her hand shot out and caught hold of him. 'Thank God for that.' She gave throaty chuckle as she squeezed him. 'I thought for a minute you wouldn't rise to the occasion.'

She pulled him forward so abruptly he lost his balance. Her hands were already tugging at his belt, ripping it off and throwing it across the room. One hand groped down inside his trousers, held and squeezed while the other snaked around his neck. Her mouth searched for his, biting and licking, her breath coming in hot gasps. And her lips were surprisingly sweet.

She straightened up suddenly. And with one smooth movement she removed her dress and threw it on the chair. Then she took O'Shea's hands and cupped them over her breasts as she straddled him, giving a long, gasping cry as he squeezed them.

Then she kissed him as if she was trying to exorcise the frustration that consumed her for all those years. Her tongue searched for his. She wriggled and groaned and gave a sudden thrust with her hips. Instantly O'Shea was inside her and he yelped in ecstasy, and she gave another loud groan and pulled at his hair.

She wrapped her legs around him so hard they flipped over and dropped off the sofa onto the rug. Her fingers tore into his back as she bit at his face and neck. Nails raked down his spine and sank deep into his buttocks making him jerk with the pain. The more he wriggled in agony the more forcefully it made her gyrate. And she groaned even louder.

'Oh, Francis! Don't stop, don't stop.'

Her breath came in great gulps and O'Shea's heart thumped in his ears as he tried to keep up with her. His elbows were rubbed raw on the rug and his knees started to ache under the weight of her body. At last she arched up and a huge shiver rippled through her.

She gave a deep, husky laugh and dropped onto her back. Her breath came in rapid, contented gasps.

O'Shea smiled down at her and her hands suddenly grabbed his thighs again.

'Don't stop,' she panted.

In the subdued light of the room the smile she gave O'Shea was amazingly beautiful. He leant down and kissed her softly on the mouth.

'Stay with me,' she whispered. 'Please, stay with me. Don't leave me now.'

Her arms snaked around his neck again and they lay still, quietly listening to their heartbeats and the crackle of the fire in the grate. O'Shea could feel her breath on the nape of his neck and the rise and fall of her breasts as they moved in tune with it.

Then she snapped awake and gave a long moan, and the whole thing started all over again.

Eventually they ended up under the bureau with Cerys clinging tightly to O'Shea as she buried her face in his neck. Somewhere nearby there was the soft ticking of a clock and O'Shea shivered.

In the buzz of the silence he was suddenly overwhelmed by a deep sense of foreboding. Whatever web of conspiracy she was leading him into, it was way too late to back away now. Panic was taking hold and he swallowed hard.

'Danny?'

'Yeah?' He almost choked on the word.

'You know I asked you earlier about some boxes?'

Boxes? Those bloody boxes again. 'What about them?'

'Did you remember?'

He looked down at her. 'Did I remember what?'

She pulled away with an irritated click of her tongue and sat up. Little goose bumps appeared on her arms.

'Look, the people who attacked those German trucks were after something special.' Her voice was cold and precise again. 'From what I overheard, they were expecting to find some boxes. How many, I don't know. But I *do* know they were pretty upset when they weren't on the trucks. Now you were there. You saw everything. Are you sure you didn't notice any boxes? Did you see anyone taking boxes from the trucks? Or maybe from the German car? Did anything unusual happen?'

'Did anything unusual happen?' O'Shea spluttered. 'The whole feckin thing was unusual. It isn't every day I'm stuck with a bayonet, you know?'

She glared at him for a moment. Then she gave another disarming smile and patted him on the bandage. 'How is it now?'

'Fine.'

'Danny,' she kissed him softly on the knee then slowly brushed her lips along the inside of his thigh. And he gasped when she took a bite of his skin. 'Please try to remember. It's very important.'

'For God's sake, Cerys!' He rubbed the bite with his hand. 'I told you already. I did *not* notice any boxes. I swear to God! If I'd seen them I'd tell you. You know I would.'

She rolled away from him and stood up, and she raked her fingers through her hair. Then she picked up her dress, pulled it on over her head and strolled back into the kitchen.

O'Shea lay where he was. It felt safer. The dark mood Cerys was carrying this morning was back and menace dripped off her. But why? It wasn't O'Shea's fault he couldn't tell her about the boxes. He hadn't seen them. And why were they so important to her anyway? The shadow of doom skipped across his heart again and he wished he'd taken his chances with the muddy lane.

He got up, put his clothes back on and followed her into the kitchen. Adam was still curled up in the blanket and breathing softly.

O'Shea sat at the table and watched Cerys as she moved around the kitchen, straightening things and poking the fire.

Suddenly she threw the poker into the corner with a loud crash and went to the door.

'I'm off to bed.' She pull it open with an irritated jolt. 'Can I get you anything before I go?'

O'Shea shook his head. 'No thanks. I don't think so.

Dark September

Chapter Twenty-Three

A few days later Bethan told O'Shea to get ready. They were leaving that afternoon. That was all she said. Then she went back out and slammed the kitchen door behind her.

O'Shea's heart was racing as he got Adam's coat and put it on the back of a chair. He checked his own coat for the sock of money and put it on top of Adam's.

Adam looked up at him with trusting eyes. O'Shea forced a smile but inside he was in turmoil. He had a very bad feeling about this. He'd convinced himself they were going to be bundled into a truck and driven away into the woods to be dispatched with a bullet to the back of the head. Whatever Cerys said about her sister, O'Shea knew Bethan was capable of doing just that.

Through the window he could see Rhys and Idris leaning against a tree with their shotguns by their sides. They were on the opposite side of the yard from the toilet, out of sight of the gate that led to the muddy lane.

If he took Adam to the toilet, could they make a run for it? They didn't have to stick to the lane. They could go straight across into the field beyond.

Cerys came in from the front room and slammed the door behind her. O'Shea gave her a smile but she brushed past him and went to the fire. She had the hard look on her face again as she clattered pots and pans on the grate.

O'Shea wasn't surprised, though. Ever since he'd told her he knew nothing about the boxes she'd totally ignored him. He tried to talk to her several times but she acted as if he was invisible.

When she did speak it was for something trivial, like did he want some tea. But before he could answer she'd be off doing something else and his reply would float off into thin air.

A couple of times she stopped and stood gazing into the distance as if she'd suddenly remembered something. But just as quickly she snapped out of it and carried on doing what she was doing.

O'Shea couldn't understand any of it. His worst nightmare was never as bad as this. It was distressing enough getting kidnapped by a bunch of deluded insurgents. But how in God's name did he get sucked into such a weird relationship with one of them?

Was he so desperate for an ally he just grabbed the first straw that was held out to him? Was he *that* easy to dupe into thinking he was her best friend? Someone she wanted to tell her life story to? Someone she trusted enough to engage in a wild passionate moment in front of a blazing fire? She even begged him to stay with her forever. *Didn't she?*

But it was all just part of a plan. Cerys wanted information from O'Shea and she wanted it fast. So she used the best weapon she had. She saw O'Shea for what he was, vulnerable and scared. The interrogation was subtle. There was no resistance.

Then in the blink of an eye he was a stranger again, that inconvenient person ... that prisoner ... who sat in the kitchen with nowhere to go.

He could feel his face burning with the embarrassment.

He wondered if she knew what was going to happening that afternoon. Were they *really* going to disappear down a bog hole somewhere?

Cerys threw down the spoon she was stirring the pots with and wiped her hands on her apron. Then she untied the apron and dropped it onto a chair.

'Come down to the front gate with us.' She brushed O'Shea on the shoulder as she took her coat off the back of the door. O'Shea looked startled.

'Come on.' Her eyes twinkled and there was a laugh in her voice. 'The walk will do you good.'

'Are you serious?' O'Shea stood up and pushed his chair back. 'You want us to go for a walk? You *do* know we're supposed to be leaving here this afternoon?'

'I know.' She picked up his coat and threw it at him. 'It's starting to rain. Put that on.'

'Look, Cerys, I'm sorry ...'

'What are you so worried about?' Again her voice was bright and bubbly. 'We're only going to meet some people. They should be here about two o'clock. We're going to meet the people who'll be looking after you.'

'What? Our new jailers?'

'Jailers? What do you mean jailers? This isn't a jail. Is it? You don't think this place is a jail? You haven't been treated like a prisoner, have you?'

Adam got up and reached for his coat.

'Not you, Adam love.' Cerys ruffled his hair. 'You can stay here in the warm.'

'You want Adam to stay behind?'

'Relax,' she rolled her eyes at him. 'You're not going anywhere just yet. We're only going to meet them, bring them back here for a rest and something to eat. It'll give you an opportunity to get to know them, won't it?'

'Thank you,' O'Shea answered dryly.

'Oh, stop worrying, will you?' She grinned as she opened the door. 'You shouldn't take any notice of what Bethan says, you know. She planned to send you to

141

North Wales all along. To that ferry place on Anglesey. You'll easily slip over to Ireland from there.'

'Really?' O'Shea followed her out the door. 'Are you telling me the truth?'

'Of course I'm telling you the truth.' She sounded irritated now. 'What did you think we were going to do with you? We're not the Gestapo!'

The pigs in the whitewashed shed were grunting and snorting. O'Shea looked at the open door.

'No. I didn't think you were.'

Clouds came in a continuous blanket from over the mountains on the other side of the valley and they sprayed everything with a thick mist.

Cerys walked on ahead. Idris and Rhys picked up their shotguns and followed her. O'Shea pulled his collar up and faced into the drizzle as he strolled along after them.

When she got to the end of the drive Cerys waited for the others to catch up. Then she swung the gate open and walked out onto the road.

'What time will they be here, did you say?' O'Shea asked.

Cerys had her hair tied back in a ponytail, highlighting her cheekbones and the soft curve of her mouth. Even with a huge baggy jumper and loose trousers pulled over big boots she still looked strikingly beautiful.

'Soon,' she muttered absently.

The vagueness had come back into her eyes. After a while she sauntered back inside the gate and they all shuffled after her. They stood under the branches of an oak trees that were hanging over the driveway. But the tree only gave shelter from the breeze because rain built up on the leaves and channelled water down over their heads.

Idris passed around a packet of cigarettes and they all took one. They had to cup them in their hands to stop them getting wet and they smoked them in silence.

Somewhere in the distance thunder rumbled and everyone shifted and looked up at the sky. A thin wisp of smoke came from the house and tapered through the trees before the wind blew it away.

Cerys flapped her arms and hovered close to Rhys to keep the wind from her. Her nose was red and her lips were thin blue lines. Idris leant against a tree with his eyes closed and his head bowed. The rain made rivers through his hair before dribbling down his face.

'How much longer do we have to wait?' he asked suddenly, clapping his hands. No one answered but they all looked at Cerys.

She shrugged. 'Not long now.'

'How long?'

'I said not long! We'll wait, all right?'

Her eyes were dark and angry again and she looked at everyone in turn. They turned away and decided to wait.

Rhys dug in his pocket and pulled out a small bottle of whisky. He took a swig that made him cough then he handed it to Cerys who passed it to O'Shea. O'Shea sucked hard on the last of his cigarette before spitting the butt on the ground. Then he took a mouthful of the whisky and gasped as it burnt all the way down to his stomach. He passed the bottle to Idris and Rhys followed it to make sure Idris didn't go mad with it.

A car cruised past the gate and everyone straightened up. A few seconds later it reversed back and pulled in by the hedge just beyond the entrance.

Chapter Twenty-Four

Cerys ran to the car and pulled open the driver's door. And she was beaming as she leant in to speak to the man behind the wheel.

From where O'Shea was standing he could only see one person in the car. Cerys stepped back, and as the man climbed out he pulled up the collar of his long overcoat. He gave a quick smile at everyone before he reached back into the car and brought out a trilby which he pulled down over his eyes. Then he threw a long white scarf around his neck.

Rhys and Idris glanced at each other. Cerys slammed the door shut and guided the driver in O'Shea's direction.

'This is Danny O'Shea. Danny is the one who'll be going back with you this afternoon. Danny, this is Mr Clooney.'

Clooney took O'Shea's hand in a strong grip. And there was something about him that made O'Shea hesitate. Had they met before? Clooney obviously didn't know O'Shea because there was no recognition in his eyes. He just smiled and said hello. Then he turned back to Cerys.

Cerys motioned for Rhys to go on back to the house. Rhys looked at Idris and his eyes narrowed. There was a hint of annoyance in them. But there was something else, too. He seemed anxious. Idris just shrugged and walked on.

O'Shea caught up with them. 'What's going on?'

Rhys raised his eyebrows but didn't answer. O'Shea looked behind. Cerys and Clooney were still on the road talking.

O'Shea sensed the tension in the way Rhys was walking. He'd swung the shotgun across his arms and snapped it shut. His eyes were like a water rat's as he scanned the trees.

'How come there's only one person in the car?' O'Shea looked from one to the other but again there was no response from the two men. 'I thought Cerys said there would to be more than one person. You know, like when she said *people* were coming? She didn't say *person*, did she? She said *people!*'

He looked back at Cerys and Clooney again. This time they were just inside the gate. And there was something strange about the way they were acting. It was as if they were reluctant to come up to the house.

O'Shea felt a prickle of sweat on the back of his neck. As he turned to Rhys he caught the look in his eyes. And he turned towards the trees just as a shadow darted back out of sight.

'Who the hell is that?'

Rhys was obviously startled. He had the shotgun cocked and aimed. But before he could do anything the shadow jumped out in front of them. A rifle cracked and Rhys grabbed his face and flew backwards, slammed into O'Shea and knocked him into the ditch.

As O'Shea rolled onto his knees he saw Clooney grab Cerys and drag her into the high grass at the bottom of the field. His white scarf flew in the wind behind him.

Idris ducked and fired and the gunman flipped backwards clutching his chest. His second shot was aimed at the trees and another gunman tumbled out of the bushes with a gaping hole in the side of his head.

'Run!' Idris grabbed the gun Rhys had dropped. O'Shea started sprinting towards the house.

'Get off the road,' Idris bellowed. 'Get into the trees.'

145

'My boy's in the house,' O'Shea yelled back. 'I've got to get Adam.'

Two shots hit Idris and he folded up, dropped to his knees and sagged forward until his face was on the ground.

O'Shea crouched low as he raced towards the house.

Bullets whined around him as he stumbled into the yard. They plopped in the mud and pinged off the wall as he threw himself behind the shed just as Bethan came charging out of the front door. She was screaming for Cerys. Gareth was pulling at her clothes and trying to drag her back into the house when another burst of gunfire came from the back of the house and spattered along the wall towards them. And Gareth clutched his chest and flew against the window.

Bethan staggered forward a few feet before she realised something had happened. She stopped and looked back in horror. Then she gave a howl of agony as another burst of gunfire slammed into her. She jerked backwards and hit the wall. And she beat at her thighs and stomach as she tried to ward off the pain and hold back the blood all at the same time.

As she wailed her eyes were darting all around the yard in disbelief. Then she saw O'Shea and she pointed a trembling finger at him. She started to walk towards him but she sagged to her knees and dropped onto the cobbles.

O'Shea stayed down in the mud as he crawled over to her. He took her head in his hands. Her whole body was trembling.

'Irish! You bastard ... you ... was it you?'

'For God's sake,' O'Shea snapped. 'What do you mean was it me?'

'Cerys ... where's my sister?' Her breath came in desperate gulps.

'She's all right. I saw her running away. She got away. But where's my boy? Where's Adam?'

'Safe,' Bethan nodded. 'He's with Rhianne. There's a secret cupboard under the stairs. No one will find him there.'

Her eyes rolled and blood filled her mouth. She coughed as she gripped O'Shea's hand. 'Why did you ...?'

'As God's my witness!' O'Shea wiped her mouth with his sleeve. 'On my son's life, I had nothing to do with this.'

Boots came crunching across the cobbles and a bayonet pressed against O'Shea's neck. A soldier ran over to Gareth, pulled him onto his back and prodded him with his foot. More soldiers gathered around Bethan and O'Shea.

An officer barged his way through and took a closer look.

'Shit!' He took off his cap and wiped his brow with a handkerchief.

Then he pulled his cap back on and rushed back out of the circle, calling loudly to someone.

Bethan tried to sit up but O'Shea held her down. A soldier took a flask from his belt, poured water onto a handkerchief and dabbed it to her mouth. She sucked hard against it.

'Irish,' Bethan's hand went to his face and her touch was already deathly cold. 'Tell Cerys *through the looking glass*. What she wants ... *Alice through the looking glass*?'

She twitched violently and her eyes bulged.

'Don't talk now,' O'Shea squeezed her hand. 'Just lie still and we'll take care of you.'

Her mouth quivered as she forced the words out. 'Don't trust ... you can't trust ...'

Her eyes rolled again and her chest heaved, and with it came her last breath.

A boot slammed into O'Shea's ribs and he toppled sideways with a yell of pain. He was grabbed by the arms and hauled back on his feet, dragged across the yard and pinned against a tree with a sickening thud.

The officer was back beside Bethan and feeling her wrist for signs of life. He swore again as he let her hand fall. And his face was dark with fury as he turned on the soldiers that were still standing around. They hurried away. He marched over to O'Shea and stood in front of him with his eyes blazing.

'I am Captain Weiss.' He spoke surprisingly softly. 'What did that woman say to you?'

'What? *Nothing*!'

'She was speaking to you. I heard her. What did she say to you?'

'She was dying. She said she didn't want to be dying.'

The fist hit him on the side of the head.

'I haven't got time for this bullshit,' Weiss screamed. 'I saw her talking to you. What did she say?'

'For God's sake ... she wanted to know where her sister was. I told her I didn't know. She was dying. She was frightened. She was talking rubbish.'

Weiss stepped back and his face was shaking in temper as he glared at O'Shea. Then he turned and walked across the yard with his sergeant.

A truck rumbled up and stopped in front of the house. O'Shea was dragged over to it and thrown over the tailboard. And he landed heavily on the bare floor. When he managed to sit up he gasped in surprise. Sitting on the bench in front of him was a man in a long overcoat and white scarf

'Are you all right, old boy?' Clooney asked.

Chapter Twenty-Five

The soldiers were everywhere. They streamed in and out of the house and swarmed like ants all over the yard. They were poking in the sheds and outhouses. They moved in a line down through the fields, beating the bushes and undergrowth with sticks. They searched behind troughs and barrels.

Things flew out of the upstairs windows and smashed on the cobbles below. Every time O'Shea heard a shout his stomach turned. His heart was in his throat waiting for someone to come running out of the house dragging Adam behind them.

O'Shea knew Adam couldn't sit still for long. He'd be frightened and confused. He'd get frustrated and start looking for his father. O'Shea prayed that Rhianne could keep him calm.

A cold, clammy sweat had O'Shea's clothes sticking to him as he sat for what seemed like hours in the back of the truck. Clooney was lying on the bench and appeared to be asleep. But O'Shea was far too agitated to close his eyes. His side was bleeding again where he'd been kicked and it throbbed like a dull toothache.

A donkey sauntered into the yard pulling a cart that rattled loudly on the stones and it stopped in front of the scullery door. The two men who came with it pulled Gareth and Bethan across the ground and threw them up onto the cart next to the bodies of Rhys and Idris. One of them gave the donkey a slap on the buttocks and they all strolled off again around the side of the whitewashed building.

Clooney sat up and rubbed his face. 'Are you all right, son?'

O'Shea shook his head but didn't answer.

'Say,' Clooney repeated. 'Are you all right?'

'What do you think, you stupid prat?'

'Nice one. Remind me not to be too concerned about you in future, won't you.'

'Yeah, right,' O'Shea snorted.

'Look,' Clooney leant forward and rested his elbows on his knees. 'Have you got a problem with me?'

'As a matter of fact, I have. My problem is I don't understand how you're sitting there without a scratch on you. How is it that you're not after getting the shite blown out of you like all the others? Eh? Tell me that, so!'

Clooney's eyes were as cold as ice and they made O'Shea hesitate again. There was definitely something familiar about him.

'*Well*?'

'Well what?' Clooney shrugged. 'What are you saying? Are you saying I ran away? Of course I bloody ran away. The minute I heard the shooting, I ran away. I grabbed Cerys and I took off across the fields. She hid under a bush and I ran. Unfortunately I ran the wrong way. Suddenly I was looking down the barrel of a gun. So what would you want me to do, eh? Be a bloody hero and go down fighting? Die with my boots on, is it? Is that what you're saying?'

His eyes were unblinking. O'Shea looked away.

'Anyway, what about you?' he said after a while. 'What's your excuse?'

'Look, all I care about right now is my son. I'm sure Bethan told you about my son, seeing as you were supposed to be taking us to North Wales today. So you'll understand why I'm concerned. You know what the Germans will do to him if they find him. So all I can think of at the moment is how to get him out of there. I've got to find a way to get to him, make sure he's safe.'

Clooney gave a sarcastic laugh. 'You're in a bloody world of your own. Have you looked outside? Can't you see the place is crawling with German soldiers? Just because they didn't shoot you earlier doesn't mean they won't shoot you now. Before your feet hit the deck you'd be splattered all over the back of this truck. And me with you. So behave yourself, will you.'

'Behave myself?' O'Shea shouted back. 'Am I supposed to just sit here and do nothing? That's my son we're talking about. He's only a child. He's not able to look after himself.'

Clooney lay back down on the bench. 'You haven't got a cigarette on you, have you?'

'No, I have not!'

'Thanks, anyway.' Clooney grinned as he sat back up. 'But how do you know he's still in the house? How do you know he hasn't gone out the back way? He could be half way to Cardiff by now.'

'He could not.' O'Shea flapped his hands in irritation. 'He wouldn't be able to think like that. He'll still be hiding in the house. He'll be sitting there and he won't know what to do. You don't understand at all, do you? He's not *able* to look after himself. He needs me. I'm all he's got. So I have to find a way to get him out.'

'Look,' Clooney leant forward again. 'If the Germans *were* going to find him they'd have done it by now, don't you think? You can see for yourself. They're packing up to leave. So he'll be safe if he stays where he is. But you acting the fool isn't going to do him any favours, is it? You won't be much use to him lying on that cart with Bethan and the others.'

Two soldiers climbed into the back of the truck and took up their positions, one on either side by the tailgate. They gave the prisoners a dismissive glance as the truck shuddered into life and rumbled across the yard and down the drive to the gate.

O'Shea watched the house until it disappeared behind the trees. The panic rising up in his throat came out as a whimper and one of the soldiers looked at him curiously.

'Do you know where we're going?' O'Shea asked him.

There was no response. He just stared back at O'Shea.

'Well, do you know? Where are we going?'

The soldier looked away. The truck rocked as it turned out onto the road and they had to grab the metal rail to stop themselves from falling off the narrow benches.

O'Shea's head ached and it thumped with every bump of the road. He glanced at Clooney who was lying relaxed on the bench. There was something very strange about all of this. Something was very wrong but O'Shea was just too confused to focus on it. But he was sure Clooney had something to do with it. He felt it in his bones.

The truck passed the donkey and cart with the bodies lying in a pile on the back. Their faces were grey in death and twisted in horror at the way it happened. One of the guards spat casually and grinned to himself. He was stocky with a huge stomach that strained against his uniform. He had a fixed sneer on his face and he was obviously annoyed with his colleague. That guard was thin and pale and unshaven with red eyes sunk into his head. He looked uncomfortable with the swaying of the truck, and when he burped a waft of alcohol breath drifted back into the truck.

Clooney sat up and scratched himself. 'Drunken bastard. I knew someone farted just then.'

'He doesn't look very well, does he?'

'Serves him right.' Clooney rested his head back and closed his eyes again.

'So where do you think they're taking us?' O'Shea whispered.

Clooney shrugged. 'I haven't got a clue.'

'Well, we're going north, that's for sure. What's up there, do you think?'

'North? What makes you say that?'

'The sun is on our left.'

The truck rumbled down a steep hill, over an iron bridge and along a narrow street of terraced houses that were all identical right down to the colour of the front doors. Rising up behind them like a huge black shadow was a mountain of coal slag. The cables that stretched all the way to the top had enormous buckets swinging from them. They rocked and swayed as they passed each other in a continuous loop, dropping the coal dust at the top and rolling back down to the colliery again.

'I told you we were going north.'

Clooney looked up. 'Are you sure?'

'I am. Shur didn't pass this place last week when they were taking us to Bethan's house? They're taking us back up to the Brecons.'

The truck drove under a mass of pipes and walkways then back up another hill and out onto a flat plateau.

'Don't you see?' O'Shea was getting louder and he had to check his voice. 'I know where we are. If we're going to do something, we have to do it now. That way we can find our way back to the farm.'

'*What*?' Clooney almost choked. 'What do you mean *do something*? What are you talking about, for God's sake?'

O'Shea nodded at the two soldiers.

Clooney pulled a face. 'You *are* joking! Look, old son, I know you've had a very bad day and you're upset and all that stuff. But what the hell are you talking about?'

'My boy is back at that house. He'll be frightened and confused and he won't know what to do. I have to get back there.'

'Listen,' Clooney growled. 'Think about this very carefully. Those are trained soldiers right there, and probably two more in the front. We couldn't take them on at the best of times. We certainly couldn't take them on right now. Look at yourself. You don't look like you'd win a fight with a dead sheep.'

'All right,' O'Shea snapped. 'We haven't got much time to argue about this. Wherever we're going, we can't be too far away from the farm just yet.'

Both guards turned together and one pointed his rifle at Clooney.

'Sorry,' Clooney smiled. He said something in German and they stared at him until they were satisfied. Then they turned back to the road again. Clooney glared at O'Shea and motioned at him to say no more.

The road cut through a narrow valley and now O'Shea realised where they were going. They were being taken back to the place of the ambush. What the hell were they going back there for?

Pictures flashed through his mind. Cerys asked him about some boxes. Bethan tortured the German in the shed because of them. Could it be the Germans thought O'Shea knew something about them as well?

The road took a steep downward turn and the truck started to pick up speed, rocking and swaying on the uneven surface. The thin soldier leant over the tailgate and started retching and his whole body shook with the effort. His colleague groaned in disgust and grabbed him to stop him falling out.

Instinctively O'Shea leapt forward and slammed into the soldier. The soldier flipped out of the truck and landed on his head before dropping lifeless onto the road.

The thin soldier looked up, his ashen face creased in confusion. O'Shea put his hands between the soldier's legs and flipped him over the tailgate. There was an almighty scream and the truck began to brake. The driver had heard the cry and seen him in the mirror.

'You lunatic,' Clooney howled.

The soldier's rifle was spinning across the floor. O'Shea snatched it up in a blind panic and fired it into the back of the cab. Canvas flew in all directions and the truck skidded, rolled over onto its side and threw O'Shea out the back as it slid along the road in a shower of stones and bits of wood.

Clooney was out too and on his feet immediately. He pulled O'Shea off the ground and across the road. 'Move, you mad bastard. Get out of here before they recover and come after us.'

They fell through the bushes and down a ditch into soft wet leaves before scurrying back up the other side and bolting across the field to the shelter of the woods.

'Which way now?' O'Shea gasped when they eventually stopped to catch their breath.

His heart pounded in his ears with a strange mixture of fear and exhilaration and it made him want to laugh. He couldn't believe what he'd done, how he'd exploded in the emotion of the moment. Flopping down onto the grass he sucked in the cold air.

'What the hell do you mean *which way now*?' Clooney dropped down beside him. 'You're the one who said he knew where we were. You wanted to escape and go back to the farm. Now you've escaped. So which way is the farm?'

'Sure isn't this *your* country?' O'Shea head was still buzzing from the rush of adrenaline. 'Are you telling me you don't know your way around it?'

Clooney grabbed him by the throat. 'If we ever get out of this, you mad Mick, remind me to break your bloody neck.'

Then he stormed off through the trees.

They walked until the sun went down and the night fell over them. And it was blacker than black and bitterly cold.

When they spotted the faint glow from a cottage in the far corner of a field they stopped and watched it for a while. The biting wind slapping against them enticed them towards it.

O'Shea could sense the tension in Clooney as he motioned with his head to move towards the warm yellow light.

Through the cracked glass of the tiny window they could see an old man sitting on a stool beside a coal fire.

His bony fingers braided a length of rope as he sucked on a long clay pipe. A young girl sat on a log on the other side.

O'Shea reached out to the warmth of the fire but Clooney grabbed his jacket and pulled him around the back towards the barn.

'We'll stay here for a few hours and get some rest. We'll be up and gone before they even know we've been.'

Clooney prised the barn door open and they slid in the gap. Then he pulled it shut it behind them. After taking a quick look around they climbed the rickety ladder to the loft. And as they crawled into the hay it rustled like a forest fire in the stillness of the night.

'How long do you think it'll take us to get back to the farm?' O'Shea wrapped himself in hay.

Clooney didn't answer.

Thick black clouds rolled past the gaps in the roof and started to spill out their rain again.

Chapter Twenty-Six

When sleep eventually came it was filled with a dream that was fragmented and confused. O'Shea was with Heather again and this time they were in the Newport indoor market. Heather loved the indoor market, especially on a Saturday morning.

Wallowing in the hustle and bustle of the place, she'd wander up and down the rows of stalls that were bulging with fruit and vegetables. And she'd laugh out loud when Idwel Roberts shouted for everyone to come and look at the size of his cucumbers.

She usually went to the flower stalls first. She was fascinated by the vast display of freshly cut freesias and chrysanthemums with their sprigs of gypsophila. The whole range of colours and the sheer diversity of fragrances made her wish out loud she had a garden of her own instead of the bland concrete back yard.

In this dream the market began to get more and more crowded. Soon people were irate and they started moving in a sinister wave, pushing and shoving in an aimless surge. Heather and O'Shea were separated and pulled away in different directions.

Then all O'Shea could see was the back of Heather's head moving towards the High Street entrance. He tried to follow her but he was blocked by the sea of people and he started to lose her. She looked back once and smiled. Then she was gone.

When he woke up he was shivering badly. Clooney was buried in a pile of hay and snoring peacefully. O'Shea snuggled back down and rolled into a ball to try and get warm. Every muscle in his body was tight and painful. He tried to ignore it and get back to sleep.

Then he was awake again. Dawn was already creeping through the cracks in the barn walls and bringing spatters of rain with it. He forced himself to stand up, and he stamped his frozen feet as he hobbled over to where Clooney had been sleeping. Clooney wasn't there.

A wild panic gripped O'Shea. It was already daylight and they were supposed to be miles away from here by now. What the hell was going on? Why had Clooney not woken him? So what was he supposed to do now? He couldn't stay here. He knew that. It wouldn't be long before he was discovered.

When he heard a distant rumble of engines he squinted through a crack in the wall. But it was hard to decide where it was coming from. He moved across to the other wall but he still couldn't see anything. But the sound was definitely getting closer, humming furiously in the morning air.

Then two motorcycles and a car came roaring through the gate up on the main road and slid down the narrow path to the house.

O'Shea threw himself back from the wall as they came around the gable in an angry growl. They circled the yard before the car crunched to a halt in front of the door. An officer climbed out, strode over to the door and rapped on it with his cane. He waited a few seconds then knocked again. A latch clicked and the door opened a fraction.

The German gave a courteous bow and spoke for a few moments before the door was pulled open. Then he stood back and waved his men into the house. Three more men got out of the car and filed past the officer, then the door closed behind them.

There was no way O'Shea was going out there now. He pushed farther down into the hay and resigned himself to a long wait.

Chapter Twenty-Seven

Sometime in the early afternoon the latch on the door gave a metallic clatter that echoed around the yard. A soldier came out and strolled across the yard with his hands in his pockets. He looked contented as he yawned and let a shiver run through him.

O'Shea watched him curiously as he sauntered over to the motorcycles. He bent down and examined the tyres, tracing the rubber with his finger. Then something on the ground caught his attention and he reached down and touched it. He studied it for a minute before trailing it across the yard with his finger. He was obviously intrigued because he decided to follow it, stopping every few yards to probe it again. It took him over to a low wall where a pile of sacks and metal containers were stacked. He grabbed a sheet of canvas and pulled it away.

Underneath the sheet was a jumble of funnels and pipes that looked like the kind of whisky still O'Shea had often seen in Ireland. The soldier ran back to the house.

Seconds later they all rushed out and they stopped a few feet from the still while the officer prodded it with his cane. He shouted at the old man to come closer. And as he shuffled forward his frail body was visibly shaking.

The officer shouted again but the old man didn't respond. And the cane was a blur as it crashed across his back. The young girl screamed and a soldier held her as the old man fell onto his knees and groaned loudly.

The officer sent two soldiers back into the house and he strutted around as the crash of breaking furniture filtered out. Then the soldiers reappeared carrying a load of papers which they threw down in front of the old man.

The officer flipped through some of the papers before searching the old man's pockets. He pulled out a wad of money which he put in his own pocket then he spoke quietly to the soldiers. They took the old man over to the wall and stood him against it. And as they raised their rifles the old man lost control and wet himself. The rifles cracked and he fell back against the wall. And as he slid to the ground he left crimson lines along the whitewash behind him.

The soldier holding the girl let her go and she ran to the body, and she cradled the head. The other soldiers picked up some kegs of whisky and traipsed back into the house without giving her another glance.

A clap of thunder came out of the sky and grumbled before it let the rain fall to wash the blood in little streams down the cracks in the cobbles.

The little girl knelt by her grandfather's body for over an hour, holding the head with its deathly white face against her chest. Her bare knees were blue with the cold and her clothes were matted against her body by the rain that saturated them.

Eventually she lay the head down and got a shovel from a shed, took it over to the field and started to dig in the heavy mud. She worked steadily until the hole was about three feet deep. Then she dragged the body slowly and awkwardly over to it, and she rolled it in with a soft splash. As she began to fill in the hole she started to sing. More thunder roared and the sky lit up.

Suddenly O'Shea noticed a soldier relieving himself against the side of the house. His head was bent and he was oblivious to the rain that turned his uniform a darker grey. O'Shea hadn't seen him come out of the house.

The soldier turned around and buttoned his trousers, and as he staggered back towards the door he noticed the little girl. He shook his head before creeping over to her. He grinned when she didn't appear to notice him, and he put his hand on her breast. She didn't flinch. So he pulled her to him, and she hung from his big arms like a lifeless doll.

He carried her across the yard to the barn and prised the door open with his foot. Then he dropped her in the hay beneath O'Shea and was on her instantly, all his control gone and groaning like a mad animal.

And all the time the girl lay beneath him her eyes were unfocused, staring past him into the distance.

Revulsion had O'Shea seething with anger. But all he could do was close his eyes in shame because he wasn't going to do a thing about it. The familiar cold fear had gripped him again and pinned him to the safety of the loft. He just didn't have the strength or the guts to interfere. So he clamped his hands over his ears to drown out the gasping and slobbering and the rustling of the hay.

Eventually the soldier gave a long sigh and fell exhausted onto his back. And the girl lay still, no change in her expression, no indication of the pain she must have felt.

After a while the soldier got up and wiped his face with his hands. He threw one more look at the figure in the hay before walking unsteadily across the floor and his shoes picked up clumps of hay as he went. He'd almost reached the door when a shout came from outside.

He shouted back and pushed the door open. Another soldier fell in the gap and steadied himself by grabbing at the first man's tunic. They dragged each other back into the barn and stood hanging onto each other, and their slurred laughter rattled around the walls until something caught the second man's eye. He strained against the dim light to see what was lying in the hay. They were still giggling stupidly as the second man went to the girl and examined her. He held her face in his large hands and squeezed her lips. But he was still hesitant. Then the first man made jeering noises and slapped him on the back. And that was all he needed.

While he was busy the first man went outside and when he came back he was carrying a keg of whisky. He slurped loudly from it, letting the whisky spill out over his chin and shirt. And he chuckled hysterically as he sat on the floor and waited for his friend to finish.

When the keg was finally empty the boredom set in and the soldiers threw it away before drifting back to the warmth of the house. The barn was enveloped in a strange, morbid silence that was only disturbed by an odd rustle of hay when the icy wind whistled through the cracks in the walls.

When O'Shea was absolutely certain the soldiers were gone he mustered enough courage to climb down from the loft and go to the girl. Her eyes had sunk deep into her swollen face and her mouth was daubed with blood that streaked her teeth. O'Shea rubbed her cold hands and whispered that it was all right now, it was all over. But he knew the words were meaningless because no one on God's earth could experience what she did and not lose their mind. This terrible thing would bite so deep into her soul it would remain with her for the rest of her life.

O'Shea sensed someone standing inside the barn door. He spun around as the dull light glanced off of the length of lead pipe in the man's hand.

'Where the hell have you been?' he snapped.

Clooney didn't answer as he bent down and touched the girl's face.

'So where were you?'

'I went out to look around.' Their eyes met for a split second then Clooney looked away again. 'I had no idea they were doing this. I thought they'd found you.'

'Oh, that's all right, then!'

'I got lost in the dark, all right? I was on my way back when I saw the Germans coming.'

The girl opened her mouth and gave an almighty scream. Her whole body vibrated and her voice was as shrill as a whistle. She looked at Clooney for a second before her eyes rolled and her head fell back. And she closed her eyes for the last time.

It was late afternoon now and the darkness of the winter was closing in fast. The rain pattered in spasms against the old wooden walls of the barn as the wind whistled around outside. An animal howled like the wail of a child then faded again into the distance.

Clooney covered the little girl's body with a blanket of hay. O'Shea looked away because all he felt was anger and shame that he'd done absolutely nothing to help her. And he knew he wasn't going to do anything now, either. He was just going to sneak away into the night in the hope of saving his own skin. So he moved to the door, and it groaned as he pushed it open.

A soldier stood there with his hand out and his eyes wide in a drunken daze. He looked up in surprise but he couldn't focus. O'Shea grabbed him, pulled him inside and dragged the door shut behind him.

The soldier's head cleared fast and as he turned to O'Shea his hand grabbed for the bayonet in his belt. But Clooney was on him before he could get it out and the metal pipe clanged against his forehead.

O'Shea took a quick look out of the door to make sure the soldier was alone then ran back to where he was sprawled out on the floor.

'What the hell do we do now?' O'Shea was impatient to get going now that darkness had fallen. His head felt strangely light and when he coughed his eyes watered.

'We have to go,' he insisted. '*Now*!'

Clooney made a gesture to wait. Picking up the bayonet, he held the soldier by the hair and drew it across his neck in a quick sweep. Blood shot out across the hay. Clooney threw the bayonet away and as he shoved past O'Shea he pulled his arm to make him follow.

The cold wind bite into them when he pushed the door open. After taking a quick look around the yard Clooney crouched low and ran across to the German car. O'Shea scurried along behind him and they knelt on the wet ground until they were sure they hadn't been seen.

Then as quietly as a shadow Clooney moved across to the motorcycles and searched through the side pouches, pulling things out and putting them on the ground. Then he slid back to the car and squatted down beside O'Shea.

'What are you doing?' A persistent tickle in his throat made O'Shea want to cough and sweat itched his body even though his clothes were soaked and the rain was cold.

Clooney popped the car door open and climbed inside without a word. O'Shea crawled around to the other side and slid into the passenger's seat. Then Clooney pulled at the wires under the dashboard and the engine gave a whine and the car shuddered.

There was silence for a second then the engine whined again.

'Come on!' Clooney growled.

Another whine and another shudder.

'Start, you bastard!'

The door of the house opened and a chorus of rowdy singing made the two of them freeze. A shaft of light cut through the darkness and fell across them, and O'Shea ducked instinctively as a shadow filled the doorframe.

A soldier stood there for a moment before his arm swept in a wide arc and a match cracked against the wall. He bent forward and cupped his hands around the flame, and the smoke came out in puffs. Flicking the match out into the night he leant back against the doorframe and looked out at the wild weather. His face lit up every time he drew on the cigarette.

The tickle in O'Shea's throat was choking him now and he clenched his teeth with the strain. The minutes dragged on until at last the soldier flicked the butt out into the yard and turned to go. And O'Shea gave a gurgling splutter he could no longer suppress.

The soldier turned and squinted into the darkness. O'Shea couldn't believe it. All that noise coming from the house and he still heard a cough.

The soldier hesitated before he stepped out into the rain and strolled towards the car. It was clear he couldn't actually see anything because he didn't look concerned. He probably thought it was his friend from the barn.

Clooney rummaged in the glove compartment and gave a yelp when he pulled out a Luger.

'Take that.' He shoved it at O'Shea.

'*What*?'

'For God's sake! Take the bloody thing. If he comes any closer, shoot him.'

'*No!*' O'Shea tried to push it away. 'They'll hear us if I shoot that thing.'

Clooney leant across, opened the door and kicked O'Shea out onto the wet cobbles. He threw the Luger after him.

The engine whined again, and this time the lights came on and blinded the soldier. He dropped onto one knee as he turned away.

'Shoot the bastard,' Clooney screamed. O'Shea screamed too as he scrambled for the gun, snapped it up and fired blindly in the general direction of the house. Unbelievably the soldier fell onto his face. Another man appeared in the doorway and the next shot caught him in the chest and threw him back inside.

The car burst into life and shot forward about ten feet before stopping again. Clooney shouted at O'Shea to stop pratting about and get in. O'Shea dived in the open door as the car spun around the yard, knocked over the motorcycles then raced up the narrow road to the gate.

Chapter Twenty-Eight

Grey clouds streamed down the valley. Sometimes a gap let a finger of sunlight dab at the shiny green fields that were still wet from the night's rain.

Lying back against the side of an old stone bridge kept the bitter wind off O'Shea. But his clothes were still cold and damp and he couldn't stop the shivering that had taken hold of him. Pain racked his chest and pulled at his stomach from the constant coughing.

Clooney built a fire and made a hot drink. He helped O'Shea swallow it then sat back against the wall and threw a large twig on the fire. Sparks blew away with the wind and smoke scattered in all directions.

Clooney's face was tight and his eyes were red from lack of sleep. He gave a long, loud yawn and let his eyes shut. And his head sagged down onto his chest. But it snapped up almost immediately and he looked around warily.

It didn't last long, though. The effort of trying to stay alert was getting harder and harder and he was sucked back into sleep.

The only thing that disturbed him was O'Shea's persistent coughing. He opened his eyes every time then let them drop again. And he slept like that for over an hour. Then he jumped up and kicked out the fire.

'Right. Let's go.'

He half-dragged O'Shea back to the car and threw him in the door, and he played with the wires again until the engine started.

'We haven't got much fuel left, I'm afraid. Keeping off of the main roads is making the journey that much longer. But you never know, we just might make it '

Trailing a cloud of dirty smoke the car bounced across the grass and out onto the road where it took off in a spray of mud and stones and bits of turf.

O'Shea couldn't tell how long he'd been dozing but it felt like hours. He rubbed his face and gave his legs a stretch. Then he looked around just as a motorcycle with a sidecar appeared in the wing mirror some distance behind.

Clooney saw it too. He grunted as he pushed the accelerator to the floor and threw the car around the bends, lifting O'Shea right off the seat.

The man on the motorcycle wasn't taking any chances and Clooney put some distance between them with each bend. But when they hit a long straight piece of road the motorcycle closed in and the soldier in the sidecar let rip with a machine gun. Bullets screamed past the car taking chunks out of the road.

'Bloody hell!' O'Shea shrieked. 'He's shooting at us!'

'No shit! You're pretty smart for a thick Mick!'

'But we're in a German feckin car. Why is he shooting at a German car?'

'Why do *you* think? Don't you remember where we *got* the feckin German car?'

When they took the next corner Clooney slammed on the brakes and made the car spin around in a circle before sticking to the road. Then he roared back the way they'd come.

The look on the motorcycle driver's face was sheer horror as he rounded the bend and saw the car coming at him in the middle of the road. He swerved but the motorcycle still clipped the front of the car and flipped into the air.

Clooney stood on the brakes and the car juddered to a halt. He was out before it stopped completely and ran back to where the motorcycle was lying upside down in a ditch. The man from the sidecar sat at the side of the road holding his leg and staring at the headless body of his driver.

Clooney hesitated for the briefest of seconds before he checked the driver's body and took the flask from his belt. He then made the other man strip to his underwear and kneel at the side of the ditch. After shooting him in the back of the head, Clooney rolled him in on top of the bike.

He dragged the driver's body off the road and let it fall on top of the other man. Then he picked up the uniform, folded it and put it on O'Shea's lap. And they drove off again, only this time more slowly.

A short time later Clooney pulled off the road, coasted onto a wide patch of grass and let the car shudder to a stop.

'Ah, well.' He pulled on the handbrake. 'It could have been worse. At least it saved us a bit of a walk.'

'What's the matter?' O'Shea's speech was slurred.

'Well, as the Yanks say, we've run out of gas.' He gave a resigned shrug. 'Sorry, old chap, but from here on in we're on foot.'

He built another fire then helped O'Shea change out of his wet clothes and into the German's uniform. It was a poor fit but it was dry.

'You know if you get caught wearing this they'll shoot you,' he said cheerfully. 'And not just the Germans, who'll think you're a spy. But also the British who'll think you're fair game because you're a kraut. But at least you won't die from pneumonia. *I hope*. So keep your head down. When we get back to the farm we'll find something more appropriate for you to wear.'

He looked up and spluttered. 'It'll probably have to be a dress, mind you, seeing as it was all women living there.'

He was still chuckling as he made another hot drink. It was weak and bitter but it didn't matter because O'Shea couldn't keep it down anyway. He just lay back in the car seat and pulled the German's jacket tighter around him. Clooney got in the driver's seat and rested his head back too.

'What about you?' O'Shea managed to say without coughing. 'Your clothes are just as wet as mine.'

'What? You don't expect me to wear the uniform of a mere sergeant, surely?' He prodded the insignia on the sleeve. 'Nothing below a Field Marshall for me, I'm afraid. One has standards to keep, after all. Now shut your gob and get some rest while you can. We have a long walk ahead of us later.'

When O'Shea closed his eyes again his head went into a spin. The awareness of what was going on around him became foggier and he kept losing track of reality. Different people wandered through his mind, people whose faces he couldn't see properly. The cold bit deeper into him, penetrating right through his skin to grate on his very bones.

When the coughing came he was forced to sit back up until the tickling in his throat eased and he was able to suck in the air again. He propped his head against the window and gazed up at the sky where patches of lighter cloud peered through the darker ones as they rolled across the top of the trees. Clooney shuffled and gave an irritated snort. But it didn't take long for his breathing to soften again.

O'Shea's eyelids started to droop, but they snapped open again. Was that a noise? He raised his head and looked around but he couldn't see anything. So he let his head sag back against the seat.

Then he really *did* hear something. It was sharp and crisp, almost like a muffled shot. As he sat up again he caught a movement behind the bushes at the bottom of the field. A shadow dropped out of sight so fast all he got was an impression. But he was certain it was a man. Rubbing the mist from his eyes he looked again. And this time he saw the glint of light on a helmet.

He slapped Clooney on the arm. 'Wake up, there's soldiers coming up the field.'

'What?' Clooney sat up slowly and reached for the water flask.

'Come on.' O'Shea shoved him again. 'There's German soldiers heading this way. You'd better get out of here.'

The bottle had reached Clooney's lips when he froze. And in a mad flurry he snatched at the wires of the car.

'That's no bloody use.' O'Shea pulled the wires off him. 'Get out and run, for God's sake.'

Clooney jumped out, ran to O'Shea's side of the car and tried to drag him out too.

'No!' O'Shea pushed him away. 'I'm too sick. Just get yourself out of here.'

'Come on,' Clooney tried to lift him again but he sagged down into the seat. 'Get out of the car, you lazy shit. Move yourself.'

'I'll never make it. I'm too sick. You'll have a better chance on your own.'

Clooney's eyes flashed and he gave O'Shea an angry pat on the shoulder before scurrying away through the bushes seconds before the soldiers started walking up the field towards them.

All the excitement brought on another bout of coughing and O'Shea leant out of the door to be sick. The soldiers came running. They lifted him out on to the grass and undid his jacket. The blood around the torn knees of the trousers and on the front of the jacket made them think O'Shea was wounded. But when they saw the bandage that Cerys put on his wound they were puzzled. It wasn't an army issue bandage. It was just a strip off an old bed sheet.

O'Shea's real wound had become angry and infected so they decided not to peel off the old dressing. Instead they put another pad on top of it and wrapped it in a clean bandage.

They kept asking O'Shea questions but he pretended to be too sick to understand. Someone took a wallet from his jacket pocket and pulled out an ID card.

'Eric Kirst,' the soldier said as he held it close to O'Shea's face.

Chapter Twenty-Nine

'How's my silent little friend today, then?' Corporal Idwel Thomas of the Army Medical Corps grabbed O'Shea's wrist and felt his pulse.

It was 6.30 in the morning. The orderlies had been through the ward half an hour earlier turning on lights and opening windows to let the crisp air blow away the sour smell of the night.

Those who were able to stand had to get up, make their beds and clean their bed space ready for the doctor's rounds. If the person on their right was too sick they had to clean his space too. It didn't matter who did the cleaning. When the doctor came at 6.15 the ward would be ready. There would be no excuses.

Patients who couldn't stand had to sit to attention in their beds while the rest stood and faced the front, their dull grey Army dressing gowns tied at the waist with the regulation cord.

'Pulse still a bit high.' Corporal Thomas let O'Shea's hand drop again.

While Corporal Thomas was checking through his notes the duty doctor Captain Pendry stood at the bottom of the bed and watched O'Shea suspiciously.

Corporal Thomas took a quick look at O'Shea's wound. It had practically healed now and he prodded the bright pink scar with his finger.

'Well, Corporal Thomas?' Pendry barked.

'Fit as a flea, Sir. Nothing physical wrong here, as far as I can see.' Thomas motioned for O'Shea to do up his dressing gown.

'Then why isn't he speaking yet, damn it?' Pendry stamped his foot. 'He's been here a week and he hasn't said a word. It won't do. Won't do at all. I need this sorted out. Do you hear, Corporal? See to it today, will you?'

Corporal Thomas looked O'Shea in the eyes and smiled, his chubby face showing just a hint of contempt for the duty doctor.

'Can't have malingerers,' Pendry snorted. 'Not even German ones. If I had my way he'd be shipped back to his unit immediately.'

He dismissed O'Shea with a nod of his head and moved on to the next patient. And the Corporal waddled after him.

O'Shea took a quick glance around the ward. Every one of the beds was occupied by men who all looked the same with pale faces and eyes glazed with pain. O'Shea had been here for six long, harrowing days and he'd seen so many people come and go it was hard to remember any of them. As soon as one patient left the ward his bed was made up and someone else was in it in a matter of minutes.

In all that time O'Shea hadn't said a single word. He couldn't afford to. But now the strain was beginning to tell. The constant struggle to keep his mind alert and his wits about him was taking its toll.

Initially his lack of speech wasn't a problem because when he was brought in he *was* very sick. They dressed his wound and fed him an assortment of pills and medicines. In a couple of days he was well enough to walk unaided to the toilet at the end of the corridor.

For some reason the British orderlies didn't take much notice of him. But when the Germans came on duty it was a different story. They viewed his silence with suspicion. He was brought in wearing a German uniform and carrying a German identity card, so it was assumed he would comply with basic German instructions. It annoyed them when he wouldn't. So they constantly poked him and screamed abuse. They didn't know O'Shea couldn't understand a word they were saying.

Corporal Thomas, however, had his own perspective on it. He insisted it was nothing more sinister than plain old shellshock.

'A good rest, isn't it,' he would say in his Caerphilly accent. 'That's all it'll take to have him back on his feet again.'

He knew O'Shea understood English because he reacted to whatever Corporal Thomas said. But for some reason he treated it as their little joke, as if O'Shea's silence was some sort of conspiracy against the Germans. And that pleased him very much indeed. He wallowed in the deception.

Pendry had a different view. He took an instant dislike to O'Shea. He knew there was nothing wrong with him physically and he was suspicious about his behaviour. And he was growing more impatient by the day. Whatever he was contemplating worried O'Shea. And that made his mind up for him.

From the moment he could think straight O'Shea had been searching for a way out of the hospital. Not a minute went by without his thoughts switching to Adam. It grieved him to think his son was out there somewhere, alone and confused, unable to look after himself properly. O'Shea needed to get back to Bethan's farm and start looking for him. And the germ of an escape plan was already percolating in his brain.

A large map of South Glamorgan in the main corridor showed Cardiff in great detail right down to street level. On the rare occasion when the corridor was deserted and

O'Shea could study it properly, he was able to establish that he was in the Royal Infirmary in the centre of Cardiff. Although he didn't know exactly where Bethan's farm was, he recognised some of the villages he'd passed through. He was positive he could find his way back there.

But first he had to get away from the infirmary.

Because he was well enough to get out of bed now he was expected to do some light work. So immediately after the doctor's rounds he had to go to the kitchens and help get the breakfast ready.

And the kitchen was his means of escape. There were so many people milling about in there, chefs cooking on the vast ranges, assistants scrubbing pots and pans and washing dishes. It would be relatively easy for him to slip out the back door unnoticed.

One major problem, though, was the clothes he was wearing. When he was brought in he was given one set of grey pyjamas and one grey dressing gown. The uniform disappeared. All that was in his bedside locker was soap, a razor, a toothbrush and a towel. Again, the kitchen would help with that. The chefs had their own little rest room away from the kitchen. It was right at the far end of the corridor next to the back door. They went there for a smoke and a beer throughout the day.

O'Shea was sent to clean it once and he saw jackets and coats hanging on the back of the door. An assortment of shoes and boots were scattered under the coffee table.

From about five o'clock onwards the chefs were far too busy preparing the evening meal to spend time in the rest room. So once O'Shea decided it was time to go his plan was simply - grab a pair of boots and a coat and slip out the back door.

Now, as he stood to attention watching the Captain
and Corporal Thomas descending on another unfortunate
patient, he knew he couldn't afford to hang about any
longer.

So this evening when he was back in the kitchen he
would seize the moment. Of course if he wasn't back in
the ward in time for evening rounds they'd come looking
for him. But with a bit of luck he'd be miles away by
then.

Chapter Thirty

When afternoon tea was brought around at half past four the night had already closed in. It was cold and drizzle streaked the big windows.

O'Shea sat up in bed and sipped the weak tea. He dunked a plain biscuit in it and looked around at the other patients. They were too wrapped up in their own misery to take any notice of him.

It was O'Shea's job to take the empties back to the scullery next to the kitchen. And his stomach was in a knot as he waited for the last patient to put his cup on the trolley. Then he pulled on his dressing gown, took his own cup and placed it on top of the pile.

The crockery rattled as O'Shea swung the trolley into the scullery and pushed it up against the sink. And he took his time stacking the dishes along the worktop. He could see the rest room from where he was standing. It was empty. All the chefs were busy pushing pans of food around the top of the cookers. Everyone else was clattering plates and dishes and chatting happily amongst themselves. They caused a wave of noise. It was the perfect moment.

He wiped his hands on a towel. And he jumped when a German orderly grabbed his arm, pointed towards the door and muttered something about Pendry. When O'Shea hesitated the orderly slapped the towel from his hands and bundled him out of the kitchen and along the corridor to Pendry's office.

The doctor was hunched behind his desk in his large neat room. His craggy face had taken on an even more anxious look as he watched O'Shea being manoeuvred to a chair in front of the desk.

Behind Pendry a short stocky man was looking out of the window. His hands were clamped rigidly behind his back, his feet were spread, and his long leather overcoat was pulled tight at the waist by a large belt.

He oozed hostility. An aura of menace shimmered all around him.

The orderly backed out of the room and pulled the door shut behind him. Pendry motioned with his head for O'Shea to sit down. And he gave a soft cough into his fist before speaking to him in German. He let the words out slowly and precisely. And as he spoke his gaze was fixed on O'Shea's face waiting for a reaction.

When O'Shea didn't respond Pendry grew agitated. His voice rose and his hands moved in emphasis. The man at the window glanced at him and then at O'Shea before turning away again.

Pendry repeated what he'd said. But this time his words were sharp and angry. When O'Shea still didn't respond the man at the window turned around and his face split into a wide beaming smile. Pendry looked startled. He rubbed his hands nervously as the man took a packet of cigarettes from his pocket and strode casually over to O'Shea. He flicked one up and held it out. O'Shea's hand was shaking as he took it.

The man was smiling but his eyes were like a shark's, cold and dead. O'Shea waited as he drew another cigarette out with his teeth and clamped it between his lips. The solid gold lighter clicked and he held the flame to his own cigarette, drew the smoke in deep then held it out towards O'Shea.

'These are very expensive cigarettes, you know.' He nodded at the packet in his hand. 'You must smoke them the right way round. You must put the end with the blue ring in your mouth.'

'Oh?' O'Shea studied the cigarette, and as he put the end with the blue ring in his mouth he leant towards the flame. He took a long drag before blowing the smoke out through his nose.

Then the cigarette froze between his lips. The enormity of what he'd just done rippled through him and he almost screamed with the fright.

His knees buckled. *For God's sake!* Six long days of not saying a single word and in the blink of an eye he falls into the simplest trap of all. Just a moment's loss of concentration and it all unravelled in a heartbeat.

Pendry's eyes narrowed in a mixture of amazement and annoyance. The man's smile faded into a slightly amused frown. He muttered something and Pendry shrugged. Then he turned to O'Shea and knocked the cigarette out of his mouth. It flew across Pendry's desk and he leapt up, beating the burning ash off the front of his white coat.

The next blow caught O'Shea on the temple and knocked him to the floor. The man dragged him back to his feet before sauntering around the desk. He stood beside Pendry who was trying to keep his face impassive. Little beads of sweat glistened on his forehead.

'Now,' the man waved a hand at O'Shea. 'We will have some answers, please. We will have them quickly and we will have them truthfully. Otherwise things will become very unpleasant. For you, that is. Do you understand?'

O'Shea wiped his face with his sleeve.

'Stand still!' the man screamed. 'You will not move until I tell you to move.'

He glared at O'Shea for a minute before his shoulders suddenly relaxed again. 'Now, your name?'

'O'Shea. Danny O'Shea. My name is Danny O'Shea.'

'And you are a British spy using a German name and wearing a German uniform.'

'*What*? No! I'm not a spy. Sure I'm not even British.'

'Then what are you doing here?' The man gave his cold smile again. 'Why are you pretending to be Eric Kirst?'

'I'm not. There was ... I was sick, that's why they brought me here.'

'You were sick and *who* brought you here?'

'I don't know. Someone ... I don't know.'

The man sprang from behind the desk. 'I will tell you who brought you here. A German patrol brought you here. This is a military hospital, as you well know. And they brought you here because they thought you were a military man. Isn't that right?'

'I don't know.'

'And why did they think you were a military man? Because you looked like a military man, didn't you? You were wearing a German uniform and you had the papers of a German soldier. That's why they brought you here, isn't it?'

O'Shea's legs wobbled.

'How did you get that uniform?' The man's voice dropped to a whisper.

'I don't know.'

The man's boot stamped on O'Shea's toes. But before he collapses the man grabbed him by the throat.

'Tell me how you got that uniform.'

'But I don't know,' O'Shea grasped the man's wrist in desperation. 'I was sick. I had a fever. I didn't know what was happening to me. You must believe me. I had no idea of what was going on. I wasn't capable of doing anything about it.'

The man pushed O'Shea away, went back behind the desk again and fiddled with some papers scattered on top of it. Then he picked some up and threw them across at O'Shea.

'Do you deny having these papers on you when you were brought here?'

O'Shea shook his head. 'I can't remember.'

The man slammed his fist on the desk and Pendry jumped.

'You will tell me the truth. Or you will be taken from here and *made* to tell the truth. And you had better believe me, we *can* make you talk!'

'For God's sake ...' O'Shea wiped his mouth with his sleeve again. 'I don't remember anything about what happened to me. I was sick, I'm telling you. Whatever happened to me was out of my control. I have no idea of what happened to me.'

The man whispered something to Pendry. They looked at the papers before glancing up at O'Shea again.

'These papers.' The man tapped them with his finger. 'They belong to a man called Eric Kirst. He was a Sergeant in the German Army Transport Corps. How did you come to be carrying them in your pocket?'

O'Shea closed his eyes and shook his head.

'Let me give you a clue. A short time ago Sergeant Kirst was found murdered by the side of a road. He had been shot and his clothes were taken from his body. His driver was murdered, too. His clothes were still on him, but his head was not. Did you know, when no one came forward to identify the killer ten local people were executed? Twelve were executed the next day. And so on. Eventually we had to look further afield. We check everything but we find nothing.'

He sucked his gums and spat on the floor, and Pendry flinched.

'Around the time Corporal Kirst was lying murdered in a ditch three soldiers, a farmer and a little girl were also murdered on an isolated farm some miles away. The killer drove off in a German staff car. Then a very strange thing happened. We get a report that Sergeant Kirst has been found in a field miles away from where he was supposed to have been murdered. He was very ill but still very much alive. And he was in the very same German staff car that was involved in the murders at the farm. Now, how do you explain that?'

Spinning around on his heels, he marched across to the window. 'Of course, in the cold light of the day, the answer is logical.' He watched the rain trickling down the glass. 'One of the Sergeant Kirst is *not* Sergeant Kirst.'

He turned around again and clapped his hands, and O'Shea jumped.

'So, what was your part in the murders at the farm?

'Nothing. It was nothing to do with me.'

'But it was you they found in the motor car pretending to be Sergeant Kirst?'

'What motor car?'

The man rushed over and slammed a boot into O'Shea's shin. O'Shea shook with the pain and gritted his teeth so hard he felt his gums bleed even more.

'You really should think twice before being clever with the Gestapo.' The man was so close his breath made O'Shea turn his head away. 'It can be so painful. But surely they taught you that in the British Military? Still, you seem to want to learn for yourself.'

'But what have I got to do with the British Military?' O'Shea spat out some blood. 'I'm Irish, I'm telling you.'

The man squared his jaw. 'This is no game! I am beginning to tire of this display of bravado and insolence. You will answer me now because this is your last chance. How did you come to be in possession of a German uniform and a German motor car, both of which were involved in the murder of German soldiers?'

'Honest to God, I can't tell you anything. All I remember is being cold and wet and sick. And a man in a motor car giving me a lift. He gave me some clothes to wear and then I blacked out. I can't remember anything else.'

'A man in a motor car gave me a lift,' the man mocked. 'What man?'

'I told you already, I don't know.'

'How did he have a German motor car? Where did he get the clothes he gave you?'

'I don't know.'

O'Shea caught the fist full in the mouth. Tears clouded his eyes.

'Who was this man?'

O'Shea shook his head again, bracing himself for the inevitable response. The blows hammered down on him until he was back against the door and down on his knees. Then the man spat in his face before walking back behind the desk.

Beads of sweat dotted his forehead and he pulled a large handkerchief from his pocket, mopped his face and blew his nose before stuffing the handkerchief away again.

'Get up,' he growled.

As O'Shea struggled to his feet he noticed Pendry watching him with what could have been pity. But he quickly dropped his gaze to his hands. The man straightened his coat and tightened the belt.

'The way I see it,' he waved his hand again. 'You are a British agent.'

'But I'm not!'

'Do not interrupt! Do not interrupt me.' His eyes blazed into O'Shea for what seemed like minutes before he continued. 'Now, for whatever reason, you were at that farm. Probably working with the farmer to produce his illicit whisky. Maybe it was a cover for you, who knows? Our routine patrol discovered you and somehow you murdered three of them. Sergeant Kirst then came across you as you made your escape and you killed him and his partner as well. Then you took his uniform and pretended to be him. But before you could do what you set out to do you got sick.'

He paused for effect.

'At least that part of your story is true, getting sick. That suited your purpose perfectly. Once you were well again you could just return to Sergeant Kirst's regiment.' He snapped his fingers. 'And no one would be any the wiser. You could do what you set out to do and everything you wanted to know would be at your fingertips. Troop movement, fuel locations, logistics, the lot. Very clever. Very, very clever.'

He thought a moment.

'But what exactly happened at that farm? You killed my soldiers, which is understandable. But why did you kill the farmer and the little girl?'

'What do you mean?' O'Shea gasped. 'I didn't kill them. Your soldiers did that. They murdered them in cold blood. They raped that little girl until she died. I didn't do that!'

The man's face twisted in a cruel grin. 'So you *were* there.' He muttered something at Pendry who just nodded again. 'You must be very good to escape from a six man patrol. How did you do that? You even killed three of them and took their motor car. Then you also killed two more trained soldiers later on, taking a uniform to help you to disguise yourself as a German soldier. Was this after you got ill? Did you see disguising yourself as a German soldier as a way of getting medical attention for yourself?'

He took out a pistol and cocked it in front of O'Shea's face. 'You have ten seconds to tell me who you are working for and what your orders are.'

He pressed the gun to O'Shea's temple.

Chapter Thirty-One

'For God's sake! I'm an Irishman. I'm no spy. You're making a terrible mistake.'

'Oh, no,' the man's laugh was sharp. 'I don't make mistakes.'

'Look, if I was a spy surely to God they'd have made sure I could speak the bloody language.'

'You won't survive, you know.' The gun pressed harder. 'No one does. This is your last chance. Five ... four ...'

O'Shea heaved and his mouth filled with bile. He gritted his teeth and he braced himself for the flash. Every fibre in his body was tingling with fear.

Pendry jumped up but the man laughed at him and pressed the gun harder into the side of O'Shea's head. Then he gave a shriek and the gun went off with a click that sounded like a bomb in O'Shea's head. O'Shea screamed as he flew across the room, clawing at his head for the wound that wasn't there. This time it was too hard to control and he was sick all over the floor.

The man was hysterical with laughter as he put his arm around Pendry and patted him on the back. Then he put the magazine back into the pistol and shoved it in his pocket.

'I'm sorry I have to go now, Mr Irishman,' he snorted. 'I have a very important appointment. It cannot wait. But you will stay here, of course. And don't worry. I will be back. Then I will have the answers to my questions. Otherwise, where you will be going they are a little bit more persuasive.'

He roared with glee again. As he went out he let the door slam behind him and it muffled the laughter that echoed along the corridor.

Pendry let O'Shea get up by himself. He staggered to the chair and flopped onto it, and he held his head in his shaking hands.

'So,' Pendry asked after a long silence. 'What exactly is going on?'

'What do you mean?'

'What are you doing here? What were you doing in a German uniform?'

'I told you already.' O'Shea's words were mumbled through his bruised lips.

'You've told us sod all.' Pendry waved his hand impatiently. 'You've been here six days and you haven't said a single word. Everyone thinks you're a German called Eric Kirst. The British don't care and the Germans think you're mad.'

He gave a faint smile and leant forward onto his elbows. 'Do you know what will happen to you now? They will take you to Gestapo Headquarters here in Cardiff. It's a terrible place. They will make you talk. You will tell them everything, I promise you that.'

'Tell them what, though? I'm not a spy.'

Pendry shrugged. 'They'll soon find out.'

O'Shea's head swam and he fell off the chair. Pendry watched him get back up again.

'What exactly are you doing? What were your plans?'

'There weren't any plans,' O'Shea insisted. 'I had no control over what happened.'

'But you were at the farm where those soldiers were killed. What were you doing there?'

'I was hiding in the barn.'

'Hiding from what?'

'Look, I was trying to get home to Ireland. I had no papers and I knew if they found me something like this would happen. All I was trying to do was take myself and my son to Ireland.'

'Your son?' Pendry's eyebrows rose. 'Where's your son now?'

O'Shea hesitated. He tried to read Pendry's expression, see what was lurking behind the tired, red eyes. But it was hard to decide if the doctor could be trusted or not.

O'Shea told him anyway. He didn't know why. Probably out of sheer desperation. A last frantic attempt to avoid the approaching retribution. All the places he'd been to, all the details of what he *did* know were just a blur now. He had no names to give Pendry, but he told him as much as he could.

'So what were you going to do?' Pendry sat back with his hands under his chin. 'How long did you think you could keep this up?'

'Until tonight,' O'Shea said quickly, as if it made a difference.

Pendry squinted. 'Tonight?'

O'Shea hesitated again. He still wasn't sure about the doctor. 'I was going to try and get away tonight.'

'Really? And where were you going to go?'

'I had a plan.'

Suspicion still lingered on the doctor's face and he gave a brief smile again. 'Did you think there's no German soldiers in Cardiff? Did you think no one would notice you wandering around the streets in pyjamas and slippers?'

'I had to take that risk. I knew you were suspicious. I knew my time was running out.'

Pendry rubbed his eyes, leaving them looking even more red and tired. 'You are a very foolish man, my friend.'

O'Shea didn't have an answer for that.

Pendry waved his finger at him. 'Why didn't you just stay in Newport and explain all this to the authorities in the first place?'

'They'd have taken Adam off me. I had no choice. I just panicked and ran away.'

'One thing's for sure,' Pendry looked up at the ceiling. 'You're too dull to be a spy.'

The noise O'Shea made was as loud as a laugh and he sat up in the chair. 'So you *do* believe me? Then help me, please.'

Suddenly Pendry's eyes had fear in them and he shook his head. 'I can't help you. The Gestapo knows all about you. It's too late. There's nothing I can do.'

'But you can't just let then take me away. You know they'll kill me. Tell them you believe my story.'

'*What*?' Pendry gave a sour laugh. 'Why do you think they'd believe *me*? Who do you think I am? I'm just a doctor. They wouldn't take any notice of me.'

'But you have to try!'

'No!' Pendry's eyes closed quickly as if to end the conversation.

Panic clutched at O'Shea's chest again and he felt more bile rise in his throat. 'Then if they kill me it'll make you as guilty as them.'

'Please! Spare me the judgment. I'm not German. I'm just a doctor who happens to be under German jurisdiction.'

'But you're still a doctor. Tis your duty to help me.'

'You're asking too much of me.' Pendry's eyes glistened and he wiped them quickly. 'I cannot help you.'

'So you'll just let them take me away and kill me?'

Pendry shrugged.

'You won't even try and save me?'

The doctor gave another sour laugh. 'Are you really as stupid as that? Have you any idea what those people do if you get in their way? Do you know how they treat people who annoy them?'

'Have you tried?'

Pendry jumped up and stormed around to the front of the desk. His hands shook as he prodded O'Shea in the chest. 'My father did. My father made that mistake. He challenged them at a rally so someone shoved a burning torch in his face and then they took him away.'

He licked his lips in anger. 'It was weeks before we saw him again. When he appeared on our doorstep in the early hours of the morning he was battered, broken and completely blind. The man didn't know who he was or where he was. And I had to treat him myself and there was nothing I could do for him. He didn't live very long after that.'

He turned sharply and went to the window. 'And you want me to risk all that for you? Do you think I have the strength for that?'

O'Shea held his head in his hands. Of course he felt pity for Pendry. But this might be his only chance, his very last chance. 'So all I am to you now is just another statistic? Can you look at me and cancel me out like a number?'

'No,' Pendry said softly. 'I don't want to see you dead. I don't want to see any more people dead.'

'Then help me.' O'Shea grasped at the weakening he thought he saw in the doctor. 'Just open the door and let me run out of here. I can look after myself after that.'

'And when our friend comes back?'

'Tell him I'm dead. Say I died of shock or something. Show them a body in the morgue. You must have enough bodies to choose from.'

'That's impossible. That same man will come back. He'll know.'

'Not if the body didn't have a face.'

'How would I explain that?'

'I tried to escape,' O'Shea stood up and went to the desk. 'Say you had to shoot me. You shot me in the head.'

Pendry thought about it. But then he waved it away. 'It's out of the question.'

O'Shea slapped the desk. 'But you must ... '

'No!' The doctor turned to the window and threw it open, and he sucked in deep gulps of air. As he looked out into the dull black of the evening his face glistened with nervous sweat.

'No,' he said again. 'I cannot help you.'

He came back across the room and flicked through the papers on the desk. Then he rummaged in a drawer before wiping his face roughly with his sleeve. And he walked past O'Shea to the door.

'I'm sorry. I cannot help you. Now I must go. I have business to attend to. You will wait here until I come back.'

He hurried out and pulled the door shut behind him. O'Shea heard the key turn in the lock.

Chapter Thirty-Two

The silence pushed down on O'Shea so hard he was struggling to breath. What he was supposed to do now? Just sit here and wait? Wait for what? To die?

He jumped up and gave the door handle a shake. It was definitely locked. Moving back to the desk he looked at the papers scattered on top of it. What did they mean? The man kept referring to them, but they were just a jumble of words to O'Shea. The room was so quiet he couldn't think straight. The only sound was his heart pulsing in his ears.

A breeze came into the room and disturbed the papers on the desk. O'Shea almost didn't notice it. Then the curtains fluttered and O'Shea turned to them in amazement. Pendry had left the window open!

Suspicion made O'Shea hesitate. He still couldn't decide about Pendry. Did he leave the window open deliberately or did he just forget?

O'Shea tried the door again. It *was* locked. He switched off the light and went back to the window, and he pulled one of the curtains back.

The office was at the rear of the hospital looking out over a garden. The ground was about four feet below the window and light came from a solitary street lamp on the other side of a high wall. Through a gate at the end of a gravel footpath he could see a road.

But he couldn't go like this, in pyjamas and slippers. So he gave a quick look around the office to see what he could find. There was an overcoat on a hook behind the door. O'Shea put it on and dropped Pendry's cigarettes and lighter into the pocket. Then he rummaged through the desk drawers.

When he pulled the bottom one open a pistol rattled against the side. O'Shea grabbed it, checked the magazine then pocketed it. If this *was* a trap he'd give the doctor a run for his money. At least now he had a fighting chance.

He lowered himself out of the window onto the soft spongy grass then rolled back into the shadow of the wall. And the wet grass soaked through his slippers as he waited.

When nothing happened after a couple of minutes he stood up and walked out of the narrow gate and into the deserted street.

Two hours later he was in a small square with a bronze statue on a concrete plinth in the middle of it. The statue was in the shadows because the only light came from a lamp attached to the side of a house.

All the streets of Cardiff were surprisingly quiet and this one was no different. It could be because of the curfew. But it was strange that O'Shea hadn't seen any patrols. Maybe it was just the *fear* of a curfew that kept the citizens indoors.

Anyway, it looked like a good place for a rest. O'Shea crossed to the plinth and as he was about to sit on it he sensed a car creep around the corner behind him.

Its lights were off but O'Shea was in the middle of the square and it was obvious they'd seen him. Before he could scramble for cover the engine gave a roar and the car sped towards him.

A flash came from one of its windows and something whined past O'Shea's head before slapping into someone's front door. O'Shea crouched and ran for cover. He yanked the gun from his pocket as more thumps came from the car and sparks flew from the bronze statue above his head.

Dark September

The car bounced on the pavement. It was almost on top of him. O'Shea turned instinctively as the front bumper brushed his leg and he fired blindly at it. The shot lit up the face of the driver who opened his mouth a second before falling sideways clutching his head. A man in the back tried to open the door but O'Shea's next shot hit his hand and he ducked back inside. The front passenger pulled the dead man out of the way and scrambled into the driving seat.

The car screeched around in a wide circle, turned its lights on and roared across the square before disappearing down a side street.

O'Shea ran in the opposite direction. Suddenly the night was alive with the crunch of running boots and the shrill of police whistles. A beam of light swept the square and latched onto him. He tossed the gun high into the air as police officers dived on him and threw him back against a wall.

His arms were stretched wide and his face pinned against the cold brickwork as they searched him. Then he was handcuffed and thrown into the back of a car that sped off into the night.

A short time later they drove through a gate in a high wall and up to the front doors of a dismal-looking building that had bars on the windows.

O'Shea was dragged out of the car and marched in through the doors, up a wide staircase and down a series of passageways where wooden benches lined the walls with tired-looking people sitting on them.

Eventually they arrived in front of a fat man in German uniform sitting behind a high desk. The police officer spoke in a whisper and looked O'Shea up and down.

'One of your lot by the look of him. A deserter, I'd say. Just an overcoat and pyjamas. No shoes. Captain's insignia but I'll bet they're not his. God knows where he came from. No ID at all.'

O'Shea was searched again and they took the cigarettes and lighter off him before marching him down another bleak passageway to a thick door. They went down more steps then along another passageway until they came to a row of uniform doors. One clanged open and O'Shea was given a firm push into the little cell. The door shut behind him and the footsteps tapped away along the concrete floor until they eventually disappeared.

A soft groan came from the out of the darkness behind O'Shea.

'Feckin hell. Sure wasn't this supposed to be a private suite?'

Chapter Thirty-Three

The little panel on the bottom of the cell door slid back and two tin plates dropped through. Their thick, colourless contents splashed over the floor as they slid across the bare concrete. They were followed by two lumps of grey bread.

'Ah, breakfast.' Liam Sullivan swung his legs off his bunk and picked up the plates, compared the weight then passed one to O'Shea.

'Breakfast in bed, is it now?' he grinned. His sunken eyes twinkled in the dawn light that came in through the bars on the little window high up on the wall. 'Sure, don't you have the life of luxury?'

He gave a little chuckle as he scooped the bread off the floor and flicked one piece onto O'Shea's bunk. Pulling a lump from the other piece, he dipped it into the paste and started to eat it with relish.

'Go on,' he nodded at the plate in O'Shea's hand. 'It will excite the cockles of your heart.'

O'Shea dipped his finger in the slop and sucked at it. Then he dropped the plate on the floor.

'Do you not want it?' Sullivan was incredulous. 'You know tis all you'll be getting until this evening?'

O'Shea didn't answer. His stomach rumbled but his mind was too confused to know *what* he wanted. He lay back down on the narrow bunk and shifted about to find a comfortable position. It had been a long, fretful night. He hadn't slept because the bed was a solid concrete block that was cold and unyielding. If he hadn't been wearing Pendry's overcoat he would have probably frozen to death.

The bare walls were polished to a shine in places where the bodies of prisoners leant against them for a few hundred years. They were also as cold as ice and had little streams of condensation trickling down them.

The cell was so small if one of them needed to move about the other one had to pull his legs out of the way.

O'Shea turned onto his back and stared up at the ceiling where a mass of little cracks merged with the cobwebs to confuse the spiders.

'I wouldn't count them all at once,' Sullivan said between mouthfuls of bread.

'What?' O'Shea turned to look at him. In the weak light Sullivan's haggard features made him look almost ghostly.

'The cracks.' Sullivan pointed at the ceiling. 'You shouldn't count them all at once. Otherwise you won't have anything to do later on, you see.'

O'Shea closed his eyes. He tried not to listen to Sullivan slopping and munching and rubbing the bread eagerly around the dregs on his plate.

When Sullivan eventually dropped the plate on the floor he sat quietly for a minute or two. Then he gave a soft cough. 'Excuse me there, ah ... Danny. Seeing as you don't want your breakfast, do you think I could have it?'

O'Shea grinned at the earnest look on Sullivan's face. Like a child asking for an ice cream. 'Yeah. Help yourself.'

'Well, I hope you're sure. Cos that's all you'll be getting for the rest of the day. You *do* know that? You'll get nothing else until this evening.'

'I'm sure.'

Sullivan's hand was a blur as he snatched the plate before O'Shea had time to change his mind. Then he sat cross-legged on his bunk and shovelled the contents into his mouth. Finally he gave a satisfied burp.

O'Shea was still in shock. He felt sick when he thought of it - how he'd escaped from the Gestapo by the skin of his teeth, how he'd been so close to getting out of the city, how he'd been so near to finding Adam again. He'd trudged for hours through the desolate streets of the city with his slippers soaking wet and his feet so cold he could no longer feel his toes. And he ended up in Cardiff Prison! Just two streets away from where he started. In fact, if this cell was on the next floor up O'Shea would see the Infirmary from the window.

What the hell was Pendry playing at? He allowed O'Shea to escape - that was for sure. He left the window open and the gun in the drawer. But what happened then? Maybe the Gestapo came back and didn't believe his story so Pendry changed his mind? Perhaps he realised the enormity of what he'd done. And he had no choice but to have O'Shea killed and his body brought back to cover his mistake?

Now it looked like O'Shea had leapt out of the proverbial frying pan and landed in the fire. How was he ever going to get out of a prison cell? He could be locked away for years. Lost in purgatory. Forgotten by the rest of the world.

Every time he closed his eyes Adam's face appeared, his big brown eyes wide with distress.

Someone kicked the cell door and Sullivan shot off the bed, picked up the plates and shoved them back out through the panel.

'They get annoyed if you keep them waiting,' he explained as the little panel on the door slammed shut again. He started pacing up and down the narrow space between the bunks, counting his footsteps in loud whispers.

'My exercise,' he panted, turning around with an exaggerated flourish. 'I have to do it every day so's to keep my blood pressure down. Otherwise my auld heart might give out on me.'

'What's wrong with your heart?' O'Shea raised himself up on his elbow. 'Sure you're not much older than myself.'

'Nothing, yet!' Sullivan walked faster, turning sharply each time he reached the wall. 'But the blood pressure is a bit high, though. I have to keep the old weight down, so I have.'

'What weight?' O'Shea laughed. 'You're like a stick insect already. And I'm not surprised if that slop is all we get to eat around here. I can't see any of us turning into that little fat fella. What's his name? Billy Bunter?'

'Will you look at the cut of yourself?' Sullivan was seeing O'Shea clearly for the first time now it was daylight. 'Is someone after using your face as a football? Or were you beaten with an ugly stick when you were a baby?'

O'Shea touched his face. 'Is it that bad?'

'It is! You look like my cousin Cornelius who's a boxer in America after he lost the featherweight title to some black fella from Alabama or Arkansas or somewhere that begins with an A. Didn't he have a face like a bag of spanners on him for weeks after that? You've probably heard of him yourself, I'd say. Cornelius Sullivan, from the Bronx. A great boxer altogether.'

'I was never a great boxing fan, I'm afraid.'

'Ah sure, everyone's heard of Cornelius, whether they're a follower or not. And I'm not saying that just because he's a cousin of mine because I've got loads of cousins in America. New York, mostly. The Bronx. But I expect you have people over there yourself. Sure hasn't every Irishman got someone in America? It isn't too surprising, I suppose, when you think about all the Irish who had to go to America to escape the famine. You're a Kerryman, didn't you say? Sure almost everyone in Kerry has a relative somewhere in the States. Uncles, aunts, brothers, sisters, they're all over the place.'

He rubbed his hands together as he reached the door again. He paused for a moment to look out of the grill, letting his forehead rest against the rough old wood. 'I wish to Jasus I'd gone there myself. I had my chance and all. But no, I had to be the big eejit and come to this God-forsaken hole of a place instead. And what for? What bloody for?'

He spun around and started pacing again. 'Anyway, what are you doing here yourself?'

'You asked me that last night. The police stopped me. I had no identification so they threw me in here.'

'No, I mean what are you doing in Wales? What are you doing in Cardiff?'

'Ah, 'tis a long story.'

Sullivan flopped down on his bunk. 'Well, I think I have all the time in the world to listen to it. Sure I'm not going anywhere in a hurry.'

'Now that's a point.' O'Shea sat up straight. 'How long do you think they'll be keeping me in here?'

'Who knows? The way things are around here at the moment you could well be forgotten. Just like the rest of us poor bastards.'

'But shouldn't I have some sort of hearing or something? Surely they'll want to know who I am, what

I'm doing here. I'll have to be seen by someone at some stage, won't I?'

'Well, I certainly didn't have no hearing.'

'Didn't you?' O'Shea studied the thin face that looked ashen beneath the mop of tight ginger hair. The haggard features were too hard to read. The deep-set eyes had dark rings around them making them appear distraught. 'What are you in for, anyway? You must have had some sort of trial before they put you in here.'

'Well, if you could call it that,' Sullivan scoffed. 'It wasn't a proper trial. It was a farce. A complete and utter bloody farce with a lot of pompous cretins trying to show some ponce of a judge how bloody clever they were. Some of them were so far up the judge's arse all you could see was their boots hanging out. And I was standing there in the middle of it all like a pawn on a chessboard. I wasn't a person. I was just a piece in a game, shuffled around for their amusement.'

He stabbed his chest with his finger and his eyes flashed with the injustice of it all. 'I was accused of something that I positively did not do. There was no case against me. There were no witnesses, no evidence, nothing. Just a few vindictive people who were jealous of me and who plotted against me. I was an innocent man but I was still sentenced to three years in jail. Three years for something I didn't do. Can you believe that?'

'But what exactly did you ... sorry, what did they *say* you did?'

'That's just it!' Sullivan flapped his arms in agitation. 'They didn't say anything specific. They said all sorts of things about me, but the charge itself was just a lot of confused legal jargon. They seemed to make it up as they went along.'

'But they obviously found you guilty of *something*, even if they *were* wrong.' O'Shea shifted position on the hard bunk and straightened his coat beneath him. 'So what were you convicted of?'

'Well, I was actually convicted of neglect of duty. I am ... I *was* a teacher, you see. Science and Chemistry. I was a resident teacher in a college near Bridgend. One day while I was on duty a student, a young Philippine boy, died. So I was held responsible. I was his Housemaster, you see. I was supposed to be looking out for him. They charged me with neglect of my duties that resulted in manslaughter.'

'Could they do that?'

'Of course they could! Wasn't I just a country boy from the bogs of Ireland? An easy scapegoat, you see. They couldn't afford a scandal at the school. It might impact on their reputation and lose them some precious revenue. So they took the course of least resistance. Find someone to blame and hang him out to dry.'

Keys rattled down the corridor and a door banged open. It was followed by a rush of noise. Lots of clattering and shouting echoed around the bare walls.

'Ah, here they come.' Sullivan leapt off the bunk and ran to the rusty bucket in the corner, lifted it to the centre of the floor and clasped the handle with both hands. A childish excitement danced across his face and he gave a squeal of joy as the footsteps got closer. Keys clattered noisily in the lock before the door was finally flung open.

'Will you come on?' he yelled at O'Shea. 'You don't want to be sitting there wasting your only bit of freedom for the whole day.'

He picked up the bucket and scurried out, and O'Shea ran after him.

'Where are we going?' O'Shea had to shout above the noise as men filled the corridor. They all headed for a door at the far end, pushing and shoving with their buckets rattling together.

'To the lav. They let us out this time every day to slop out our buckets and have a quick wash. But it's not for long, though. Maybe ten or fifteen minutes. So we can't waste any time. We'll take turns carrying the bucket. That way one of us can have a longer wash while the other one swills it out. So you get in line today and I'll slop out. All right?'

Sullivan shuffled away and O'Shea tagged onto the end of a line in front of a row of chipped and cracked porcelain sinks. The din was deafening. The prisoners laughed and joked and pushed each other playfully. The man at the sink had just a few seconds to wash and wipe himself before he was hustled away by the person behind.

O'Shea could see Sullivan swilling the bucket in a big tank. Then he washed it under a standpipe and ran across to join the end of the line.

When O'Shea eventually reached the sink the water was already coated with a thick scum. The soap was just a thin strip now, and when O'Shea hesitated it caused a hush to fall over the prisoners. Everything stopped. The only sound in the whole toilet block was the trickle of water lapping over the edge of the tank behind them.

A hand jabbed O'Shea in the back. He spun around and found himself looking up at a giant with a bald head and a sneer on his face.

Someone muttered to the big man and he laughed, then he poked O'Shea again. O'Shea staggered back against the sink and cracked his elbow against the tiles. He gritted his teeth and straightened back up. And it was only then he noticed the man's face. Stone hard with scars on both cheeks and across his forehead.

The mean lips widened as the man looked around at his friends. They sensed entertainment, a moment's relief from the tedium. So they shouted encouragement at him. His hand shot out and gripped O'Shea by the throat. A roar erupted as he lifted O'Shea off the floor and pinned him to the wall.

Sullivan came running through the mob, grabbed the man's arm and spoke to him in German. The man growled and dribble trickled down his chin, and he spat at Sullivan's feet. But the grip on O'Shea's throat loosened and he pulled away.

'Have your bloody wash. *Quick*!' Sullivan pushed O'Shea towards the sink. 'They have to wash in your water so you'd better wash in theirs.'

The guards started shouting out in the corridor. They hammered the wall with their batons and everyone hurried. Sullivan used the end of a towel to dry himself.

'Come on,' he grabbed O'Shea by the shirt and pulled him along. 'We have to show the guards we're keen to get back to our cells. Otherwise they think we're being awkward and they get very angry. Sure didn't they kill two fellas a couple of weeks ago because they were dawdling?'

'*What*?'

'Oh, they did. They beat them with their clubs. Then they threw them in the slop tank and left them there until the truck came to take the slop away. Sure they don't mess around, these guards. They're like the bloody Black and Tans, you know? They kill you for the fun of it, and no questions asked.'

Two men stepped out in front of Sullivan and blocked his way. The bigger one tried to ruffle O'Shea's hair and when O'Shea slapped the hand away the man laughed out loud.

'So, the priest's got a new boyfriend, eh?' he announced to everyone around him. 'And what's your name then, sweetheart?'

'Looks like they've already had a fight, by the state of his face,' the second man added. 'Lover's tiff, was it, sweetheart?'

They both laughed this time. Sullivan held the bucket in front of him and barged through them. And O'Shea used his shoulder to knock one of them back against the wall.

'Just as well no one dropped the bleedin' soap in there,' they shouted after him. 'It wouldn't have been safe to bend to pick it up, would it?'

Chapter Thirty-Four

Back in the cell Sullivan sat on his bunk with his knees under his chin. He avoided looking at O'Shea.

'So?' O'Shea was also propped against the wall with his feet tucked under him.

'What?'

'You know what!' O'Shea snapped. 'You're a priest.'

'I am *not*.' It came out in a splutter. 'What makes you think I'm a … Ah sure, you're not taking any notice of that lot out there, are you? They're all nuts. Aren't they all criminals, the lot of them? Robbers and thugs, that's what they all are. How could you believe a single word they tell you?'

'Then why the hell would they say a strange thing like that?'

'They made a mistake, that's all.' He waved his hand dismissively. 'Someone got the wrong end of the stick, that's all.'

'What stick? That's a very strange stick if you ask me.'

Sullivan wiped his nose and pulled a face. 'That waste tank is smelling worse lately. Still, you'd stink too if you had buckets of crap dumped on you every day and then got left for weeks until someone came to clean you out. Do you know they get the poor Jews to do that?'

O'Shea didn't answer. Sullivan was annoying him now.

'How's your neck, by the way?' Sullivan asked after a while.

O'Shea touched his throat. 'It could have been worse.'

'Well, you shouldn't be so bloody particular, should you? You shouldn't cause a fuss until them fellas are used to you. I never said a word for the first few weeks I was in here.'

'But what did I do?' O'Shea swallowed to check how sore it was. 'The dirty water took me by surprise, that's all.'

'You know they thought you were an officer, don't you?' He nodded at O'Shea's overcoat. 'That big fella, the German, he hates officers. They say he's in here because he stuffed a hand grenade in an officer's mouth and blew him to smithereens. Then there you are in an officer's coat showing off because the water's a bit dirty. I only managed to save your life because I told them you got the coat off of a dead officer. And I sort of implied you were the cause of the officer being dead in the first place. So if I was you I'd pull off all those insignia and ribbons and things, just to be on the safe side.'

'God, I'm glad he believed you. It would be awful to be killed because of some stupid misunderstanding.'

'Oh, so you think it's all right to be killed deliberately, do you?' Sullivan had a strange look on his face.

O'Shea wasn't sure what he meant. So he asked him.

'Your predecessor,' Sullivan nodded at the bunk. 'The fella whose bed you're using, he was killed deliberately. Sure, I know he was weird. One of those big strong types who just lies there and stares at the ceiling all day and doesn't say a word. I suppose he was just counting the cracks like the rest of us. There's nothing much else to do in here except count the cracks.'

'So what happened to him?'

Sullivan jumped up on his bed and stretched to look out of the window. 'Come up here and look at this.'

O'Shea climbed up beside him. The huge courtyard was less than a foot below the window. It was surrounded on all sides by high red-bricked walls. A patchwork of windows looked down into the yard. And over in the far corner an iron grill covered an arch that led to another yard beyond.

'That gate over there is the only way into this yard.' Sullivan pointed to the grill. 'If you walk in that gate you usually don't walk back out again. Do you see that wall over there?'

One of the walls was bare of windows or doors. And it was pockmarked with bullet holes.

'That's where they took him, one day last week. But something happened to him between the time they took him from this cell to the time he appeared out there because he was a mess when I saw him again. It looked like he was glad to die. But how can you tell?'

He jumped off the bunk and went to the door. 'Have you ever seen someone die?'

O'Shea sat back on his bunk. 'Oh yes.'

''Tis really horrible.' Sullivan's voice was soft now. 'One minute they're walking and talking, the next they're just a lump of dead meat on the floor.'

'Well, I suppose when your time comes … '

'When your time comes?' Sullivan scoffed. 'Well, just who decides when your time comes, eh? If someone lobs your bastard head off with a big machete, isn't it he who decides when your time comes? If someone stabs you up the arse with a bloody big bayonet, surely tis he who decides when your time comes. Isn't it?'

His eyes flashed and saliva trickled out the corner of his mouth.

'Hey, take it easy, will you?' O'Shea laughed at the ferocity of the tone. 'All I was saying ...'

'Yeah, all you were saying!' Sullivan licked his lips and rested his head back against the wall. 'So what *were* you saying? When your time comes? Are you saying you have some sort of time switch inside your head and when your time comes you just drop dead by whatever means are at hand at that moment? Are we all born with this clock of doom inside our head? Are we all destined to live only for as long as this clock permits? Are we?'

'Well, I don't bloody know.' O'Shea still had a chuckle in his voice. 'How do I know? We live. We die. We all have to die sometime.'

Sullivan jumped off the bed, went to the bucket in the corner and pressed his head against the wall. The bucket rattled with the first rush which slowly turned to a trickle. Then he did up his trousers and turned back to O'Shea.

'But who sets this clock, though?' He was undeterred by O'Shea's lack of seriousness. 'Who is it that can take your life in his hand and say *you, my boy, you will live six years*. Or *you, my girl, you will live till you're ninety*. Who is it that can do this thing?'

'Well, who do *you* think decides these things?' O'Shea threw the challenge back at him.

Sullivan clicked his fingers. 'You're a Catholic, right?'

'Well, I was baptised a Catholic, yes.'

'Then you must believe in God!' Sullivan's eyes opened wide, giving them a more haunted look. 'You must believe in someone sitting up in the sky looking down on us and telling us what to do.'

O'Shea gave another little laugh and Sullivan forced himself to stop a smile.

'Ah, so you *are* a priest, then.'

Sullivan's hand shot up in horror. 'No. I am *not*!'

'Well, you could be, the way you're preaching at me now.'

Sullivan squeezed his eyes shut and shook his head. Then he let his breath out in one long exasperated sigh. 'Actually, I *did* want to be a priest once.'

O'Shea waited for more but Sullivan just rubbed his eyes with his fingers.

'Then why didn't you?' He had to ask.

Sullivan looked up at the ceiling as he considered the answer. Then he gave another long sigh. 'Well, I did try. When I was seventeen I actually went off to study for the priesthood. But of course I realise now that it was for all the wrong reasons. I was vain, I suppose. And if I was really honest, I was also afraid of going out into the big bad world and fending for myself. The priesthood seemed a cosy option. Unless they sent you to a jungle somewhere and you got eaten by the natives. Anyway, in Ireland it's a great honour to be a priest. For yourself *and* for your family. Everyone knows there's a priest in the family and they ask you to bless them and say mass for them. Tis a wonderful thing altogether.'

'So what happened?' O'Shea asked after a pause.

'Well, the spirit was willing all right, but the flesh ... well, the sins of the flesh. We know all about them. They've destroyed greater men than me, I'm afraid.'

'What do you mean? You don't mean ...'

Sullivan shrugged.

'But I thought you said you were in a priest's college?'

'Well, I was. But it was an ordinary fee-paying college too. The main building was for non-religious boarders. All the students in the main college weren't Catholic, you see? So the trainee priests lived in a small house down by the lake and attended classes up in the

213

main college. Of course the domestic staff came from the nearby town. And they were mostly girls.'

'And you couldn't leave them alone!'

'Something like that.' Sullivan smiled to himself. Then he put his fingers to his lips. 'You wouldn't have a cigarette on you, by any chance?'

O'Shea shook his head. 'They took them off me last night.'

'Pity. I haven't had a fag for weeks. That's another bad habit I picked up in college, smoking. A waste of bloody money.'

'Give them up, so!'

'Ha bloody ha! As if I have a choice in here. Anyway, didn't I hear they're bad for your health? Couldn't you cough yourself to death from smoking them? Which brings us back to the other point there. If you smoke, doesn't that mean you decide for yourself when you'll die?'

'Ah, you're not going to start all that again?'

'Sure, why not? Tis a legitimate argument, isn't it? Is there a God or isn't there?'

'Well, what do you think?'

Sullivan stood up and stretched. 'I think, in all probability, there is not. I think we come into this world in the process of evolution and, as Shakespeare said, we strut and fret our hour upon the stage and then we're heard of no more. The end.'

O'Shea sat and thought about that.

Chapter Thirty-Five

A few days later a group of men was waiting for them when they went into the toilet. They should have realised something was wrong because there was a strange lack of noise they walked down the corridor. Normally they couldn't hear themselves think. But this time there was a suppressed murmur and an odd look of expectation on the faces of the others as they rushed past.

Some of them gave a furtive glance at Sullivan and sniggered out loud. For some reason Sullivan didn't seem too concerned about it and he marched briskly into the toilet towards the line of men waiting by the sinks.

Suddenly O'Shea was grabbed from behind and slammed back against the wall. Sullivan turned to see what was happening. And when he saw the way the men had bunched up behind him he went ghostly pale. He looked around slowly and his face creased as he tried to back away. But the prisoners had already formed a circle around him and there was nowhere left for him to go.

'We have a surprise for you today, priest,' one of them laughed. 'Seeing as it's Sunday and all.'

They took him by the arms and dragged him across the floor, and they shoved him face down on the row of sinks. Someone reached through the gap from the other side, took his wrists and pulled them so his head and shoulders were wedged in the small space. Then they gave a huge roar as his trousers was pulled down around his ankles and his legs were kicked apart.

'We want to give Horse a treat, since it's his birthday, like!' one of the prisoners said. The cheers grew even louder as a small thin man with pinched features came out of one of the cubicles wearing just a towel around his waist.

'Horse,' they roared. 'Here's your birthday treat.'

Horse let his towel drop and there was a gasp of approval as he raised his arms above his head and rolled his hips provocatively. He turned around slowly to show everyone that what they heard about him was no exaggeration.

O'Shea was stunned. It was obvious now why they called him Horse.

Sullivan was grabbed by the ankles and his legs forced apart. Horse did a slow shuffle up behind him, preparing himself with tantalising slowness and prolonging the entertainment to the wild approval of the men. They surged around him and O'Shea lost sight of Sullivan. Then he heard a desperate scream. For a brief moment he saw the top of Sullivan's head rise up then disappear again. The applause drowned out everything else.

O'Shea was panicking now. He struggled but they had his neck in a stranglehold.

Suddenly the guards were banging on the walls with their batons and the prisoners scattered, laughing and shouting as they scurried back to their cells.

They threw O'Shea to the floor and gave him a few kicks. And he waited until they'd all disappeared before he staggered back to his feet.

Sullivan's face was ghostly white and his eyes unfocused as O'Shea lifted him off the sinks. He was bleeding badly and mumbling incoherently. O'Shea had to practically carry him back to the cell.

When O'Shea laid him on the bed, he curled up and turned his face to the wall.

Chapter Thirty-Six

The gate in the yard gave a slow agonising screech as it was hoisted up by a couple of rusty chains. In the dismal grey morning the noise it made echoed eerily off the bare red-brick walls.

O'Shea jumped up onto Sullivan's bed to see what was happening. Faces began to appear in the other windows too as an army officer in a menacing black uniform lead two columns of soldiers through the archway. One column snaked left along the far wall and the other one went down the right hand side.

The officer strutted into the middle of the yard and his heels clicked as he yelled an order. The soldiers' boots hit the ground like a clap of thunder. He shrieked again and the two columns turned inwards. Seconds later a sleek black Mercedes staff car came through the arch and crunched to a halt inches from the officer's back.

The man in the back of the car stood up and chopped off a salute. He glanced up at the faces now filling every window and gave a satisfied smile. The soldier in the front seat handed him some papers. He cleared his throat as he studied them for a moment before shouting loudly in German.

'What's going on, Liam?'

Sullivan was still stretched out on his bunk. He grunted and rubbed his nose, but he didn't answer.

'*Liam*!'

'Well how the feck do I know?'

'Then come up here and take a look!' O'Shea gave him a poke with his foot.

Sullivan swore loudly and went to turn away, but he caught the look on O'Shea's face and decided he wanted to know after all. He scrambled up beside O'Shea and studied the performance, and he shook his head.

'I haven't got a clue.'

The German's voice rose and fell as he turned his head to make sure everyone heard his message. When the cold breeze ruffled his coat he pulled the collar up high and gave a quick shiver. Then he took off his cap and wiped his forehead. And when he put it back on he made sure it was straight by giving the peak a quick tug.

He glanced at the papers in his hand again before continuing his announcement. And as he turned towards them O'Shea felt Sullivan tense up. He craned his neck to get a better look and his hands squeezed the window bars.

'Oh, sweet Jesus!' he gasped, and his head clattered against the window sill. 'Oh, thank you, God. Thank you, thank you!'

He knocked O'Shea out of the way as he threw himself off the bunk and started pacing frantically up and down the cell.

'Thank you, Jesus,' he whimpered and clasped his hands under his chin. 'Thank you, thank you, thank you.'

'*Liam*! For Heaven's sake. What's the matter with you? What's going on?'

'See him out there?' Sullivan eyes filled with tears and overflowed onto his cheeks. 'Sure isn't he the same fella who saw me the last time he was here. I've prayed for this moment, Danny boy. Every bloody night I've prayed he'd come back and give me another chance. I just knew he'd come back and get me out of here.'

'What do you mean? How's he going to get you out of here?'

'Because he's *the man*!' Sullivan was agitated by O'Shea's stupid questions. 'He's the fella who

218

interviewed me the last time. He's the one who'll get me away from this place.'

Sullivan was breathless now. He sagged onto the bed and rubbed the tears away with the back of his hand. 'I hope to God he remembers me, that's all.'

O'Shea climbed down and sat opposite him. 'Liam, you're not making any sense, you know? How's that fella going to save you? How do you know him, anyway?'

Sullivan rolled his eyes and pulled himself back against the wall.

'Well, I can't say I actually *know* him exactly. Tis just that after the Germans invaded he came here to do some sort of census. You know, to find out who was in here? And why. They were looking for people to put to work, as far as I know. Some of the prisoners were taken away immediately. And some were even enlisted into the prison service right here. Can you believe that? Right here, where they were prisoners themselves? Anyway, he's back again now and all I can say is thank you God.'

'So you think he's doing another census now? Is he going to question all the prisoners again?'

'Oh, I think so.' Sullivan started crying again and he blew his nose on his sleeve. 'Sure tis great news altogether. Haven't I prayed for this moment every day of the week? And it couldn't have come at a better time for me, you know. After what those bastards did to me yesterday. What they did to me yesterday certainly made my mind up for me.'

'Liam, you've lost me there, I'm afraid.' O'Shea patted him on the knee. 'I don't understand how a census will help you get out of the prison.'

'Look,' Sullivan shot off the bunk again, staggered over to the door and leant back against it. 'Do you remember I told you I was a teacher, Science and Chemistry? Well, when I saw that fella out there he immediately assumed because I was Irish I would naturally be anti-British. Which is understandable, of course. So he suggested I take up a research position at the University Hospital here in Cardiff. The gist of it was I would be involved in some ... shall we say unsavoury ... research. You know, the kind of stuff that would be taboo under normal circumstances? And any volunteers I might require for this research would be readily available to me from the local population. Anyway, they asked me a heap of strange questions, like what did I think of the Jews, what did I think of the gypsies, what did I think of the cripples and the mad people? And the English, too. One or two other things as well.'

He fell silent and his breathing was heavy and erratic. And when he continued his face was a sad mask. 'Of course I considered it. I'd be lying if I said I didn't. The rewards would have been tremendous and I was sorely tempted, I can tell you. After all, I'm only a humble country boy and I crave riches as much as the next man. But for some inconceivable reason known only to God Himself, I just couldn't do it. My conscience wouldn't allow me to become involved in something that impacted so drastically with my basic convictions, my natural belief in the sanctity of human life.'

He rubbed his face roughly with his hands as he paused again.

'Sure I know the English were mad bastards,' he almost shouted, causing O'Shea to jump. 'What with the Black and Tans and all that. And I know the way they treated the Irish people was unforgivable in any language. The way they murdered and plundered and ravaged us, well, t'was an outrage and it cut deep. Oh yes, it left a scar on every Irishman that ever walked on two legs and a lot of them can never forgive, let alone forget.

But, sure, it was never the fault of the ordinary Englishman in the street, was it? Weren't they treated just as bad themselves, hanged for stealing a loaf of bread, deported overseas for stealing a purse? I read some books when I was sitting there in my flat in the college with nothing to do. And you know, didn't some of them make me weep at the way the poor people of England were treated by their own ruling elite, their so-called political masters. The workhouses, the slavery, well, it gave me a sort of insight into the kind of people the ordinary English really are. Not the fat pompous farts, the so-called officers and gentlemen, but the ordinary God-fearing working man.'

He looked at the floor as he chewed his fingernail.

'Anyway, I knew that, bad and all as that stuff was, sure wasn't it all in the past. It was just another page in the history books. But this Nazi thing, well that's actually happening right here and now. And I just wasn't sure I had the stomach to be a part of it. So I told them no. And by Jasus didn't they turn nasty with me! You wouldn't believe how pissed off they were. They beat me black and blue and kicked me all the way back down to this cell right here. I still get the fits because of it, you know. My nerves just explode and I take off. All my guts are damaged too. They're slowly giving out on me day by day. And what happened to me yesterday only made things worse. I can't stop bleeding, you know. And I can hardly walk either.'

He sagged onto the bed with a loud groan and rested his head back against the wall.

'I actually believed I'd be able to see my sentence out, do my time with a clear conscience. Pay my price and be on my way. But not now. Not anymore. When I see the man today I'll sell him my soul. I'll do anything he wants as long as I can get out of this dreadful place.'

O'Shea sat on the bunk beside him and took hold of his arm. 'Will you take me with you, Liam?'

Sullivan pulled away and jumped to his feet.

'*What*?' His eyes were darting all over the cell in panic and spittle dribble down his chin.

'Take me with you,' O'Shea pleaded. 'When you see the man today, tell him you need to take me with you. Tell him I'm Irish, the same as you.'

'I can't do that,' Sullivan spluttered and a strange fear danced in his eyes. 'How can I do that?'

'You can!' O'Shea grabbed him by the collar, hauled him up to the window and pressed his head roughly against the bars. And Sullivan didn't resist. He hung like a rag doll from O'Shea's hand and dropped his head onto the windowsill.

'Look out there!' O'Shea shouted at him. 'Somewhere out there my son is all alone and in serious danger. Now you can help me get out of here and find him before it's too late. You have to help me. Please, Liam! You have to try.'

The cell door flew open. A guard bellowed and waved them out with his rifle. Sullivan practically ran out of the cell. The guard pulled O'Shea off the bunk and shoved him after Sullivan down the corridor that reeked of damp and stale urine. More prisoners were already there. Everyone looked confused.

Eventually the guards herded them out through a narrow opening in the arch wall. And by the time they arrived in the yard most of the other prisoners were already bunched in little huddles. The car was gone.

A bitter easterly wind came over the rooftops and whipped at them mercilessly. It bit right through O'Shea's clothes. He hugged his coat and moved closer to a large group of men, using them as a windbreak. Sullivan stood by the wall with his shoulders hunched. His face had a strange look on it and spittle glistened on his chin.

Soldiers with batons persuaded the prisoners to form one long line that snaked all the way around the yard and faced inwards. Then the man in the black uniform jumped up on a table in the middle of the yard. The muttering faded to an uneasy silence as the prisoners looked at him with trepidation in their eyes.

A gust of wind made him hold onto his hat, and when he spoke his voice was blown away with it. Everyone surged forward to catch what he was saying but O'Shea still couldn't hear a word. All he could do was stamp his feet and blow into his frozen hands.

After what seemed like hours the man jumped off the table and the soldiers started moving some of the prisoners out through the arch. The rest were then separated into four lines.

As they separated O'Shea grabbed Sullivan's arm. 'Help me, Liam. My son is all I have left. Help me find him.'

Sullivan hesitated and blinked several times. Then he gave a reluctant nod.

'I'll try,' he answered a second before he was roughly pushed into another line.

A table had been set up in each corner of the yard and an officer stood next to it. A clerk sat behind the desk taking notes. Each line of prisoners was manoeuvred towards a table. And when the man at the front was questioned by the officer and had his details taken he was bundled away. Then the next man shuffled forward and the rest of the line crawled after him with an agonising slowness.

By the time O'Shea reached the front of the line he was completely numb from the cold and shivering badly. All the guards were tired and irritable. He'd lost sight of Sullivan by then.

O'Shea glanced up at the officer who was wiping his streaming nose with a handkerchief he then stuffed angrily into his pocket. He blew on his frozen hands and rubbed them together. His face was deep pink and his nose and lips had turned a lifeless shade of blue.

The officer's tired hooded eyes blinked a few times before they turned and looked at O'Shea for the briefest of moments. And O'Shea's heart gave a thump in his chest.

Something tugged at the curtain of his memory. Something that he didn't like. And when he instinctively stepped back he was pushed forward by the man behind him.

Where had he seen those sharp, brutal features before? Tredegar? No! That was too raw. He would remember something like that.

The hospital? No, he would have remembered that too. It must have been before that.

One more step and O'Shea was in front of him. The officer sniffled and rubbed his nose before snapping a question.

O'Shea frowned. He didn't understand the question.

The officer looked up when no answer came. And in a flash O'Shea remembered the sneering, angry face and cold, soft voice snarling at him while his hands were pinned against a tree and Bethan was lying dead in the middle of the yard.

It was Captain Weiss.

The trimmed eyebrows rose and the tired impatient eyes burnt into O'Shea. He asked the question again, this time with much more venom.

O'Shea shrugged. Weiss grunted and stepped around the table, grabbed O'Shea and threw him back against the wall. A soldier rushed over and held O'Shea's hands against his side.

'I don't understand,' O'Shea yelped with the shock of his head hitting the wall. 'What are you saying to me?'

Weiss pressed his finger under O'Shea's chin and jerked his head up. 'You don't speak German?'

'I'm afraid I do not, sir.' O'Shea grimaced as the finger pressed hard against his windpipe.

'Is that not the coat of a German officer?'

O'Shea tried to look down at the ragged overcoat but the finger increased the pressure and he gagged.

'No, no.' O'Shea spluttered. 'Well, *yes*! A German coat, to be sure. But tis not mine, you see. It was given to me by a very kind gentleman who had no more need of it.'

'A very kind gentleman?' The red eyes glinted. 'And did this kind gentleman have a white beard and a red suit? Was his name Father Christmas?'

A strained laughter trickled down the line. The finger eased up on the pressure and O'Shea gasped. 'Ah no, sir. Not at all, sure. I don't think it was.'

Weiss sighed and took his finger from O'Shea's throat, and O'Shea was dragged back around to the front of the table again.

'Answer my question now. What is your name?'

'Danny O'Shea, sir.'

'Why are you here in this prison?'

'I didn't have any papers, sir.'

'Why not?'

O'Shea coughed and covered his mouth with his hand. Was it possible Weiss had no recollection of him?

'I ... they got burnt, sir. In the fire.'

Weiss sneezed and caught it with his hand. He rooted in his pocket, dragged out the handkerchief again and rubbed his eyes with it before looking back at O'Shea. His intense gaze demanded an explanation.

O'Shea looked at his hands. 'When you ... during the invasion ... ah, during the ... well, my house got bombed and everything was destroyed. So I was arrested and put in here.'

Weiss stuffed the handkerchief back in his pocket. 'Have we met before?' His eyes seemed to be even redder.

'No,' O'Shea said too quickly. 'Well, I don't think so, sir. No.'

There was a stressful pause. 'Are you sure?'

'Yes, sir. I'm sure.'

'Strange.' Weiss pursed his mouth. 'I rarely forget a face. Still, I'm sure I will remember. I always do. Anyway, what is your trade?'

'I was a dockyard worker, sir.'

'Doing what, exactly?'

'Just manual labour. Anything and everything.'

'Follow that line and you will be examined by a doctor.' He dismissed O'Shea with a flick of his hand. O'Shea almost bowed with relief before scurrying over to the group of men bunched up near the arch.

He tried to disappear amongst them. But he couldn't resist a quick glance back at Weiss. And his face drained when he saw the officer still watching him, his brow wrinkled in concentration. O'Shea looked away and pushed deeper into the group.

It was a long, agonising hour before the medics finished checking O'Shea's group and by then there was no feeling left in his feet or hands. As the prisoners were commanded back into line and marched off through the arch they stamped their feet to get the blood flowing again.

O'Shea said a silent prayer as they came out on the other side. And he was so thankful to be away from the oppressive presence of Captain Weiss he didn't notice the commotion in the yard behind him.

Some prisoners looked back as boots came rushing through the arch, and when one of the guards gave a scream the line stopped dead. O'Shea bumped into the man in front and yelped in surprise as he was grabbed by the arm.

'I told you I always remember a face.' The officer's eyes were like little grey pebbles and he gave a snort. 'And I'm so glad I remembered yours. I think you and I have some unfinished business.'

He glanced at the guards. 'Take him to the reception suite.'

Chapter Thirty-Seven

O'Shea's footsteps died in the thick stained carpet as the guard walked him up to the solitary desk at the far end of a bare room. They stopped a few feet in front of it.

The low ceiling had emulsion peeling off it and the weak afternoon light glistened on the brown gloss walls.

Weiss was sprawled on a high-backed chair with his legs stretched out and his arms folded across his stomach. He studied O'Shea impassively, letting his gaze wander from his feet to his head and back down to his feet again. Only his eyes moved. And they moved very slowly. The silence buzzed in O'Shea's ears and he swallowed hard to clear them.

The guard gave a sharp cough and O'Shea glanced at him. And when he looked back at Weiss the eyes were still watching him.

'So!' Weiss raised himself up in the chair with an exaggerated slowness. 'Isn't this a nice surprise, seeing you again? I thought you were already dead. You must be like a cat with nine lives.'

He waited for a response. He didn't get one.

'So, what have you got to tell me?' The corner of his mouth harboured the impression of a smile, but it was devoid of any trace of compassion.

'What do you mean?'

'Please!' Weiss waved his hand. 'You *know* what I mean. You were at the farm the day that lady died. She spoke to you. She said something to you before she died, and I want you to tell me exactly what it was.'

'Sure how do you expect me to remember that?' O'Shea spluttered. 'She was after being shot, for God's sake. She was in pain. She was afraid. She knew she was going to die and she was terrified. All she said was where's my sister? She only wanted to know where her sister was.'

'Where are the boxes?'

'*What* boxes?'

The half-closed eyes didn't flinch.

'The boxes,' he repeated calmly.

'But I don't know what you ...' O'Shea's voice cracked and he swallowed hard again.

'Please don't play games with me,' Weiss sighed wearily. 'We know all about the boxes. What we don't know is where they are right now.'

O'Shea shrugged and Weiss tapped his fingers on the desk.

'Don't make me ask you again.'

'But I really don't know what you mean.'

'Stupid boy. Who are you trying to impress?' Weiss uncurled himself from the chair and ambled around to the front of the desk. He stood to attention in front of O'Shea with his hands by his side and his head back so he was looking down his nose.

Then his hand shot out and grabbed O'Shea by the face, and he squeezed his mouth so his lips were pursed.

'I am very, very tired today.' He held O'Shea like that for a minute before pushing him away. Then he knocked him with his shoulder as he went back behind the desk and dropped onto the chair.

'The reason you are here right now is because some boxes have gone missing.' He stifled a yawn. 'I need to know where those boxes are. I believe you already *know* where those boxes are. So let me assure you it is very much in your best interest to tell me where those boxes are. Otherwise ...'

He left the rest unsaid as he leant forward and put his elbows on the desk.

'Anyway,' he continued with a totally insincere smile. 'Tomorrow is Christmas Day, as you know. Now I am not an ungenerous man. So I will give you until then to think about your predicament, my friend. So when you come back to see me again full of the joys of the season you will not hesitate to share your information with me.'

With the slightest nod of his head he ended the conversation and the guard marched O'Shea out of the room and back down two flights of stairs to his cell.

The cell door was yanked open and O'Shea was bundled inside. Then the door slammed behind him and shut out all the light. He felt for the edge of his bunk and dropped down onto it, and he rubbed his eyes to help them adjust to the darkness. When he opened them again he was surprised to see a shape lying on the other bunk. He jumped up and took a closer look.

'Liam?'

Sullivan turned over and raised himself onto his elbows. 'Danny? Is it yourself?' He sounded distressed.

'What happened, Liam? How did you get on? Did you see your man?'

Sullivan gave a stifled cry and shook his head.

'But why not?'

'Sure they wouldn't take any notice of me, Danny.' His voice wobbled. 'I tried to tell them I had to see the Colonel urgently, but they ignored me completely. I tried to explain to them how important it was, that it was imperative I see the man himself. I was so desperate, so I was. Then one of them hit me in the face and threatened to shoot me if I didn't feck off. Did you hear that, Danny? He was going to shoot me!'

He buried his face in his hands and his body shook as sobs spluttered through his fingers.

O'Shea went to put his hand on Sullivan's shoulder but sat back down instead. 'Look, Liam, just take it easy, will ya? You never know, he might still be here tomorrow. You might still be able to see him then.'

'No. There's no way I'll get to see him now. I'm stuck here for the rest of my life. I'm stuck here and I don't know what I'm going to do. For God's sake, what am I going to do? I'm so confused, Danny. I just don't know what I'm doing any more.'

'Look ...'

'I've got a horrible feeling in my bones I won't be able to survive in here for much longer.' He was mumbling through his hands. 'My mind can't take it, you see. All those arse-bandits waiting for me if I go for a wash. But if I stay in here and don't go out at all I'll climb the feckin walls. It's their revenge, you see. They're paying me back for the dirty mortal sin I committed, for offending God Himself and the church and everything to do with it. They're getting their own back, you see. And you can't blame them, can you? Don't you think I should be punished for what I did, Danny boy?'

'Punished for what, Liam? What did you do that was so terrible?'

'I told you already!' His voice had an edge now. 'The boy who died in the college. It was all my fault. I caused the death of a beautiful, loving young boy who didn't have a bad bone in his poor little body.'

'Ah, no,' O'Shea was trying to sound comforting. 'You can't go blaming yourself for that. How can ...'

'You haven't got a feckin clue, have you?' Sullivan sat up and wiped dribble from his chin. 'Didn't you hear

what they called me out there? They called me a priest!
Well, yes! I *am* a priest. I *am* a bloody priest. So there!
Isn't that just grand, now? And don't tell me you didn't
believe them, too?'

'Look, you're getting yourself all worked up.'
O'Shea gave him a gentle pat on the arm. 'You have to
try and calm down.'

'Ah, tis way too late to calm down now. I ruined
everything, my job, my family. They were devastated.
They didn't believe a word of it, of course. How could
they? Their son, the priest. How could he do such a
thing? Never to God!'

He rolled back his head and gave a shrill laugh. 'Did
you hear that? God, I said. As if I still believe He really
exists. And yet I find myself praying to Him every night
because I'm afraid if I don't I'll be damned forever. So I
lie there in the dark and I pray. And my mind goes back
to the happy days in the old village church with its
candles and its smell of incense and the tight-lipped
people kneeling and praying to the Blessed Virgin for
their sins.'

His voice shook badly now. O'Shea coughed into his
hands. 'Liam, come on now!'

'Oh, God. Sweet Jesus, I wish I was at home. I wish I
was back in Ireland with the green fields and the
mountains and the rivers. Oh Danny, what am I going to
do?'

'I wish I could tell you.' O'Shea leant his head back
against the cold damp wall. 'All I can say is try to be
patient.'

'Try to be patient?' Sullivan shot off the bed and
threw himself at the door. 'Do you know how long I've
been in this bloody hole? Look at the back of the feckin
door. All those scratches there, see them? Well, there's

one for every day I've been in here. And do you know how many scratches there are? Seven hundred and twenty six. Almost two whole years. Two whole miserable feckin years. And you say be patient?'

He dropped back onto his bunk and curled up with his face against the wall. And he sobbed pitifully until he fell asleep.

Chapter Thirty-Eight

Christmas Day dawned bitterly cold and if you closed your eyes and thought hard enough you could almost smell it. The crispness smarted of jingle bells and flakes of snow sticking to the windows. The world should be glowing with excitement and expectation. Coloured lights twinkling, seasonal toys in the shops. Children wide-eyed at Father Christmas clanging his bell and snowflakes drifting lightly onto his beard.

But the breakfast today was no different from any other day. And O'Shea still had to wash in the same dirty cold water with the rest of the subdued prisoners.

Sullivan stayed in the cell.

'You'd think they'd let the holy ones go to Mass on Christmas Day,' he grumbled when O'Shea got back. 'But no. They don't have any respect for Christmas and that's for sure. I bet they think tis just another day, the dirty pagans.'

O'Shea lay on his bed and closed his eyes, and he tried to focus on anything other than Sullivan's continuous ramblings. They were getting more and more vague as he talked non-stop about places and events that merged into one another in confused sequences.

O'Shea always lost track of what time scale Sullivan was talking in because he would flit from something that happened when he was a child to something that happened just a week ago. It all became a blur to O'Shea. He would drift off to sleep only to wake again to the drone of Sullivan's voice going on and on and getting more intense and increasingly muddled.

The only break O'Shea had was when he went for a wash and slopped out the bucket. He was apprehensive about going to the washroom after what happened to Sullivan, but it was either that or lose his sanity. To his great relief they appeared to have lost all interest in him anyway.

He noticed too that there were a lot less people in the washroom. And there was no sign of Horse and his cronies.

Unfortunately when he got back to the cell Sullivan was still mumbling in his strained, whining voice. O'Shea threw himself face down on his bunk and pretended to go to sleep.

Sullivan dwelt repeatedly on the boy who died in his college. It was Christmas then too, and almost everyone had gone home. One person who couldn't go home was a young Philippine boy. Sullivan called him Fred because he couldn't pronounce his real name. Fred's parents were diplomats, and they'd sent their son to various boarding schools since he was six years old.

He was now fifteen and he hadn't seen them for over a year, and he was homesick and very lonely. As his Housemaster Father Sullivan was responsible for Fred's welfare over the holiday period and they spent a lot of time together playing snooker and darts. They even played chess at which Sullivan was useless.

Gradually Father Sullivan realised there was a fondness developing between him and Fred, and he knew in his heart it was not a healthy one. Such closeness was fraught with danger, not just morally but also in the eyes of the law. He'd seen many a colleague come to grief because of it. So he tried to distract himself from those feelings by avoiding any unnecessary contact with Fred unless there was someone else present.

But on the Christmas Eve Father Sullivan was going for a shower when he realised Fred was already in the washroom. His instincts told him he should not go in. He did anyway.

The next day Sullivan was physically sick with the guilt of what he'd done. Whichever way he tried to colour it, the reality was he'd taken advantage of a very vulnerable young man. And now his whole world was about to collapses around him. It was such a stupid thing to do. He couldn't believe he was so weak, so incapable of resisting what was just a moment's pleasure.

Now he was terrified to face the day. It took enormous effort to go about his business as if everything was all right. He fretted about how Fred was going to react.

How Fred reacted wasn't what Sullivan wanted. Fred had found a friend, someone who understood his difference, who understood what he'd suppressed all his life because he was ashamed of it. Father Sullivan gave him the love he craved for, love he'd been starved of for as long as he could remember.

Sullivan tried to convince Fred that such a liaison was not only illegal in the eyes of the Catholic Church, but also illegal in the eyes of the law. It had to stop. No one must ever know what happened between them.

The holidays were soon over and the rest of the pupils and teachers drifted back. It was obvious to Sullivan if he and Fred weren't careful someone was bound to notice and they would both end up in prison.

But Fred wasn't prepared to just abandon something so precious. He pleaded for the two of them to run away together, to go where no one would know them. Fred would pretend to be his son, his butler, his handyman, anything.

Sullivan was adamant. They had no future together. There was nowhere on God's earth they could go to and not be chastised and vilified. It could never work. He told Fred they were not to have any more contact outside of the classroom. And he'd already requested a transfer to a different parish somewhere else in England.

They found Fred's body hanging in the shower the next morning.

Of course there were people who'd already noticed the closeness between them. Body language was something that could not be hidden. There were other signs too that aroused suspicions and they'd grown out of all proportions. So when the college gathered witness statements it was hard to decipher which was fact and which was total fabrication. But it didn't matter. They wanted someone to blame for such a disgraceful blot on the character of the college. They had their scapegoat. Sullivan got three years in Cardiff jail.

'My old parish priest told me a good thing once,' Sullivan was still talking in the background. 'Imagine you're standing on the shore and a huge ship goes by with all the lights and the flags waving and the funnels billowing out clouds of smoke. Then the man standing next to you says; *that's a grand ship indeed. Whoever built that is brilliant.*

But the fella on the other side says; *what do you mean built it? Nobody built that. It just evolved. It was just a lump of molten metal millions of years ago, then over the years it grew into a skeleton, and eventually a skin developed on it. Then decks grew, then doors and portholes and funnels. Engines formed, and shafts and lights and propellers. Then life came upon it, and it started to float about the seas, all by itself.'*

He gave a shrill laugh. 'What do you think of that?' His hand flapped in the air. 'Is Man like the ship? Was it created or did it evolve? Were eyes that can see things away in the distance and in a fraction of a second focus on something right up close just something that evolved? Was the human brain that's as sharp as a razor and able to analyse and make critical decisions in a heartbeat, something that just came about by chance? Voices that can communicate in thousands of different languages? But if it was built, who built it? Who is powerful enough to build a thing like that?'

He sat up straight. 'I knew God once. I was so close to Him, walked with Him. And then I went and lost Him. And now I don't even know where to look for Him anymore.'

Out in the yard the old gate creaked and footsteps clattered on the cold bare concrete. Sullivan looked up startled, then jumped up on the bed to look out of the window.

'Oh, Sweet Jasus!' His voice was high as he gripped the bars. 'Not on Christmas Day, surely! They can't ...'

O'Shea climbed up beside him and watched the soldiers herding five figures across to the killing wall. A woman was bent and wrapped in a shawl, and her thin hands held onto the two little children. A man held a little boy's hand as they all shuffled over to the wall and stood against it.

'Dear God, no,' Sullivan cried. 'Not today, not now!'

His hands turned white with the grip he had on the bars

'Will you look at them? Ah, will you just look at the poor little things. Why do they have to kill the little children? What have the children got to do with any of it? Why can't they just leave them alone? For God's sake, they're only babies.'

The boy let go of the man's hand and was edging away from the group, his eyes darting around the yard in blind terror.

The woman kissed the other children and held them tightly. The little boy covered his face with his hands and his little legs took him off at a gallop across the open ground.

He didn't get far. A soldier crouched and fired his machine gun. The bullets howled along behind the boy and his panicked gasping changed to a gurgling scream as the shots hit him.

Sullivan screamed too as the boy danced violently and slammed against the wall outside their window showering Sullivan and O'Shea in a spray of red and grey mist.

Sullivan flew back off the bunk, beating the air and wailing hysterically as the guns chattered again. Then there was silence.

Sullivan sat on the floor with his mouth quivering as he whispered the Lord's Prayer. Outside the soldiers took the bodies away as the first snow of Christmas began to fall and cover the evidence with a soft and perfect white sheet.

Dark September

Chapter Thirty-Nine

They came for O'Shea in the early hours of the morning when it was still pitch black. The cell door crashed open and a beam from a flashlight pierced the darkness and blinded him before he had time to react. Then he was dragged off the bunk and out through the door by shadowy figures who never spoke a word.

Sullivan was facing the wall and snoring. He didn't move.

This time the room was smaller with just a chair in the middle of the floor. The bulb dangling from the ceiling had a black metal shade and the light it threw down encompassed the chair and left the rest of the room in shadow.

O'Shea was slammed down on the chair. And he sensed someone standing just beyond the edge of that shadow.

There wasn't a sound until a match cracked and the flame lit up a familiar face. Captain Weiss flicked the match away as he took a slow drag on the cigarette. Then he blew out three little circles of smoke that drifted across to O'Shea and brushed his face.

'I dreamt about you last night.' Weiss appeared to glide out of the darkness and into the circle of light, and in the blink of an eye he was standing in front of O'Shea. O'Shea jerked back and looked around at the guards but they were just dark unmoving shapes.

'I dreamt about your face,' Weiss continued. 'Your sad eyes, how pitiful they look when you're frightened. And believe it or not I felt a great sadness for you. You've got yourself into such a mess and there's no one to help you get out of it. No one, except yourself. Please stand up.'

O'Shea stood up, conscious that Weiss had moved even closer now and their feet were almost touching. Suddenly the flat of a hand crashed against the side of O'Shea's head. His knees buckled but the guards were quick and they caught him before he fell.

'My friend.' Weiss stepped back and stretched his shoulders. 'My foolish, foolish friend. You will never know the trouble you caused me. The agony, the frustration you have brought down upon me.'

He sucked hard on the cigarette. Then he gripped it in his teeth and slapped his hands together. O'Shea cringed.

'The man that was shot yesterday, did you see him?' Weiss blew the words out with the cigarette smoke.

O'Shea considered his answer carefully. 'Yes.'

'Did you not recognise him?'

'No. I don't think so.'

'You should have. His name was Pendry. He was a doctor. He was in charge of the Cardiff Royal Infirmary, which is just down the road from here. But you know the place, don't you?'

He smiled at O'Shea's surprise. Then he tapped the side of his nose. 'It seems the Gestapo has a keen interest in you. Did you know that?'

He crept back into the shadow again. 'Or should I say, they are interested in someone of your *description*. And as you know when the Gestapo becomes interested in someone, everyone pays attention. Pendry should have known that.'

'What? Are you saying Pendry was shot because of *me*?'

'Pah! Pendry was a fool.' The disembodied voice was cold. 'He had a wonderful chance to be part of the New

Order but he chose not to be. Germany has a deep admiration for the British soldier, his reliability, his loyalty, his fighting capability. That's why Berlin was happy to incorporate certain regiments into the administration of the Reich. Pendry was an excellent doctor, but he couldn't adjust to the new disciplines. He betrayed our trust. And you played an important part in that betrayal. *You* were the patient the Gestapo was looking for, is that not so? You were in Pendry's care and you disappear off the face of the earth. How very silly. How very amateurish. What was even more ridiculous is you turned up here the same evening wearing his coat.'

'But the children ...'

'What *about* the children?' Weiss snapped. 'If you find a bad piece on an apple, do you not cut it out? If that bad piece is gone too deep do you not throw it all away so it won't contaminate the rest of the apples? Berlin does not like bad apples!'

Again a circle of smoke puffed out from the shadows.

'Anyway, that is not why you are here. Now I could send you straight to Gestapo Headquarters if that is what you wish. But I ask, do you really want to subject yourself to such torment? I believe you would rather spare yourself all that pain and worry. So give me a reason not to send you there. Tell me about the boxes.'

'But I told you already. I don't *know* about any boxes.'

'For God's sake, why are you being so difficult? You shouldn't even be here in the middle of a war that is no concern of yours. You're not even British. In fact you probably dislike the British, and with good reason. You could be rid of all this right now if you just co-operate with me. I can give you freedom, anything you want.

Money to get you home to Ireland. So why let yourself be treated like a dog? Why allow yourself to be subjected to the most appalling torture when you could walk out of here right now a free man?'

He waited for an answer.

'But I don't know about any boxes,' O'Shea groaned after a long tense moment. 'Honest to God. If I knew I'd tell you. But I don't.'

Weiss shot out of the shadow and O'Shea fell back down on the chair.

'What we are interested in are four small leather cases about the size of large shoe boxes. And they are priceless. They contain the result of years of research by some of the greatest minds in England. Men of vision who discovered a way to create a power so awesome the whole world will sit up and take notice.'

He leant down and studied O'Shea's reaction. 'They were found in a secret laboratory in the Welsh mountains. Disguised as an ordinary little factory, of course. Called Obren Industries. Obviously we knew of its existence for years. But it still took us weeks to decipher all the work that went on there.'

He stood up to his full height again and gave a last suck at the cigarette before dropping it on the floor and crushing it with his boot. 'And what we eventually uncovered was so astonishing it had to be shipped to Berlin immediately.'

He looked down at the floor as if he was trying to find the right words. Then he snapped his fingers. 'But our top secret operation was not so top secret after all. The boxes were stolen. And they have not been seen since. But my instincts tell me you know something about their whereabouts.'

'But I don't ...'

Weiss rubbed his nose. 'Tell me, how long do you think you can endure the attention of the Gestapo? How much pain do you think you can stand before you tell them what they want to know about the murder of German soldiers on a farm near here?'

O'Shea couldn't answer.

'Look at yourself.' Weiss flicked his shirt. 'Look at your clothes. Rags, filthy tatters! And your hair. Look at the lice dropping off it. You are thick with dirt and smelling like a gypsy. Look how thin you are, like a bag of bones. So why go on like this, my friend? Why not just tell me where the boxes are and you can have a nice hot bath, a haircut and some fresh new clothes. You can kiss your cellmate goodbye and walk out of here a free man. What do you say?'

O'Shea's mind reeled as darts of panic flashed through his brain. 'But I never saw any boxes. I swear to you. We were ... '

'We?'

'Me. Just me. All right, I *was* there when your trucks were attacked. But it was nothing to do with me. I just happened to be passing by and I tried to keep my head down. But I did see that big fella Gareth looking for something. That's all I can tell you. Honest to God, I don't know *what* he was looking for. In fact I thought he was going to kill me when he discovered me hiding in the bushes.'

Weiss gave a yelp. 'I know all that!' He ran forward and raised his hand, and his eyes were blazing in anger. But he dropped it again. 'You're not telling me anything I don't know already. The other German officer, what happened to him?'

'I don't know. I never saw him after that.'

'Let me tell you something, young man. I am a captain in the German Security Forces. I have been a captain for a number of years, and I was due to be promoted to major and given a staff position back home in Berlin. It was a job I was very much looking forward to, being with my family, being home. My last assignment before I was to leave England was to arrange the safe transportation of four little boxes from Brecon in Wales to Berlin in Germany. A simple, routine assignment. However, as it was also top secret I handpicked my own people. People I trusted and with whom I had worked before. Berlin was waiting in anticipation. If this research proved to be correct it would be a major breakthrough in the world of armament. And the Third Reich would indeed endure for a thousand years. My name was on the lips of the Fuehrer himself.'

He took out a packet of cigarettes, pulled one out with his teeth then shoved the packet back in his pocket. He took his time lighting it before flicking the match at O'Shea. O'Shea dodged it, but not the long stream of smoke that followed.

'But someone discovered the plan and unbelievable as it sounds they stole the boxes. And yes, my name was still on the lips of the Fuehrer but for all the wrong reasons now. This time it was concerning a posting to the more exotic location of the Russian north. That is if I should live that long. So you understand my impatience, don't you? I need to find those boxes. And I need to find them very quickly. You, my little Irish friend, are going to tell me where they are.'

'But if I don't know ...'

The blow knocked O'Shea off the chair and he yelped as he hit the floor. Weiss stepped back and spoke to the guards and they stood back by the door. Then he stooped down and pressed a finger under O'Shea's chin.

'Where are the boxes?'

'Honestly, sir, I just don't know.'

The finger pressed harder. 'Where are the boxes?'

O'Shea turned his head and tried to pull away. 'I told you. I don't know.'

The side of the hand cut across his throat and he doubled up with a muted cry.

'Please do not lie to me.' Weiss was using his soft voice again. Then a boot collided with O'Shea's chest and turned him onto his back. And Weiss bent down and held the tip of the cigarette inches from his eyes.

'The lady who died on that farm, my sources tell me you were fond of her sister. I'm told you would be upset if anything unpleasant was to happen to her.'

He waited for a response. And he gave a wide smile when O'Shea gave a shocked gulp.

'Very good.' He spoke to the guard and nodded at the reply before turning back at O'Shea. 'Just a few miles from here there's an old building. A disused mansion, I believe. Your friend has already been taken there.'

He disappeared into the shadows and emerged holding a phone which he shoved at O'Shea. 'This is connected to that building. So now you must tell me where the boxes are or my men will proceed to amuse themselves with her. And I promise you they are not as gentle as I am. They can extract the maximum amount of pain with the minimum amount of damage. So please, spare her from such a fate since she is just an innocent like you. All you have to do is tell me where the boxes are and I will pick up the phone and she will be free to walk away.'

Now O'Shea was confused. This had to be some kind of trick. He was positive Cerys played a part in what happened at the farm - that she and Clooney were somehow involved. They were so obvious the way they held back at the gate while insisting the others went on ahead. They must have known soldiers were waiting in the trees. Why else was Clooney wearing that ridiculous white scarf? They looked prepared for what was going to happen. They *knew* it was coming yet they didn't warn anyone. No, they *had* to be part of it.

So why was Weiss pretending Cerys was about to be tortured unless O'Shea revealed where the boxes were? It *had* to be a bluff.

But what if he was wrong? What if Cerys *wasn't* involved with Weiss? What if it was just a misunderstanding, a romantic liaison with Clooney she didn't want broadcast to the world? She could have been totally innocent and got captured later.

His heart sank. If they found Cerys, did it mean they'd found Adam and Rhianne too?

If the Germans *did* find Adam he certainly wouldn't be alive anymore.

The thought of it made O'Shea feel sick. He'd lost the game. He knew nothing about the boxes but he was going to end up dead because of them. His hope was it would be quick. Maybe if he could provoke Weiss he would end it right now. Make him really mad. Make him react and lash out, and kill O'Shea right there and then.

'So if I told you what you wanted to know, what would happen then?' O'Shea had no strategy, no plan. He was just trying to crank up the tension.

'You would both be free to go.' Weiss smiled but there was something cold and deadly about the way he said it.

'You feckin maggot. Do you really think I believe that?'

'I do not care *what* you believe. You don't actually have a choice. Either you tell me where the boxes are or you will be forced to watch a beautiful young lady being horribly mutilated. Remember these men are professional. They have destroyed people who have been trained to resist interrogation and who have had a wealth of experience to call upon. Your lady friend could last for days, all the time pleading, begging for the end, begging to be released from all of this. Begging *you*, remember. Because you alone have the key. But I'm sure it will not go that far.'

Again he smiled and O'Shea cringed. The fear inside him had morphed into a sort of morbid resignation and it manifested as an angry scowl. Weiss saw it and his smile dropped.

'Well?' he tapped the watch on his wrist. 'Your time is running out. You now have only to the count of five. One, two, three ...'

O'Shea hurled himself at Weiss and grabbed for his throat. But Weiss sidestepped out of the way. A guard spun O'Shea around and dropped him back down on to the chair.

'Nice try,' Weiss laughed.

'Go to hell, you mad German bastard!'

'Hell?' Weiss pursed his lips. 'Hell is just a figment of your imagination. There is no such place. But the word *might* be used to describe something of the utmost horror, a pain that robs you of all sense of dignity and self-respect, a pain that leaves you broken and empty, mindless and pitiful. If that word is appropriate to the world you are about to enter, dear boy, then it is *you* who is going to hell.'

He gave the guards a nod and they grabbed O'Shea, and they dragged him down the stairs and out through a small door to a car parked discreetly in the shadows well away from the front doors of the prison. They threw him into the back seat, then got in on either side of him. And the car crept out through the gate and down the wet streets of Cardiff.

Chapter Forty

When they were a reasonable distance from the prison they picked up speed. And as they swept through the outskirts of the city the dawn was breaking with a cold light that had no colour in it at all.

O'Shea was panicking. What was going to happen to him when they reached the derelict building? He feared the pain Weiss had promised. He felt desolate, wearied by the thought that if the Germans had found Cerys then Adam and Rhianne had probably been found too. So there was no reason to go on living anymore.

He wished he could just end it all right here.

He took a sideways glance at the guards. They were both young and fit and their faces hadn't yet acquired the hardness that comes with the horror of war. They gazed out of the windows at the blur of trees that sped past. They were not the least bit concerned about their prisoner. They obviously didn't consider him a threat.

The one on the left frowned when he realised O'Shea was looking at him. He tried to look hard but it didn't work. He was too young.

The driver was a little man at least sixty years old. A clump of grey hair stuck out from under his hat and his thin bony hands shook whenever he took them off the steering wheel. He glanced at O'Shea in the mirror, but he didn't seem too concerned either. He was just the driver. He didn't care.

What would they do if O'Shea tried to escape? They'd have no choice but to shoot him.

So how could he make this work? A blow with his elbow to the face of the soldier on his right then grab the door handle? Baby Face wouldn't be expecting it. A quick kick and he'd be out on the road with O'Shea inches behind.

Then he'd brace himself. He'd probably run. It would be human nature to run. Then it would be finished. All over.

He closed his eyes and took a slow breath, tensed his body and braced his arm for the first blow. But the car slowed down and turned into a road that was thick with trees.

It made a left into the driveway of a large derelict house and crunched to a halt beside another car almost hidden at the bottom of the overgrown garden.

O'Shea was dragged out of the car, pushed through a side door and down a long corridor strewn with rubbish. A huge door at the end led into a dark-panelled drawing room.

A robed figure with a ferocious face glared down at them from a giant portrait above the enormous fireplace. Heavy stained curtains hung loosely around the windows and a naked light bulb dangled from the ceiling on a single strand of flex. Furniture was piled in one corner and rubbish littered the rest of the floor.

A girl sat in the middle of the room. As O'Shea and the guards came in she turned her head and her ash blond hair moved in a wave around her shoulders. But she couldn't move her body because her hands were strapped to the arms of the heavy wooden chair. Her hair was matted with dirt and her face was swollen. Her bruised eyes were almost closed.

And she was wearing the same baggy jumper and the same big boots she had on the last time O'Shea saw her - at the farm waiting for Clooney to arrive.

O'Shea froze with the shock and the soldiers bumped into him. Baby Face stiffened when he noticed her too and he looked startled. The other soldier gave a snort and his face folded in a mask of anticipation.

The two men standing behind the chair scowled at the new arrivals.

'You're late.' The man on her left slapped a cane against the leather boot of his black uniform and bounced up and down on his toes. 'We have been here for hours waiting for you.'

He waved O'Shea to a chair opposite Cerys and told the soldiers to go and guard the door.

As O'Shea sat down he couldn't take his eyes off Cerys. She struggled to focus on him. And when she did she shook her head.

The man in black slapped her then marched over to O'Shea and clamped his hands to the arms of the chair with rusty iron shackles.

'Now,' he tapped the shackles with his cane. 'You will be aware of what is happening here. Unless you are a fool, of course. But I will explain anyway since all you English *are* fools.'

'But I'm not English,' O'Shea said weakly.

The spit hit him in the face and he yelped in surprise.

'Fool,' the man in black shouted. 'You are a fool. Now, you are here for one reason and one reason only. To tell us the whereabouts of certain boxes. We have been given our orders. And we are to extract this information from you by whatever means we think fit. Do you understand me?'

He nodded to the man in plain clothes who picked up a long thin needle from a small table by the fireplace.

'What is in those boxes, we do not know,' the man in black continued. 'What we do know is Berlin wants them. And they do not care how they get them. So they do not care if the girl has to die to make you tell us where they are. Of course we will endeavour to keep her alive for as long as possible, you understand? Although I am sure she'll wish she was dead long before that.'

The other man walked behind Cerys with the needle. She wriggled frantically and tried to watch him with eyes full of panic. And when O'Shea turned away a hand smashed into his face.

'You will look,' the man in black screamed. 'You will watch every moment of what you are causing. All this is because of you.'

The man in plain clothes lunged with the needle and Cerys jumped. And her mouth opened a second before the scream came.

Chapter Forty-One

'Open your eyes!' A fist slammed into O'Shea's face one more time but it was too numb now to make any difference. He felt the pressure that made his head jerk back. But there was no more pain there. Just a strange dull sensation.

But there *was* a lot of pain from his wrists. The skin was rubbed raw by the shackles as he struggled to distract himself from the horrendous screams that came from Cerys every time the man in black administered his own brand of persuasion.

She was unconscious now, slumped in the chair with her head on her knees. Blood glistened where lumps of her hair was torn out.

The men from the Gestapo considered her for a few minutes. The one in black had taken off his jacket and his shirt was spattered with blood. His eyes were red and totally mad.

He gave O'Shea another slap and pushed his head back. 'You must not look away.'

Then he danced back to Cerys and woke her with a shock by throwing a cup of cold water in her face. Both of them sniggered as she spluttered back to awareness. Her head came up and her eyes opened, and she looked around for a moment before the reality of what was happening hit her. Terror flooded her face.

O'Shea's throat was raw from pleading with them to listen to him. How many times did he have to tell them? He knew nothing about any bloody boxes! Bethan said nothing about boxes. Why couldn't they see he was telling the truth?

Surely to God he would have told them by now if he did? No one in their right mind could watch someone being brutalised like this and not concede. O'Shea would have told them long before it ever got to this stage.

Several times he was tempted to make something up. Tell them a pack of lies, *anything*, to get them to stop. But he knew it would never work. They weren't stupid. They'd keep him here while they checked it out. And then they'd come back with a vengeance and make things worse. If that was possible. They would actually relish prolonging the final agony.

The man in plain clothes took a bone-handled dagger from a sheath on his belt, leant over Cerys from behind and slid it down the front of her jumper.

She whimpered, making pitiful animal noises as she tried to pull away. He grabbed her hair and sliced through her clothes in vicious cutting movements until they were ripped open down to her waist.

He put the dagger back in the sheath, took a bunch of keys from his pocket and undid the shackles one at a time. Then he pulled the sleeve off each arm and snapped the shackles back on her wrists again. Next he pulled the belt off her trousers and tugged them down roughly, taking her boots off with them in one swift movement. Then he picked up all the clothes and threw them into the fireplace.

His tongue darted in and out of his mouth like a snake's as he drew the dagger again, and he gave the tip a dramatic flick as he walked behind Cerys. He leant over her, lifted one of her breasts and draw the blunt side of the knife slowly across it.

'So ripe.' He looked across at O'Shea. 'Ripe and firm, perfect for harvesting.'

Both the Gestapo men laughed. Then the man in plain clothes flew across the room slashing the air with the dagger. He stopped with the point of it an inch from O'Shea's face.

'Do you know what time it is?' His foul breath wafted across O'Shea's face.

'Do I know *what* ...?' O'Shea tried to pull away from the sliver of polished metal that was almost touching his eyeball.

'It's lunch time.' He gave a strange high-pitched snort. 'Time for lunch. And since we're in Britain we will be typically British and take a whole civilised hour. What do you think, old chap? Marvellous, what?'

He put the dagger back into the sheath and wiped his face with a dirty handkerchief. Then he kicked O'Shea on the shin.

'Ponder this, English. What you have seen today, the patient will recovery from. In a few weeks or so, of course. There will be no permanent damage. Even her face will heal and she will once again be a beautiful young woman.'

He licked his lips again. 'However, when we return from lunch we will be forced to use a different kind of persuasion altogether. This is something from which the patient will *not* recover.'

He patted O'Shea's face and sauntered over to where his colleague was waiting.

And as they headed for the door he gave a sudden little dance and skipped out of the way of something on the floor in front of the two guards.

Baby Face was leaning against the wall with his head bowed and his rifle held loosely between his legs. His face was a pasty grey and his eyes had a look of distress in them as he stared at the floor

The other soldier was standing to attention with his back straight and one hand smartly by his side. The other hand was holding the tip of his rifle.

His face was pale too, and he looked like he was in shock. In front of him was a large pool of vomit.

The man in black shook with disgust and his face turned purple. Both soldiers jumped when he gave an almighty roar and ran to the fireplace. He grabbed some of the clothes he'd ripped off Cerys, threw them at the soldier and ordered him to wipe it up.

The man in plain clothes was ranting too and he slapped Baby Face across the side of the head before storming out into the garden. He was followed closely by the man in black.

The soldiers looked sheepish as they picked up the clothes and started to clean up the mess. But they didn't speak.

Cerys had fainted again. O'Shea cried silently at the mess she was in. Her beautiful face was contorted in pain and her naked body was punctured all over and streaked with blood. And he was powerless to help her.

Through the broken window he could see the Gestapo men leaning against the car eating sandwiches. They washed them down with wine swigged straight from the bottle. Their callousness made O'Shea sick and his stomach heaved, but there was nothing left to bring up.

The man in black was stuffing the last crust of bread into his mouth as he came back into the room. The other man followed and he looked at O'Shea with cold dead eyes as he wiped his mouth on his sleeve.

'I hope you gave our little problem some thought while we were out to lunch,' he mocked. 'I hope you reflected on the consequences of your next answer.'

O'Shea's legs shook uncontrollably and he grated his torn hands against the shackles to block his mind from what was about to happen. *Just get on with it*; he wanted to scream. *Do your worst. Just get on with it!*

'Tell me,' the man in black grinned as he picked up a scalpel. 'Where are the boxes?'

Now O'Shea's whole body was trembling. What in God's name was he supposed to say? He didn't know about any boxes.

But the moment he shook his head the man in black ran at Cerys and drew the edge of the scalpel around her breast. It took a second for Cerys to realise what happened. She looked down in disbelief. Then she gave a howl that immediately turned into a demented wail.

'Well?' the man in plain clothes was barely able to conceal the mirth in his voice as he snapped at O'Shea again.

O'Shea sobbed and shook his head again. It was the only answer he could give. And the man in black slashed with the scalpel one more time.

O'Shea's head swam and fell down onto his chest. The man in plain clothes was in front of him in an instant and he lifted O'Shea's head back up by jamming his finger under his chin.

'Open your eyes.' His voice was eerily soft. 'Do you remember what I told you this morning? How we can keep someone alive for twenty minutes after they are disembowelled? Believe me, we can make this last a lot longer than twenty minutes. So please, tell me the truth.'

The man in black was a lot more enthusiastic with his next cut and Cerys howled in agony.

And the soldier by the door gave a loud choking heave. Then he vomited so hard it reached the Gestapo men as it spattered across the floor.

Both men jumped out of the way with a torrent of curses, and the man in plain clothes went red with anger. He flew at the soldier and hit him repeatedly in the face, knocking him back against the wall. Then he wiped his face with his sleeve and rushed back to Cerys.

And for the benefit of the soldier who was now struggling back onto his feet, the man in black did another cut. Only this time it was slower and more exaggerated.

The soldier cringed as he watched the attack with wet, embarrassed eyes. He wiped the trickle of blood from the corner of his mouth as he bent down to pick up his rifle.

Cerys was silent now. Shock had made her mute. Only the contortion of her face showed the ferocity of the pain she was feeling.

The soldier sucked at his bruised lips and looked down at the rifle in his hands. And when he pulled back the bolt the click it made was unbelievably loud in the big bare room.

The man in black spun around with an angry growl. And he froze when saw the look in the soldier's eyes that transformed his face into a dark and dangerous scowl. His hands went up instinctively as the soldier lifted the rifle and pointed it at him. The flash came a split second before the crack and the man in black flew backwards, collided with Cerys and knocked the chair over.

As the man in black hit the floor his colleague moved with the speed of a cat. He pulled a Luger from his belt and fired as he dropped on his belly. Three shots caught the soldier in the chest and he bounced off the wall before crashing to the floor.

Baby Face gave a panicked cry and his eyes flickered in confusion. It all happened too fast. The noise of the gunshots buzzed in his ears. All he could see was the Gestapo man on the floor with a gun in his hand and his friend wriggling in a pool of blood at his feet. Instinctively he whipped up his rifle and pointed it aimlessly into the room. The Gestapo man fired off another shot, sprang to his feet and threw himself behind the fallen chair.

The bullet hit the doorframe above the soldier's head and he ducked. He couldn't understand what was happening. He could see one prisoner still strapped to the chair in the middle of the floor. The other chair was on its side but that prisoner was also secured. The man in the black uniform was on his back with his arms spread wide. And his partner was crouched behind the upturned chair as if he was hiding from something. So who fired the shots? Who killed his pal?

He was still waving the rifle all over the place when the Gestapo man jumped up and made a dash for the window.

He fired twice over his shoulder as he scurried away and the soldier fired back. The shot tore a lump out of the Gestapo man's back and slammed him into the wall. But he managed to stay on his feet and fire his gun one more time, and Baby Face disappeared back through the open door.

The Gestapo man gave a demonic chuckle as he looked down at the gaping wound in his chest. His eyes blazed with a strange fury as he pushed himself away from the wall and stood up straight. There was a large spatter of blood around a chip in the plaster behind him. He staggered back into the room and when he noticed O'Shea his eyes rolled as they tried to focus on him. When they did he gave a loud splutter and steadied himself by spreading his legs wide apart. Then he raised his arm, aimed the gun at O'Shea's head and pulled the trigger.

The response was a dull click. He looked down at the gun and sighed. Then he gave a resigned shrug and fell on his face.

Chapter Forty-Two

An oppressive silence came down on the old house. The quietness was so intense it buzzed in O'Shea's ears. He couldn't grasp what had happened. A minute ago his eyes were clouded with tears of frustration at the terrible butchery being inflicted on Cerys.

Then everything changed in a heartbeat. A rifle shot, and the man in black was sprawled on the ground. From the angle of his head it was obvious he wasn't getting back up. Cerys was strapped to the upturned chair and from the look on her face she wasn't getting back up either.

Then more shots and the second man was staggering towards O'Shea waving a gun in his face seconds before he dropped dead too.

And both of the guards were down. Now O'Shea was the only one left. But he was chained to a heavy chair and the keys for the shackles were in the pocket of a dead man well out of his reach. At this rate it wouldn't be long before O'Shea joined them.

Then he heard what sounded like a moan from outside the door. He craned his neck and caught a glimpse of Baby Face struggling to his knees, his body quivering with the effort and sweat pouring down his face.

But it was all too much. He flopped back onto the floor with a whimper. O'Shea let his head drop down on his chest. The beat of his heart tapped in his ears.

A loud crash snapped him awake again. Baby Face was on his feet and hanging onto the wall with one hand. His other hand clutched his groin and blood dripped from between his fingers.

There was a look of shock on his face. His mouth quivered and his eyes rolled back in his head. Then his knees buckled and he sagged against the doorframe and slid back down on the floor.

But he had incredible determination. Despite the pain he rolled back on to his knees.

'Come on!' O'Shea shouted at him. 'Don't give up. Get me out of this chair and I'll can help you. You can do it. *Come on.*'

Then O'Shea remembered this was a German soldier and he probably didn't speak a word of English. But their predicament was the same in any language. Baby Face would know his life depended on setting O'Shea free. So when he began to crawl across the floor leaving behind a trail of blood O'Shea let out another yell of encouragement.

It took an agonisingly long time to reach the chair, and when he grabbed O'Shea's hands to lift himself up the shackles grated against bare bone.

'No!' O'Shea screamed. 'My hands! *Please*, let go! *My hands* ...'

Baby Face grabbed at his clothes instead and it caused a tsunami of pain so severe a cloak of darkness hit O'Shea as if someone had switched off a light.

When his head cleared again he was relieved to find the dead weight had gone from him.

A movement out of the corner of his eye made him look around. Baby Face was pulling at the body of the Gestapo man.

'Which one of them's got the bleedin' keys?' Baby Face muttered as he rummaged through the pockets. He pulled out all sorts of bits and pieces and flung them away. Then he flashed a weak grin, sagged back on his heels and waved a bunch of keys at O'Shea.

But as he turned back to O'Shea his smile died in a spluttering cough. He spat out a mouthful of blood and his head hit the floor.

And he stayed like that long enough for O'Shea to start panicking again. All hope had vanished like fog in the morning sun.

But a few minutes later Baby Face gave another gurgling cough, wiped his mouth with his sleeve and started crawling over to O'Shea again. The keys jangle along the ground behind him.

O'Shea was laughing and crying at the same time as he yelled encouragement. Then he howled with pain when Baby Face grabbed at him again. The soldier's hands shook as he struggled to find the right key. And it took six excruciating attempts to get it into the lock of the shackle.

O'Shea could feel what little strength he had left pouring out of him and he had to grit his teeth to stop himself from fainting. When the shackle dropped from his hand he pushed Baby Face away in sheer desperation. Baby Face flew backwards with a surprised curse.

Tears smarted O'Shea's eyes as he coaxed the key out of the lock with his lifeless fingers. When it eventually popped out he undid the second shackle in a mad flurry of movement. Before the pain overwhelmed him he tumbled out of the chair and landed on top of Baby Face.

Baby Face groaned as O'Shea rolled away and lay flat on his back. And he drifted into a blissful state of unconsciousness.

Chapter Forty-Three

Bitter cold rain blew in the broken window and sprayed over O'Shea. As he pulled his coat tighter around him the pain from his wrists screamed and he snapped awake.

It didn't take him long to remember where he was. He rolled onto his knees and shuffled to his feet, holding his injured hands against his chest.

The Gestapo man's thick leather overcoat was still on the chair. O'Shea eased his battered hands through the sleeves as he swapped it for the dirty old one he was wearing. There was something heavy in the pocket and when O'Shea checked he found a small handgun and two clips of ammunition. He left them there.

His hands were too sore to undo the shackles that held Cerys to the chair, so he left her where she was and covered her with the jacket of the man in black. He wanted to clean her up, wash her face, but he felt it would be much more dignified to just leave her alone.

Baby Face groaned when O'Shea slipped the length of rope under his arms and around his chest. Then O'Shea wrapped the rope around his own shoulder and a pool of blood splashed from the soldier's lap as O'Shea dragged him out the door and along the hallway.

The day was fading quickly now and dark clouds rolled in over the horizon. O'Shea gave one more determined heave and hauled Baby Face down the grass bank and over to the car. He propped the injured soldier against the door then went around to the driver's side. One of the keys on the bunch Baby Face took from the Gestapo fitted the ignition. O'Shea turned it and the engine purred into life.

O'Shea shuffled back around Baby Face and opened the door, but when O'Shea tried to lift him into the seat Baby Face pushed him away.

'It's no good, mate. I'm finished. You see to yourself.'

O'Shea let go of his arm. 'Your accent. You're not German …'

'No.' Baby Face gave a slight shake of his head. 'North of England. Cumbrian Penal Corp. It was either this or sixteen years for armed robbery. This looked like the best option at the time.'

He tried to laugh but convulsed instead with a fit of coughing.

'Look,' O'Shea grabbed his arm again. 'You're in a pretty bad way. I can help you but first I have to get you out of this cold. So come on. Give me a hand.'

'It's too late for all that shit.' Baby Face pushed him away again and looked at O'Shea with red eyes in a ghostly white face. 'But you can do something for me.'

He rummaged in his jacket pocket and pulled out a wallet, flipped it open and shoved it at O'Shea to look at the picture of a pretty young girl.

'She lives in Whitehaven. That girl in there reminded me of her. That's why I was so upset. So if you make it will you do me a favour? Do you think you could …' Tears filled his eyes and dropped onto his cheeks. 'Just tell her I love her, will you? Please tell her …'

He rubbed his face and his hands jerked with sobs that came out loud and pitiful. O'Shea sat back on his heels and thought of Heather. He knew how this girl was going to feel tomorrow when someone called to give her the dreadful news.

Dark September

A gust of wind brought a flurry of snow and it stayed on his hair for the briefest of moments before magically disappearing again.

Chapter Forty-Four

The pain from his wrists had dulled into a sort of numbness now and O'Shea could just about tolerate it as he drove through the night. The snow came down thick and fast, fat flakes settling and covering the landscape in a blinding white carpet. It was impossible to see where the edge of the road touched the grass verge. Or where the ditch began on the other side.

O'Shea was struggling to stay awake. The glare of the headlights on the snow burnt his eyes. When he blinked he thought he'd never open them again.

Every bit of his body ached and he was close to collapse. But, amazingly, he was still alive. He'd been so near to death again and yet he'd survived by the skin of his teeth. He'd gotten away with just a few bruises and a couple of battered wrists. Maybe Sullivan was right. Maybe there *was* someone up there looking out for you.

So O'Shea said his own prayer of thanks as he drove like a lunatic to get as far away from Cardiff as he possibly could.

He had to leave Baby Face behind, still holding the photo of the pretty girl in his lifeless hands. O'Shea took some money from his wallet and the food the Gestapo had left in the house.

A map of Wales in the glove compartment of the car had a lot of scribbling on it, including a cluster of notes written in German. The town of Caerphilly was circled in red and the word Weiss had a question mark beside it. O'Shea presumed the circle marked the location of the house they were in so he took directions from that. He found Ebbw Vale and marked the road down as far as

Abertillery. If he could get that far he'd have a good chance of finding Bethan's farm.

Of course he was clutching at a very elusive straw. He knew that. But if he was ever going to find Adam again he'd have to start in the obvious places first. There was a tiny chance Adam hadn't been found, that he was still at the farm waiting for someone to come back and tell him what to do.

When O'Shea got to Ebbw Vale it was as silent as a Trappist monk's cell. Thick snow lay in one long sheet down the whole length of the town. And it was completely undisturbed. Not a single soul had ventured out in it. They had more sense. Their warm cosy shadows danced and flickered from behind curtains as O'Shea cruised quietly along the main street.

It took him down a steep hill and around the enormous steelworks that was belching smoke and steam. Then it swung back up another steep hill and along the lonely road to Cwm.

By now the glare of the snow merged everything into one big blob and all the roads looked the same. And O'Shea couldn't decide whether to turn left or right at a four way junction.

He took a chance and went straight across. Now he had no idea which way he was heading. He could be on the road back to Cardiff for all he knew.

He could see nothing, hear nothing, just the purr of the engine and the thump of the wind as it buffeted the car. He had no choice but to keep going straight on. He couldn't risk turning back in case someone had noticed his tracks and were curious.

When the road suddenly dropped away to his left he instinctively slammed his foot on the brake and the car shuddered as it tried to get a grip on the road. But it was too heavy and the snow was too thick. The back end began to spin.

The pain from his wrists was like an electric shock when he grabbed the gear-stick and wrenched it down a notch. But still the car went around in a circle and thudded sideways into a high wall. The engine stalled and there was total silence.

A mass of snow blew through the narrow beams of the headlamps and stuck all over the window now the wipers had stopped. It caused the inside of the car to slow darken and turn it into a strangely soothing cocoon.

Now he'd stopped driving and let go of the wheel O'Shea let his head rest back against the seat. Just for a moment. Just to gather himself before he carried on again. He was so very, very tired. He needed to close his eyes.

A crow squawked and its shadow fluttered past. And O'Shea jumped and opened his eyes. Snow completely covered the car, inches thick and bathing the interior in a strange ghostly light.

He strained to hear if there was any activity outside before he wound down the window and flicked off a sheet of fluffy snow that was left behind.

A perfectly clear sky created a premature dawn and it shimmered on the layer of pure white that covered everything in sight. Clumps of snow topped the evergreen bushes on either side of the avenue and the weight of it bent the smaller branches. Birds were making tracks that led nowhere.

A crisp breeze blew away the stuffiness from inside the car. O'Shea shivered and rubbed his hands together. They were so cold he thought they might be frostbitten. He couldn't feel his fingers at all. When he pumped them to get the circulation going the scabs on his wrists cracked. Warm blood mixed with puss seeped out of them.

He knew he couldn't sit there for long. He was too exposed. This looked like a main road and someone could wander by at any moment. It was time to move on.

He needed to look around the car first to see what damage was done in the collision. He braced himself, whipped the door open and jumped out. Apart from a few dents there didn't appear to be anything to cause concern so he dived back in and turned the key in the ignition.

The engine coughed once and kicked into life. O'Shea flipped on the wipers and scooped a wedge of snow off the windscreen. Then he put it into gear and eased it away from the wall. The car bounced back onto the road and moved slowly around the bend in the street. And he slammed on the brakes again and slid six feet before stopping against the kerb.

It took a moment to grasp what he was seeing. A string of houses on either side of a road that dipped down a long severe slope and rose back up abruptly on the other side.

A shriek caught in his throat. Could this be true? Was this that odd little village they'd passed through when he and Adam were taken to Bethan's farm? Surely there wasn't another one like it in the whole world, balanced on the side of a mountain and bent like an English longbow. This was amazing. What were the chances of him ever finding it like that? And in the dark as well?

'Thank you, God.' He looked up at the sky as if he expected a response. 'Thank you, thank you, thank you!'

Then he said another thanks you to Sullivan's guardian angel.

He put his hands inside his jacket for a moment to ease the throbbing and glanced around. He was stopped in the middle of the road. But there was no sign of activity around the place. Where were all the people? Surely someone must be out and about. He had to get moving. At least he had some idea of where he was now, and where he was going.

He released the hand brake and let the clutch out gently and the snow crunched beneath the wheels as he moved forward very carefully. If he remembered correctly the turning to Bethan's farm was right at the top of the slope opposite.

His main concern was judging the speed to get back up the hill on the other side. The snow was pretty thick. If he went down too fast he'd probably lose control at the bottom and skid into one of the houses. But if he went too slowly there wouldn't be enough momentum to carry him all the way to the top on the other side.

So he held the speed at a steady twenty until he was ten yards from the bottom then put his foot to the floor. The car shot forward and splashed through the slush where the road flattened out before rising sharply again.

The sheer weight of the car carried it half way up the slope. Then the wheels started to lose their grip and the momentum began to die. The rear end slid sideways and O'Shea struggled with the wheel to keep it steady. The speed dropped to fifteen, then ten miles an hour.

After another twenty yards it was down to less than five miles an hour. And he was still thirty yards from the top. He rattled the wheel, willing the car to give it one more push. But now the needle was almost at the bottom of the dial.

A huge oak tree hanging over a wall had a patch in its shadow where the snow was so thin it was almost transparent. It was only about twelve feet away but the car was losing power fast. The back end oscillated as the tyres compounded the snow and turned it into solid glass. Then it slid slowly across the street and right into the patch. When the wheels touched solid ground they propelled the car forward with a jolt and it shot all the way up and over the top of the hill.

Chapter Forty-Five

Laughing with relief O'Shea drove on for another quarter of a mile. But he couldn't find the turn for Bethan's farm. He was sure it was closer to the top of the hill than this. It was a small turning, just wide enough for the truck, but it appeared to have completely disappeared now.

He pulled over, got out of the car and walked back to where he had a clear view down into the village. This *had* to be the right place. He could distinctly remember the way the woods swept up the enormous hill behind one row of houses, and the sheer drop behind the other row that let you look down onto a river.

Maybe his memory wasn't as precise as he thought it was. Maybe he'd misjudged the distance to the turning. It *was* months ago. And under very strange circumstances as well.

He decided to drive on another mile but by then he was certain he'd gone too far. He turned the car around and rolled back along the earlier tracks.

Then he saw it. A huge drift of snow had formed a ridge against the wall on one side of the gap making it invisible as O'Shea approached it from the village side. But from this direction it was obvious.

He raced the engine to build up enough power to plough through the snowdrift. But it was surprisingly soft and it exploded in a cloud of white spray as the car sliced through it and went sliding and spinning along the narrow lane.

A short time later O'Shea was at the final crossroads. He jumped on the brakes and the car skidded across the junction, slid another ten feet and juddering to a stop inches from the gate to Bethan's farm.

He paused for a moment to clear his head. His hands were shaking but he wasn't sure if it was from the cold or from apprehension. What was he going to find at the house? All kinds of scenarios filled his head and some of them were too horrible to dwell on.

He got out of the car and stood perfectly still listening to the sounds of the countryside. The screech of the rooks in the trees, an animal yelping in the distance. But there was nothing to cause concern so he opened the gate and leant a large stone against to stop it swinging back. Then he drove slowly up the long narrow path to the whitewashed building.

His eyes were everywhere as he cruised up to the back door of the house. There was no sign of people. The snow was crisp and untouched. Nothing had disturbed it.

He parked the car as close to the wall as he could and got out cautiously. When he lifted the latch on the scullery door it gave a dull click and swung open with a prolonged creak.

The house was bitterly cold. The kind of cold that penetrates the fabric of a building that hasn't been heated for a long time. Cobwebs on the windows were as thick as net curtains and so grey with dust you couldn't see out. There was absolutely no noise. It was as if the house was holding its breath.

If Adam was still here there was no obvious sign of him.

What did Bethan say? They were safe behind a secret panel under the stairs? Was it possible they were still using it, scurrying back there whenever they heard someone coming?

But the dust was so thick on the stone floor it was obvious nobody had walked through it recently.

Still O'Shea stooped down and gave a loud thump on the panel. 'Adam?'

His voice echoed in the quietness of the house.

'Adam, tis your dad. I'm after coming back for you, son.'

But there was no response. Perhaps they were hiding upstairs. Maybe they lived upstairs in case someone *did* turn up unexpectedly. It would give them time to get under cover.

His footsteps caused little puffs of dust to scatter over his shoes as he crept up the stairs. He looked in all the rooms but there was no sign of anyone being up there for a long time either.

Disappointment squeezed his heart and smarted his eyes. He'd been hoping against hope that his son was still here. Now that hope had evaporated in the blink of an eye.

When he turned to look out of the window his head seemed to float away from him and he had to sit on a bed. The surge of despondency brought on a dreadful weariness and he realised he was on the verge of exhaustion. He hadn't slept for days. He'd been battered and bruised and he desperately needed to lie down and rest.

But before he could do that he had to get a fire going and fix himself something to eat. So he forced himself to go back downstairs. There was a pile of logs by the fireplace and a box of matches on the mantelpiece. Using the pages from books he brought from the living room he got a fire going.

By then a dark gloom had descended on him and he didn't have the energy to shake it off. He pulled a stool up to the fire and sat staring into the flames.

His stomach rumbled. A large copper jug in the alcove was full of water so he poured some into a pot and hung it on the hook above the fire. Then he went in search of food.

He found tins of soup in one cupboard and a tin of marrow fat peas and assorted vegetables on a shelf above the sink. He emptied them into another pot and hung that over the fire too.

While he waited for the concoction to brew he poured salt into a basin and added some of the hot water from the first pot. And he soaked his sore wrists in it before wrapping them in strips he cut from a pillowcase.

The fire was well alight now and it threw waves of heat all over the kitchen. But instead of bringing comfort to O'Shea it seemed to aggravate the tightness in his weary body. Every bit of him ached. And he couldn't resist it any longer. He needed to lie down and sleep. And he needed to do it right now.

Back upstairs he checked all the rooms again and decided the bed in the front room was the most inviting. The room was bitterly cold. He needed to get a fire going in here too so he went back down to the kitchen and shuffled some of the burning logs into a bucket.

He threw some more logs into another bucket and carried them back up to the room, and he built a huge fire in the grate.

In one of the wardrobes he found a thick pair of corduroy trousers that fitted him reasonably well. They could have been Bethan's but he didn't care. He also found a cotton shirt, a woollen pullover and a pair of thick socks. It took him less than half a minute to change, and he threw the German pyjamas and slippers into the fire. He would look for some shoes later.

Pulling the leather overcoat back on he dropped onto the bed and pulled the big eiderdown over him.

The daylight was already fading when he woke up. And he was concerned to find he had a splitting headache as well as aching muscles. He recognised the symptoms immediately. He was having a relapse of the dreadful illness that landed him in hospital in Cardiff.

He tried to sit up to judge how bad it was but his head started swimming and a dry tickle in his throat became a rasping cough. He was perspiring heavily too, the prickly sweat agitating the skin on his back and neck. At the same time he felt desperately cold.

He knew he had to keep the fire going. Rolling awkwardly out of the bed he shuffled across to the fireplace and threw some more logs into it.

Then he sat on the floor as close to it as he could. But the warmth brought on an even more severe shivering and sweat trickled down his forehead in little streams.

His eyes burnt with tiredness and he shook his head to keep them open. And when the spinning started again his stomach heaved and he threw up all over the floor.

When he mustered enough strength to crawl back into bed he lay still and willed himself to sleep. Unfortunately when sleep *did* come it was fretful.

He felt strangely disconnected. He was conscious of being in bed but also detached from it. His mind was agitated, full of confusion. He saw faces and shadows all over the place, darting in and out of a dark prison cell. And cars racing recklessly through thick, heavy snow.

He tossed and turned, sat up then fell back down again. He shouted and swore, and shook his head. He couldn't make himself fully conscious. But he couldn't fall totally asleep either. It was one long and uncomfortable night.

Chapter Forty-Six

The next day dawned bright and clear. A sharp breeze fluttered the curtains as it whistled down the chimney and stirred the grey ashes in the fireplace.

O'Shea lay perfectly still. He was relieved the spinning in his head had stopped. Now he had a chance to focus his mind on what he was going to do next.

From his previous experience he knew the sickness wasn't finished yet. It was going to get a lot worse before it got any better so he needed a plan. While he still had the strength to do it he needed to gather as much food and water as he could. And also plenty of wood,

It took him over an hour to get the fire going again and heat up the rest of yesterday's stew. While it was simmering in the pot he gathered as many logs as he could find and stacked them close to the grate.

He brought up buckets of water and some more tins of food, and he put them beside the logs. By the time the sun went down he'd built a cosy little nest for himself.

But all the activity took its toll and now he desperately needed to rest again. He climbed back under the eiderdown and listened to the wind lashing at the window.

The next day his world exploded. The shaking and the coughing was so bad just lifting a piece of wood to throw on the fire was too painful. So the flames faded and he grew weaker.

Lying on his back he stared through stinging eyes at the ceiling. And he was sweating so much the eiderdown was soaked. But now the fire was dead the sweat quickly chilled and brought on a worse shivering.

Dark September

By nightfall the room was even colder. But O'Shea just didn't have the strength to get the fire going again. He groaned in desperation, knowing he would definitely die unless he had some heat. But not even the fear of a slow lingering death could squeeze another ounce of strength out of him. He could do nothing but lie there and shiver.

The darkness closed in and blocked out all sounds of life, and a desperate fear welled up inside him. He hadn't felt like this since he was a child and he was accidentally locked in the school and had to spend the night alone in the dark and ghostly quiet corridor.

Now he sensed that same terror. It bit deeper and deeper, making him hide his head under the eiderdown. And even when he got sick he couldn't bring himself to look out at the blackness.

Then he heard it. A noise somewhere deep in the house. His heart pounded. And suddenly he wasn't lying down anymore. He was walking across the room and the day was fine outside. The sun was shimmering on the green leaves of the trees.

And he wasn't afraid anymore. In fact, he felt great. He heard people talking out in the corridor but when he pulled the door open only a cold wind came in. The corridor was bare and covered in dust and cobwebs.

But he was convinced he'd heard someone talking. Maybe they were in another room. He pushed against the wind that was pinning him back as he tried to get to the next bedroom. And when he shoved it open he recoiled in astonishment.

Sullivan was sitting on the bed grinning at him.

'Sure how are *you*, Danny Boy?'

'What the feck …?' O'Shea pinched his leg. There was no feeling. This was all just a horrible dream. He laughed with the relief of it. But when he tried to turn away his feet were pinned to the spot.

'I just wanted you to know something.' Sullivan pointed a shaky finger at him. 'I know all about you. You kill people.'

'What are you talking about?' O'Shea knew he'd spoken but no words came out. His mouth was as dry as cotton wool.

'Oh, you know all right, you little shite,' Sullivan roared. 'You know all right. I only hope the devil takes your rotten soul.'

Now O'Shea was looking out of a window into a big courtyard and people were dropping like flies onto the snow. He turned back to Sullivan as the door opened behind them and Gareth walked into the room.

Rhys came in after him. They carried their shotguns in their arms and their eyes were glossy and unreal. They stared past O'Shea out of the window.

O'Shea choked on the cry. How the hell did *they* get here? They were dead. He saw them die.

No, no! He was still dreaming. He pinched himself again and again there was no pain. He told himself to wake up, it was all just a horrible dream.

But why was it so cold? In dreams you don't feel pain so how could he feel so cold? Yet his feet were numb and his fingers felt like they were wrapped in thick gloves.

Surely he wasn't awake? These people couldn't be real. He'd only come here to find Adam. All he wanted to do was find his son.

He pulled the door open and again everything was dark. A bitter wind whistled up the stairs almost blowing him off his feet. And when he turned back the room was empty.

His feet grew heavy as if he was walking through deep water.

Try another door. It opened with a creak and the wind howled in. There was no one there either.

Blood oozed out of the bandages on his wrists. Then a door slammed downstairs. Whispering? Someone was whispering.

'Sullivan!' O'Shea called his name but his eyes were so blurred he couldn't see anything.

A shaft of light came from somewhere down below, like a door opening. Had someone come in the front door? O'Shea still couldn't see.

A shadow? A small shadow! His eyes wouldn't focus properly.

Someone was coming up the stairs, footsteps soft and cautious. Hesitating? Why? Could they see O'Shea? O'Shea had to get down out of sight.

Now the figure was closer and O'Shea could see it better. Blonde hair? The light danced on it for a split second and O'Shea's heart leapt.

Heather? It was Heather!

He jumped up as she stepped silently towards him. The footsteps were light. Not like an adult.

But it had to be Heather. Her hand reached out and he took it and it was so soft and warm.

She stepped into the light and O'Shea saw her face, her beautiful brown eyes shining in her soft pale face. His knees started to crumble and he sagged down onto the floor.

Now he was being helped back into the bedroom. He shivered violently and sweat dripped down his neck. He was dropped onto the bed and the eiderdown was wrapped around him. Then the coughing started and he creased up in agony.

After a while he became aware of a fire glowing brightly. The warmth coming from it touched him like the rays of the sun. His head was lifted gently and a sweet liquid was held to his lips. Then his head was lowered again.

But why couldn't he open his eyes? He pinched himself again and this time there was a sharp pain. This time he wasn't dreaming.

A hand rested lightly on his brow. O'Shea reached up and took it and his fingers coiled around it. It was small and warm. He squeezed it. And this time he forced himself to open his eyes.

The light from the fire danced on the blond hair and sparkled in the big brown eyes. O'Shea gave a cry of astonishment.

It was Adam!

O'Shea smiled as he closed his eyes again and let the sleep of exhaustion swallow him.

Chapter Forty-Seven

A strip of sunlight came in the window but it didn't bring any warmth with it. So now the room was bitterly cold again. The fire had died down and all that was left was a few tiny embers.

O'Shea had no idea what time of day it was. The sun was low in the sky and the day was fading. But at this time of year it didn't mean anything. It could still be early afternoon.

He'd been wide awake and very uncomfortable for hours now, but he was still too sick to move.

He didn't even have the strength to lift his head off of the pillow. Whenever he tried to make himself more comfortable he'd start coughing again. Sometimes the coughing lasted for over a minute and left him sick and totally drained.

So whether he liked it or not he was forced to lie on his back and keep perfectly still. And the self-pity he was wallowing in was exaggerated by the total silence of the house.

There hadn't been a sound from the place all day. Not a creak or a groan. Even the noises nature makes and which should be filtering into the house from outside weren't there. Nothing penetrated the stillness so there was nothing to distract O'Shea. And his mind kept wandering back to the bizarre nightmare from the night before.

He still couldn't figure it out. How much of it actually happened? Did he really get out of bed and go wandering around the house? And if he'd found Adam again, where was he now? O'Shea knew his son had been in the room because he'd reached out and touched him. Adam was there, standing beside the bed. But where did he go? Why hadn't he come back to see his father?

And who was with him? O'Shea knew he hadn't dreamt *that* bit because someone lit the fire. And it certainly wasn't Adam. He just wasn't capable. So who did? And someone fed him a warm drink too. Could it have been Rhianne?

His emotions flickered from frustration to anger and they touched on all the areas in between as he tried to make sense of it all.

Of course there were bits of the dream he wanted to cling on to. The moment he thought he was with Heather again. When he felt the closeness of her body, the touch of her hand, the warmth of her breath on his face.

His heart ached to be with her and when tears stung his eyes he questioned his reason for clinging onto this wretched life. What was there left to live for? He'd gone around in a complete circle. He'd been beaten to a pulp and everyone whose life he'd touched had died on him. So what was the point of going on?

Then he remembered Adam and his emotions bounced off in the opposite direction.

And it made him realise he had to do something about this ridiculous situation. He'd been lying there for too long now. It was no good. The only way he was ever going to find Adam again was to get up and start looking for him.

He clinched his fists and forced himself to sit up. And as he swung his legs onto the floor he caught something out of the corner of his eye.

Someone was standing by the door.

'*Adam*?' The force of his voice startled him.

Adam watched his father in silence. There was no expression on his face.

'Adam.' O'Shea started laughing with relief. His boy was back again. 'Thank God you're safe, son. You'll never believe how good it is to see you.'

He beckoned for Adam to come closer. The boy didn't move.

'Where have you been? Have you been in the house all this time, you little sod? While I've been going out of my mind worrying about you? I searched this house from top to bottom, you know? I couldn't find a trace of you anywhere. Didn't you hear me scrambling around, shouting for you? It must have been a bloody good hideout, that's for sure.'

O'Shea waited for an answer. Adam didn't move.

'Look, come over here to me, son. Come here to your old da and tell me how you are, will you?'

The excitement had drained what little strength O'Shea had left and he sagged back against the headboard.

'Adam, come over here to me, will you? Come over here and say hello to your old da. What are you standing over there for? Come here and sit on the bed and tell me all about it.'

But still there was no reaction from Adam. O'Shea raised his head again and looked over at him. The boy looked back with a blank stare.

Then O'Shea recognised the vacant expression in Adam's eyes and he felt an instant squeezing of his heart.

Adam didn't even know who O'Shea was!

In the short time his father was away Adam had completely forgotten him. When he looked at O'Shea now all he saw was a stranger.

When the cough came it was sudden and intense and O'Shea doubled up on the bed gasping for air. Adam moved towards him. For a brief moment he put out his hand but he let it drop to his side instead. He wasn't sure what was happening so he stepped away again.

Once the coughing subsided and O'Shea was able to catch his breath he forced himself to sit back up and drop his legs onto the floor. And he sighed when he looked up. The boy was looking back at him through big brown eyes and he was the image of his mother.

O'Shea reached out again but Adam moved back by the door. Sweat dripped from O'Shea's eyebrows and into his eyes. And every limb in his body had turned to putty.

Somewhere downstairs a door opened and shut again and O'Shea snapped back up onto his elbows.

'Who's that, Adam?'

Adam gave the faintest shake of his head but his expression didn't change. He watched O'Shea without blinking.

'Adam, who is that? Is that your friend downstairs?' O'Shea was trying not to let the impatience sound in his voice. 'Is that Rhianne? Is Rhianne still here in the house with you?'

The boy's forehead creased and he looked like he was going to say something, but he bit his lip instead.

'C'mon, son,' O'Shea pleaded. 'Just tell me. Who else is in the house with you? Who's that downstairs?'

The room started spinning and O'Shea gave his face an angry wipe with his sleeve. 'For God's sake, son, will you stop just standing there staring at me and say something. Who else is in the bloody house? Who else is here with you?'

Adam was startled. He turned and shot out of the door. O'Shea heard him running down the landing.

'*Adam!*'

The shout nearly choked O'Shea and he started coughing again. He sagged back onto the bed and cursed out loud as he gasped in pain. When the attack eventually stopped he lay still and breathed through his nose. And he wondered how he was ever going to coax Adam to come back.

Still, at least the boy was alive. And O'Shea was grateful for that. It was the only reason he'd come back to this God-forsaken hole. Now all he had to do was get well again. And when the time was right they'd be on their way to Ireland.

He let his eyes close. And when he opened them again he was surprised it was still daylight. He felt sure he'd been asleep for ages. Then he sensed Adam standing by the door again.

'Son,' he croaked. 'You're back. Where have you been?'

'I had to see my friend.' Adam's voice was high and nervous.

'Oh?' O'Shea was relieved. Adam had spoken to him at last. 'Who's your friend, son? Is it Rhianne?'

Adam frowned. He didn't seem to know.

'I was with my friend,' he said again.

'Look, son.' O'Shea sat up and got his feet back on the floor. And he rested on the edge of the bed for a moment. 'We have to get that fire going again. Tis freezing in here and I'm very sick. I'll catch my death of cold if I don't have some heat very soon. Do you know what I'm saying?'

Adam blinked, looked at the fireplace and back at O'Shea again.

'Do you think you could ask Rhianne to come up here and light the fire for us, son?' O'Shea pleaded. 'Will you ask her? Please?'

When the boy didn't seem to understand O'Shea felt a familiar surge of impatience and he had to choke back a scream. It was the same mixture of disappointment and frustration he remembered feeling when Adam was old enough to start school and O'Shea desperately wanted him to learn to read.

He had all the books children his age were reading. And O'Shea went over them with him every day, week after week. But none of it seemed to sink in. Adam just couldn't understand any of it. He wasn't able to grasp the simplest word. O'Shea knew it wasn't the boy's fault but still it frustrated him so much he wanted to shake him until he did.

Now all these years later O'Shea was lying helpless on a bed feeling sick and sorry for himself and desperate for help. And still Adam wasn't capable of understanding what was going on around him.

'Will you look at the feckin state of me?' O'Shea cried. 'I'm like this because of *you*. All this is because of you! Don't you know how I suffered these past few months trying to get back here to find you? I was terrified out of my mind I was going to lose you? Have you any idea what…'

But he couldn't finish. All he could do was take a deep breath and remind himself none of this was Adam's fault.

He rubbed his nose on his sleeve and tried to sit back up, but Adam had already shuffled back out the door.

This time O'Shea *did* heard the murmur of voices. He strained to listen but all he could hear was a deep drone. It was definitely a man's voice.

Instinct made O'Shea reach into the pocket of the Gestapo overcoat he was still wearing. He'd been too sick and weak to bother taking it off. The gun was still there. He looked at it quickly then put it back.

Adam came back into the room and this time he went right up to the bed. 'Dada, if I light the fire will you tell me where the boxes are?'

Chapter Forty-Eight

'*What*?' O'Shea snapped up straight but his head swam violently and he dropped back down onto his elbow.

'If I light the fire will you tell me where the boxes are?' Adam's voice quivered.

O'Shea couldn't control the laugh that came out like a gunshot. 'Oh, Adam! Who put you up to this? It can't be Rhianne, that's for sure. Unless she has a very deep voice.'

Adam blinked and stepped back.

'Who's that outside the door, Adam?' O'Shea nodded towards the landing. 'Is Rhianne with someone else?'

'My friend is out by there.'

'But isn't Rhianne your friend? Is that her out there?'

Adam shook his head. 'Not Rhianne. My friend is out by there.'

'Then who the hell is your friend? And where is Rhianne?'

Adam backed away towards the door and his head shook slightly.

'Rhianne is gone,' he said. 'My friend took her away. He said she'll come back when I light the fire and you tell me where the boxes are.'

O'Shea closed his eyes and sighed. 'Adam, what are you talking about? Who's your friend and what boxes is he looking for?'

'My friend is out by there,' Adam stuttered and his eyes glistened. 'He wants you to tell me where the boxes are. If you tell me I'll light the fire and he'll bring Rhianne back.'

'Look, son, will you go and ask your friend to come in here and talk to me? Please.'

Adam looked at the door then back at his father, but he didn't move.

'For God's sake! Whoever you are, come in here and show yourself and stop pratting around.'

Adam turned and faced the door as if waiting for someone to appear. But no one came.

'Adam, son,' O'Shea waved his hand at the boy. 'I promise you as God's my witness I know nothing about any boxes. I've told the Germans a million times. I've told the Gestapo a million times. If I knew anything about the bloody boxes wouldn't I have told them a long time ago? Wouldn't I? Do you think I'd have gone through all this shite if I'd known where they were?'

Adam's eyes were wet now and O'Shea desperately wanted to hold him, comfort him, protect him from whatever evil was lurking out in the hallway.

'I promise you, son, I don't know where those boxes are. All right? Please believe me. On your mother's soul, I promise you. But I need you to help me now. Please ask your friend to come here and just light a fire and get me something to eat, will you? Please. I need your help, son.'

Adam scurried back out the door again and his footsteps clattered away off down the stairs.

O'Shea made a desperate attempt to get up and follow him. But the effort was too much and he dropped back down onto the bed. And he cried with frustration.

What the hell was going on? Who was out there on the stairs? Could it be Clooney? If it was, why didn't he just show himself instead of conducting this charade?

Anyway, how would Clooney know O'Shea was at the farm? Unless someone followed him? Was this part of some weird, elaborate plot? Was he actually *supposed* to escape from the Gestapo and come back here?

He heard the front door open down below and then slam shut again and rattle the windows.

They were leaving.

They were actually abandoning him. But worst of all they were taking Adam with them!

A wave of panic gripped O'Shea. He couldn't let them just walk away with his son. Not now. Not after he'd found him again.

He sat up but the dizziness hit him like a fist and stopped him dead. He had to wait for his head to settle before he could put his feet on the floor. Then he stood up and held onto the bedpost. He was determined to go after them. Or die trying.

The crack of a gunshot made him jump and the echo from it rippled off across the fields. There was a sharp cry and a thud. A child's cry. Then feet running away, crunching on the snow.

O'Shea staggered to the window and his head smacked off the glass as he tried to see what was happening outside.

A figure in German uniform was tugging at the door of a car parked next to the one O'Shea came in. He looked up at the window and O'Shea jerked back in shock.

It was Captain bloody Weiss!

The car door flew open and he dived in. The engine thudded into life and roared as the wheels strained to get a grip on the packed snow. Then it shot forward, clipped the gable of the whitewashed shed and slid around the corner. Then it bounced off down the long drive to the front gate.

O'Shea stumbled out onto the landing and down the stairs. The adrenaline numbed him against the pain that gripped his aching chest. A bitter wind whipped at him when he pulled open the front door.

'*Adam*?'

The word blew back in his face. He stepped outside.

Footprints in the snow disappeared around the side of the house. O'Shea staggered after them. He stopped at the corner and peered around, dreading what he might see.

Adam was sitting against the wall by the scullery door with snow settling lightly on his hair. His eyes were large and round as they looked up blankly at the cold grey sky.

A thin trickle of blood bubbled from a hole in his cheek to form a line down to the corner of his mouth.

Chapter Forty-Nine

O'Shea slid across the snow and dropped to his knees beside Adam. He brushed the snow from his face and pressed his hand against the wound to stop the flow of blood.

'Adam, for God's sake say something!' O'Shea's eyes smarted and blurred his vision. 'Speak to me, son.'

He tried to scoop the boy up in his arms but he was too limp, too heavy. So he held the cold face in his hands and tried to squeeze the life back into him.

'Adam, don't do this to me, son! Wake up. Please wake up.'

But Adam's eyes had already glazed over and they looked past his father into the distance.

'No, no, no!' O'Shea screamed. 'Just hold on. Hold on now and I'll get you back into the house.'

He ran at the scullery door and kicked it open. Then he grabbed Adam under the arms but still couldn't lift him.

He started to drag him along the ground but his feeble legs couldn't take the strain and he collapsed on top of his son.

Then all O'Shea could do was hold Adam's head to his chest and rock him in his arms. The wind was like a blast of needles. It shook the trees and blew snow in little blizzards and scattered it over them.

A pair of shoes shuffled into O'Shea's vision.

He looked up wearily. He knew he should recognise the man in the long coat. But his brain was too numb.

'What's going on?' the man asked. And then O'Shea remembered. He couldn't forget that voice.

'*Clooney*?'

Clooney stepped back in surprise and studied O'Shea's face.

'Look what they've done, Clooney,' O'Shea sobbed. 'They've killed my son. They just shot him. They shot him like a dog and they drove off and left him to die out here in the snow.'

'Who did?' Clooney stooped down beside them.

'Weiss! Captain bloody Weiss! You *know* that German piece of shite. Well he wanted something I couldn't give him so he took my boy's life instead, the mean spiteful bastard.'

Clooney looked closer at O'Shea, then down at the child on the ground. 'Who are you?'

'What do you mean *who am I*, you stupid prat?' O'Shea had to suck back a cough.

Clooney studied O'Shea again and suddenly his eyes registered the face and he stood up straight.

'Holy shit!' He was obviously surprised. But there was something else too. *Anger*? He certainly wasn't delighted about it. 'How the hell did you get here? You should have been ... what happened to you?'

'So you do know me, then?'

'Yes.' Clooney struggled for words. 'It's just ... well, your *face* ... it's all black and blue. It's hard to tell *who* you are.'

'Weiss did that as well.' O'Shea was shivering violently now as he held Adam tightly. The cold from the boy's face stung his own.

O'Shea sensed someone else standing beside Clooney but he couldn't be bothered to look up. He was too distressed to care anymore.

Clooney muttered something out of the side of his mouth and O'Shea heard a shocked gasp. And this time he did glance up. And even though she was wrapped in a big coat with a scarf around her neck O'Shea could see her face was flushed and her eyes were annoyed.

'How the hell did he get here? Did you know about this?' Her tone was sharp and Clooney put his hand out to her.

'All right, Cerys. Just shut up. We'll sort it later.'

It took a moment for the name to filter through the chaos of O'Shea's mind. And when it did he looked up at her in astonishment. 'What did he call you?'

She shook her head and looked away, pretending not to hear.

'He called you *Cerys*?' Disbelief modulated O'Shea's voice so it came out as a hoarse shout. 'You lying shit. How the hell can you be Cerys?'

'What *are* you talking about? Of course I'm bloody Cerys.'

'You're lying! Why are you saying that?' O'Shea held Adam tighter. 'What's going on here? How can you be Cerys? I saw Cerys die! I was there. I saw what happened to her. So what kind of sick game are you playing here?'

Cerys rushed towards him but Clooney put out his hand again. 'Stop it! Both of you. Now I don't know what you're thinking, Danny. But she *is* Cerys. I promise you.'

O'Shea's chest heaved as the sobs came again. He closed his eyes and rested his head on Adam's shoulder. Everything had merged into a blur of confusion once more.

This was so unreal. He was sitting in the snow holding the body of his son in his arms and now someone he'd seen die before his very eyes was standing right in front of him. *Talking* to him. He just couldn't think straight anymore. He started rocking Adam again.

'What happened to him?' he heard Cerys ask.

'Weiss shot him,' Clooney told her. There was silence for a moment.

'Why?'

O'Shea shrugged. 'I don't know. I don't know anything anymore. I don't know what he was doing here. I don't know how he found me. I don't know what he was looking for. I don't know why he shot Adam. And I don't even know what he was doing with Adam in the first place.'

Clooney took his glove off, grabbed Adam's wrist and searched for a pulse.

'Don't touch him!' O'Shea tried to slap the hand away. 'Don't touch my son, you miserable shite.'

Clooney pushed O'Shea back with his free hand.

'He's still got a heartbeat,' he shouted to Cerys. 'I can feel it. Come on. Let's get him into the house. Quickly now.'

'What?' Cerys hesitated. 'But he's so ... look at his eyes.'

'Shock.' Clooney tried to prise O'Shea's arms from around the child. 'We have to get him out of this cold.'

'Don't touch him.' O'Shea held the boy tighter. 'I'll do it myself. I'll carry him myself.'

O'Shea gave one desperate heave, lifted Adam into his arms and shuffled to his feet. But as he turned towards the door his whole world went into a mad spin. And a deep and total blackness crashed down around him.

Chapter Fifty

When O'Shea came down stairs Cerys was sitting in a rocking chair in front of a blazing log fire. She glanced up and the light made the rings around her eyes look even darker.

She pulled her cardigan tighter around her shoulders, turned back to the fire and ignored him completely.

Adam was at the table doodling on a slate with a piece of chalk. The bruising on his face was almost gone now. There was just an inch long scar on his cheekbone below his eye.

According to Clooney it was the cheekbone that saved his life. He thought the bullet hit the wall before it impacted with Adam's face and glanced off the bone. Then it embedded itself under the skin close enough to the surface for Cerys to pick it out with tweezers. A fraction of an inch higher and it would have gone through his eye and killed him.

O'Shea smiled and went to give Adam a hug but the boy gave an unconcerned blink, turned away and carried on doodling.

O'Shea felt totally deflated. He didn't know *what* he expected when he came down stairs for the first time in over a week. But for some strange reason he thought he'd get a better reception than this. It took a lot of effort to drag himself out of the bed and all the way down to the kitchen. And he certainly didn't expect to be totally ignored.

He'd planned to say something witty to announce his arrival but suddenly it all seemed so pathetic. And standing there brooding caused a surge of weakness to sweep over him and he had to hurry across to the table and rest against it.

He pulled out a chair on the inside and dropped down on it, and Adam gave him a furtive look but didn't stop writing.

Cerys sneezed into her hands. And as she wiped her mouth on her sleeve she glanced over at O'Shea and this time she held his gaze for more than a second.

Her face was pale and gaunt. The lines around her eyes gave her a haunted look as she rocked back and forth in the chair. Her hair had lost its shine and it hung limply around her shoulders.

O'Shea could relate to how she was feeling. Of course he could. She'd been through an appalling time. And like him she'd lost people who were close to her.

But what he *couldn't* understand was why they were both sitting here now wallowing in their own pocket of misery and not saying a word to each other. It confused him. There was a strange anger in her and it appeared to be aimed at him. It was as if she begrudged him turning up again. It was as if he'd done something terrible and she resented him for it.

Yet she helped Clooney get him back into the house after he'd collapsed in the snow. They dropped him into an armchair in the front room and as he drifted in and out of consciousness he was aware of them putting Adam on the sofa next to him. Then when they were satisfied the boy was all right they dragged O'Shea up the stairs, threw him on the bed and pulled the eiderdown over him.

The next morning when he opened his eyes Cerys and Clooney were standing by the bed. He jumped up and called for his son.

'Calm down.' Clooney held O'Shea's arms down on the bed. 'He's fine. He's got nothing worse than a black eye. There's no permanent damage. When the swelling goes you won't even know he'd been injured.'

The relief was like a shot of neat adrenaline and O'Shea laughed and sobbed at the same time. 'I thought he was dead. I really thought my boy was dead. He was so cold, so … thank God you arrived when you did, that's all I can say.'

Then he pointed a shaky finger at Cerys as he strained to sit up again. 'But where did *you* come from?'

Cerys and Clooney glanced at each other and O'Shea caught the faintest shake of Clooney's head.

'How can you be here?' he repeated. 'I saw you with my own eyes. You were dead.'

But instead of answering the question Cerys took O'Shea's face in her hand, prised open his mouth and poured some vile concoction down his throat.

As he coughed and spluttered they both walked out of the room and pulled the door shut behind them. Then everything went blank.

He woke with a start when the door clicked open again and Cerys appeared beside him with a bowl of soup on a tray. He felt groggy and weak. The light in the room told him it was late afternoon.

'What the hell did you give me?' He tried to raise himself up onto his elbow. 'I went out like a light. How long have I been asleep?'

Clooney appeared and helped him to sit up. Then he perched on the bed as Cerys put the tray on O'Shea's lap. O'Shea took a sip of the soup and put the spoon down again.

'I still don't understand how you're alive.' He watched Cerys for a reaction 'I know what I saw. I just don't understand …'

'Neither do we.' Clooney took the tray and put it on the chair. 'All I can say is it wasn't Cerys.'

'But I saw her. They tortured her and they killed her.'

'Who did?'

'Weiss.' O'Shea felt his strength drain and he lay back on the pillow. 'Well, not him personally. But he arranged it. He got the Gestapo to do it.'

'But what made you think it was Cerys?' Clooney folded one leg over the other.

'I saw her.' O'Shea pointed to the end of the bed. 'She was this close to me. *This* close.'

There was a long pause and O'Shea noticed heat coming from the fireplace. He glanced over and smiled. 'I didn't hear you light that.'

Clooney glanced at it too and then took a long breath in through his nose. 'Why would Weiss want to torture Cerys, though? What was he trying to get out of her?'

'Not *her*. Weiss thought *I* knew something. He assumed if he tortured Cerys in front of me I'd tell him everything.'

There was another pause.

'And did you?'

'No!' O'Shea snapped. 'How could I when I …'

'You bastard!' Cerys rushed back over to the bed. 'You let her *die?* You watched her being tortured and you …'

'Because I didn't *know* anything,' O'Shea yelled. He tried to grab her arm but Clooney jumped up and pushed his hand away. Cerys huffed and went over to the fire and stood with her back to them.

'Look,' Clooney turned back to O'Shea. 'We're just trying to figure out what happened, that's all. You obviously saw someone you thought it was Cerys. So it's no wonder you're confused. Especially when she's here in the room with you. And it must have been horrible seeing someone tortured like that.'

He sat back down on the bed again. 'But what's confusing me is if the girl died because you wouldn't tell Weiss what he wanted to know, why didn't he just torture *you* until he got whatever he wanted? I mean, why did he bring you back here?'

'No, no,' O'Shea groaned. 'Weiss didn't bring me here. I managed to get away from Weiss. After Cerys … after the girl died there was a bit of confusion. I was lucky. I stole a car. It was a sheer fluke I found this place again.'

'But why would you want to come back here anyway?'

'I thought Adam might be here. Unfortunately Weiss was here as well.'

'So he followed you?'

'I don't know,' O'Shea started to cough again and he pressed the blanket to his mouth. When he finished he lifted himself up onto his elbow.

'No, Weiss couldn't have been here when I arrived. There was too much dust. It was all over the floor and it obviously hadn't been disturbed for a while. The place was freezing as well. So nobody had been here for ages. So he must have come afterwards so …'

He jumped up and swung his legs out of the bed. 'But that means he already *had* Adam! He must have found him some time ago and took him away. Held him somewhere else. No wonder there wasn't any sign of him when I got here.'

The weakness overwhelmed him again and he flopped back and dragged his legs back onto the bed. 'I don't understand any of this. What the hell is going on? And you know what that means, don't you? If he found Adam he found Rhianne as well.'

Clooney cleared his throat. Cerys came over and stood beside him, and she slid her arm around his shoulder.

'Then that would explain who the girl was,' Clooney said softly.

O'Shea groaned. So *that* was why the poor wretch looked so familiar. Weiss had been playing mind games with him right down to the smallest detail. The way her hair was combed. The same clothes Cerys wore. Making sure her face was bruised to obscure her real identity.

His stomach turned when he remembered the screams.

'Weiss must have had a reason to follow you back here.' Clooney's voice droned on in the distance as O'Shea tried not to dwell on the last image he had of the poor girl lying dead on the floor. 'Perhaps when Rhianne died on him he decided to let you escape just to see where you'd go. And you came *here*. But the Germans already searched this place and they didn't find anything of interest. So what made Weiss think *you* knew something? Was it something you said? Something you mentioned? Something he recognised even if you didn't?'

O'Shea realised Clooney was talking to him and he spluttered.

'For God's sake. How could I have said anything when I bloody well don't *know* anything?'

'Well he obviously thought you did.' Clooney continued as if he was talking to himself. 'I mean, why go to all this trouble? Pretending Rhianne was Cerys and torturing her in front of you? He was sure you knew something. And he was going to drag it out of you, one way or the other.'

O'Shea went to shout at Clooney again but a cough squeezed his throat and he bent double in agony.

Cerys appeared with a bottle. When O'Shea managed to open his mouth to take a breath she puckered his lips and poured some down his throat in one quick slug. It was sharp and bitter but before he could react Cerys let his head fall back on the pillow.

'This will ease the cough and help you sleep for a few hours.' Then she and Clooney walked out the door.

It didn't take long for the medicine to work. It spread a warm glow from the back of his throat right down to his stomach. His whole body relaxed and the tickle in his throat faded.

But for some reason his mind refused to let go. A whole bundle of questions wafted through his brain, teasing him, mocking him. But they were too fleeting, too wispy for his exhausted mind to focus on.

He shook his head to make them go away but they wouldn't. He was so tired. He just wanted to sleep.

Still the questions nagged at him. So what if Weiss discovered Adam and Rhianne when he searched the farm? Surely he would have seen they were a couple of frightened children hiding from soldiers in their own home. That wouldn't be unusual. And it certainly wasn't a crime, was it? So why would Weiss pay any attention to them?

And if he did mistake Rhianne for Cerys, wouldn't that imply he actually *knew* Cerys in the first place? How?

An even more intriguing question tumbled into his mind. What would possess Weiss to even *think* O'Shea had feelings for Cerys? Why would something like that even enter his mind in the first place?

No, someone planted it there. Whoever it was, they were very persuasive. They convinced Weiss that torturing Cerys would make O'Shea reveal what he knew about the boxes.

But what would mean …

Then the medicine kicked in.

Chapter Fifty-One

Over the next few days Cerys fed O'Shea the thick, bitter medicine every four hours. And within a very short time he was well enough to sit up and eat properly again.

But the whole time Cerys was attending to him she never said a word. And that unnerved him. She did everything in total silence. She rushed into the room, placed the tray of food on his lap and poured the medicine into his mouth directly from the bottle. She wiped his face with a wet cloth and disappeared again without ever looking directly at him. Without speaking a single word.

O'Shea wanted to talk about the things that were bothering him, but he never got the chance. She deliberately didn't engage with him. She was in and out in the blink of an eye.

He thought she'd want to know about Rhianne. Her own sister. Her only surviving relative. He thought she'd want to know exactly what happened to her. But she didn't.

And O'Shea had the feeling she already knew.

Now as he sat at the table in the kitchen listening to the crackle of the fire and the scratching of Adam's chalk on the slate he became aware that he stank rather badly.

He was still wearing the long leather overcoat. He hadn't taken it off since the day he arrived. Consequently he reeked of stale body odour. But he didn't have the strength or the inclination to take a bath. Or have a shave, even. And so far nobody had said anything about it.

The latch on the back door rattled and a gust of cold air rushed in as the door flew open. Clooney came clattering into the scullery, pulled two dead rabbits from the gamekeeper's bag hanging from his shoulder and dropped them onto the draining board. He threw a handful of onions into the sink.

'Ah, you're up.' He nodded to O'Shea. 'About time, too. I thought you were going to hibernate up there for the rest of the winter.'

Cerys gave him a half smile then turned back to the fire.

'Is that kettle boiled?' Clooney asked her.

She lifted the lid to take a look. 'Would you like some tea?'

'Please,' Clooney took off his overcoat and threw it over the back of a chair. He took off his jacket too, and as he flung it on top of the overcoat his wallet dropped out and landed in the middle of the table. He'd already turned away so he didn't see it slide across the table and fall on the floor beside O'Shea's feet.

Adam glanced down at it but decided to ignore it and carried on drawing.

'How're you feeling, anyway?' Clooney shook the dregs from the teapot into the fire as he spoke to O'Shea. 'Do you feel well enough to skin those rabbits in the scullery? We could have them for supper if they're ready.'

'Probably. Well, yes. I think so,'

'Don't sound so worried,' Clooney laughed. 'It's not that difficult.'

'No. That's not what I'm worried about.'

Clooney looked at him curiously. 'So what *are* you worried about?'

'Oh, I don't know.' O'Shea picked up the wallet and put it on the table. 'I was just thinking about that mad German fella, Weiss. What happens if he comes back? He'll find you two here as well.'

'Why would that be a problem? This house belongs to Cerys now.' Clooney poured boiling water into the teapot and put it on the floor beside the fire. 'This is why we've come back. Especially now the dust had settled. It's quite safe, you know.'

'Is it? Weiss knows I'm here now. And he knows Adam is here too. He could come back looking for us. And that wouldn't be healthy for you two.'

'Why do you think that?' Clooney laughed as he put three mugs on the ledge beside the fireplace. 'Anyway, why *would* Weiss come back looking for you now?'

'He might!' O'Shea snapped.

Clooney poured tea into the mugs and handed one to Cerys. He walked over to the table with the other two mugs and put one in front of O'Shea. Then he sat down opposite and cupped the last one in his hands. Adam shifted his slate out of the way.

'Well, aren't you worried?' O'Shea sipped the tea. 'What will you do if he does come back?'

Clooney grinned. 'Dandelion tea.' He nodded at the mug in his hand. 'Beautiful, isn't it. From our very own crop out there in the yard. Sorry we don't have any cake to go with it, though.'

O'Shea picked up the wallet to give back to Clooney but it slipped from his fingers and flipped open on the table. The dim light from the lamp picked out the words 'Obren Industries' on an identity card inside the sleeve.

O'Shea picked it up again and took a closer look. The photo showed a young Clooney. It had the word *Security* stamped across it.

'You work at Obren Industries?' O'Shea looked up at Clooney in total surprise.

Clooney took the wallet and smiled at himself in the photo. 'What would *you* know about Obren Industries?'

'I know it's up in Brecon. Or somewhere near Brecon, anyway.'

'Just outside.' Clooney's smile faded slightly. 'But how do you know so much about it?'

'Weiss told me.'

Now Clooney's smile faded completely.

'Did he now?' And O'Shea was unnerved by the way Clooney was looking back at him. His eyes had narrowed and were tinged with menace.

O'Shea tried to hold his gaze. Had he touched a nerve? He had an ominous feeling about the way this conversation was going. But he was determined not to let Clooney know he was flustered. He rubbed his eyes with his left hand and let his right hand drop onto his lap. Then he slid it into the pocket of the overcoat. His fingers shook as he touched the gun and he had to grip it hard to control them. It took an effort to flick off the safety catch.

He didn't know what he was going to do with it, but just feeling it gave him comfort.

'So you *do* work there, then?' O'Shea picked up the mug and sipped his tea.

'*Used* to.' Clooney looked cautious. 'But not anymore, I'm afraid.'

'Oh? Why's that?'

'Well, let's say the invasion changed everything. Our new bosses had a bit of a skirmish, didn't they? They needed to decide who they could keep, and who they … well, *couldn't*.' He took some bread and nibbled on it.

'Well, actually, it was more like a purge. They obviously saw it as an opportunity to get rid of the dead wood.'

'That's understandable.' O'Shea nodded and took a sip of his tea. 'But I thought their policy was to keep the people who knew the business. Keep them doing the job they know best. It causes less disruption that way, surely.'

'Well, not in our case.' Clooney tone softened slightly. 'The thing is, there was an unfortunate incident and it had some very grave consequences for the security team that was on duty at the time. Something went missing. It was supposed to be top secret and known to only a handful of bodies. So the proverbial poo hit the proverbial fan. And the resulting mess stuck to everyone in the nearby vicinity. And some who were outside the vicinity too. So, as you can imagine, they decided if the security team couldn't prevent it from happening in the first place, they would have to get someone else to do the job. It was as simple as that.'

A cloud of jigsaw pieces fluttered around the parameters of O'Shea's mind. He knew they were critical bits of the puzzle, but when he tried to focus on them they disintegrated into blobs of nonsense. He looked over at Cerys but she was still gazing into the fire and she didn't appear to be listening.

He gave a deep sigh and sipped his tea noisily.

'What?' Clooney asked.

'Nothing. I just don't understand any of it. I have a headache and I feel like crap. All I want to do right now is get myself fit, take Adam and bugger off home to Ireland. Preferably before Weiss comes back and has another crack at me.'

'But why are you so sure he'll come back?' Clooney's eyebrows rose with the question. 'I thought he decided you were a complete waste of time. You couldn't give him what he wanted and you pissed him off, so he shot your boy and left. So what reason would he have to come back now?'

'I don't know.' O'Shea took another sip of the tea. 'The man's a complete feckin lunatic. He's obsessed. He's going to keep coming back till he finds what he's looking for.'

'Which is what, exactly?' Clooney sat back in the chair.

O'Shea studied him for a moment, trying to decide if he already knew the answer to that. But the cold grey eyes held O'Shea's stare and it was impossible to read the poker face.

'Well,' O'Shea continued to watch the face looking for anything that would betray its mendacity. 'Weiss told me British scientists in Brecon had developed an amazing new weapon and he was responsible for getting it back to Berlin as soon as possible. It was all top secret stuff but still someone robbed it from under his nose.'

'Why would Weiss tell *you* all this?' Clooney took a half-smoked cigarette from his pocket, cracked a match against the floor and sucked in a lungful of smoke. 'I mean, how come you two were having such a cosy chat in the first place? Because it sound very unlikely to me that someone like Weiss would tell someone like you about something like that.'

'Well,' O'Shea tapped the table with his finger. 'He wanted me to know how important the weapon was to him. And to his career in the army. Even to his future health. And how determined he was to get it back.'

'But why *you*?'

'Because he saw me talking to Bethan after she was shot. He got it into his fat head she knew where the weapon was and she'd told me. But she didn't! I swear on my son's life. She did *not* tell me about a weapon or boxes or anything else. But Weiss wouldn't accept that. He threatened all sorts of retribution if I didn't co-operate. And I got the impression he didn't believe the attack on his truck was random either. You know, by some pissed off local eejits trying to impress their mates. He suspected someone close to home. Someone with inside knowledge.'

O'Shea caught the twinkle in Clooney's eye.

'It was you, wasn't it?' he spluttered. 'You had something to do with this, didn't you? You worked for Obren Industries. You were on that security team when it ... you'd have all the information you needed, the place, the time. Of course, you'd have...'

'As if I could organise something like that.' Clooney actually laughed. 'Who do you think I am? Robin bleeding Hood? Anyway, if it *was* true and I did rob the weapon, where the hell is it now?'

'Ah, I've been thinking about that,' O'Shea tapped his nose. 'What if Weiss was being cautious? What if he sent the real boxes by a different route and sent an empty truck as a decoy? That would explain why there was nothing on the truck when you attacked it.'

Clooney took another sip of his tea and his face was strangely calm as he looked back at O'Shea. 'Think about this, then, clever dick. If Weiss had taken the stuff by a different route why is he still chasing you for it? I mean, if he had it in the first place, why is he still looking for it?'

O'Shea bowed his head. 'That, I'm afraid, I do not know.'

Cerys stood up and pulled her cardigan around her shoulders. 'Why are you talking to *him* about all that?

It's got nothing to do with him. It's none of his bloody business.'

She sauntered over and sat at the table beside Clooney, and she rested her head on his shoulder. The poor light made her skin as pale as ivory.

Clooney kissed the top of her head. 'It won't make much difference now whatever we tell him. It's all gone to pot, anyway. The whole bloody lot is gone belly up. So it doesn't matter who knows about it now, does it?'

Cerys picked up Clooney's mug and took a sip from it. Then she closed her eyes and leant back against him, and he put his arm around her waist.

'Well, I still don't think you should be discussing our business with *him*.' Her voice was weary. 'I don't trust him.'

Chapter Fifty-Two

Before O'Shea could reply a tickle in his throat started him coughing again. Tears welled up in his eyes and he had to bury his face in his hands as he gasped for breath. It was almost a minute before he managed to calm down again.

He wiped his eyes with his sleeve and looked up. Three pairs of eyes stared back at him. And all of them were impassive.

'Nice,' he said sarcastically,

Cerys rolled her eyes and nodded towards the scullery. 'What about those rabbits? Weren't you supposed to be getting them ready for me to cook? You'd better hurry up if you want any supper tonight.'

O'Shea ignored her. 'So what *did* happen that day? How did the weapon just vanish into thin air? Someone must know what happened. And I have a sneaky suspicion that someone is you.'

'The thing is ...'

'Don't tell him, love!' Cerys she sat up and pulled away from Clooney. 'Just tell him to get on with the rabbits. I'm starving.'

Clooney took an irritated breath through his nose. 'As I was about to say, the plan was simple. Ambush the trucks and capture the weapon. What could go wrong? It was fool-proof. And the fact it was top secret was in our favour. Only a handful of people even knew of its existence. And even fewer people knew it was being taken to Cardiff in the back of an army truck to be put on a plane. No one was going to miss it for hours and that would give us a head start.'

'I knew it,' O'Shea snapped his fingers. '*You* planned the whole bloody thing, didn't you? You and Bethan, you were all in it together. You found out about the weapon and somehow you managed to discover the route they were taking. Good God, the Germans must be awful sloppy if you were able to just snoop around and discover all that secret stuff.'

'For God's sake!' Cerys jumped up and shoved her chair back. She looked like she was going to spit at O'Shea but she stormed back to the fireplace and dropped back into her rocking chair.

Clooney shook his head and took a swig of his tea. 'I didn't have to snoop around anywhere, actually.' There was a smirk on his face again. 'No, no. Weiss already had all the information we needed.'

'Weiss?' O'Shea sat up straight. 'What do you mean? Are you telling me Weiss himself ... *what*? *Weiss* gave you the information? Weiss was involved with you in this?'

'Oh, yes,' Clooney gave another smug laugh. 'Right from the very start, I'm afraid. The moment he realised how valuable this amazing new weapon was his greedy little eyes lit up. He decided that if he could nick it for himself and sell it on to some interested party, he would be set up for life.'

'But what ...all this shite and he ...how do you know all this?'

'How do you think? He couldn't do it on his own, could he? No, something this big would take planning. And resources. And he couldn't trust his German colleagues to help him. They'd be singing about the glorious Motherland as they strung him up by his credentials from the nearest church tower. No, what he needed was someone with local knowledge. Someone who was easily coerced. Or enticed with the promise of great rewards.'

O'Shea was stunned. He tried to speak but his throat dried up.

'Look, the Germans aren't stupid,' Clooney pointed with his finger. 'For years they've had spies in this country. So when the invasion started they knew exactly where to go.'

O'Shea pulled a lump off the bread, dipped it in his tea and slurped it noisily.

'Anyway,' Clooney continued, 'they landed at Obren Industries long before we even knew the invasion had started. Paratroopers dropped down on us like a cloud. They knew exactly what they were looking for. But they didn't know how advanced our scientists were, and that the prototype was out on the range undergoing final trials. In the heat of the moment the paratroopers blew it to smithereens. So it took another few weeks for their own scientists to decipher the paperwork. And when they *did* they got very excited. The British scientists confirmed the prototype had already undergone tests and only needed some minor adjustments. However, rather than risk building another one in Britain the Germans were instructed to get the papers to Berlin immediately.'

He glanced over at Cerys. She looked up, pulled a sour face and turned her back on him.

'In the meantime, though,' he continued, leaning back casually in his chair. 'Weiss got himself into a spot of bother. He assumed the local lasses were the spoils of war to be taken at leisure. To be fair, a lot of the girls did succumb willingly. It was understandable, I suppose, considering the reputation of the Germans. Self-preservation, isn't it?'

Dark September

He wiped his forehead with the palm of his hand. 'Anyway, one young girl who worked in reception was having none of it. She was a good chapel girl, you see. They found her body stuffed behind a cupboard in the stationary room. She'd been raped and strangled. Someone discovered a crucial piece of evidence showing Weiss was involved. But instead of turning him in, they hinted he might prefer to buy the evidence back. Weiss, you understand, was a married man with children back home in Germany. His wife was also a church person. Catholic, I think. And her father was high up in the German Army. An aristocrat, too, by all accounts. Anyway, Weiss thought he could raise the money by playing cards. He was a good card player, you know. But luck wasn't on his side so he slipped deeper and deeper into the mire. Of course, like a cornered rat, his crooked little mind was open to any opportunity that might help him climb out of the nasty little hole he'd dug for himself.'

'How do you know all this?' O'Shea interrupted. 'Don't tell me you were involved in the blackmail too?'

'No,' Clooney said with mock indignation. 'Actually, Weiss approached *me*. One night, right out of the blue. He wandered over to me in the local pub and offered to buy me a pint. I must say I was a bit uneasy at first, you know? He isn't an easy man to like. There's something rather nasty about him. But, for some reason I thought he looked lonely that night, like he just wanted someone to listen to his moans and groans. Then he bought another pint, and another. Eventually we were both as pissed as rats and falling over each other like life-long pals. I didn't know at the time, of course, but it was all a set up. Weiss knew all there was to know about me. As you can imagine, with me working in such a sensitive job the

Secret Service had already monitored us very closely. So Weiss now had access to all our files. He knew about my association with Bethan and my sympathies with the Nationalists.'

He looked at Cerys again. She was still glaring into the fire. 'Bethan had a high profile in local politics. Have you ever heard of John Frost of the Chartist movement?'

'I have,' O'Shea nodded. 'Bethan was a direct descendant. Cerys told me all about it.'

Clooney smiled approvingly. 'Well, there you have it. Weiss knew how Bethan felt about Wales. She dreamed of independence from the English. She was ripe so he fed her a dream. He supplied her with weapons and money to put together a team capable of doing a quick and efficient job for him. You know, he even had the lads up on the Brecons training with the weapons? Can you believe the nerve of the man?' He gave a loud laugh and sipped his tea.

'Anyway, as I said, the plan was so simple it just couldn't fail. He would tell us where and when, Bethan would take the stuff off of the Germans, and then he'd sell it on.'

'Who was he going to sell it on to?' O'Shea put his cup down. 'How was he going to get it out of the country, for a start? The Germans would be like lunatics looking for it. They'd seal the borders tighter than a duck's eyelid. Surely he knew that?'

'Oh, that was the easy part,' Clooney smiled. 'Weiss already had a buyer. The Americans have no wish to be in this war but they still want to keep ahead of the game. A weapon like this would make sure they were well ahead of everyone else. Especially the Germans. And they were going to pay serious money to get their hands on it, too. Weiss was going to share that money with us.'

'But what did Bethan think about that? I mean, how could the money buy her independence for Wales?'

Clooney shrugged and looked at Cerys again. 'Well, she may not have been told the *whole* truth, exactly. She was led to believe she could use the *weapon* to negotiate with the Germans. You know, bargain with them for a neutral Wales based on the Irish Republic.'

'Naw,' O'Shea let it go of the gun and took his hand back out of his pocket. 'I can't believe Bethan would fall for that shite. She was no eejit. Would she take the word of a German and not even ask what *he* had to gain from it? Surely to God she'd question his motives?'

'Actually, she didn't know Weiss was involved. She believed the suggestion came from the Nationalists' Army Council. And like I said, she was blinded by a vision. She was shown a dream and she followed it.'

'Some bloody dream,' O'Shea snorted. 'More like a friggin' nightmare. So how did it go so wrong?'

'Well,' Clooney gave a weary sigh. 'Weiss hid the boxes himself before we were supposed to ambush the trucks. He figured his colleagues would believe the insurgents stole them and it would cause a nice little diversion. While they were looking for us in one direction, he'd be off on his toes in the other.'

'However,' Clooney took a final drink of his tea before banging the mug on the table. Adam jumped, glared at him then carried on scribbling on the slate. 'When Weiss went back to collect the boxes from his hiding place the cupboard was bare. Someone had double crossed the double crosser.'

'But what made him think Bethan had anything to with that?'

Clooney considered the question before answering. 'The lads were given clear instructions. For everyone's sake no German was to be left alive after the attack. But one of the officers who helped Weiss hide the boxes was not amongst the casualties. So he either got away and helped himself, or he was kept alive by the lads and brought back here. And if he *was* brought back here he was persuaded to share his story with Bethan. Either way he disappeared off the face of the earth.'

Clooney read something in O'Shea's face and his eyes narrowed. 'What? He *was* brought here? But of course. You'd know because you were brought here at the same time '

'Yeah. He *was* brought here,' O'Shea agreed. 'Adam and I were in the truck but I did see him in the car with Gareth.'

'So what happened to him?'

'They fed him to the pigs.'

Cerys was suddenly paying attention. 'How do you know that?'

'I saw them. The first night we were here. I went out to use the toilet, and I saw Bethan and Gareth questioning the German. It wasn't very nice. Anyway he went and died on them so Gareth threw his body into the pigs.'

'Shit,' Clooney spat. 'So what did he say to them? Did you hear what he said to them?'

'No, I was too far away. But he obviously told them something important because they looked pleased. Then they drove off in the German's car.'

'I *knew* it,' Clooney jumped up and stomped around the kitchen. 'I bloody knew it. I told you, didn't I? I told you Bethan knew where the stuff was all the time.'

Cerys was suddenly alert and she stood up too. 'Then that means the boxes must still be here on the farm.'

Clooney raked his fingers through his hair. 'But where, though? We've been through the place with a fine-tooth comb. The Germans pulled it to pieces as well. There's nowhere left to look.'

'What about the ...' O'Shea said.

They both stopped and looked at him. He hesitated.

'What?' Clooney asked.

'Well, Adam and Rhianne were hiding in a hole under the stairs. I just thought ...'

'No,' Cerys clapped her hands. 'We've looked there.'

She took a sharp intake of breath and looked at O'Shea. Her face had a strange expression, as if she'd said something he wasn't supposed to hear.

He tried to grasp it but it fluttered away too quickly. Clooney sat back down and rested his head on his arms. 'The boxes have to be here.'

He turned to O'Shea. 'You were the very last person to speak to Bethan. Are you absolutely sure she didn't tell you something? Give you some sort of a clue?'

'For God's sake!' O'Shea felt his face redden with the rush of anger. 'How many more times have I got to tell you? Do you really think I'd have gone through all that shite if I knew where the boxes were? Do you think I'd have watched Cerys ... *Rhianne* being sliced to pieces if I knew? My own son was shot because I couldn't tell your buddy where the stupid boxes were. My son nearly died because I didn't bloody *know*! For God's sake, what more can I say? Bethan was lying on the ground with the life pouring out of her and she was bloody scared. She was terrified and she was asking for Cerys. She was calling for Alice in bloody Wonderland.'

Cerys snorted. 'She was calling for what?'

'She called Cerys Alice in Wonderland.'

'Alice in Wonderland? What the hell does that mean?'

'How the feck do I know?' O'Shea shouted. 'She was *your* feckin sister. She was calling for *you*. She said *tell Cerys Alice in Wonderland*. Then she died and Weiss appeared. I never saw her after that.'

Cerys settled back into the chair, picked up her mug and took a long drink. 'Well, I haven't got a clue what she meant by that.'

'Well, that's what she said, anyway.' O'Shea closed his eyes. He could still see the chaos when the farm was raided, the bullets spitting against the ground, the fear on Bethan's face. 'Tell Cerys *Alice in* ... something. Tell Cerys *Alice through the looking glass!* That's it. Something like that, anyway. I can't remember now. It was so quick, and then she was gone.'

O'Shea sat back down and put his face in his hands. The only sound was the crackling of the fire and the whisper of the breeze in the chimney.

'Oh my God!' Cerys sprang to her feet. Her chair scraped the ground as it shot backwards and fell upside down. The mug dropped out of her hand and shattered on the stone floor.

Clooney jumped up too and caught her by the elbows. 'What's the matter? What's happened?'

He helped her to another chair and sat her down.

'Of course!' she was saying. 'It was so bloody obvious. I *should* have remembered it. How the hell could I not have remembered? How could I not have guessed? I should have realised. All this time it was so ...'

'Cerys!' Clooney still had a grip on her elbows. 'What are you saying? Are you saying you know where the boxes are?'

'Oh, yes.' Her eyes danced with excitement. 'I think I do.'

Chapter Fifty-Three

The morning was black and bitterly cold. An icy wind whipped at their faces but at five o'clock in the morning they were just too tired to care.

They piled as much food as they could carry into three canvas satchels, threw them into the trunk of the German car and scrambled inside as fast as they could out of the cold. Adam and O'Shea got in the back and it was like climbing into an industrial freezer. They'd wrapped themselves in whatever extra clothes they could find but they still needed a thick blanket around them.

'Come on!' Cerys snapped as Clooney started the engine and revved it a couple of times. 'Stop farting about and let's get going.'

Clooney's breath came down his nose in little annoyed puffs of condensation. He threw the car into gear and released the handbrake, and as they pulled away from the house Cerys hugged herself into a ball.

She was extremely agitated. When she first realised where the boxes were the colour flowed back into her cheeks. But the initial euphoria quickly turned into frustration as she tried to explain to Clooney what Bethan meant by *Alice through the looking glass*.

'Look, calm down,' Clooney held his finger to her lips. 'You're not making any sense. Just slow down. Take your time and start at the beginning.'

'Right,' Cerys pushed his hand away. 'Just stay here. I'll show you.'

She ran up the stairs and they could hear her clattering around in her bedroom. When she came back down again she was clutching a small creased photograph of a group of children playing on a beach.

'I should have known all along.' She slapped the photo with her hand. 'I can't believe I didn't think of it before. God, I'm so stupid. It was right under my nose all the time and I didn't see it.'

Clooney took the photo from her and scrutinised it. 'What are we looking at?'

'That!' Cerys tapped it with her finger.

'What? That's just a ... do you mean the waterfall?'

'Exactly.' Cerys snatched the photo back, took it to the fire and studied it again.

'That waterfall is our *Alice through the looking glass*. That's what Bethan was trying to tell me.'

Clooney pulled his chair closer to her as she told them about her uncle Rhodri who had a farm near Penarth. It was right on the coast and stretched for about three miles along the edge of the sea. It was mostly just rugged cliff, but there was one small inlet with its own little sandy beach accessible down a narrow path from the farmhouse.

The photo showed Cerys and Rhianne on that little beach digging for crabs with their cousins Paul, Barry and Leigh. She thought Bethan took the photo. She was older than her sisters so she spent most of the time with the boys' mother, Sian.

Because the beach was so secluded the children believed it had a special magic all of its own. It was their very own treasure island.

And most exciting of all, it had a waterfall.

A small river meandered through the farm and it was often swelled by water from a network of irrigation ditches. So by the time it reached the cliff it was powerful enough to create a wild and noisy waterfall as it cascaded down onto the beach.

That particular summer was exceptionally hot, though. And one day the waterfall just petered out into a fine mist. Leigh was first down on the beach that morning and he came running back up to tell the others that he'd found a secret cave. But it was halfway up the cliff and the earth was so loose it was impossible to climb up to it.

However, when the tide came in that evening it was as calm as a village pond and the children were playing about in their uncle's boat. And they went to investigate the mysterious cave. They discovered a ledge just below the mouth of the cave that was wide enough for them to crawl along.

The cave was no more than twelve feet deep and five feet high, but to the children it was enormous and absolutely enthralling. Imaginations ran wild and the cave became their secret hideout, their sanctuary from invading pirates, their headquarters, their very special place.

The next day Sian made them a picnic and when the tide came in again they all sailed across to the cave. Bethan even helped them collect some wood and build a small fire.

A week later it rained and the waterfall was back. And this added to the enchantment of the secret cave because the children could still crawl along the ledge and get to it behind the wall of water.

They took another picnic and sat around the fire telling stories. One story Bethan told them was about a girl called Alice who walked through a looking glass into a magic world. And the waterfall became their very own looking glass.

Then the holiday ended and they all went home. And as the years drifted by all contact with the cousins faded.

Cerys forgot about her time in the magic cave behind the waterfall.

Bethan didn't. It was the perfect place to hide things.

But Clooney wasn't convinced. It was all too bizarre, too much like a fairy story. *A cave behind a waterfall?* That old chestnut!

And how did Bethan have enough time to collect the boxes from where Weiss left them, take them to the coast, hide them and get back to the farm all in one night? And how did she get the boxes up into the cave? She would have needed help, a boat and a high tide.

And if everyone knew about the cave, would she risk leaving the boxes there?

No, Clooney thought it was too farfetched. Bethan would have wanted the boxes close by. She'd want them where she could keep an eye on them, probably right here on the farm. And like he said, she just didn't have time to do anything else.

But Cerys was adamant. What else could she have meant? *Alice through the looking glass* was their childhood fantasy. Why else would she have said something as bizarre as that? Especially if she knew she was dying?

They argued loudly and aggressively well into the night. But eventually the highly emotional Cerys persuaded Clooney to at least go down to the cave and take a look. What did they have to lose?

'All right,' Clooney slapped his knees as he stood up. 'If that's what you really want to do, my little chicken, then we'd better get some stuff together to take with us. Just in case.'

He went into the scullery and came back with three old canvas satchels. And an arm full of tins that he dropped with a crash onto the table. 'We'll take one bag each. Fill it with what you think you can carry. Food and some dry clothes. And anything else you think you might need. We could be gone for a few days.'

Cerys took a bag and started rooting in the cupboards and stuffing all kinds of things into it.

'Come on,' Clooney waved the third bag at O'Shea.

'Sorry,' O'Shea rested his head on his arms. 'Not me, I'm afraid. I'm a sick man. I'm ready for my bed. And I think Adam is too. But you two carry on. Don't worry about us.'

'Oh, no,' Clooney slammed the bag on the table. 'Now that we've decided to go, we all go together. All right? So start filling. There's no time to waste.'

He grabbed some more tins from the shelf and dropped them into his bag. 'Now I know there isn't much fuel left in that car outside but I think it should get us to the other side of Cardiff. I have some friends down there in Radyr so if we get that far we'll leave the car and go the rest of the way on foot. Hence the need to take enough supplies with us.'

When he turned around O'Shea still hadn't moved. 'What are you doing? Why aren't you filling the bag?'

'Look,' O'Shea sat up. 'How can I go with you? I'm too sick. I just want to go to bed and get some sleep. Anyway, this has nothing to do with me anymore. So you two just carry on, all right? I'm really not interested anymore, so just ...'

'I'm afraid it doesn't work like that.' Clooney put his bag on the floor. 'If the boxes are where Cerys thinks they are we won't be coming back here, will we?'

'So what?' O'Shea laughed. 'You don't really think I'll be upset by that? I'm not likely to miss you, am I? No, I'm just going to rest here for a while. Then when I'm well enough me and Adam will be off to Ireland.'

'And what if Weiss comes back?' Clooney's eyes were as cold as flint as he stared hard at O'Shea.

O'Shea shrugged and looked away. He detected a dangerous inflection in the way Clooney asked the question. But what did he mean? Did he mean now O'Shea knew where the boxes were, he'd be in grave danger from Weiss?

Or was Clooney implying that, because O'Shea was in grave danger from Weiss they couldn't risk leaving him behind? Not alive, anyway.

'Look, Danny boy,' Clooney pulled out a chair and sat opposite O'Shea, 'I know your priority right now is to get your boy to Ireland. I understand that. But you might not believe this, our original plan was for Weiss and me to take the boxes to Ireland too. His American contact works out of the embassy in Dublin and he was going to send a boat to take us and the boxes to Dublin.'

He waited for O'Shea to respond. O'Shea blinked a few times but didn't speak.

'So what I'm saying is, you help us find the boxes and we'll take you and your boy to Ireland with us. Not only that, you'll get a share of the proceeds too. We'll all be far richer than we've ever dreamed of. Then you can go your way and we'll go ours, and you'll never have to set eyes on my ugly mush again. If that's what you really want.' He gave a mock pout. 'So what do you say, Danny boy? We've been in this together since day one, so we need to stick together now. We need each other now more than we ever did before, right?'

O'Shea gave a cynical smirk. There was more sincerity in a dead fish than there was in Clooney's eyes right now. But what choice did O'Shea have? And it could be his big chance to get Adam to Ireland.

Of course he was aware Clooney only wanted him along for insurance. Just in case the boxes weren't in the cave after all. What if he'd misunderstood what Bethan actually said?

Apart from that, what if O'Shea suddenly remembered something else, some other important little detail? No, Clooney certainly wouldn't want O'Shea sitting here by the fire sipping tea if Weiss *did* decide to come back.

'Look,' Clooney seemed to read O'Shea's thoughts. 'As an act of faith I'm making you quartermaster of our little band of brothers. You'll be in charge of the finances. Which means you'll have to pay for the transport to get us to Ireland. So we'll need some hard cash to get things rolling.'

He put his hand in the pocket of his coat, pulled out an old sock and threw on the table. 'Yours, I believe.'

O'Shea picked it up and looked at the wad of money stuffed into it. It was Mrs Mead's sock.

'I almost burnt it,' Clooney laughed. 'I found it when I put that German uniform on you that day in the car. I thought why is this lunatic carrying a stuffed sock around with him? It's lucky for you I checked what was in it. So, Mr Quartermaster, are you with us?'

Chapter Fifty-Four

When they reached the gate Clooney jumped out, flung it open and kicked a rock into place to hold it there. Then he shot back into the car, slammed the door behind him and they were off again in a shower of stones and grit.

They kept away from the main roads by sticking to the narrow lanes and some had bends so vicious the car skidded off the road several times. One time they had to rummage around in the pitch dark for stones to shove under the wheels and give them traction in the thick mud.

By the time they reached the outskirts of Radyr the car was spluttering and running on fumes. Clooney had no choice but to freewheel down the long street, keeping the speed in check with reluctant taps on the footbrake. Then he swerved abruptly at the bottom of the hill and turned into a lane between some battered fences and a rusty corrugated shed.

He made the car spin around in a tight circle before it crunched to a stop under a huge tree. Thick branches hung down so low they almost touched the roof of the car.

'This is it, old girl.' He nudged Cerys with his elbow and she shot up straight. She rubbed her eyes and sighed, then gave him a wicked scowl.

As they stumbled from the warmth of the car onto the damp spongy grass the insipid dawn was greeted by the chirping of birds hidden in the branches above their heads.

Unsure of what they were supposed to do now, they stretched their arms and legs and waited for Clooney to say something. But he didn't. He went around to the trunk, grabbed his satchel and strode off down a dusty track at the back of a row of small cottages.

'Oi!' Cerys called after him. 'Where the hell are *you* going?'

When he didn't respond she grabbed her own satchel, slung it over her shoulder with an angry flourish and hurried after him.

O'Shea shook his head, took his bag by the strap and he and Adam followed after them.

When Clooney reached the end cottage he pushed open the little gate and strode up the cobbled path. He gave a few quick raps on the door and it was opened immediately by a middle-aged lady who gave a howl of delight when she saw him.

'Agnes,' Clooney beamed. 'You got my message, then?'

Agnes was still chattering excitedly when a man appeared behind her, reached out his hand and drew Clooney inside.

Cerys waited for O'Shea to catch up before she followed Clooney up the path. When they reached the door they were practically dragged into the kitchen by Agnes and invited to sit around the long pine table.

Everyone was talking at the same time and the noise bubbled with an obvious, comfortable familiarity. Agnes threw more rashers of bacon into a frying pan sizzling on the big range, and the aroma from it made O'Shea drool.

When the kettle started boiling she poured the water into an enormous teapot. She was still talking as she clattered a bundle of knives and forks down onto the table.

'It won't be long, now.' She smiled over at O'Shea. 'We'll have you sorted again in no time. There's nothing like a nice hot cup of tea to start the day, is there?'

'Thank you.' O'Shea smiled back.

Agnes hesitated for a second. Then she took a closer look at O'Shea.

'Francis, I didn't know you had a brother.' She gave Clooney a big grin.

O'Shea looked up in astonishment. Suddenly he realised what bothered him about Clooney right from the start. *For God's sake!* How did he not notice the uncanny resemblance between them? When he first saw Clooney something registered in his mind. The colour of his hair - light brown with a hint of ginger. The same sallow complexion with its spattering of freckles. Clooney's face was fuller and the eyes were a deeper grey, but they could definitely have been related.

So why didn't O'Shea see it at the time? Was he too distracted by what was happening around him? Or had the brutal events that followed minutes later deleted all memory of what initially bothered him? His pulse thumped in his ears and he had to swallow hard to clear his mind.

'No, no.' Clooney gave a gleeful wave of his fork. 'We're not brothers. We're not even related.'

'Surely to God ...'

'No, really. He's not even Welsh. He's Irish.'

O'Shea sensed Cerys watching him and when he looked up her eyes were narrow and cold. He felt she was waiting for him to react to something. What else had he missed? Was it something to do with Clooney again?

He studied Clooney, watching him flirt openly with Agnes. Agnes scooped the food onto large plates and handed them around. And her husband Allan put a pile of toast in the middle of the table.

'Tuck in.' Allan put a slice of toast on Adam's plate. 'There's some brown sauce in that bottle on the sideboard. If you ask Francis he'll pass it over. Give it a good shake and you might get some to plop out.'

Then suddenly it clicked and O'Shea groaned out loud. Of *course*. They called him Francis!

When Agnes handed him a plate O'Shea put it on the table in front of him. But his hunger had evaporated. His guts felt too heavy to eat. All this had landed on him so fast his brain was struggling to unscramble it.

So Clooney was the mysterious Francis. The husband Cerys said she hadn't seen for years. She said she didn't even know where he was anymore. And all the time she was lying. But why did she need to concoct such an elaborate story about being deserted, abandoned by a man who couldn't face the responsibility of having a baby?

And what was the charade about believing O'Shea was Francis?

O'Shea *knew* Cerys was odd right from the beginning. The mood swings, the ramblings about losing her baby. That could have been true, of course. But her obsession with the boxes? That was something else.

Maybe she couldn't help it. It was easy to dismiss it as the fantasy of an emotionally fragile young woman. What if she actually *had* some sort of mental disorder? What if she had an obsession to embellish her life to elicit sympathy for herself?

All the rest made sense now too. The way she acted that day down by the gate when Clooney got out of the car. She wasn't the least bit surprised to see him. In fact she was as giggly as a schoolgirl. She *knew* he was coming.

The whole scenario from that appalling day started to replay itself in O'Shea's head. He squeezed his eyes to block it out, but it was too late.

He smelled the rain again, tasted the unease about being taken to Liverpool. He remembered the way Rhys and Idris were behaving. They were obviously surprised when they saw who was in the car. But it wasn't just that. They were annoyed, too. O'Shea sensed animosity between them, which was why they stomped back to the house the way they did. They reeked of suspicion. Was it the strange way Cerys and Clooney were behaving?

The hairs on O'Shea's neck prickled as he remembered how they hung back while the others went on ahead. As if they knew something was going to happen. And why was Clooney wearing that silly white scarf? Because it made him stick out like a sore thumb? Because it kept him safe?

'Have some tea, love.'

Agnes put a mug on the table in front of Adam. Everyone was talking and eating and passing things to each other.

Then something else popped into O'Shea's head. All the time they'd been together he never heard Cerys call Clooney by his proper name. She always called him *love*, or *pet.* She never once called him Francis.

After breakfast Clooney and Allan disappeared while Agnes piled the dishes in the sink. Adam took the tea towel and helped her wash up.

O'Shea went out to the garden and lit a cigarette. Cerys came out too and went down the lane to the car. When she came back she walked straight past him without looking up.

'You all right there, Mrs Clooney?' He tried to sound lighter than he felt.

Her face clouded and she paused at the door. 'Yes.'

'So it *is* Mrs Clooney, then?'

'*What?*' She turned with her hands on her hips and her eyes flashing.

O'Shea took a long drag of his cigarette. 'Look, I'm sorry if I'm a bit slow sometimes, but …'

'What *are* you on about?' Cerys rolled her eyes.

'You and Clooney! What else do you think I'm on about? He's your husband, right?'

'So?'

'So isn't he the one you haven't seen for …*what*? How many years? Isn't he the one who's supposed to have abandoned you and your baby? And you didn't even know where he was anymore, remember?'

'As I just said. *So*?' Her mouth was a thin, tight line. 'What the hell has it got to do with you?'

'Nothing, I suppose,' O'Shea spat out the butt and rubbed it in the ground with his foot. 'I was just wondering why you told me all that crap about yourself back there in your house. What was it all about, Cerys? I'm just curious. What's going on inside that head of yours? The question is do you even know yourself?'

'Oh, who cares?' She turned around to go back in the door.

'Maybe *I* do.'

'Why?' Her eyes blazed again. 'It's none of your business, is it? It's got absolutely nothing to do with you so keep your bloody nose out.'

'Well, I'm sorry!' O'Shea gave a dry laugh. 'But I happen to think it has a lot to do with me.'

'How?'

'Well,' he was suddenly unsure of what to say. 'Ever since I met you I've had nothing but grief. And most of it is down to the lies you told me. You told me such a huge pack of lies …'

'Oh, piss off!' Cerys spun around and stormed back into the house.

Chapter Fifty-Five

It was mid-afternoon before Clooney and Allan turned up again. Clooney called Cerys and O'Shea into the front room where he had a large map spread out on the table. He pushed the door shut and took a quick look out of the window.

'Right.' He gathered them around the map and pointing at it with a pencil. 'This is where we are right now. And this is where the cave is. Now if you look here you'll see there's an old jetty about quarter of a mile from the cave. According to the locals it hasn't been used for years. Apparently it was built by the nearby colliery to transport coal overseas. But all that's gone now. Anyway as I told you before, the original plan was to take the boxes to Ireland and pass them on to our buyer. But obviously that didn't go to script. However, I've managed to contact the buyers and we've reopened negotiations. So it's back to plan A. They've arranged for a trawler to pick us up at that jetty and take us, and the boxes, across the Irish Sea to Dublin.'

'But what if the boxes aren't in the ...?'

'Forward planning,' Clooney tapped the map with the pencil and left a deep mark which he tried to rub out. 'We have to assume they are.'

He looked around suddenly, crept over to the door and opened it quietly. Satisfied no one was spying, he closed it again.

'Now, look,' he drew everyone into a conspiratorial huddle. 'As far as Allan and Agnes are concerned we're on the run from the Germans and we're trying to get to Ireland. The less they know, the better it is for everyone. So we have to keep it that way. Obviously Allan knows about the trawler picking us up near Uncle Rhodri's farm because he was there when it was arranged. But that's all.'

He looked at O'Shea. 'Right. I'll need fifty pounds.'

'Fifty pounds? What for?'

'For the trawler, what do you think?' Clooney said dryly. 'I have to give it to Allan to give to the skipper. When he gets us to Ireland he gets another fifty pounds.'

'Bloody hell,' O'Shea groaned. 'You could sail around the world on a luxury liner for fifty pounds. What are you hiring, the Queen Mary?'

'Just give me the bloody money, will you?'

O'Shea handed him the sock.

'Another thing,' Clooney added. 'The trawler can't pick us up until the day after tomorrow. He can only come alongside when the tide is high around three o'clock in the afternoon. But to make absolutely sure we're ready and waiting for him, I think we should leave straight away. What do you think?'

'Fine. I'll get Adam and take him out to the car.'

'No, we're walking. That's why we need to leave now.'

'You *are* joking!' O'Shea put his hand out for the sock. 'We have a car right outside the door and we're walking? Why?'

'Well, how far do you suppose the car will take us with no fuel in its tank?' Clooney threw the sock at him. 'Or have you forgotten we only just made it here? If we had fuel don't you think we'd have driven all the way to the farm already? Or did you think Agnes cooks such an amazing breakfast I couldn't resist stopping by for it?'

O'Shea pulled a face and Cerys glared at him. 'What's that look for?'

O'Shea shook his head. Cerys glared even more viciously. 'Come on! Spit it out. If you think you have a better idea tell us about it.'

'No, no.' O'Shea avoided her eyes. 'I was just wondering how your husband is clever enough to arrange for a trawler to pick us up in some God-forsaken dot on the map and take us all the way to Ireland. Yet he couldn't manage to get a lousy gallon of petrol for the car.'

'Ha bloody ha,' Cerys snorted and turned away.

'Anyway, how far is it? What about Adam? He's only a child. He can't walk far.'

'It's not that far.' Clooney was getting impatient. 'We'll just have to carry him if we need to. And if we stop farting about and go now we'll have plenty of time to rest along the way. We should be there by this time tomorrow, anyway. So let's go.'

'I won't be carrying him,' Cerys mumbled sourly. 'You bring him, you carry him yourself.'

'Thank you.' O'Shea still didn't catch her eye. 'You're so considerate it warms my heart, it really ...'

'That's enough!' Clooney pushed between them, put his arm around Cerys and drew her towards the door. 'Come on, we're going. Now!'

Chapter Fifty-Six

They'd been walking for two hours when Clooney took them through a gap in a hedge and up a steep embankment onto a railway line. By then the sky was one big black cloud making the winter evening close in around them much earlier than expected.

'This line leads all the way to Barry Island,' Clooney called over his shoulder as they scrambled onto the oily stones. 'It'll be easier to follow this in the dark. And it'll keep us off the road as well.'

'What do you mean follow it in the dark?' Cerys groaned. 'Are we going to walk all night?'

'It's still early yet.' Clooney put his arm around her shoulder and guided her towards the sleepers. They took a few slow, careful steps together to get in stride. 'We'll have a rest soon.'

O'Shea hitched his bag onto his shoulder, put his arm around Adam and traipsed after them. It took a while to get used to the pace of the sleepers.

A couple of hours later Clooney stopped. In the dark, O'Shea walked into him.

'What's the matter?'

'This is it,' Clooney pointed at the tiny railway station directly in front of them. It was practically invisible among the trees and they were on top of it before O'Shea even knew it was there.

They all bunched together as they followed Clooney up the slope and onto the platform. Even though the place seemed deserted, Clooney was still cautious as he moved quietly across to the waiting room door.

The door wasn't locked. Clooney went in first and looked around, and when he gave the all-clear the others followed him. They dropped their bags on the floor and flopped down on the wooden bench that lined the wall.

Clooney lit a match and studied a timetable.

'Good, there's nothing coming through here until eleven fifteen tomorrow morning.' He flicked the match into the fireplace. 'So this is our chance to get some sleep. But we'll still have to take turns on lookout just to be on the safe side. If no one minds I'll take the first shift. Three hours each, that should be enough.'

'That's fine by me.' O'Shea helped Adam to stretch out on the bench with the bag under his head. 'Wake me in about three hours. If you can. I'm exhausted. I could sleep for a week.'

'God, I'm so cold.' Cerys coughed into her hands. 'Shouldn't we light a fire or something?'

'No,' Clooney answered quickly. 'The town is less than half a mile away. If someone sees a fire up here they might come over to have a look.'

'No one's going to see us here.'

'They might!' Clooney's voice was strained. 'We can't take that chance.'

Cerys gave a grunt, rubbed her arms angrily and lay down on the bench opposite O'Shea.

O'Shea closed his eyes. He was just glad to be resting. A niggling headache stung the back of his eyes. His clothes were damp from walking and his shoes were soaked with wet mud. This certainly wasn't the best way to get over an illness. He would love to feel the heat from a blazing fire too. But Clooney was right. They couldn't take that chance. So he pulled his coat tighter around him and rested his head on his arm.

He woke with a start. The grey light of the morning was already creeping in through the small window. And he could hear the hum of activity. It sounded like voices. And footsteps walking on stones by the railway lines.

A train puffed and hissed as if it was shunting back and forth behind the main building. Iron couplings clattered in rhythm with the scrape of metal wheels on metal tracks.

O'Shea rolled off the bench and looked around the room. And his heart skipped a beat.

Adam was gone.

He ran across to Cerys. She groaned when he shook her. 'Get up. Something's happening. Adam's not here and there's someone outside. I think a train's arrived and they're parking it behind us.'

'What are you on about?' She rubbed her face as she looked around. She didn't notice the urgency in O'Shea's voice. 'Where's Francis?'

'He's not here,' O'Shea snapped. 'That's what I'm telling you.'

'Where is he, then?' Cerys practically fell off the bench and cursed as she scrambled back to her feet.

'I don't know. I just woke up.' O'Shea realised he was almost shouting and he checked himself. 'I don't bloody know where he is. But my son is gone too and that worries me a lot more.'

He tiptoed to the door and opened it a fraction. But he couldn't see a thing. All the activity seemed to be at the back of the building. He closed the door quickly, went to the window and wiped a hole in the condensation.

Cerys followed him and craned her neck to look out. But all they could see was the woods and a swathe of wild undergrowth.

The train sounded like it had stopped. The engine gave one last spurt of energy before it went silent. But men were still talking and moving around. Gradually they became less animated and eventually faded away as if they'd wandered off in the opposite direction.

'What's going on?' Cerys had a sob in her voice.

'I don't bloody know. But I think we should…'

Cerys glanced over O'Shea's shoulder and the look of sheer horror in her eyes made O'Shea spin around.

'Well, well, well!' The soldier standing in the doorway grinned back at him. He looked Cerys up and down and his face became a dirty leer. 'And where did you two strays come from?'

O'Shea's hand went in the pocket of his coat but the soldier swung the machine gun from behind his back. He cradled it in his arms and made sure it was pointing at O'Shea. Cerys reached for O'Shea's hand as the soldier sauntered across to the window and took a quick look outside.

'Right, you,' He waved O'Shea back against the wall. 'Stand over there and don't move.'

Then he grinned smugly. 'And you, darling. Over here and sit down.'

As Cerys dropped on to the bench the soldier sat beside her and put his hand on her knee.

'Stop that,' Cerys yelped and tried to push his hand away.

'Wow!' The soldier gave a spluttering laugh. Then he pushed the barrel of the gun against her cheek as he stood up and leant over her. 'I like a bit of spirit.'

'What do you want?' Cerys tried to shrink away from him but he held her down as he drew a line with his finger up the front of her body. When he got to her face he grabbed her mouth and squeezed it tight so her lips pouted.

Her eyes were terrified as he bent down to cover her lips with his mouth. When she tried to pull away from him again he banged her head against the wall.

Then he laughed even harder as he licked her face and sucked at her lips again.

It was all happening so fast O'Shea couldn't think straight. He considered rushing the soldier and taking him by surprise. But he was still so unbelievably weak after his illness he dismissed that stupid idea. But he still had the gun in his pocket.

He'd have to be quick, though. And accurate. Go for a head shot. He had no idea how many more soldiers were outside but with the element of surprise he and Cerys might just get out the window. They could be in the woods before anyone had time to react. In fact, if he was quick enough he could block the door with one of the benches. That might give them a few more precious seconds.

But the window was very small. And he couldn't make out if it was locked or not.

He took a deep breath and braced himself. He had no choice. It had to be quick. And it had to be now. His fingers cradled the butt of the gun as he clicked off the safety catch.

'*Evan*!'

O'Shea jumped when another soldier crashed in the door with an angry yell. He glared at O'Shea with a warning to keep his distance. And his face had a look of pure revulsion as he stormed across to the first soldier.

'What the hell are you doing, you stupid prat?' He grabbed Evan by the jacket. 'You know you're not supposed to touch those people.'

'Isn't she gorgeous, though?' Evan was chuckling as he banged her head against the wall again.

'Don't be so bloody stupid, you mad clown. You'll be put on a charge for this, you know that!'

Evan grabbed at her breasts, and the more Cerys whimpered the more he laughed. He slammed his hand between her legs so hard she recoiled backwards up onto the bench.

The second soldier slapped Evan across the back of the head, pulled him away from her and threw him back across the room.

'For God's sake,' he shouted. 'What's got into you? If you get caught doing this you'll be dead. I'm telling you now, what you're doing is worse than shagging a sheep. You just don't touch those people. You *know* that.'

'Get off me,' Evan sulked. 'Who's going to know, eh? Just give me five minutes with her. That's all I'm asking. Then I'll get rid of her. Who's going to know? Those woods out there are thick. They'll never find her in that.'

'Look at me!' The second soldier stabbed Evan with his finger. 'Don't you realise the kind of trouble we'll be in if anyone finds them here with us? They'll want to know how they got off the train in the first place. The way you're acting, they'll think you *let* them off just to satisfy your stupid lust.'

'What?' Evan looked at O'Shea with total revulsion. 'I just found them in here. I was going ...'

'Well, they'll think you're involved! And me with you. Either that or we weren't doing our bloody job properly and we let them escape. Either way we're in serious trouble. We'll have to get them back on the train without being seen.'

'How're we going to do that?' Evan went to the door and looked out. 'The corporal is over in the engine. He'll be there all day in that nice warm cab. He'll see us if we go out now dragging these two behind us. Let's just blow a hole in them and leave them here. Pretend we never saw them.'

'And nobody would hear a bloody thing?' the second soldier scoffed. 'Nobody would come running to investigate the shots? I always knew you had shit for brains. You're lucky we're related. Otherwise I'd just leave you to it and watch you hang. No, we'll just lock them in here until the next batch arrives. They're due any minute now. We'll hide them in here then slip them out when everyone's busy. So come on, let's get back and show our faces before we're missed.'

He waved the gun at O'Shea and nodded dangerously.

'If you make a sound, pal, you'll be dead before you can blink. Just remember, if you're found in here by our comrades you will be shot immediately. So behave yourselves, right? Just keep quiet and wait until we come back for you. Do I make myself clear?'

O'Shea sat back on the bench and looked down at the floor.

Chapter Fifty-Seven

'Oh, my God,' Cerys sobbed as soon as the door was shut and a bolt slammed into place. 'Where did they come from? How did they know we were here? What are they going to do to us? Where's Francis? Have they got Francis? Do you think they've got Francis? I don't understand ... why didn't he warn us?'

'I don't give a shit about him.' O'Shea ran to the window and tried to pull it open but it was stuck down with years of dried paint and neglect. 'I want to know what happened to my son. What have they done with Adam?'

A terrible hopelessness welled up inside him. None of this made any sense. Surely he hadn't fallen into such a deep sleep he didn't hear soldiers come into the waiting room and take Adam and Clooney away?

And why would they just take those two and leave O'Shea and Cerys?

No, this was all wrong. There had to be some other explanation. But O'Shea didn't like the first one that sprang into his mind. He shook his head in frustration and paced up and down the room.

Cerys curled up on the bench. She was sobbing and praying at the same time.

'Where the hell is Francis?' She rubbed angrily at her face with her sleeve. 'He'd know what was going on. He'd know how to get us out of this mess. I can't believe he'd just go off and leave me like this.'

'*What*?' O'Shea sniggered. 'Well, it wouldn't be the first time, would it?'

'What do you mean by that?'

'You know what I mean! You told me he ran out on you once before. So did you really expect him to stick around now he's got what he was looking for all along?'

'Don't you dare say that.' She swiped the air with her hand. 'Did you have to say that? He's still my husband, you know.'

'So where is he, then? He was supposed to be on watch, looking out for us. Where's my son? How did he let them take my son? You'll just have to face it. Your prat of a husband has abandoned us. I wouldn't be surprised if he'd arranged all this in the first place.'

'No,' Cerys blubbered. 'He wouldn't do that to me. They must have surprised him. Otherwise he'd have come and warned us. You know he would. You don't understand. He's not like that.'

'No, you're right!' O'Shea agreed. 'I *don't* understand. I don't understand how he's conveniently not here when those soldiers wandered in and found us. Don't you think that's odd? Or are you too blind to see what's happening right in front of your eyes. *He's left us behind!* He took off in the night and left us behind. I wouldn't be surprised if he left a note for the Germans telling them where to find us. Just to make sure we were delayed long enough for him to collect the boxes and be off to Dublin on the boat.'

Cerys shuddered and took a deep breath through her nose. 'I don't believe you.'

'Please yourself.' O'Shea hit the window in frustration. 'I knew in my bones I shouldn't have trusted him. Or you, for that matter. I should have taken Adam and left when I had the chance. I knew you and your whole weird family was rotten to the core. I knew I shouldn't have come with you. I should have stayed behind at the farm and taken my chances.'

'*Me and my whole weird family*? What do you mean by …?'

'You're all mad, the whole bloody lot of you. I can't figure any of you out. Everything you say is a pack of lies. You wouldn't know the truth if it jumped up and spat in your eye. Not a single one of you makes any sense.'

'Don't you talk about my family like that.' Tears fell down her face and she wiped them away with an angry swipe of her hand. 'They're not … don't you talk about them like that!'

'But tis true, isn't it. Nothing any of you ever did or said made any sense. You're all away with the bloody fairies. You make things up as you go along. You're all crackers. Everything you say is made up. There's no consistency in any of your stories.'

'What's that supposed to mean? Are you saying we were telling lies? When did we ever lie to you?'

'*Hah*!' O'Shea kicked at the wall, marched up to the window again and pressed his head against the glass. 'Well for a start, if all that stuff you told me about Clooney deserting you because you had a baby is true, why on earth did you get involved with him again? If he caused all that grief and upset everyone in your family why did Bethan even *speak* to him? I don't understand it. If she hated him so much why did she go along with his crazy plan to attack the German trucks?'

'Because he promised to give her what she always wanted.' Cerys sat upright and shook the hair from her face. 'Francis already told you. Bethan had a dream. She wanted a free, independent Wales and they promised to give it to her.'

'Holy Mother of God!' O'Shea spun around to face her. 'How the hell could she swallow that pile of old shite?'

'Well, she *did*. You don't know her. This wasn't just about a free Wales. It was about power. It was about recognition. It was about status. She saw herself as some sort of national hero. She was going to go down in history. Every town in Wales would have a big bronze statue of her in their town centres.'

O'Shea gave a curt laugh. 'Well, she must have been seriously delusional. As I said before, how could she swallow that pile of old shite without a stiff drink?'

'I don't know.' Cerys sagged back and held her face in her hands. 'All I know is what Francis told me. He said he approached her a few times over a period of weeks. He drip-fed her little bits of information and built up her trust. Weiss was very clever, you see. He planned every meeting down to the smallest detail. He had access to some Secret Service files so he knew who the active members were. Francis only had to drop a few key names into the conversation to convince Bethan he was high up in the movement. When he told her about his job in Obren Industries she was really impressed. He told her he was risking his life every day by spying on the Germans. And it was vital that she never, ever mentioned his name to anyone. Not even the other members of the movement. She had to swear not to tell a single soul about him or he'd just walk away. Then the movement would look unfavourably on her and her family.'

She leant her head against the wall and closed her eyes.

O'Shea swore under his breath. His whole body rippled with frustration. He couldn't just stand here doing nothing. They had to get out of here. If he could only get a look outside, see how many soldiers were actually out there on the platform, maybe he could plan something.

He walked over to the small door that led to the ticket office and rattled the handle. It was locked. Anyway, it didn't lead anywhere. He gave it a kick. Cerys jumped.

'It really *was* all lies, wasn't it?' She sat up and her eyes were wide and fretful. 'Francis lied when he said he wanted her to do a special job for him. She actually believed it came directly from the very top. She could barely contain herself with the excitement. She was ecstatic. Francis had to remind her it was top secret. A lot of lives, and the future of the movement itself, depended on her discretion. And he was *so* convincing. Bethan never doubted he had the full authority of the movement. It was like fishing. He threw her the bait and let her nibble at it. Then as soon as she was hooked he reeled her in. Hook, line and bloody sinker. Whatever a sinker is.'

She watched O'Shea for a few minutes, waiting for him to say something. But he was too distracted trying to find a way out.

'But I swear to God, I didn't know anything was going on until you arrived the farm. First you turn up, then all those other people start arriving too. And everyone is on edge. They're all arguing with each other. They're asking what went wrong. And what happened to some boxes.'

She wiped her nose on her sleeve. 'They were pointing the finger at each other so I knew something bad had happened. That's why I asked you about those boxes. I thought if I could find out what happened to them it might help Bethan sort out whatever the problem was.'

O'Shea was back at the window trying to prise it open. It wasn't working. When he turned around he caught the look Cerys was giving him.

'What?'

'Are you listening to me?' she snapped. 'I'm trying to tell you what happened.'

'Well don't!' O'Shea swatted it away. 'I don't feckin care. All I care about right now is my son.'

Chapter Fifty-Eight

'For God's sake! I'm just trying to explain to you. I was doing it for Bethan.' Cerys wiped her eyes and curled her legs up under her. 'And isn't that sad? Someone my age so desperate to please someone who treated her like rubbish? You saw how she put me down while *she* strutted around like she was really important. She believed they asked her to take part in this *thing* because she was so special. So there's no great mystery about it. She just wanted the power. It's as plain and as simple as that.'

'As plain and as simple as that?' O'Shea repeated sarcastically.

'Well, there you have it.'

'But you must have known Clooney was stuck in it somewhere. He was *your* husband, for heaven's sake.'

'No. I *told* you. I knew nothing about any of it until the day you came to the house. The shit had already hit the fan by then. I overheard the conversation in the front room between Bethan and the other men. They were accusing each other of all sorts of betrayal and stuff. Apparently there was an attack on some German trucks but whatever they were hoping to find wasn't there. And suddenly everyone was suspicious of everyone else. The atmosphere was hysterical. Absolutely horrible. I was petrified. I felt things had gotten out of hand and something terrible was going to happen to us. And when Bethan and Gareth drove off in the car Francis appeared. He'd come looking for my help.'

O'Shea gave a caustic snigger. 'I don't believe a word of it. I'm sorry, but it's total crap. If what you'd told me was true and he'd really deserted you all those years ago, he'd need more neck than a giraffe to just wander back in and pick up where he'd left off. What's even harder to believe is that you let him! As I said, *weird*. The whole bloody lot of you.'

'He was under enormous pressure.' Cerys spoke as if O'Shea should have known. 'Weiss was demented. He put a lot of time and effort into getting those boxes and now he was spitting fire. He'd risked everything. Even his life. And he wanted answers. For some reason he thought Bethan knew what happened to his precious boxes so Francis was sent to the house to see what he could find out.'

'Ah, now I get it.' O'Shea dropped onto the bench opposite her. 'That's why you were so nice to me that night. Because Clooney thought I might know about the stupid boxes.'

'No,' she gasped. 'What are you saying? Are you saying I ... because he *told* me to? What do you think I am? Are you saying I'm a prost ... a whore?'

'Something like that.' O'Shea glared back at her. 'The strange thing is, Cerys, you only had to ask me. You didn't have to treat me like I was some sort of simple eejit. I was on your side, believe it or not. Still, now I know why your mood changed so drastically.'

O'Shea stood up and walked the length of the room like a caged rat. He went to pull the handle on the front door in the tiny hope it was unlocked, but he stopped himself. Someone might be passing by and hear him.

'The stupid thing is,' he glared at Cerys as he strutted by again. 'The first time I saw you I thought you were such a beautiful looking girl. You had a lovely, gentle sort of way about you. You reminded me of ... someone. But then something happened.' He snapped his fingers.

'You turned into a different person. You were all bitter and twisted. I have to tell you, I didn't like what I saw.'

'People change.' Cerys shivered and hugged herself.

'Yeah. Especially when their mysterious husband turns up out of the blue.'

'It was nothing to do with him.' She gave another quiet sob.

'Really?' O'Shea flapped his arms and spun around.

'Really!' Cerys mimicked him. 'Not that it's any business of yours, but the reason my mood changed so drastically was because I found out my whole life was a lie. So you can give yourself a pat on the back for noticing it. Everything about me is a big fat lie.'

O'Shea snorted. 'What does *that* mean?'

'It means my mood changed because I discovered I'm not the person I believed I was.'

She sat up straight when O'Shea shook his head and stabbed a finger at him. 'Then tell me how *you'd* feel if you found out your mother didn't die giving birth to you after all. Something you were blamed for every day of your life and you were beaten with the guilt of it for as long as you could remember? How would you feel if you found out that she actually killed herself? She jumped out of an upstairs window because someone she worshipped let her down yet again? That she was so ashamed she couldn't face the world anymore?'

'Your father?'

'Not him. It was nothing to do with him. You must have noticed that Bethan is ... *was* a few years older than Rhianne and me. Fourteen years older, to be precise. She was an only child, you see. The miracle baby her parents dreamed of. After years of trying, after years of frustration, she was the answer to their relentless praying. So obviously she was worshipped, spoilt rotten.

She could do no wrong in her mother's eyes. They were chapel people too. So you can imagine the shame when Bethan comes home one day, still in her school uniform, and tells them she's pregnant. She'd only just turned thirteen.'

She looked at O'Shea for a reaction, but he turned away and scratched his head.

'And do you know what hurts the most? The way I found out about it! I wish to God I hadn't because now Bethan is gone none of it really matters anymore. It makes no difference to anyone now because they're all gone.'

A train whistle blew somewhere in the distance and they both looked at the door. But outside on the platform everything seemed to be quiet. O'Shea gave a long sigh and sat back down.

'It was Francis turning up made me discover that particular skeleton in the family cupboard.' Cerys was unable to let go of the story. 'Seeing him again after all that time, well, I was ... you know? He told me what happened up in the mountains. I knew something had happened from what you'd already told me. But I promise you, Bethan never told me anything. She always treated me like that, too stupid to understand. She treated me like I was still ten years old. Anyway, Francis told me the stuff was missing and it was all very frightening, wasn't it? I didn't know what she'd got herself into. I was worried about her. I just felt I had to do something to help her. So while she was out I had a look in her bedroom.'

She gave a long shiver and hugged herself again. 'I don't know what I expected to find there. It was something I'd never done before in my whole life. We were forbidden to go into her room and we were too scared do disobey her. Now I know why. What I found there made me physically sick. There was a box full of papers, letters and things. And wrapped in a sheet of pink paper were two birth certificates. Rhianne's and mine. I couldn't believe what I was reading. Both of them had the mother's name as Bethan Elizabeth Frost. Father unknown.'

O'Shea was intrigued now. 'Are you saying Bethan was your mother?'

'Yes. From the letters in the box I worked out Mama took the pregnant Bethan to a convent in England. And Mama stayed with her until the baby was born, which was me. Of course the family pretended the baby was an unexpected blessing for Mama. A beautiful sister for Bethan. And I was brought up thinking my mother was my big sister.'

'Oh, dear,' was all O'Shea could say. 'Did Bethan know you found out?'

'No, she did not!' Cerys looked at him as if he was mad. 'Anyway, Mama and I were only home a few months when Bethan, who was still spoilt rotten and who was still worshipped by the both of them, told them she was pregnant again. This time with a different boy.'

She gave a deep sob and let her hair fall over her face. 'My mother wasn't feeling well at the time, as you can imagine. She was struggling to cope with a new baby and run the farm as well. So the news hit her like a bomb. She put me to bed and ran a bath for herself. Then she just opened the window and threw herself out. Somehow they managed to convince everyone Mama actually died from complications after giving birth to me. And that's what I always believed. It was a guilt I had to carry around my whole life.'

'Does Clooney know about this?' O'Shea asked after a long awkward pause.

'Oh, yes. But do you know what the hardest thing about this? My father. He pretended Rhianne was the child of his fancy woman so no one would know what a little whore his precious daughter really was.'

A little line of spittle appeared in the corner of her mouth and she licked it away. 'He put up with years of back biting and snide comments. He was banned from the chapel and almost run out of the army as some kind of pervert. They couldn't tolerate him having a child by another woman when his own wife was hardly dead and buried. But no one corrected that impression. Someone in the family must have known the truth. Someone would have worked it all out.'

'I can understand why you'd be upset.' O'Shea felt he needed to say something to keep his mind off his own pain.

'No you bloody can't.' Cerys clapped her hands angrily. 'You'll never know how betrayed I felt. How angry and deceived I *still* feel. You'll never know how I carried that guilt like a cross on my back for the whole of my life. I thought I'd killed my mother. When I think how I put up with Bethan's tantrums, the spiteful remarks. I allowed her to intimidate me and bully about the sacrifices she had to make to raise us. What she had to give up, how we destroyed her chances of ever getting married and having children of her own. God, it makes me so angry.'

O'Shea was suddenly conscious of increased activity outside. It sounded like another train was approaching. They both went to the door and tried to look through the crack.

Dark September

The train arrived with a flurry of steam and slowed down as it clattered past the platform. Then it stopped and there was a lot of shunting and thudding as it was parked behind the first train.

Chapter Fifty-Nine

The door flew open, hit O'Shea in the face and threw him back into the middle of the room. The two soldiers rushed in, dragged both of them outside and pulled them down a narrow path that tapered around the back of the station. O'Shea was still dazed and couldn't see who else was on the platform. Everything happened so fast it was just a passing blur.

Evan took delight in prodding Cerys on the buttocks with his machine gun. And he giggled manically to himself.

They passed another soldier with a long buttoned-up overcoat who looked at them with amused eyes. As they rounded the corner they were hurried up to a row of cattle wagons parked in a sidings.

They both paused. There was a strange humming noise coming from the wagons. Evan gave them a vicious shove as a man in railway uniform lifted a long iron bar off the wagon doors. And O'Shea's mind reeled when the doors were pulled apart.

The wagon was full of people.

A mass of deathly white faces stared down at them. Faces of all ages, men, children, women, all with the same haunted resignation in their eyes. The smell that poured out of the carriage made O'Shea stagger.

Cerys buried her face in O'Shea's chest. Evan pulled them apart and shoved them towards the sea of bodies as the man in the railway uniform started beating at the legs with a walking stick to push them farther back into the wagon.

Cerys pulled away and tried to run but Evan grabbed her hair and put his arms around her waist. As he lifted her up into the wagon he took great satisfaction in groping her viciously before he threw her heavily onto the floor.

The man in railway uniform hit O'Shea repeatedly with the stick to encourage him to follow her. Then the doors were slammed behind them and the iron bar was dropped back into place.

Within seconds hands were grabbing and pulling at their clothes for something to eat. The floor was swamped with a mess of thick putrid sewage,

O'Shea struggled to breathe as he pushed the clawing hands away. He was gagging on the overpowering smell and forced to inhale through his nose. And his stomach heaved.

Cerys wrapped her arms around him and forced him back against the door. A mass of bluebottles pattered against their faces and she screamed. And it all came up and spurted out over O'Shea's back. Hands grabbed at his clothes to get at it. Cerys went limp but they were packed too tight and she had no space to fall.

'Where's Francis?' she wailed. 'How could he do this to me? What's happened to him? Oh my God! Do you think they've caught him too? Do you think he's somewhere on this train? Or did the bastard just slip away in the middle of the night like you said. Nothing else matters to him, the selfish pig. Nothing! Not even me.'

She looked at the faces that surrounded her. 'Who are these people, anyway? For God's sake! This is like something out of a nightmare. I can't stand it. I can't stand it. Let me out! Get me out of here!'

The middle-aged woman who was pressed against O'Shea's back looked up with bloodshot eyes. 'Foolish girl,' she sneered. 'Who do you think you are? Why are you so special? Why should they let you out and not us?'

'But who are you? Why are you on this train?'

'You don't know?' A mocking sneer creased the lady's face. 'You are a Jew and you don't know this? What world have you been living in these past few months? Have you not been listening?'

'A Jew?' Cerys yelped. 'What do you mean, a Jew? I'm not a Jew. We're not Jews. We're chapel, Church of Wales. Tell them, Danny. Danny's Irish. We're not Jews.'

'Then you must be a gypsy,' the woman said dismissively. 'Either way it does not matter now. Where we're going it is no matter. Gypsy, Jew, whatever.'

'No,' Cerys cried. 'They've made a terrible mistake. They've got it all wrong.'

The woman closed her eyes and her lips moved in her own silent prayers.

'I'm sorry,' Cerys whimpered. 'Dear God, Lord, I'm so very sorry for what I've done. Please forgive me. Please let them see their mistake and get me off of this train and I promise I'll do anything You ask of me for the rest of my life. Please, God, please.'

The hours crept by with a horrifying slowness. The numbness in O'Shea's legs got so bad he was forced to prise the people around him out of the way with one mighty shove so he could change position and ease the raging pain.

He managed to turn around completely and the relief made him groan out loud. He closed his eyes and savoured the moment.

Cerys was now against the door and she still had her arms around O'Shea's neck. And she was crying softly and rubbing her head against his shoulder as she hung from him like a limp doll.

Pressed up against her was a young woman with eyes that sank deep into her pale face. When O'Shea looked at her she lifted a tiny child from somewhere between them and held him so his face was against O'Shea's. The boy's skin was cold and clammy.

'Mister, my baby?'

Even with the child's mouth close to his ear O'Shea couldn't hear his breathing. He lifted the head back and the mouth hung open, and the half-closed eyes stared away into the distance.

'I'm sorry,' he whispered.

The mother gave a soft whimper and lowered the boy back down between them. Then she started screaming and there was a surge of pressure as everyone panicked and tried to see what was happening. The noise rose to a deafening pitch as others starting shrieking too because they were getting crushed where they stood.

Cerys cried as elbows and shoulders battered them. And it was several minutes before the noise abated and they could breathe again. But the stench had been stirred up and it made O'Shea's head swim with each gulp of putrid air. A panic rose up from the pit of his stomach. He swallowed hard and tried to distract himself from it.

'Please God,' Cerys sobbed. 'Please get us out of this place and I swear I will never tell another lie for as long as I live. I swear I'll tell the truth about what happened, what I've done. Only please get me out of here.'

Rain pattered against the roof of the wagon and the weak light that filtered through the narrow grills got even dimmer as angry clouds flooded the sky.

Apart from the initial flurry of activity they couldn't hear anyone moving about outside. And not one vehicle drove along the road that ran parallel to the railway line.

It was as if they were hidden away and forgotten about. Now, as the darkness seeped in around them the murmuring faded. They weren't given any food or water and the dehydrated, dejected passengers resigned themselves to a long uncomfortable night.

When O'Shea became conscious of a tapping on the outside of the wagon he pressed his head against the door and strained to listen. Cerys raised her head and looked at him. 'What is it?'

'I don't know.'

It came again, this time farther along the wagon.

'It'll be the guards checking the wheels.' The old lady gave Cerys a contemptuous look. 'They'll be getting ready to move us again.'

'What do you mean?' Cerys cried.

'That is what they do. They move us at night. In the daytime they keep us out of sight. They don't want to upset the sensibilities of the general public.'

'Oh, dear God. What's going to happen to us?' Cerys screeched and tried to pull away.

O'Shea put his hand over her mouth. 'Shush! *Listen*. That tapping, it's as if someone is trying to send a message. You know, like Morse code? Tap, tap, then a space, then another tap, tap.'

'Rubbish,' the lady griped. 'It will be the guard, I'm telling you.'

The noise came back along the wagons again. And as it got closer O'Shea could hear the crunch of feet on the stones.

'Cerys?' a voice called in a loud whisper. 'Where are you?'

'My God.' O'Shea slapped the door. 'It's bloody Clooney!'

He thumped the door with the heel of his shoe and repeated the rhythm of the tapping.

'Is that you, Clooney?' O'Shea was unable to keep his voice down in the excitement.

The gravel crunched back towards them.

'Yes, it's me. Where are you? Where's Cerys?'

'We're here.' O'Shea kicked the door again. 'We're just in here.'

There was a lot of grunting as the iron bar was dragged out of the way and lowered carefully onto the ground. Seconds later the door cracked open an inch and Clooney's face was shiny in the faint light.

'Right, when I pull this door open I want you to jump out and follow me as fast as you can. Do you understand? Don't fart about. There might be shooting but with all those other people running about as well there should be enough confusion for us to get away. All right?'

'Where's Adam? Have you seen him?'

'He's safe. He's with me.'

'He's with *you*?'

'Yes!' Clooney snapped. 'Now get ready. Here we go.'

Clooney pulled the two doors together. They opened out like giant wings and Cerys went with them. Clooney reached up to catch her but she landed awkwardly and they both tumbled backwards onto the oily stones.

They were back up and running across the track before O'Shea had time to follow them. He wanted to jump clear of the stones but he'd been standing too long and misjudged the weakness of his legs. So he dropped straight down and his legs collapsed under him, and his head clanged against a wheel with a solid crack.

It threw him around in a complete circle and for the next few yards he was on his hands and knees as he scurried after Clooney. And his nerves screamed as he waited for the shooting to start.

But nothing happened. He tumbled into the bushes and glanced back at the people in the wagon. Their faces were eerie in the weak light. None of them moved.

'Come on, for God's sake,' he called to them. 'Get out while you have the chance. What are you waiting for?'

They stared blankly at him.

'Over here,' Clooney barked. 'Get a move on, you prat. I told you not to fart about.'

Clooney and Cerys were lying in a ditch about thirty feet ahead of him.

'What are they waiting for?' Cerys pointed back at the open doors in disbelief. 'Why won't they run for it?'

'God knows,' Clooney muttered as O'Shea slid into the ditch beside him. 'But we have to go. We can't wait for them to make their minds up.'

'I can't see Adam,' O'Shea said. 'Where is he? Where's my son?'

'He's all right. He's just up by there.'

'So what the hell happened?'

'We haven't got time for this. We need to go before they come to check the train. When they see the doors wide open they will not be happy pussycats.'

'Don't give me that shit,' O'Shea grabbed Clooney by the shirtsleeve. 'I want to know …'

'All right!' Clooney slapped his hand away. 'Your boy needed the toilet so I took him outside. But while we were busy soldiers came and sat on the bench outside the waiting room. They looked like they were there for the night so we had no choice. We slipped away and waited to see what was happening.'

He held out his hand and Cerys took it. 'Lucky for you we did. Otherwise I wouldn't have saved your stupid fat arse tonight. Are you happy now? So come on!'

Together they moved towards the open field behind them and in the blink of an eye they disappeared into the blackness of the night.

Chapter Sixty

'I don't believe it!' Clooney pulled at a lump of weeds as he sat back on his heels. 'We've lost a whole bloody day, and now this!'

The four of them were crouching behind a cluster of blackberry bushes on the edge of a stretch of moorland that went on for miles.

'It'll take us half a day if we have to go around. Then we'll be too late. We'll miss the bloody boat.'

'Well, that's not our fault.' Cerys gave a sullen pout. 'They'll just have to wait for us, won't they?'

'No, they will not!' Clooney threw the fistful of weeds at her. 'They're not going to risk *that*. Anyway, they'll be governed by the tide. So whether we're there or not, when the tide turns they'll have to leave or get stranded. Apart from that, if they hang about too long the Germans might see them and blow them out of the water.'

'No they won't.' O'Shea spat out the bit of grass he was chewing and wiped his mouth with his sleeve. 'They're fishermen. They'll be in a trawler. Isn't that what fishermen in a trawler are supposed do? Bounce around on the sea catching fish?'

'Listen to me!' Clooney spun around on his heels. 'Those trawlers only fish where they're told to fish. If they're outside their zone they get investigated. And our friends wouldn't like that. So we better be there to meet them because they're not going to hang around for us. Do you understand?'

Cerys and O'Shea both nodded wearily. They were too tired to argue. Being trapped on the train for all that time had taken its toll on them. They were still buzzing from the shock of seeing the underbelly of the New Order. And no matter how hard they tried to rub it away, the appalling smell of death still lingered in their nostrils and clung to their clothes. That Clooney rescued them and probably saved their lives was no comfort at all.

After escaping from the train they followed Clooney without question and stumbled after him across fields and meadows in the pitch black. He seemed to know where he was going, though no one else did. And they weren't about to challenge his judgment.

After several hours they found their way suddenly blocked by a high dry-stone wall. The huge stones were heavy and loose, and any attempt to scramble over them would have brought them crashing down. So they had no choice. They would have to follow it and find a way through.

It didn't take long. After less than half a mile they discovered a rusty gate. In the dark it looked as if it was leading onto a narrow lane. But when they scrambled over it they were amazed to hear the familiar crunch of stones under their feet. They looked closer and found tracks. It was a railway crossing.

Clooney was adamant they were back on the line to Barry! When he proposed they follow the tracks again O'Shea and Cerys just nodded meekly. He didn't bother to wait for their answer anyway. He'd already gone marching off clicking his fingers impatiently for them to hurry on.

Several more brutal hours of slipping and staggering they had to leave the track again and follow Clooney's directions to the coast and Rhodri's farm.

But just as dawn was unzipping a sliver of light along the horizon they arrived at the edge of this enormous marshland.

They sagged to their knees and glared down at it in total disbelief. Clooney's face was dark and angry at yet another frustrating delay.

'Why can't we just go straight across?' Cerys sat on her hands. Her eyes had dark rings around them and her mouth was drawn into a thin colourless line.

'Then we'd be out in the open.' Clooney nodded towards a group of workers arriving to cut peat in the corner of the bog. 'And we'd be in full view of all those people over there.'

'So what?' Cerys noticed them too. 'Surely to God they wouldn't take any notice of us.'

'That depends who they think we are.' Clooney gave an agitated wave of his hand. 'But I'm more worried about walking across that bog. After all the rain it'll be like treacle. And it'll be riddled with bog holes. The mud will be like glue. People have lost their shoes in that kind of mud. Even their clothes.'

He gave his face another angry wipe with the palm of his hand. 'But we've got to be at that jetty before three o'clock this afternoon. So what do you two want to do? Go the long way around? Or take a chance and go straight across?'

'We really haven't got a choice, have we?' O'Shea sighed. 'As you said, it'll take twice as long to go around. Apart from that, we don't know what other problems we might come across if we *do* go around.'

'What about the people over there? Should we worry about them?'

'I don't think so.' O'Shea scratched his chin. 'I haven't seen a town for a while, have you?'

'What?' They both looked at him blankly.

'Well, if there's no town, it's likely there won't be any soldiers either.'

'What are you saying?'

'Well, tis obvious, isn't it? If your fellow Welshmen decide to cash us in for the thirty pieces of silver they'd have to go to the nearest town, fetch the soldiers and come all the way back here. How long would that take? Hours? So even if it takes us a few hours to cross the moor we'll be well lost in them trees over there by then.'

'True.' Clooney had that sarcastic smirk on his face again. 'However, you might not have them in Ireland yet, but over here we have these funny little things called telephones. Maybe you've heard of them? You stick one bit in your ear and you talk into the other bit, and someone miles away can actually hear you. They're amazing. There's probably one in that big house just over the hill. The Germans could be here before you had time to evacuate your bladder near that bush.'

'Look, let's just go straight across,' Cerys groaned. 'It's a risk we'll have to take. So come on. We're wasting time.'

'Okay,' Clooney jutted out his chin. 'Then I suggest we move quickly, all right? Once we start walking we keep going as fast as possible. Strike out for the woods with everything we've got. Don't give yourself time to think. Do we all think we can do it? What about the boy?'

'Don't worry about him,' O'Shea said. 'He'll be all right.'

'Does anyone want to rest awhile? Say ten minutes?'

But no one wanted to. Their senses tingled with nervousness and they were impatient to be on their way. Their minds were already out on the moor and struggling.

'Anything you don't need, push out of sight into the thick grass. Everything else tie on tight.' Clooney stood up and slung his satchel over his shoulder. He didn't seem to notice he was the only one with a bag now. The other two were left in the railway station waiting room.

'Right, come on!' He stomped off at an incredible speed and half-slid, half-trotted through the clumps of weeds and bushes. His keen eyes scrutinised the ground and he danced across what looked like dry patches. But the mud still oozed out to fill his shoes.

Cerys ran to catch up with him but there was no way O'Shea could achieve that kind of pace. He was restricted to a more sedate stride as he guided Adam by the arm and manoeuvring him down the slope.

The people in the bog stopped and watched them for a moment. But after the initial curiosity they lost interest and carried on cutting lumps of turf and spinning them up onto the reeks.

When O'Shea and Adam landed on flat ground it was a lot firmer than expected. Clooney found an animal track that weaved through the larger patches of wild heather and avoided most of the wetter areas. And it wasn't long before a wide gap opened up between him and O'Shea.

A strange resentment started to fester in O'Shea's stomach. He could taste its bitterness. Was it because Clooney didn't look back once to see if he and Adam were all right? Anything could have happened to them. But Clooney didn't hesitated for even a second. He just ploughed on with his head down. And soon he and Cerys morphed into a couple of dots in the distance.

Now the strain was causing O'Shea to slide and stumbled as he danced around puddles. When Adam fell for the third time O'Shea crouched down beside him. 'Look, get on my back, son.'

Adam didn't hesitate. He gave a sigh of relief as his father scooped him off the ground, adjusted his weight and started walking at a much faster pace.

Clooney and Cerys had vanished into the trees a good twenty minutes before O'Shea reached the edge of the woods. But he knew roughly where they went in. And as he followed their track feeble sunbeams filtered through the branches in mottled streaks. They highlighted the dark browns and the deep greens of the ivy clinging around the roots of the trees like long thin reptiles.

O'Shea tried to ignore the bite of apprehension in his stomach, the tinge of suspicion that Clooney was going to keep on walking and leave O'Shea behind to fend for himself. After all, if the boxes were where Cerys thought they were, he really didn't need O'Shea anyway.

O'Shea got a more comfortable grip on Adam and marched on.

Chapter Sixty-One

About forty feet into the woods O'Shea spotted Clooney sprawled out on a log with his hands folded on his chest. Cerys sat on the ground beside him with her back propped against his legs. Neither of them acknowledged O'Shea when stumbled up to them.

He stopped by the log and let Adam step onto it, and he rubbed the life back into his arms. He stamped his feet too but they were so wet and cold it made no difference.

'Thank you for waiting.' O'Shea smiled but neither of them responded.

Cerys wiped her face with her sleeve as Adam jumped off the log and sat down the next to her.

'Right.' Clooney jumped up and picked up his bag. 'We can't stop here all day.'

'Oh, no.' Cerys laid her head back against the tree trunk.

O'Shea hadn't managed to sit down yet so he gave a weary groan and rubbed his tired eyes. 'He *is* right, though,' he said reluctantly. Then he took Adam by the hand and helped him back on his feet.

'I am.' Clooney took Cerys by the arm and helped her to her feet as well. 'So c'mon. A few more miles and we can have a proper rest.'

It was strangely warm under the trees. The clouds had cleared and the shadows caused by the weak sun had turned into dancing silhouettes, slanting and weaving in front of them.

When they reached the top of a steep hill they looked down over fields that stretched away to where a silver strip of water glinted like polished steel on the horizon.

As they studied it quietly they were each lost in their own thoughts. A soft breeze brought a hint of the sea with it.

'Oh my God!' Cerys jumped up onto a large rock. '*Look!* That's it. Right over there. You can see the bay from here. You can see the bay. Oh thank you God. Thank you.'

Clooney jumped up onto the rock beside her. 'Thank you from me too, God.' He wiped his neck with a handkerchief. 'So what do you want to do? Go on? Or rest here for a few minutes?'

'Well, how far do you think it is?'

'Only about four or five miles, I'd say.'

No one spoke for a moment then Cerys gave a long shiver. 'Well, I'm shattered. But I'd rather get there first and then rest. So I say we go on.'

'Right.' Clooney slapped his hands together and stomped off into the trees on the other side of the clearing.

It was well over an hour before the trees thinned out again and they found themselves in another clearing. The sun was at its highest point in the sky when they looked down and saw the sea again.

Cerys grabbed Clooney's arm. 'Look! That's it! That's Rhodri's farm. See, the one with the big stone barn? You can just see the little river on the far side of it.'

'Bloody marvellous,' Clooney cheered. 'Where's the path to the cave?'

Cerys paused and scratched her head. 'I think that's it on the left of that field with the cattle in it.'

'You *think*?'

'Yes, I *think*,' she snapped. 'I haven't been here since I was a little girl, you know. That was years ago. But I'm almost sure it went to the left of that field. Yes, that's it. It went down past that big chestnut tree over in the corner.'

'So the jetty must be over to the left?'

'I don't know. I didn't even know there *was* a jetty. No one ever said. Or if they did, I don't remember.'

'Perhaps it's around the back of that big rocky outcrop.' Clooney shaded his eyes with his hand. 'According to the map there's a path along the cliff. It's only a short distance from the farm so it should be easy to find.'

Cerys squinted against the light. 'I remember there was a small gate near a path but we were told not to go near it. Dangerous, Bethan said. Maybe that's the path to the jetty.'

'Bloody marvellous,' Clooney said again. 'This calls for a celebration. Crack open a nice can of something and let's eat to the future.'

They sat on the trunk of a fallen tree. Clooney passed each of them a can of beans which they ate cold as they studied the flow of the land that rolled away in front of them.

'So who's a clever boy, then?' Cerys hugged Clooney as he rummaged in his bag and took out another tin. 'I always knew you could do it.'

Clooney looked very pleased with himself. 'Of course it's all down to the planning, you know? Get yourself a good map, a compass and, of course, a lot of natural talent. The trick is in the detail.'

'Detail?' It came out sharper than O'Shea meant.

Clooney's eyes narrowed. 'Yes. *Detail*!'

O'Shea stuck the tin opener into a can of peaches and sliced through it.

'Come on, then!' Clooney said. 'Spit it out.'

O'Shea shook his head. He was so tired he wasn't sure what he meant. It was as if someone else was doing the talking and he was detached from it all.

'Tis just the way you said *detail*. And *planning,*' was what came out.

'Meaning what?'

'Well, forgive me for saying so, but all your plans so far haven't exactly turned out the way you wanted them to, have they?'

O'Shea took a long slurp of the peach juice before handing the can to Adam. 'But then, the best laid plans of men and mice, eh? Isn't that how it goes?'

Clooney didn't answer. He dug his knife into another tin of beans and ripped off the top in one twist.

'Of course I'm not saying it was all *your* fault or anything, you understand?' O'Shea continued. 'A plan is just like a bubble, isn't it? One little prick and ...' he snapped his fingers.

'And the prick is who, exactly?' Clooney didn't look up.

'Whoever you want it to be. The problem with you is you've got so many bubbles in the air it's hard to keep track of them all. But most of them have popped already, so it probably doesn't matter who the ... well, you know what I mean.'

Clooney scooped at the beans with his knife and ate them noisily. When he finished he dumped the empty tin under the bushes. 'Go on, then. You're dying to get something off your chest. Let's have it.'

'Look,' O'Shea was trying to find the right words to make sense of what was hopping around inside his head. 'I'm just an ordinary working man, right? I live in a completely different world from you. I worked in Newport docks fixing electric motors on cargo ships. I took home a modest wage to my family every Friday. And the highlight of my week was a couple of pints and a game of darts down the pub. Nothing grand. Just a basic, simple life.'

He took the tin from Adam and poured some slivers of peach into his hand before handing the tin back. Then he sucked the peaches into his mouth and chewed them slowly.

'I don't belong in the kind of circles you move in,' he continued. 'All that wheeling and dealing. All that intrigue. Which is why, when my wife died, all I wanted to do was take my son to Ireland where I thought he'd be safe. A neutral country. No war. I wasn't asking anything from anyone. I didn't want any fuss. I didn't want to bother anyone. And I certainly didn't want any of the shite that's happened to me since and that's for sure.'

Cerys threw her empty tin into the bushes and wiped her mouth with the back of her hand. 'What's he on about?' she asked without looking at anyone.

Clooney gave a mock frown. 'Yeah, what *are* you on about?'

O'Shea sighed. 'What I'm trying to say is I take people at face value. Call me naive if you like. Or stupid. Whatever. I just haven't got the devious kind of mind you need to live in your world. I'm not very quick at picking up the little deceptions, the little hints of dark deeds. I haven't got a clinical mind that sees everything in black and white. Terrible things happened to me and I missed the reasoning behind them. I just floated along and took each day as it came. Of course questions come into my head, but they disappear again before I can digest them.'

They were both studying him now.

'What kind of questions?'

'Well, the one that bothers me most is what happened the day Bethan was killed. It was obvious you two knew something was going to happen because you hung back by the gate while the rest of us went up to the house. And why were you wearing that ridiculous white scarf?'

Clooney looked down at the scarf he still had around his neck and he tucked it inside his coat.

'You could be seen for miles in that thing,' O'Shea added. 'But was that the whole idea. You'd stand out like a sore thumb and you wouldn't be mistaken for a target when the fireworks started?'

Clooney laughed out loud. 'That's very good for a bog trotter.' He stood up and brushed himself down. He looked totally relaxed. Happy even. Was he feeling like that because he was so close to the prize he could almost reach out and touch it? Did he believe he'd soon have the precious boxes in his greedy little hands and he'd be on his way to a new and wonderful life?

'But the fact is,' he sat back down on the tree trunk, pulled a bottle of water from the bag and took a long drink from it. 'No one was supposed to get hurt.'

O'Shea gave a sharp laugh and Clooney's face clouded. 'It's the truth! No one was supposed to get hurt!'

He passed the bottle of water to O'Shea who handed it to Adam. 'Why do you think Cerys took you and the two lads down to the gate in the first place? It was to draw you away from the house. With you three down by the gate Bethan and Gareth would be alone in the house. They'd have no choice but to come out nice and quiet when Weiss surrounded the place. They would have been perfectly safe if they'd done what they were told.'

'For God's sake,' O'Shea blustered. 'And you expect me to believe that shite?'

'Look, we believed the boxes were somewhere on that farm. We really ...'

'Why?'

'Well, because the day before the robbery Weiss gave instructions to the two officers in charge of the convoy. He told them it was top secret, straight from Berlin. They were to take the boxes to a certain pub and rent a room at the back. They'd be absolutely safe there because the landlord knew he wouldn't look good hanging from the lamppost outside his front door if anything happened to them.'

'So,' he stabbed the air with the knife. 'Apart from Weiss, the only people who knew where those boxes were hidden were those two officers. So, as you can imagine, Weiss was not a happy bunny when he went back to the pub the next day and found the boxes gone. Someone collected them the night before. Someone with a German military identity card.'

Adam handed O'Shea the bottle of water and he took another quick swig before passing it to Cerys.

'The thing is, Bethan had clear instructions. No German soldier was to be left alive. For obvious reasons. Yet one of those officers was not amongst the bodies left on the mountain. And one of the staff cars was also missing. So either that officer escaped in the car, went back to the pub and took the boxes. Or, as Weiss suspected, he was taken back to Bethan's farm in the missing car.'

He pointed at Cerys with the knife. 'Then my lovely wife confirmed it. A German car did turn up outside Bethan's front door. But she didn't see any Garman officer. However, you told us yourself the officer *was* at the farm. So the officer turns up at Bethan's one day, and the very next day the boxes are gone. Well, it could only mean one thing. He was persuaded to tell Bethan what he knew about the boxes. Of course we assumed Bethan brought the boxes back to the farm and hid them there. We didn't realise she was so bloody smart.'

He stood up and started putting his stuff together. 'Anyway,' he pulled his coat tighter around him before slinging the bag over his shoulder. 'Sorry to interrupt this very interesting conversation, but I think we'd better make a move. The sooner we get to the beach the better.'

Chapter Sixty-Two

Cerys and O'Shea stood up too, and O'Shea felt in his pocket to make sure the gun was still there.

'Anyway, I just wanted to …'

'Oh, for God's sake,' Cerys snapped. 'Just shut up, will you?'

'No, I will not,' O'Shea snapped back. 'You have to realise everything I had in the whole world was taken from me. Right now all I have left is my boy and a load of questions. They may be stupid questions but they're questions that I'd like answers to. If that's all right with you? Anyway, what does it matter now if I know the truth? Everyone else is dead.'

Cerys tutted and stormed off after Clooney.

'For instance …'

'Jesus!'

'For instance,' O'Shea caught up with Clooney. 'If Weiss double crossed you the first time, what possessed you to trust him again? And if Bethan had the boxes, why didn't you just ask her what happened? She trusted you. She believed you were on the same side.'

Clooney grinned. 'You haven't the faintest idea how Bethan's mind worked, have you?'

'Well …'

'Look,' Clooney waved his hand around. 'Bethan was a dreamer. She wanted a free Wales, yes. But she also wanted the glory. She was chasing rainbows. She was hoping for greater things for Wales, but with herself at the head of it. But she was no fool. She was a very smart lady. And very devious. And when she realised she'd been double crossed she was confused. She was disappointed too. But she was not one for just rolling over and curling up in the corner. No, no. She went straight into counter-attack mode. First off, she trusted the Nationalists completely. So she didn't think for one moment *they* betrayed her. No, it had to be simpler than that. It had to be someone in her own camp. So that's why, when she *did* get hold of the boxes, she hid them where the bad guys would never find them in a month of Sundays. Then, once she'd found the people who betrayed her and dealt with them, she would continue with her original plan. An independent Wales.'

Adam stumbled and O'Shea ran to help him. And when he caught up with Clooney again Cerys stepped between them. Clooney chuckled and she gave an irritated growl before sliding her arm around his waist.

'It was just unfortunate for Weiss that Gareth suspected something when the stuff wasn't on the truck and decided to keep the German officer alive,' Clooney added.

'Just leave it, for God's sake.' Cerys groaned again. 'Concentrate on what we're supposed to be doing.'

'Yes, dear.' Clooney gave her a patronising pat on the back. 'Anyway, Bethan had no idea what the real value of those boxes was. This is something that will change the concept of warfare as we know it. So whichever country has it will be the ultimate world power. What would a tiny, insignificant little country like Wales do with it? Can you imagine Wales as the greatest power in the world? How could they possibly develop it? How could they possibly keep hold of it? Could they stop the big boys taking it off them? No, this thing is huge. It's bigger than any of us. Weiss, me, anyone. It belongs to either America or Russia. Even Germany, if they were willing to buy it back. And guess who has the most money?'

He punched the air and walked on. Cerys still had her arm around his waist and she had to trot to keep up with him.

'Anyway, you can forget about Weiss and his lot.' Clooney practically sang the words as he did a little happy jig. 'We've got it now. Me and Cerys. And you, of course. We'll take the stuff to Ireland and the Americans will pay us handsomely for it. We'll be set up for the rest of our lives. We'll go to some beautiful, warm country and live the life of luxury. And spend our days idling about in a boat on a river.'

'What about all the others, though?' O'Shea called after him. 'What about Bethan and all those who died trying to get their hands on this thing? What about Rhianne? And my son? He almost died because of this stuff.'

'For God's sake,' Cerys yelled back at him. 'Don't keep on. No one was supposed to die. Do you really think we wanted that to happen? Why do you think I took you down to the road to meet Francis? It was to make sure no one got carried away. Weiss would tell Bethan he'd captured me and he'd exchange me for the boxes. He'd take the boxes and we'd all go our own separate ways. But no one was supposed to be hurt.'

'And you really believed Weiss would let Bethan just walk away?'

'He would. If one of you hadn't started shooting. *You* started it. If you hadn't started shooting none of this would have happened.'

The trees began to close in again and Clooney had to beat a path through the bushes with a piece of branch.

'Sorry, but there's still something I'm missing here,' O'Shea said. 'When I was put in the back of the truck that day, you were already in it. You'd planned to take me back to where the ambush happened because you thought Bethan told me something. She was hardly cold on the ground but still all you could think about was …'

'Well, what did you *expect* us to do?' Cerys pulled away from Clooney. 'She was dead. It was too bad, but that's the way it was.'

'But she was your sister, your very own …'

'She was *not*' she yelled. 'She was *not* my bloody sister. I told you. She was my mother. And this was my chance to get away from her. To escape from her evil, nasty clutches once and for all. I had one chance to escape from her bullying and her vile tongue and I was going to grab it with both hands. And God help anyone who got in my way.'

'Cerys.' Clooney put his hand out to her but she brushed it away.

'No,' she stamped her foot. 'All my life she was there, hammering home the guilt. Undermining everything I ever did. Plaguing me, haunting my every living moment. How could she have done that to me? I was her daughter. Yet she was so full of spite towards me. Everything I did, she ruined. Everything I wanted, she destroyed. She even tried to destroy you, Francis. She made it look like it was all my fault. But it was her all the time, chipping away at something that was so fragile it eventually shattered. And you had no choice but to run away from me. She smirked that day, you know? She smirked in my face because she couldn't grant me that one little piece of happiness.'

'Cerys,' Clooney said again. 'Please. Stop upsetting yourself. You'll waste energy. You'll need all your energy to get to the beach.'

'But she wasn't supposed to be killed.' Cerys wiped the wet from her eyes. 'Honest to God, we never meant that to happen. But even then she still tried to cheat me. She still tried to stop me from finding my own happiness. And do you know what? When I saw her lying there in the yard it was as if a huge weight had been lifted off my shoulders. In that one moment it was as if I'd suddenly been set free. I was free. I'm free of her now. I'm my own person now. And no one is ever again going to treat me like something that dropped off a dog's bottom.'

Suddenly Clooney stopped and looked back through the trees. Cerys bumped into him.

'Listen!'

Everyone stopped and turned to see what he was looking at.

'What's the matter?' Cerys took hold of his sleeve.

'*Listen!*'

They listened, but all they could hear was the rustling of the branches.

Then slowly it came, faint and chilling.

The whimper of hounds.

Chapter Sixty-Three

'Oh God, no.' Cerys shrieked and let go of Clooney's sleeve, staggered backwards through the bushes and started beating wildly at the air with her hands. 'Please, God, don't let it be dogs. Tell me they're not chasing us with dogs.'

It took Clooney a moment to react and by then Cerys was running away through the trees, slapping branches out of the way with her flaying arms. He took off after her and he had to grab her clothes to make her slow down.

'Stop it.' He wrapped his arms around her. 'They're still a long way off. If we keep a cool head we can outrun them. We're nearly at the coast, right? Now if we can make it to the beach we can hide amongst the rocks and the dogs will never find us there. All right?'

'Oh dear God.' Cerys gripped on to his coat. 'Why can't they just leave us alone? I can't take any more of this. You won't let them get me, will you? Promise me you won't let them get me! Shoot me first. Anything, only don't let them get me.'

'Of course I won't let them get you, sweetheart,' Clooney squeezed her tighter. 'Come on, now. We'll be all right, I promise you. Just follow me and we can make it to that beach in one piece. Just trust in me.'

He took her hand and coaxed her into the trees. And suddenly they were out of sight.

'What are we going to do now?' O'Shea shouted in their general direction.

'What do you bloody think?' Clooney yelled back. '*Run!*'

O'Shea grabbed Adam by his jacket and hurried after them. His heart thudded in his ears. Despite what Clooney said he knew those dogs could move faster than he could drag Adam. Whatever way he looked at it, it was only a matter of time now. With dogs it was a relentless push until they wore you down. And the dogs were often let off their lead. They caught up with the runner long before the handlers did and usually there wasn't much left for the handlers to take back with them.

'Come on!' Clooney's voice blared from somewhere in front of them.

'What's the bloody use?' O'Shea shouted back. But still he grabbed Adam tighter and picked up a faster pace. Sprigs flayed them and scratched their faces like tiny claws.

Clooney was moving a lot slower now to allow Cerys to keep up with him, and he constantly glanced over his shoulder at the noise of the dogs. Though he tried hard to hide it, there was a frightened look in his eyes.

The ground sagged under O'Shea's feet and he toppled down onto the soggy turf. Adam tried to catch him but it happened too fast, and he was knocked sideways into the bushes. Clooney bawled at O'Shea to get back up, but he only managed two more steps before his face was back in the grass again.

'What are you doing, you stupid prat!' Now Clooney was standing over him, grabbing his hair and shaking his head. 'We're almost there. Smell the sea. If we make it to the sea we're safe.'

'I can't. I'm finished. Take Adam and go on. You can make it without me.'

'Oh no,' Clooney barked. 'If you stay, the boy stays. It's as simple as that. I'm not his bleedin' mother. I'm not taking responsibility for him if you're too piggin' useless to do it yourself. What's the matter with you? Do you know what those dogs will do if they catch you?'

'I'm sorry. I've got no feeling in my legs. Please, just take Adam. You'll have a better chance without me. I'll try to hold them off for you.'

'How?' Clooney screamed in his face. 'They'll be all over you in seconds.'

'Look, just leave me ...'

The sky grew darker and almost immediately a spatter of huge raindrops hit O'Shea on the neck.

'Shit,' Clooney flapped his arms. 'That's all we bloody need.'

Within seconds the few drops had turned into a heavy shower. It beat on the trees before cascading down through the bare branches to splash furiously on the ground.

'Come on.' Clooney turned to go. 'Get going or we won't be able to move in a minute.'

'No, wait.' O'Shea tried to grab his sleeve. 'This could be our chance.'

'What? Are you stupid? We're going to get bogged down in this.'

'No.' O'Shea scrambled to his feet. He was suddenly invigorated by the fleeting chance of avoiding the dogs. 'Don't you see? The rain will wash out our scent and the dogs won't be able to follow us.'

'Where the hell did you get that idea? They're not that far behind, you know.'

'But if we can get up into that tree they'll never see us.' O'Shea pointed to a huge chestnut that had thick ivy clinging all over it. There was plenty of cover in the wide branches. The rainwater was already pouring down it to form pools around the base. 'They'll never expect us to do that. The dogs won't be able to pick up our trail. They'll walk right past us.'

'You must be bloody joking,' Clooney scoffed. 'They're going to be here in a minute. They're not stupid. They'll see us straight away. Our best bet is to keep running while we still have the chance.'

'We can't outrun them,' O'Shea argued. 'We're too tired. We're too weak. This is the only way.'

'You're mad. I know what dogs can do. There's no way I'm staying here for them to catch up with me. Come on, Cerys.'

A huge dog came bursting out of the bushes and Clooney went spinning back against a tree with the shock. The streak of grey wolfhound hesitated for the briefest of moments as it landed in the clearing, a shower of dribble spraying from its jaws. There were too many targets. It hunkered down as it tried to decide which one to attack first. Then it flew at O'Shea with its jaws wide open to rip out his throat.

But O'Shea's hand was already in his pocket and clutching the gun, and it gave a muffled pop when he tugged the trigger. The dog was less than a foot away when the bullet caught it in the throat and it gave a yelp before tumbling sideways into the bushes. O'Shea threw himself in the opposite direction and collided with Clooney.

Clooney was paralysed with terror. His face was ghostly white and his eyes wide in disbelief.

'Get up the tree,' O'Shea yelled at him.

'Cerys first,' Clooney gave O'Shea an embarrassed shove.

Cerys held up her arms as they lifted her between them, and when she was high enough she grabbed the branch and hauled herself up onto it. Then she leant down, took Adam's outstretched hands and hauled him up beside her with one easy pull.

O'Shea made a stirrup with his hands and supported his back against the tree.

'Do it this way,' he told Clooney.

As O'Shea lifted Clooney, Cerys grabbed his clothes and pulled him up the rest of the way.

When he'd sorted himself out Clooney lay on his stomach and reached down to O'Shea. But even when O'Shea jumped as high as he could Clooney's hand was still out of reach.

O'Shea looked around for something to use as a footstool, but he couldn't see anything strong enough to take his weight. Time running out. He took a few steps back, launched himself at the tree and stepped up onto it as far as his stride would take him. But the bark was covered in slimy moss and his shoes had nothing to grip on. He slithered back down with a thud.

'Shit, shit, shit.' He rubbed his head furiously where it made contact with the tree. ''Tis no use, I'll have to find another tree.'

'No time,' Clooney ducked back out of sight. 'Here they come. Get down, get down.'

O'Shea flung himself behind the nearest bush and landed on the dead dog. He rolled away from it as the first soldier came into view with his collar pulled up against the driving rain and the dog's lead in his hand. The wind carried his voice as he called his dog and gave a long broken whistle.

Cerys and Clooney were out of O'Shea's view. But the soldier was directly under them now and he would certainly see them if he decided to look up. He didn't. He was too wet and cold and more concerned about his dog. So he carried on walking away through the woods.

The next three soldiers had their dogs back on their leads and the rain made them creep along in a reluctant huddle. The excitement was gone out of the dogs now and their whimper had lost its edge as they traipsed past in sullen silence until they too were eventually swallowed up by the trees.

It took at least ten minutes before Clooney was satisfied the soldiers hadn't doubled back to retrace the scent. Then he dropped down out of the tree and rubbed the cramp from his legs.

'Well, that wasn't a very big patrol. Either they're spread out over a wide area, or they're not really that interested in us at all. What do you think?'

'I don't know.' O'Shea swiped the rain off his face. 'I'm no soldier.'

'No.' Clooney looked him up and down and his eyes had a cautious sparkle in them. 'So where did you get that gun?'

O'Shea reached up to catch Adam as Cerys lowered him down, and he guided the boy to a log and sat him on it. Then Cerys yelped as she slung her legs over the side and dropped quicker than she intended. Clooney rushed to catch her and they both tumbled on the muddy ground.

'Well?' Clooney's face had turned a deeper shade of purple as he pulled Cerys back to her feet and swatted the mud off his coat. 'That gun. Did you have it with you all this time? Back at the house, when you were sick?'

O'Shea's answer was an ambiguous shrug and a smug pout. Cerys went to say something but Clooney gave his coat an aggressive tug and walked away with an angry swagger. 'Come on. We haven't got much time before the boat arrives. We need to get a move on. But keep your eyes open. We can't afford any more surprises.'

Chapter Sixty-Four

Clooney was agitated now they'd lost so much precious time and he wasn't prepared to lose a minute more. So when they left the cover of the trees and were out in open country he took a desperate risk. Instead of skirting around the perimeter of the fields and using the natural cover of the hedges he cut straight across. Even with the thick mist floating in off the sea they could still be spotted from higher ground.

Their route took them through the middle of Rhodri's farmyard and close enough to the house to be seen from the windows. But for some reason there was no sign of life anywhere. It was unnaturally quiet. No dogs barking. No chickens squawking. No people moving around. Cerys stopped to look over the low wall that skirted the vegetable garden.

'Come on.' Clooney gave her an impatient shove. 'Stop farting around. We haven't got time for a social call.'

'But where is everyone, though?' Cerys whispered. 'There's not even a light on. It's not normal on a farm. There's usually people moving about at this time of day.'

'Look, just be glad it's raining and they're all looking for something to do in the cow shed.' Clooney tugged her sleeve. 'The less people around, the less chance of us being seen. And the less explaining we'll have to do. So which way do we go now?'

Cerys pulled away from him with an exasperated grunt and headed down a narrow track around the edge of a small meadow. It tapered through a gap in the hedge and brought them down on to the beach.

The rain had lightened into a thin drizzle now but the sea was a dirty grey with waves that heaved and dipped and threw up huge angry strips of white foam.

'Good grief, isn't it small?' Cerys cried above the roar of the waves. 'I don't remember it being as small as this. It seemed enormous when we were kids. When we were little kids this beach was absolutely massive.'

'Are you sure it's the right place?' Clooney gave a stroppy wave of his hand.

'Of course I'm sure.' She danced around him. 'Look over there. See? There's the waterfall, isn't it. And up there's the gate I told you about. The one to the jetty.'

'Can you see the cave?'

'You won't see it from here.' Cerys had to shout. 'Not in this weather. The waterfall's too heavy. But you can see the ledge by there. If you follow that ledge you'll find the cave behind the waterfall. The tide's coming in fast and it won't be long before you can take a boat over to it.'

Waves rolled in and crashed down like thunder. At one point they reached the bottom of the cliff and threw spray high into the air before retreating again rolling a pile of stones behind them.

'How the hell did you take a boat out in this?' Clooney lifted the bag off his shoulder, threw it down and walked to the edge of the water. 'You told me you sailed a boat in this. Look at the size of those waves. You'd be tipped upside down in a flash.'

'We *did*!' Cerys had exasperation in her voice. 'When the weather's tidy it's like a pond by here. Sometimes it was so mild you couldn't get a breeze to put up a sail.'

'Well, we can't take a bloody boat out in it now, can we?' Clooney took a kick at the bag on the ground.

'There has to be another way. I'll just have to climb up to the cave and pass the boxes down to you.'

He started running across the shingles towards the cave as the next wave raced up the beach behind him. He tried to dance out of the way but it was too fast and it knocked him back against the rocks.

He jumped back up and ran out of the way of another wave, and he kicked at a clump of seaweed as he glared at Cerys. 'So where's this famous boat, then?'

Cerys looked around. 'There used to be an old tree stump over by there. It was tied to that. But it obviously isn't there anymore.'

'You did *have* a boat?'

Cerys rolled her eyes.

Clooney kicked at the seaweed again. 'Well, we have to find a way to get those boxes down before that friggin' boat gets here.'

'What friggin' boat?' O'Shea mocked. 'You don't think they'll come now? How'll they find us in this weather? It's like looking for a flea on an elephant's bum.'

'They'll find us.' Clooney's eyes bulged with annoyance. 'They *know* this place. They've used that jetty a million times. So when I give them the signal they'll come in and pick us up, all right?'

'When you give them a signal? Do you think they'll actually *see* you flapping your bloody hands in the air from way out there?'

'I won't be flapping my arms, you moron.' Clooney pointed to the bag on the ground. 'I've got a lantern. Those guys know *exactly* where the jetty is. They're professional seamen. So when the time is right I'll light the lamp and give them the signal. Then they'll come in and pick us up. In the meantime stop asking stupid bloody questions and start thinking about how we're going to get up to that cave.'

O'Shea shrugged and guided Adam to a cluster of rocks under a large outcrop where he was sheltered from the rain.

'Listen,' Clooney called to O'Shea. 'Why don't you go along the shore and see if you can find a boat. And keep a lookout for the trawler, too. Come straight back here if you see it. We don't want them thinking you're some escaped lunatic out for a walk and frighten them off. Cerys, you stay here and watch the boy. I'll go back up the path and see if I can find a rope or something. Maybe I can get down to the cave from above.'

'You can't,' Cerys protested. 'The cliff is too dangerous. It's too fragile. It breaks away just by looking at it. There's nothing to tie a rope to anyway up there.'

'There's no other way.' Clooney started walking back up the path.

The stretch of coast that tapered away from the beach had long, high slivers of rock going all the way down to the water's edge. The strips of sand between them could easily hide a boat, but O'Shea doubted it. Because when the tide came in it completely covered those rocks and a boat would be carried away with it when it went back out.

O'Shea decided to look anyway, just in case. He waited for the waves to roll in. Then as they washed back out again he skipped around the tip of the rocks. He hopped from one inlet to the other along the whole length of the shore right up to where the rocks blended into the cliff itself.

There was no boat. He turned back.

It was impossible to see Rhodri's beach because of the rocks so O'Shea had no idea if Clooney had found a rope. Or even a boat. For all he knew they could have reached the cave already, taken the boxes and be on their way to the jetty to meet the trawler.

The spray and the drizzle were getting heavier now and the tide had come in a long way. It swirled around the front of the rocks in furious little whirlpools and O'Shea had to scramble over the jagged tops to get from one inlet to another. Which meant it was taking him a lot longer to get back. Panic started to creep up on him.

It was probably what Clooney wanted anyway. There was no doubt he was planning something. And sharing his future with O'Shea certainly wasn't a part of it. So if O'Shea missed the boat Clooney wouldn't be broken-hearted. The thing was, what would Clooney do with Adam?

The last stretch of rock was almost ten feet high. The waves came rolling in around O'Shea and lapped at his ankles as he searched for a decent foothold. When he found one he heaved himself up and grabbed at the top with both hands.

As he straightened up and got ready to fling himself over the top a familiar sound blew at him in the breeze - the rumble of angry voices. He paused, then stretched up very slowly. Through a tiny split in the rock he could just see Clooney waving his arms and stomping around in angry circles on the shingle.

'How the hell do I know?' he howled above the noise of the waves. 'He's thick as shit ... probably half way back to Cardiff by now!'

O'Shea could also see Adam squatting under the outcrop about thirty feet away. He was keeping dry as best he could, but he looked bored and miserable as he lobbed stones into the pool of water by his feet.

By shifting position O'Shea could see Cerys too. But she wasn't looking at Clooney. There was someone else on the beach.

From where O'Shea was hanging on the rock he couldn't make out who it was, so he moved his foot onto another small ledge. Then he could see the side of a man's face.

The shock made his heart pulse with the violence of an express train. The man wasn't in uniform now. But there was no mistaking him. It was Weiss.

O'Shea dropped off the rock like a sack of spuds and fell on the sand. His mind was a haze of furious anger. His wet hands shook as he pulled the gun from his pocket and hammered it against the rock.

He never expected to see Weiss again so he hadn't paid much thought to how he'd feel about it if he did. What he actually felt now was a blinding revulsion that made him want to jump over the rock and pound him into the ground. His mind shrieked for revenge, for blood, for brutal retaliation.

Chapter Sixty-Five

It took all of five minutes for O'Shea to calm down enough to climb back up on the rock and take another look. He shoved the gun back in his pocket, and this time he used a different foothold to give him a better view of the beach.

The first thing he noticed was a long groove in the shingles where someone had dragged a small boat down to the water's edge. Clooney kept looking at it while Cerys paced around him nervously. She'd picked Clooney's bag off the stones and slung it over her shoulder, and it flapped against her leg every time she moved.

'So,' Weiss spoke in a cold, menacing voice. 'You've come all this way and gone to all this trouble, and you want me to believe you're just spending a pleasant day by the sea? Do you think I'm a fool? Do you not know me at all? Because I know *exactly* why you're here. And I insist you share with me your good - how would you put it - *fortune*? After all, are we not still colleagues? Partners even?'

Clooney's response was a high, hysterical splutter. Weiss straightened up, and as he moved closer to Clooney O'Shea could see a pistol in his hand.

'Are you saying we're *not* partners?' Weiss emphasised the question by waving the gun at Clooney.

Clooney's face was red with rage and thick dark veins pulsed in his neck. 'How did you know we were going to be here? Who told you about this place?'

'Really?' Weiss chuckled as he gave another wave of the gun. 'You *must* have known I'd have the farm watched. I *did* intend coming back with some colleagues, just to give the place another sweep. But then I thought of a better plan. I would let you lot carry on as normal and see what happened. See where you went, if you took an interest in any specific part of the farm. Unfortunately the man I had watching the place choose to relieve himself at the very moment you decided to drive away. The poor man. It *was* the early hours of the morning. And it *was* cold and dark. He had children too.'

Weiss wiped his nose on his sleeve. 'Anyway, we lost you again. And I almost gave up all hope of ever finding you. So it was pure chance I was in the officers' mess the night before last and I heard that a German staff car was found down a lane near Radyr. Now *that* car was booked out to *me* a couple of weeks ago, and it was stolen later in Cardiff. Of course I knew where the car was all along because I'd seen it parked outside your farmhouse. But, naturally, I was curious to know what it was doing in Radyr. Why had you taken it *there*, of all places? More importantly, where did you go afterwards?'

He gave a sinister smile and paused for effect. 'It didn't take long to find out. The first house we called on took about two minutes to tell us that the people who came in the car went straight to the house of your friend Agnes. Agnes, as you would expect, was very loyal, very brave. But her husband was not so strong.'

Weiss took a handkerchief from his pocket and blew his nose. 'When he saw us nail her hands to the tree in his garden he volunteered to tell us everything we wanted to know.'

Weiss chuckled when Cerys cringed and turned away. O'Shea got a mad urge to take a shot at the back of his head. He shoved his hand back into his pocket and squeezed the handle of the gun. But he wasn't confident enough. His hands were too wet and cold. And they were shaking badly. He knew he would only get the one chance. If he missed, Weiss would not.

Then what would happen to Adam?

O'Shea let go of the gun, removed his hand from the pocket and wiped his eyes.

'So,' Weiss shouted, and his voice was high and impatient against the noise of the sea. 'Tell me what they sacrificed their lives for. Tell me where the boxes are.'

Clooney shook his head and stared out to sea.

'Look,' Weiss waved both hands in emphasis. 'Your friend told me about your uncle Rhodri, that he's arranged a boat to take you to Ireland. Good plan. Almost as good as mine. So why don't we reform our association, rekindle our partnership? And together we can all catch that boat. What do you say? After all, there will be more than enough recompense for all of us.'

Clooney and Cerys looked at each other, and it was clear by Clooney's face that he was furious. He obviously didn't trust Weiss one little bit. But he also hated being in a situation where he had no control. However, he was looking down the barrel of a gun so his options were limited.

'What do you want to do?' He turned angrily to Cerys.

Cerys jumped back. She was startled and confused. 'Well, I don't know! Don't ask me. You're not putting this on me.'

'For God's sake.' Clooney clenched his fists and punched the air. 'We haven't got time to think about it.'

'You haven't got time?' Weiss repeated and rubbed his chin. 'How very interesting! Of course *I* have all the time in the world. So please, continue your little debate. Take all the time you need.'

'*Well*?' Clooney shouted at Cerys. 'What are we going to do? Or are we just going to stand here and freeze to death while the tide comes in around us?'

'I told you, I don't bloody know!' Cerys shouted back at him then she slapped her hands against her sides, turned her back on him and gave a scream of frustration.

Clooney took a few steps towards her but turned to Weiss instead. 'All right. But we need some guarantees.'

Weiss gave a smug shrug of his shoulders. 'What kind of guarantees?'

'That *all* of us get on that boat safely and unhindered. And *all* of us get off again in Dublin safely and unhindered. And *all* of us benefit equally from any monies acquired from the transaction of our merchandise.'

'Anything else?' Weiss didn't flinch as he gave his answer and this caused Clooney to hesitate. He glanced back at Cerys who just shook her shoulders and pulled a face that said she had nothing else to add.

'There is one more thing.' Clooney nodded at the surrounding cliffs. 'Did you come here alone?'

'Why do you ask such a question?' Weiss raised his eyebrows in mock offence. 'Are you saying you don't trust me?'

'Oh, I trust you as far as Cerys could throw you with one hand. You've probably got some horrible destiny lined up for us already. But remember we know where the stuff is, and you don't!'

'But I have the gun.' Weiss gave a sickly, irritating grin. 'And like I just told you, I also have all the time in the world.'

Clooney's groan was almost like an animal in pain, and he spread his hands in exasperation. 'All right. But we'll have to hurry. The boat will be coming around that rock any minute now. It can only wait for a short time. If it doesn't see my signal, it'll turn around and go away again.'

'So,' Weiss waved the Luger at him. 'What's keeping you? I imagine it's like *Treasure Island*, ten paces from the big rock then five paces to the left. Am I right? So go and dig them up.'

'That's the problem, I'm afraid.' Clooney pointed at the other side of the beach. 'They're in a cave behind that waterfall over there.'

Weiss studied Clooney for a moment before stepping back a few paces and taking a quick look at the waterfall.

'But we can't get to it from above,' Clooney added. 'I had a look. The cliff face is too unstable. It crumbles if you touch it. And there's nothing to tie a rope on to anyway. Not even a bush. Apart from that the river is swollen and much too strong. The only way to the cave is to take a boat over to that ledge and crawl the rest of the way.'

'In this weather?' Weiss looked astonished. 'In that little boat? This should be interesting.'

'Well, with the three of us rowing it might just work.'

'The three of us?' Weiss was even more surprised now. 'No, no, no. I'm afraid not. I'm not a very good sailor. I got sick on a swing when I was a child. No, no, no. I could never go out in a small boat like that. Especially in a sea as rough as this. So I'm afraid you'll have to go and retrieve the boxes all by yourself.'

'No,' Cerys shrieked. She ran to Clooney and grabbed his arm. 'We can't go out in that. Not just the two of us.'

'Not the *two* of you, my dear,' Weiss corrected. 'Just him. *You* will stay here with me. You will be my insurance, just in case.'

'You're not serious?' she wailed. 'You can't expect Francis to go out in that all by himself? It's too rough, for God's sake. You need more than one person to row a boat in this weather. You can't go, Francis. Not alone.'

'Look,' Clooney wiped his face on his sleeve in frustration. 'We haven't got much bloody time left. The trawler will be here any minute now and we have to be ready for it. So if I have to go alone, so be it. But I have to go now!'

'But why do you have to go now?' Cerys was hanging onto his clothes. 'We don't have to take it to Ireland today, do we? Why do we have to go today? Please, Francis, can't we leave it until the weather gets better and we can get to the cave? Leave it until tomorrow when the sea is calmer. Please, Francis.'

Clooney pushed her away and headed towards the boat, grabbed the rope on the front and started dragging it into the water.

'We can't leave it any longer,' he shouted as the waves washed around his feet. 'It has to be now! I've waited too long for this. We have to take it to Ireland now. Today! We'll be safe there. So I have to get the boxes now if we're to be ready when that trawler comes.'

'But you can't do it on your own.' Cerys was crying hysterically as she tried to get at him again. 'Please, Francis. Please leave it. Why can't you just leave it until tomorrow? We can always get another boat another day. It doesn't have to be now.'

The tide was coming in faster around O'Shea's legs. It hit the rocks and covered him in a heavy spray, and suddenly he was knee deep in water again. The force of it started to drag him back out with it. He grabbed at the rock with both hands but the sharp stone cut into his palms and he had to let go.

When he hit the sand he sank into it, and the power of the ebbing water sucked it from around his feet with such energy it flipped him onto his back.

The shock of being submerged in the bitterly cold water made him struggle for breath, and he fought furiously to get back onto his feet.

By the time he got back up on the rock again Clooney was already in the boat. He was struggling with the oars as breakers hit him head on and lifted him up like a toy before letting him crash back down again. Cerys ran up and down the edge of the water with her arms flapping at him, her voice lost in the wind.

The next wave hit O'Shea in the middle of the back, lifted him off the rock and slammed him back down onto the sand again. Then he was upside down and gasping for breath and the tide was bellowing in around him. It rushed back out again and left him wriggling like a beached fish.

It took a massive effort to get back on his feet. Then the next rush of water bore down on him and he had no choice but to go with it. He let the wave pick him up and lift him to the top of the rock.

Grabbing at the shards of stone he flung one leg over the top, straddled it for a second then gathered his other leg under him. Then he kicked with both feet to push himself away from the sharp rocks. He landed heavily and went sliding across the loose shingle.

Weiss spun around in surprise. He tried to leap out of the way but O'Shea's legs still caught him on the back of the knees and he tumbled on top of him.

Dark September

Chapter Sixty-Six

The pistol shot out of the German's hand, clattered across the stones and landed in a puddle. O'Shea was stunned by the impact of Weiss landing on him, but he knew he had to get to it first.

Rolling onto his side he pushed hard with his shoulder. But Weiss was already scrambling back to his feet. O'Shea grabbed at his legs and Weiss staggered, and his arms grabbed empty air as he tried to stop himself hitting the ground too hard.

Cerys moved quickly too. She gave a fretful yelp as she ran to the gun, kicked it out of the puddle and along the beach. And her hair scattered around her face as she raced after it. Then before O'Shea or Weiss realised what was happening she'd picked it up and waved it at them.

'Stop,' she screamed. She held the gun with both hands and stood with her legs apart. 'Don't move, either of you. I'll shoot you if you move. I mean it. Don't make me use this gun. I will, you know. I'll shoot you both if you try anything.'

O'Shea pushed Weiss out of the way and got to his feet. Cerys took a few steps backward and gave a series of quick glances at Clooney bobbing and bouncing through the thrashing swells. Her head flicked from Clooney to O'Shea and back to Clooney again. This time she held the gun in one hand and waved at Clooney with the other.

'Francis, come back,' she screamed. 'You can come back now. I've got the gun. You'll be all right. Come back out of there now! Please, Francis.'

It was obvious Clooney couldn't hear her. The noise from the sea was thunderous. She danced angrily and fired two shots in the air.

Clooney still didn't hear her. She turned the gun back on O'Shea.

'Don't point it at me, you fool,' he yelled. 'Point it at that evil bastard by there. Shoot him. What are you waiting for? Shoot the pig. Put a bullet between his piggy little eyes and blow his bastard brains out.'

Weiss was on his feet now as well and he casually brushed the dirt from his clothes. Cerys turned the gun on him, but when he gave her a disarming smile she pointed it back at O'Shea.

'Shoot him,' O'Shea insisted. 'What are you waiting for? Do it now. Kill him now. If you don't he'll kill you. And Clooney. He'll kill us all if he gets the chance. So you'd better pull the trigger now while you still can.'

Weiss gave a throaty laugh, clasped his hands behind his back and took a step forward.

'Go ahead, my dear. However,' he waved at O'Shea. 'You *do* know she'll shoot you also?'

'I don't care,' O'Shea yelled. 'I just want to see your brains spattered all over the sand. I want to see you shot down like you shot my son.'

'Like *I* shot your son?' The frown Weiss gave was deep and puzzled, and he glanced at Cerys. 'You think *I* shot your son? Is that what she told you?'

Cerys looked as if she couldn't quite hear the conversation because she continued to glance at what Clooney was doing.

'This has nothing to do with her,' O'Shea retorted. 'She wasn't there. Anyway, I *know* you shot him because I saw you.'

'Did you?'

'Yes! You know I did. I was up at the window. I saw you. You shot my son and just walked away and left him to die in the snow.'

Weiss frowned again. 'You must have the most remarkable eyesight to see something that didn't actually happen. Perhaps you were - how do you say? - hallucinating?'

'Don't lie!' O'Shea screamed at him. '*You* shot him!'

'Obviously you know very little about guns, my friend.' Weiss looked straight into his eyes. 'As you can see, my gun - the gun your friend is pointing at you right now - is a 9mm pistol. Now if I shot your boy with that from where I was standing at the time, I promise you he would not have survived. No, the bullet that hit your son was fired from a small calibre weapon. Probably a .22 rifle. And from a greater distance.'

O'Shea studied the sneering face, but the cold eyes gave no indication if he was lying or not.

'What are you saying?' O'Shea looked at Cerys but she still seemed to be distracted. Her eyes were darting between them and Clooney as she hopped from one foot to the other.

Weiss waved his finger at her. 'Do you want to tell him what happened, my dear? Or shall I?'

Cerys suddenly snapped awake, aware of what Weiss was saying to her. She jerked the gun at him.

'You see, my friend,' Weiss continued before she had time to answer. 'The shot was actually aimed at me. Obviously I like to think she wasn't actually trying to *kill* me, you understand. No, no! I like to think she was merely trying to stop me from leaving.'

'Shut up,' Cerys screamed. Her hand was starting to shake from holding the gun. 'Just shut your mouth.'

'She looks so pretty, doesn't she?' Weiss chuckled. 'So sweet, like a delicate little angel. But inside that beautiful chest there beats a very black heart. So believe me when I tell you, she will probably kill the both of us any moment now. She will kill your precious little boy too. And she will not think twice about doing it.'

'What's he talking about, Cerys?' O'Shea had to swallow hard before the words would come out of his mouth. 'What's he mean, the bullet was meant for him?'

'I said shut up!' Cerys yelled again, and the gun waved dangerously between the two of them.

'The problem was this, you see?' Weiss dismissed her with a contemptuous shrug. 'They didn't know you'd come back to the farm. They'd been away, staying with friends apparently. Anyway, they were coming across the field when they saw me coming out of the house. They didn't know what I was doing there but their suspicious minds assumed I'd discovered the boxes.'

Weiss looked out at Clooney in the boat then back to O'Shea. 'Realising I was about to leave they began to panic, thinking it was all slipping away from them once again. But they were too far away to do anything about it. Your friend there was carrying a rifle for shooting rabbits so she took a wild shot in my direction. As I said, I like to believe she was only trying to make me stop to ask me what I'd discovered. Fortunately for me, when she saw she'd hit the boy she hesitated just long enough for me to run to my car and drive away.'

The wind blew another sheet of drizzle across the beach and hit O'Shea's already soaked clothes. His head was reeling both from the cold and the confusion of what he was hearing.

'No,' he snarled eventually. 'I don't believe a word of it. You're a lying bastard! You're saying all this to try and justify what you did. You had her sister killed and then you shot my son. And now you're trying to wriggle out of it. Well, it won't work. I don't believe you.'

Weiss gave the faintest of shrugs. 'Then ask yourself what he was doing with me in the first place?'

'Who?'

'Your son,' Weiss nodded at Adam. 'We didn't find him the day we searched the farm. In fact we had no idea he even existed, so how did I discover him? How did I know he was hiding under the stairs in the farmhouse?'

O'Shea looked at Cerys for an answer. Her eyes flicked from him to Weiss but she didn't respond.

'Cerys,' he screamed at her. 'Do you hear what he's saying?'

Weiss took another step closer to Cerys. She watched him, but the movement was so natural she didn't even register it.

'Look, when you escaped from the truck with Mr Clooney you disappeared off the face of the earth.' Weiss stood up to his full height as if to lend authority to what he was saying 'Everyone thought you were dead so we lost all hope of ever finding the boxes again. In the meantime I was demoted to the Penal Corps and promptly assigned the mundane task of recruiting prisoners for the armed forces. One of the places I had to visit was Cardiff Prison. And guess what happened?'

He gave a loud, sharp laugh and clapped his hands together before wiping the rain off his face in a quick, smart movement. 'But of course you know *exactly* what happened. I found you, my dear boy. Alive and well and hiding in a cell there. Imagine my excitement! But you were so stubborn. You were not going to tell me anything. So I consulted with Mr and Mrs Clooney as to what we should do next. We knew Bethan told you

415

something before she died. But what? And how could we persuade you to share it with us? We discussed many things.'

Cerys took another furtive glance at Clooney who was still bobbing about in the wild sea, looking more and more desperate the nearer he got to the cliff. He was obviously struggling to keep control of the little boat as it rushed in towards the waterfall then shot back out again before he could get a grip on the ledge.

Cerys gave a little squeal and covered her mouth with her hand. 'Please make him come back,' she pleaded without looking at anyone.

Weiss went to move towards her but she swung around and held the gun in both hands again.

'Look what you've done,' she cried. 'You made him go out there. This is all your fault.'

All three of them turned to look at what was happening. Through the heavy spray they could see the waves throwing the boat all over the place.

One enormous swell picked it up and seemed to hold it level with the ledge. Clooney saw his chance and got to his feet. He leant right out of the boat and it looked like he could jump across the gap. But the sea dropped from under him quicker than he could blink and he had to throw himself back into the boat. He grabbed the sides with both hands as it shook violently and carried him back down out of reach again.

'See how she blames me and not you,' Weiss teased. 'But of course that's understandable. You're aware she thinks you have feelings for her, aren't you? You look amazed? But she told me herself. Didn't you, my dear?'

Cerys wasn't listening. She had the gun pointed in their direction but she was too engrossed watching Clooney kick out in frustration every time the boat brought him to within an inch of the ledge only to throw him away from it again.

'That's why she suggested if she went to see you and pretended her life was in danger, you'd tell her everything.'

Another smarmy grin danced on his mouth. 'However, there were one or two little doubts about this. Would you really believe her life was in danger if she turned up looking beautiful and obviously very healthy? No. So we agreed she should look like she really *was* in trouble, look as if she'd been beaten up a little bit. But your friend, like the rest of us, doesn't relish pain. Unless, of course, it's happening to someone else. So she came up with this ingenious plan. It turned out she had a sister who looked uncannily like her. And she was certain that, being a good Christian, her sister would willingly swap places with her.'

'What a sick thing to ... I don't believe you! That's sick.' O'Shea choked as he recalled the horror of what happened in the house in Cardiff. 'No one on God's earth would do that to their own sister.'

'Really?' Weiss looked at him with eyes that were mocking and mischievous.

A flurry of jigsaw pieces spun into O'Shea's mind and started to click into place more clearly than they'd ever done before. They almost made a whole picture, but now he wasn't sure if he really wanted to see it after all.

'So what convinced you it was Mrs Clooney in that house in Cardiff?' Weiss was obviously enjoying his moment. 'Not her beautiful face, obviously. She'd already been ... disguised? Her hair, maybe? Or was it the clothes? The same clothes she was wearing the last time you saw her?'

Cerys was definitely listening now. Her face was full of anger as she waved the gun between the two of them. 'It wasn't like that,' she shrieked. 'She wasn't supposed to be hurt like that. She was only supposed to be bruised a little bit. Just to convince you it really was me. But that lunatic handed her over to the Gestapo.'

'Then tell him the rest of the plan.' Weiss gave a cackle of a laugh, and a spray of spittle flew from his mouth. He swung around and prodded O'Shea in the chest. 'The plan that day was to persuade you to tell us everything you knew. But suppose it didn't work? Guess what the next step was going to be?'

O'Shea couldn't. He backed away from Weiss.

'Will I tell you what the next step was going to be?' Weiss was delighted with the response he was getting. 'We were going to use the boy. That boy sitting under that rock over there! It would be interesting to see how long you kept quiet under those circumstances, don't you think? Remember, this was also your beautiful friend's suggestion.'

'No,' O'Shea groaned. 'You're making that up. You're ...'

'I'm not, I'm afraid,' Weiss shrugged. 'You must understand, your friends were unhinged by then. They were seduced by the promise of how rich they would be if only they could find those elusive boxes. They believed the Americans would give them more money than they could spend in a lifetime. It was their chance to get away from this country, this war, and start a new life wherever they wanted. There was nothing they wouldn't do, nobody they wouldn't sacrifice, to achieve that.'

'But not a child. Not Adam. He's just a ...'

'Why not?' Weiss raised his eyebrows in surprise. 'I have seen much worse than that. I have seen mothers handing over their children, betraying their own husbands. Fathers betrayed their own sons, gave their daughters as favours. When the fabric of society starts to unravel, my friend, the basic instinct of survival takes priority.'

Cerys watched Clooney more intently. He was so determined to get into the cave that the next time the sea carried the boat close enough he took a mighty leap. He hit the side of the cliff and somehow managed to get his elbows on the ledge.

Clooney had tied the rope around his arm to stop the boat drifting away from him. But the rope was too short and it was preventing him from pulling himself all the way up onto the ledge. Now when the boat dropped away from under him again it looked as if it might pull him after it.

Another wave rolled in and picked the boat up again, and this time Clooney was able to throw his whole body up onto the ledge. But as he scrambled to his feet his legs shot from under him. He fell on his face, and his arms flayed wildly as he slipped back over the side.

This time the wave seemed to flick the boat much higher into the air. And it appeared to hover about a meter above his head before it suddenly slammed down on top of him with a shocking crunch.

Cerys gave a horrified scream and raced to the water's edge.

For a long, sickening moment, Clooney was pinned against the cliff with his arms flapping wildly. When the next wave came it pulled the boat away, and the rope tightened around his arm and dragged him after it. The waves closed over him and he was lost in the mayhem of the swollen, pounding sea.

Chapter Sixty-Seven

Cerys was hysterical. She charged into the water only to be thrown back out again. It was several minutes before the boat reappeared with Clooney still tied to it. It bobbed over the top of the breakers before being flicked up into the air and dashed against the side of the cliff where it splintered into a thousand bits. A web of broken wood pinned Clooney to the cliff for a moment. Then he slid down out of sight and he didn't come back up.

Howling like a wounded animal Cerys ran in little circles and the wind scattered her hair all over her face. When she turned back to Weiss her eyes had a total madness in them. 'You bastard!' She staggered across to him. 'You made him go out there in that stupid boat. You made him get killed.'

She pointed the gun at his face and pulled the trigger. Weiss flinched as the gun gave a loud click. 'You could have stopped him,' she yelled again as she shook the gun. 'Why didn't you stop him?'

The gun clicked a second time. As she shook it again Weiss leapt at her. And before she could move out of his way he chopped her across the throat with the edge of his hand and grabbed the gun off her as she fell to the ground. She lay still, staring up at the sky with eyes that were wide open in surprise.

Weiss whipped the magazine out of the gun, cleared the breech and slammed it back in so quickly O'Shea had no time to react. In the blink of an eye both Cerys and Clooney had been killed right there in front of him, and he was stunned by the suddenness of it all.

Holding the gun loosely in his hand now, Weiss pointed it in O'Shea's general direction and stooped down by Cerys. He felt for a pulse in her neck, gave the faintest shake of his head and closed her eyes.

'What a pity.' He pouted in mock concern as he stood up again. 'And such a beautiful woman, too. Still, they'll be together now. It's what they would have wanted, don't you think?'

O'Shea spotted the fishing boat appearing out of the mist as it rounded the headland. The faint throbbing of the engine came in with the wind but Weiss had his back to it and didn't seem to notice. Though he knew it was a pathetic, futile gesture, for some odd reason O'Shea felt he should delay alerting him to it.

'So,' Weiss tugged at his coat and pulled his collar around his neck as he squinted into the rain. 'At long last. We've reached the end of the chase and I'm the winner. I've won the prize. And there's no one left to share it with.'

O'Shea shivered and he too pulled his coat tighter around him as he took a step closer to Weiss.

'But that was your plan all along, wasn't it?' He made a show of rubbing his hands together before putting them into his pockets and hunching himself up against the cold. 'You never planned to share it with anyone from the start.'

Weiss was beaming all over his face and his eyes twinkled with self-congratulation. 'Yes. You are right. But isn't it ...?'

'Look, Dada, I can see a boat.' Adam was standing on a rock and pointing out to sea.

O'Shea groaned as Weiss spun around.

'Oh dear,' Weiss grinned as he pointed at it with the gun. 'What a shame. They've come all this way for nothing.' He glanced over at the waterfall and gave a casual nod. 'Unless you know of a way to fetch the boxes down for me.'

'No.' O'Shea put a sob of rejection in his voice and choked on the words. 'I don't think that's possible right now, with the sea so rough.'

His bitterly cold fingers throbbed as he curled them around the butt of the gun and released the safety catch. And he moved a step closer to Weiss. He wasn't confident of hitting him from where he was. He needed to get nearer.

The trawler was almost in line with the approach to the jetty, and it rose and dipped with the swell of the sea as it waited for the signal.

'Then I will have to come back for them another day. At least no one will accidentally fall over them. It's the perfect hiding place, yes?'

'But other people know about that cave. Bethan's uncle Rhodri ...'

Weiss gave a cruel smirk and shook his head.

'What?' O'Shea groaned. 'What did ...?'

'Well, I naturally assumed the boxes were hidden somewhere around here. So I asked the farmer and his wife. They never mentioned a cave. Or a waterfall, come to that. I had a whole day with them, you understand. And they certainly wouldn't have prolonged the ... ah ... *conversation* for as long as they did if they knew about a cave behind a waterfall. Trust me, if they ever knew about the cave, they'd forgotten about it long ago. No, I think that cave is well and truly forgotten about.'

He gave a long exaggerated stretch, spreading out his arms as if he was totally at ease with the world. Even though O'Shea had moved another step closer to him he didn't seem bothered by it. O'Shea's body language said he was defeated. It said he was tired and very afraid.

People in that frame of mind rarely fought back. They just resigned themselves to their fate.

The trawler was starting to turn around. O'Shea moved another step closer to Weiss as he curled his finger around the trigger of the gun.

'Anyway,' Weiss said with an impatient wave of the gun. 'It is time for us to say goodbye, my friend. I can't say it was a pleasure knowing you. But I am sorry all the same.'

'No! Wait ...' O'Shea took another pleading, faltering step towards him. 'What about my boy?'

Weiss glancing around at Adam who was still absorbed with the trawler. 'What about him?'

'Well, what are you ... please, you don't have to do this. You could take him with you to Dublin. I'll give you an address. You could send him there and they'll look after him. Please, do what you want with me but don't hurt him. Take him with you. He won't be any bother, I promise you. Take him to Ireland with you.'

'What makes you think I'm going to Ireland?'

'On the trawler,' O'Shea nodded towards the jetty. 'When you get on the trawler.'

'No, no,' Weiss corrected him. 'I'm not going on the trawler. Well, not today anyway. No, I have to stay here to keep an eye on my... *investment*? Apart from that, I have to tidy up a few loose ends here also. I will use this opportunity to clear my name. For my family's sake, you understand. Maybe I will even secure a promotion when I present you - well, your body - to the Gestapo. Along with your confession. It seems you were involved with the outlawed resistance. Also your friends Mr and Mrs Clooney. So many questions will be answered, and the credit will go to me. Of course they'll assume the boxes were destroyed. The lunatics who stole them were too stupid to understand their value and they burnt the lot in a fit of clumsy rage.'

He put his hand over his eyes and squinted out at the trawler again. 'No, I will not be going on the boat today, I'm afraid.'

A smile played on the corner of his lips that indicated the discussion was over.

The trawler seemed to be holding its position.

'So you're going to kill my son?'

'But would you really want him to live after you're gone?' Weiss almost looked like he cared. 'How would he survive if you're not there?'

'But why do you have to kill either of us?'

'Oh, come now,' Weiss tutted. 'You must be realistic about this. Do you really expect me to just let you walk away? I would spend the rest of my life looking over my shoulder? I'm truly sorry but I have to close this chapter now.'

He raised the pistol and lazily pointed it at O'Shea's heart. At the same time the gun in O'Shea's pocket popped and blew another hole in the cloth. Weiss jerked when the bullet hit him in the middle of the forehead.

His eyes flashed in surprise and he dropped straight down with a thud.

Chapter Sixty-Eight

O'Shea staggered back and took some long hard breaths. For a moment he was paralysed with relief and he wanted to scream. But the slap of the cold breeze stung him back to reality. The boat was waiting, but it wouldn't wait for long.

'Adam! Get over here quick,' O'Shea screamed as he ran to Cerys. Clooney's bag was tangled around her neck and he had to roll her onto her side before he could pull it off her shoulder. He emptied the contents onto the stones.

It was possible the trawler men wouldn't let them on board if they didn't have the boxes with them. But O'Shea *did* have a sock full of money. They would be going back to Dublin anyway. Why not take a couple of paying passengers?

He picked up the lantern and pulled on the tab to open the little flap at the back. The wick was already primed and soaked in paraffin. He flicked through the rest of the stuff but he couldn't see anything to light it with. Clooney hadn't brought any matches.

How the hell could he forget matches?

Unless they were in his pocket when he went out in the boat. O'Shea ran across to Weiss and searched through his pockets, but all he found was the usual rubbish - a pen, a handkerchief, a penknife, a pile of loose change and some keys.

He ran back to Cerys and rolled her onto her back. He took everything out of her pockets but again there was nothing that resembled a match. Or a lighter.

In desperation he grabbed the bag again and turned it inside out. And he gave a cry of relief when he found a box of matches stuck in a crease near the bottom.

Hunching himself into a ball and turning his back to the wind, he yanked one out and scraped it along the strip of sandpaper. It flared up but the wind blew it out almost instantly.

He lit another one but that blew out too, so he dropped to his knees and curled himself into an even tighter ball. Tucking the lantern inside his coat, he tried again.

The next match held its flame just that little bit longer and O'Shea threw it onto the wick. There was a whoosh of blue light as the paraffin ignited, and he slammed the flap shut.

He held it like a fragile egg as he ran to the edge of the sea and splashed knee deep into the water. When he was absolutely sure it was well alight and unlikely to be puffed out by the wind, he waved the lantern as high in the air as he could.

The trawler had turned completely around now and her bows were pointing back out to the Irish Sea. It looked like they'd waited long enough. Now they probably weren't even looking in the direction of the shore.

In that instant O'Shea realised the trawler men would be looking for a signal from the *jetty*, not from some obscure bay. They probably couldn't even *see* the bay in this weather.

A breaker threw a spray of water into the air. The wind caught it and scattered it all over O'Shea, and in that moment he thought he heard Weiss taunting him again.

'What a shame,' Weiss mocked in his head.

The slap of the cold water took O'Shea backwards a few yards but he managed to stay on his feet. He turned and ran back up the beach towards the gate that Cerys showed them.

'Adam,' he yelled as he slid and wobbled across the loose stones. 'Grab that bag and follow me. Hurry, son!'

Adam looked at the bag, then at the contents scattered all around it, then back at his father again. All the time O'Shea was waving the lantern like a lunatic hoping the men on the boat might just catch a glimpse of it.

Adam decided to just grab the bag and follow his father and his little legs went in all directions as he tried to negotiate the slippery stones.

The path was overgrown with a thick mess of weeds and brambles. It slowed O'Shea right down as he tried to batter his way through it. All the time he was checking the lantern was still alight as he waved it furiously.

Adam had the bag over his shoulder and his head was bowed in concentration as he trotted after his father. Satisfied that he was coping all right, O'Shea rushed on.

The rain grew heavier and the wind blew it in sheets across the top of the heaving sea. And O'Shea panicked when he lost sight of the trawler.

Then he heard something else. And he froze. Standing perfectly still, he strained to filter out the rest of the noise that filled the air around him. It was a barking dog.

He couldn't be sure, but it sounded like it was coming from the beach below him. He crept to the edge of the cliff and he could see the two helmets moving on the other side of the rocks. From the way they were behaving it was obvious they'd found the bodies of Weiss and Cerys. A huge Alsatian dog was jumping around them and barking excitedly.

O'Shea leapt back and looked around for the trawler. It had drifted in closer but it was still pointing out to sea. They appeared to have stopped so it was possible they were still watching for a signal. But for some reason they weren't responding to this one.

Of course it was possible the signal was supposed to be something specific, not just a lantern swinging in the breeze. Maybe they could see it, but it wasn't what they were looking for.

Adam caught up and was looking at him with big trusting eyes. The dog down on the beach grew more animated and a dreadful thought hit O'Shea as hard as the cold slap of the wave. If the dog picked up their scent and followed them onto the jetty, they would be trapped. There was nowhere left to run.

In a last desperate attempt to get the attention of the trawler O'Shea pulled out the gun and fired a shot at it.

He saw a tiny flash where the bullet sparked off the metal wheelhouse. He fired again and this time the window pinged, turning the glass into a cobweb.

Almost immediately two faces appeared at the shattered window and watched O'Shea jumping up and down waving the lantern until it nearly fell off its handle.

The faces disappeared again and nothing seemed to happen. Then just as O'Shea was about to throw the lantern in frustration the screws of the trawler gave a loud rumble and churned up an angry surge of water.

O'Shea screeched with delight as the trawler shuddered into reverse, turned in a desperately slow arc and lined itself up for the approach to the jetty.

The dog sounded like it was getting closer too. Either he'd picked up the scent and was following it, or the soldiers heard the shots and decided to investigate.

Either way O'Shea knew that once they were up on the path they couldn't fail to see the trawler.

Crouching down he pulled Adam back into the bushes and out of sight. Hopefully, if the boat had to pull away and leave them behind, the soldiers might decide not to come any farther down the path.

Waves splashed over the top of the jetty and swirled around their feet as the trawler made its approach. But the angle was too difficult and it bumped against the side where it hovered for a second before the impact pushed it back out again.

The dog barked furiously on the path behind them. The trawler touched the jetty again and this time it held its position for a little bit longer as it rubbed along the side with a loud creak of rubber on concrete.

There was no time to hesitate. O'Shea grabbed Adam and charged across the exposed jetty. Immediately a shout came from behind them and was followed by a burst of running boots.

Two men appeared on the deck of the trawler and screamed at O'Shea to run faster. The man in the wheelhouse struggled to keep the trawler steady as the waves rocked it and thumped it against the jetty. O'Shea lifted Adam off his feet, swung him up in the air and threw his feet over the guardrail.

'Grab him,' he yelled. 'Quick, there's soldiers coming.'

The men crouched down instinctively. Then one of them reached up to catch Adam who was lashing out wildly with his arms and legs.

When O'Shea let go of his arms Adam collided with the man, but he still managed to grab a fistful of coat and pull the boy down onto the deck. He dropped down beside him and dragged him along the wet boards and down a hatch as the other man began to push the boat away with his feet. There was a loud crack and a spark blew a chip out of the concrete just inches from his toes. He pulled his feet back in quickly.

The swell of the sea lifted the trawler high in the air again before O'Shea could regain his balance and he skidded to an abrupt halt and fell onto his knees.

There was no way he could jump up that high. He needed to take a few steps back and make a run at it. If he judged the moment the boat dropped back down he might make it. But he didn't have much time. The gap between the boat and the jetty was beginning to widen.

As he scrambled back to his feet he caught a flash out of the corner of his eye a moment before a vicious blow hit him in the side. The force lifted him off his feet and threw him backwards into the sea.

Within seconds water was filling his mouth and stinging his eyes, and the pain was burning red-hot through his chest. His lungs tightened. He couldn't draw breath. Instinct yelled at him to swim for his life but the pain was crippling and preventing him from moving his arms. He was being pulled farther and farther down under the pulsing, rolling sea.

Then everything turned eerily silent. As the darkness closed in around him a strange calmness started to soothe him. Everything appeared to be slowing down. And in his mind he heard himself laugh.

Was this it?

After everything he'd been through, all the killing, all the deaths, all the destruction, *was this it?*

Heather floated into his vision and she was beaming all over her face. And O'Shea's heart gave a leap of delight. He reached out and she took his hand, and her beautiful brown eyes sparkled as she drew him in closer to her. A tremendous warm glow spread right through his whole body.

There's no reason to hang on any longer now. Is there? I might as well just let go.

He sensed Heather shake her head. 'Danny, you must go back! You must go back for Adam!'

Now O'Shea's heart felt like a lump of lead. He seemed to be getting lighter, as if he was floating back up to the surface. The terrible dragging force pulling him under the water was easing up. And he sobbed as Heather's hands let go of his and her face faded into the bubbling, thrashing expanse of dark water.

He was grabbed by his hair and the water fell away from him as he was hauled over the side of the trawler and dropped onto the deck.

'Is he breathing?' someone asked as fingers were shoved down his throat. When he started choking, rough hands pulled him onto his side and seawater came gushing out of his mouth.

Everything rocked madly. His head pulsed with the throbbing of the engines, and all the time there was the clatter of gunfire and the pinging of bullets on the metal bulkhead.

'Where was he hit? Can you see?'

The rough hands pulled at him again. When they found the tear in his coat they yanked it open and pulled his clothes up.

'No exit wound. A few broken ribs and a bad cut. But he'll live. That's if we can move a bit faster and get out of range of those jokers who're shooting at us.'

'Are you sure this is him?'

'I don't know,' came an anxious reply. The man turned O'Shea's face towards him to get a better look. 'I only met him the once.'

'But is it him, though?'

O'Shea's head was lifted up abruptly. He tried to open his eyes but his head was dropped down again before he had the chance.

'Well he's got the lantern I gave him, so it must be him,' said the first voice.

'But is it?' the second voice argued, his words rapid and irritated. 'We must be sure.'

'Looks like him, though. He's got the same dap and ...'

'Is it him or isn't it, for God's sake?'

'Yes!' There was a slight hesitation, then a more positive grunt. 'Yes, I think so.'

When the first man slapped his face O'Shea jumped with the surprise of it.

'You said there would be two people,' the man shouted at him. This time there was a more positive, harder edge to his voice. 'You and a woman, you said. So where's the woman?'

'Dead,' O'Shea croaked and started coughing. 'On the beach.'

'And the boy? No one said anything about a boy. So who is he?'

'He's my son. He's my … is he all right? Where is he?'

'He's grand. Don't worry about him. But we need to know where the ...'

The trawler rolled heavily and a wave washed over the deck. The men grabbed onto O'Shea as they slid a couple of feet along the wet boards.

The shooting faded as the boat increased speed, juddering and shaking as it crashed through the swells of the angry sea. A loud whoop came from inside the bridge.

'*Jasus!* That was feckin close. But the bastards won't catch us now.'

O'Shea was dragged across to a doorway, pulled inside and lifted onto a long seat. Adam was already wrapped in a blanket and perched on a bunk on the other side of the cabin. His hands gripped the bar across the front of it.

'What about your luggage?' someone asked O'Shea as he pulled up his shirt to look at the wound.

'Luggage?' O'Shea pulled away from the probing fingers.

'We were told you'd be bringing luggage with you.' The man slapped a huge pad on the wound and wrapped a strip of bandage around it. 'Something important. We had to look after it carefully, give it our full attention. We were not to let it out of our sight.'

O'Shea's mind flashed back to the carnage on the beach. And the final words of Captain Eric Weiss. 'They never mentioned a cave. Or a waterfall. Trust me, if they ever knew about the cave, they forgot about it long ago. No, I think that cave is well and truly forgotten about now.'

O'Shea gave a huge sigh. 'There's no luggage, I'm afraid. It got lost along the way.'

He tried to sit up, but his stomach heaved and he threw up another pile of seawater. He started choking again and it rapidly turned into a prolonged rasping cough. And the strain on his throbbing head became too much. He fell back and close his eyes. Someone threw a blanket around him and dabbed his face with a wet cloth.

Despite the agony there was a huge surge of relief too. It flowed through his body from his toes to the top of his head, and he had to suppress the urge to laugh. They were actually on their way to Ireland.

So they thought he was Clooney! Well, let them think it. At least until they got to Dublin. Then they'd have all the time in the world to explain.

He tugged the blanket up under his chin, turned to the wall and allowed the weariness to wrap itself around him. Then it all went very quiet.

The End